FLOWERING JUDAS

JANE HADDAM

THORNDIKE PRESS
A part of Gale, Cengage Learning

WITHDRAWN

GALE
CENGAGE Learning·

Detroit • New York • San Francisco • New Haven, Conn • Waterville, Maine • London

GALE
CENGAGE Learning™

LIBRARY OF CONGRESS CATALOGING-IN-PUBLICATION DATA

Haddam, Jane, 1951–
    Flowering Judas : a Gregor Demarkian novel / by Jane Haddam.
        p. cm. — (Thorndike Press large print mystery)
    ISBN-13: 978-1-4104-4159-1 (hardcover)
    ISBN-10: 1-4104-4159-8 (hardcover)
    1. Demarkian, Gregor (Fictitious character)—Fiction. 2. Private investigators—Fiction. 3. Armenian Americans—Fiction. 4. Missing persons—Fiction. 5. Cold cases—Fiction. 6. Large type books. I. Title.
PS3566.A613F58 2011b
813'.54—dc22   2011031065

Published in 2011 by arrangement with St. Martin's Press, LLC.

Printed in the United States of America
1 2 3 4 5 6 7 15 14 13 12 11

This book is for
Robert Piepenbrink
because it contains, within it,
everything he hates in
murder mysteries.

ACKNOWLEDGMENTS

It would be nice if, when I finished a book, I went directly to the next page and wrote my acknowledgments, but I've got to admit — what I do is wander into the living room, collapse on the love seat, and channel surf until I realized I've just spent fifteen minutes watching large, mostly fat men with too many tattoos shouting into the faces of people whose cars they want to repossess.

Or something.

And, right now, the spell check on this computer is telling me I've spelled "something" wrong. This gets harder all the time.

Let me just thank my editor, Keith Kahla, who's kept Gregor afloat these many years, and his assistant Kathleen Conn, who puts up with me with more grace than I have the right to expect. Let me thank my agent, Don Maass, as well, and Carol Stone and Richard Siddall, two of the best friends I — or anybody else — have ever had.

And then let me thank the large group of enthusiastic readers — including Linda Dumas, Mike Fisher, Mary Featherston, Sue Daniels, Lynda Standley, Lymaree, Joan Kreuser, and I don't remember who else — who spent an entire afternoon on Facebook with me, working out the intricacies of amateur tattoos.

If I've forgotten anyone, I apologize. I tried writing it all down, and then lost it.

And finally, let me send a note to Robert: having heard for years now about the list of requirements for your owning and keeping a book in hardcover, I just had to see if I could get you to do it when the book broke all your rules. . . .

— Litchfield County, CT
Thanksgiving, 2010

■ ■ ■ ■

PROLOGUE

■ ■ ■ ■

We all believe in fairy-tales, and live in them.

— G. K. Chesterton

1

The first person to see the body hanging from the billboard on Mattatuck Avenue was Haydee Michaelman, and she wasn't paying attention.

"It only stands to reason," Haydee was saying to her friend Desiree, as the two of them stood by the side of the road, waiting to cross.

It was a hot night at the end of August, and the traffic on Mattatuck was insane. Later, Haydee would wonder why everybody had managed to miss that thing up there. She wouldn't wonder for long. It was "The Billboard," after all. It was that big sign asking if you'd seen Chester Ray Morton. It had been up there for twelve years. Nobody looked at it twice anymore.

Haydee's backpack was heavy with books, and she had been walking. She and Desiree walked out here three times a week to save the bus fare. Then they took the bus back home, because Desiree didn't like to walk in the dark. Haydee thought she was an idiot.

You were not supposed to cross Mattatuck Avenue right here. There was a crosswalk about three hundred feet down the road. The problem was that the crosswalk was nowhere near the entrance to Mattatuck–Harvey Community College, and it was another five hundred feet from the entrance to any of the actual buildings. Haydee wanted a car of her own. Lots of the other students had cars. Some of them had really impressive cars. Some of them even had trucks.

"The yard was dug up all around the place this morning," Haydee said, "and then it was dug up over near the garbage shed. With a shovel. I know what digging with a shovel looks like."

"I'm not saying you don't," Desiree said. "I'm saying it doesn't necessarily have to be. Have to be Mike, I mean. I mean, I know you don't like him, but —"

"It's not that I don't like him," Haydee said. "It's that he's a prick, that's what it is. Don't ask me what my mother thinks she's doing. Don't ever ask me that. But he knows I've got it stashed someplace. He knows."

"I'm sure he knows," Desiree said.

"At least he doesn't grab at me," Haydee said. "That was the last one. Asshole. But Mike knows I've got it stashed, and he's not going to pretend he doesn't want to steal it. He stole it the last time."

"I know he did," Desiree said. She sounded a little desperate. "I know he did, but —"

"There aren't any buts," Haydee said. "Twelve hundred dollars I had that time. I was supposed to buy a car with it. Now what are we doing? We're standing here waiting for the frigging traffic to thin out, and we're probably going to be late for English class, and you know what that's going to do. She's going to give us that look when we walk in that says, well . . . whatever it says."

"I don't think she's so bad," Desiree said. "I just wish she'd be, you know. Stricter. Like high school. I get work done faster when they're stricter."

"It isn't high school," Haydee said.

Just then, a car went by with three boys in it. It was one of those fancy-ass small Jeeps, and Haydee knew all three of the boys in it. They were in the same English class she was going to. They were probably on their way there. Or maybe not. People with cars like that didn't always come to class.

Of course, people without cars, people from the place Haydee was from herself — they didn't always come to class, either. Haydee looked over at Desiree. Desiree was wearing cropped Lycra pants that hugged her big thighs and a flowing, sparkly T-shirt that looked wrinkled all along the back. She was also wearing high heels. Haydee had given up wearing high heels the second week of the semester. They hurt her feet when she walked here.

"Anyway," Haydee said. If anything, the traffic seemed to be getting worse. "I know he's looking for it, and he knows I know he's looking for it. I've got it someplace he won't think of, because he doesn't think. You've got to give it to Mike. Every time he goes to jail, it's for a crime of opportunity."

"What's a crime of opportunity?"

"When people steal stuff because it's just lying around. You know, when people leave their keys in the car or their purses on the picnic table when they go off to chase their kid, or something like that. Did I tell you he was in jail again last week?"

"I know he was in jail," Desiree said. "The police came and arrested him in front of everybody. I thought that was a domestic disturbance, though."

"Nah. He shoplifted enough beer to make a Budweiser river right in front of the cashier at the Quik-Go, and when does that make sense? He's in and out of the place half the week. It's not that they wouldn't know who he was. And there was a tape. I mean, for God's sake, the man is an idiot. And a prick. And he's not going to steal my money this time. I've got a plan."

"You could stick it in a condom and put it up your, you know, junk," Desiree said. "I saw that on television."

"I've got a much better plan. I'm going to do what real people do. But maybe it's not such a bad idea, having him digging up the place. I mean, I didn't bury it. He's not going to find it by getting down in the dirt and knocking the trailer off the blocks. If he causes another plumbing problem, maybe my mother will kick him out."

"I don't think so," Desiree said.

"I don't think so, either," Haydee said. "Do you ever think about it? What it would be like to be, you know, somebody else? Maybe somebody like Dr. London."

"Nobody is like Dr. London," Desiree said. "She's weird."

"Yeah," Haydee said. "I know."

"She's even weird for a professor."

"I know," Haydee said again.

15

"And I was just saying, about the digging. It doesn't have to have been Mike looking for your stuff. I mean, you know, the place is haunted, and that kind of thing. Maybe it's the ghost of that guy that got killed there —"

"Ghosts don't dig holes in the ground," Haydee said, "and besides, nobody knows if he was killed there or anywhere. They don't even know that he's dead. And that was a long time ago. The police have already dug the hell out of everything. You'd have to be an idiot to go digging around our place now."

"Yeah," Desiree said.

Haydee saw a break in the traffic just a little way up the road. She turned her head the other way and saw a break there, too. There were no cars coming down the long curving entryway, either. If they got the light, they'd be able to get across. She grabbed Desiree by the arm and said, "Get ready."

It was just then, at the very last second, that Haydee looked up at the billboard right on the other side of Mattatuck Avenue and thought she saw something, something moving up there, swaying back and forth in the nonexistent wind.

Then the light changed and the traffic

16

stopped and they ran. They ran with their backpacks banging against their backs. They ran as fast as they could.

You had to cross Mattatuck Avenue when you had a chance to, or you didn't cross at all.

2

For Kenny Morton, the idea of spending his time writing English papers at Mattatuck–Harvey Community College was ridiculous, and he would never have agreed to it if he didn't think his mother was about to have a nervous breakdown.

"She just wants us all to be normal," Kenny's sister, Suzanne, said, when their parents were first pushing Kenny to go to school. "She just wants us all to be the way we would have been if Chester hadn't disappeared."

"Even if Chester hadn't disappeared," Kenny said, "I wouldn't be going to Mattatuck–Harvey and studying English. What am I doing this for? Can you tell me that? Why am I bothering? It's not like I'm not making a living."

"And there's that, too," Suzanne had said. "Why do you do that? Don't you know how much it hurts them that you're not going to go into the business? And why wouldn't you

17

go into the business?"

The business was Morton Rubbish Removal, and Kenny had nothing against it except the obvious. His father wasn't about to give him any serious responsibility when he was only eighteen, and he wasn't going to give it to him now, when he was twenty-two. That was not how Kenny's father did things.

"She wanted all of us to get an education," Suzanne had said.

And now, four years later, with the light beginning to fade a little outside the living room windows, Kenny was standing in the hall with a stack of books and a state of mind so foul, he was ready to kick something.

The books were something called *Current Issues and Enduring Questions* and *The Everyday Writer.* Kenny didn't think he needed to be told how to write stuff. He wrote a perfectly good business letter, and he was even better at working out a cost benefit ratio, and nobody had had to teach him either in school. He had a deal set up in Crayfield for Saturday that was going to net him over ten thousand dollars if he handled it right. He had an appointment for Wednesday that meant taking a vintage Model T out on Route 7 just to show some

18

guy it could run. He had work to do, and the work paid him. He did not need to waste his time writing a two-and-a-half-page paper comparing and contrasting high school and college.

Mark was in the kitchen with their father and mother. There had been a lot of low murmuring all day. Kenny thought if he had to do this crap, he might as well get on with it and do it.

Mark came in from the back, looked at Kenny's books, and shrugged.

"She's upset," Mark said.

"I can hear she's upset," Kenny said.

"You can't blame her for being upset," Mark said. "The last time one of us left home, he went missing. And you know she's convinced Chester is dead."

"I'm convinced Chester is dead," Kenny said. "But that's not the point. I mean, for God's sake, Mark. I can't do this anymore."

"Can't do what? Live with your family? Lots of people live with their families."

"It's not the living with them I don't like."

Mark looked away. "It's not an unreasonable thing to ask. That you be in school, I mean. You can't just lounge around the house and not do anything."

"I don't lounge around the house and not do anything. I've got a business. I'm not

19

selling drugs, and I'm making more than enough to live on my own. And if she doesn't want me to do that, then let's cut this crap about school and stop treating me like I was six."

Mark looked at the floor. Kenny wondered what it was his brother thought about all the time. The hallway was all polished up and pretty the way their mother liked it. It had some kind of long-haired carpet on the floor, and little pictures of kittens in frames on the walls. The place made Kenny claustrophobic.

"Maybe," Mark said, "you should give up the fancy cars and come to work in the business."

"They're antique cars, not fancy cars," Kenny said. "And the business wouldn't pay me enough money. Never mind the fact that it wouldn't stop all this crap about school. Look, all I want to do is concentrate on my own business, open a showroom somewhere, expand the Web sites, do what I have to do. And not go to school. There's no point to it."

"There's always a point to school," Mark said.

He looked so smug, Kenny wanted to hit him.

Then the door at the back of the hall

opened, and their father came in. Their father was the largest man Kenny had ever known. He was six foot three if he was anything at all. Chester had been tall like that. Kenny was not.

Stew Morton came down to where Kenny and Mark had faced off, and looked at Kenny's books. Then he looked anywhere at all except at Kenny's face.

"Your mother's crying," he said.

"I've been trying to talk to him," Mark said.

"Nobody needs to talk to me," Kenny said. "I'm not going to do this anymore, Pop, that's all there is. This is the last of school, I really mean it. I'm going to finish this course. I paid for it. I can't get a full refund. I'll finish it. But that's it. I'm done."

"It's not school your mother is crying about," Stew said. "It's you. Moving out."

"I won't move to the damned trailer park," Kenny said.

"How do you think she feels? I'm not asking you to stay forever. She doesn't want you to stay forever. She just wants you to stay until it's cleared up."

"It's been twelve years," Kenny said. "Maybe you have to accept the possibility that it's never going to be cleared up. There are cases like that, Pop. There are cases that just don't get solved."

"This one will get solved," Stew said. "She's got the FBI interested."

"No, she doesn't," Kenny said. "She's tried them before. They just aren't going to come across. They can't even do it unless they can prove a crime has been committed and that it had something to do with crossing state lines. We don't even know a crime was committed here —"

"Your brother wouldn't just run off without telling anybody," Stew said. "And he wouldn't have left all his things in that trailer. Your mother talked to him at eight o'clock on the night he went missing, and he was going over to that woman's house — he was going —"

"Yeah, I know. He was going over to see Darvelle. I was here when all this happened. And it's beside the point. I'm not going to school anymore. That's the end of it. And I'm not going into the business. That's the end of that. And if you can all live with both those things, that's one thing, but if you can't, you can't."

"Your mother won't force you to go to school anymore," Stew said. "I've talked to her about it."

"You talked to her about it before," Kenny said. "She lets up for a few weeks until she thinks the crisis has passed, and then she's right back at it. I've found a place over in Morris Corners. I can move in on the first of September. I'm not going to live in Chester's trailer park."

"What happens if you go missing?" Stew said. "It will kill her. It really will."

"I'm not going to go missing," Kenny said.

He looked at Mark and then back at his father. Then he took his books and went out the back door.

His truck was parked in the driveway behind Mark's, a big red pickup he used to haul stuff around. He wasn't about to use more than one vehicle as long as he could help it. It was always possible to make money if you just watched your expenses. That was the genius of the Internet. It was great for keeping your expenses under control.

Kenny climbed into the cab of the truck and sat back. He could look up and down their street and see the flyers posted on every telephone pole. The flyers had been there since Chester had been missing a week, and his mother refreshed them every week or two. She went around to the grocery stores and gas stations and put up new ones. She made hundreds and sent them out by bulk mail.

Kenny got the truck started and took a deep breath.

If he ran into Chester on the street, he'd kill him right there.

Everybody's life would be better if they only had the body.

3

Shpetim Kika knew a few things, in spite of having been brought up on a sheep farm in Albania. One of the things he knew was that everything was better under capitalism, except morals, which were a mess. Sexual morals were a mess, that is. On the bribery and corruption front, Shpetim could scarcely believe how clean this place was. It had taken him only a few weeks to figure it out. If you gave some politician money to give you a job, they put both you and the politician in jail, and they didn't care what political party you belonged to or who was the president in power in Washington. There were good things and bad things about this. The good things were that you got the job if you were good at your work, and you didn't get accused of something and thrown in jail so that somebody with better connections could get it instead. The bad things were that you had to work your ass off.

They had been working their asses off all

day on this particular job. They would be working their asses off for at least another two hours. They'd stay as long as the light lasted. It was late August and the days were already beginning to go dark a little earlier. It wasn't much earlier, but still. It was coming. The fall was coming. The winter was coming. They had to have the shell up before the first snowstorm, or they were never going to get this thing done on time.

"It's a matter of track records," Shpetim said to his son, Nderi. Then he made a mental correction and said, "Dee. What a name for a man. Dee."

"People find Nderi too hard to pronounce," Nderi said. "I find Nderi too hard to pronounce."

"We've got to bring it in on time and on budget," Shpetim said, "or as close to both as possible. It's our first job for the state. If we do it well, we'll get another one. There's a lot of money in doing construction for the state."

"We'll get the shell up in time," Nderi said. "Don't worry about that. If you're going to worry about something, worry about the electricians. It's the wiring that keeps me up at night."

"You shouldn't be keeping up at night," Shpetim said. "You should be rested to come to work in the morning. And you should consider a girl. It's time you were married."

"I have considered a girl."

"A Muslim girl."

"I have considered a girl who will convert."

"Yes, all right," Shpetim said. "I know. I'm not comfortable."

"She's even Albanian," Nderi said. "Born and brought up in Albania. Only came here three years ago. Modest to a fault, if you ask me."

"Eh," Shpetim said. "It's that you're young. You don't really want those things you see on TV."

"Every man alive wants those things I see on TV," Nderi said, "but not in a wife, I agree. But Anya is not like that, and you know it. She's willing to convert, and you know it. She has no family —"

"You don't think that's strange?" Shpetim said. "You don't think there's something wrong with that?"

"I think we know enough people who saw half their families vanish into Soviet jails, they weren't the ones there was something wrong with. There's no family to object to her conversion. Give it up. I will get married to her, one way or the other. You can't

26

prevent it. This is America."

"Then calm your mother about it first," Shpetim said. "Just because you can't sleep nights doesn't mean your mother should be keeping me up. Have they stopped work over there? What is going on?"

The two of them were standing at the edge of the site for the new technology building at Mattatuck–Harvey Community College, standing at the door of the little shed they had built at the very beginning of the job. The shed was the place where they could do paperwork if they had to in the middle of the day. They had every man in the business out here working. Shpetim himself came out here to work, even if he couldn't lift heavy objects anymore. Nderi could lift them. He could pick up steel girders as if they were made out of bread dough.

"It's not like we're Arabs," Nderi said. "Our women don't go veiled. They don't even wear the hijab most of the time. She won't have a hard time fitting in. And Albanian cooking is Albanian cooking."

"They've stopped work over there," Shpetim said, pointing across the site to where poured concrete and steel reinforcement bars were sticking out of the ground. A half-dozen men were in a little clutch right next to a pile of concrete blocks. The earthmover next to them was puffing away, using up fuel, but not actually doing anything.

"They can't just stop like that," Shpetim said. "What do they think they're doing?"

"I want you to help me talk Ma into letting Anya come for dinner some night," Nderi said. "That's how you start this kind of thing. You have the girl to dinner. And I want Ma to meet her."

"Your mother has met her."

"I want her to meet Anya *formally*," Nderi said.

One of the men broke away from the clutch and began to walk across the blasted landscape toward Shpetim and Nderi. It was Andor Kulla, looking — Shpetim couldn't put a name to how he looked.

"There's something wrong," Shpetim said.

"There's always something wrong," Nderi said.

Andor walked up to them and stopped. Shpetim was about to start shouting, but then he didn't. He didn't know why.

"Why are you not working?" Shpetim asked. "What are you all doing, standing around like that? You know we've got a deadline."

Andor looked up, then down, then back the way he had come. The other men were all standing in their clutch, looking at Shpetim and Nderi and Andor. Andor turned back.

"You've got to come," he said. "We found something."

"Found something? Found what?" Shpetim asked.

Andor shook his head and turned away. "This is the last place they saw him alive, isn't it?" Andor said, walking back across the site as he talked. "That kid. Ten, twelve years ago. This was the last place anybody saw him alive."

Shpetim felt something drop right inside him, as if his intestines had fallen loose and were about to come out. He hurried after Andor, walking over the pocked earth as quickly as he could. Nderi came with him, moving faster.

This is what I need, Shpetim thought. *Something to bring all the work on the site to a halt. Something to make me a suspect in an investigation.* He had no idea what kind of investigation. The men must have found a body. That was the only thing that made any sense. They must have found a body, or a skeleton, and this would be a crime scene, and the work would stop, and they would be blamed for it. There would be blood. There would be policemen. It would be the end of everything he had started out to do here, and then he would have to go back to Albania.

Except that he couldn't go back to Albania. He was an American citizen now.

Shpetim got to where the men were standing and looked around. They backed up, and he could see that there was a hole where the earthmover had been digging earlier in the day. He looked into the hole expecting to see a ghostly skeleton hand reaching up out of the dirt.

What he saw instead was the top of a bright yellow backpack, full of something.

4

For Darvelle Haymes, life in Mattatuck, New York, was a matter of putting one foot in front of the other. That was what she had been doing when Chester went missing, and it was what she was doing now, as the day began to fold in on itself and the dark began to creep in around the edges. She pulled her Honda Civic into the driveway of her small brick ranch house and turned the engine off. She took the key out of the ignition and looked around. This was a reasonably good neighborhood for Mattatuck. She'd only been able to buy the house because, being a real estate agent, she'd seen

30

it go on the market, underpriced, five days before anybody else knew it was there.

She got out of the car and looked around again. The telephone pole at the curb was just a telephone pole. The community bulletin board at the bus stop was empty. She thought about going into the house right away, and then she thought better of it. She marched down to the street and looked around. All the telephone poles she could see were just telephone poles.

Darvelle went back up the driveway and then through the breeze-way and into the house by the side door. She could have parked the car in the garage, but she didn't want to.

She got into the kitchen and put her purse down on the counter next to the microwave. She stood still for a moment and listened for any sounds she shouldn't hear in the house, but the house was as quiet as the community bulletin board was blank. She got her cell phone out of her purse and headed for the living room.

The living room had track lighting. Kyle had put it in for her the week after she moved in. That was the first week the telephone poles had been covered with flyers, and the first week she'd found the crazy old woman trying to get in through a window in the back.

Darvelle sat down on the couch. Her hair was a mass of red running down her back. Her nails were long curves of violet with sparkles in them. The nails matched her suit. She punched, and then held down the number 2 on her phone and waited until it started ringing.

Kyle picked up right away. "Holborn," he said first — but Darvelle wasn't worried about that. He was just trying to appear professional in front of the people he worked with.

"Don't worry about it," Darvelle said. "I just got home. Everything seems to be fine. She didn't come back and put more flyers up while I was gone."

"Come back? Was she there before?"

"Well, she must have been," Darvelle said. "When I left to go show the Petrovski house, the street was full of flyers again. What does she think she's doing? I didn't own this house when Chester disappeared. He never got near this neighborhood, as far as I can tell."

"She thinks you killed him," Kyle said.

"I know she thinks I killed him," Darvelle said, 'but it stands to reason that if I had killed him, I'd have left his body in the place I was living in then. I wouldn't have carted it halfway across the city to put it in the flower beds here. Not that I have any flower beds. I hate flower beds. In the winter they look like crap. And in the summer they bring bees and you're trying to show the house and the clients are running around freaking out."

"Did you check the whole house?"

"No," Darvelle said. "Nobody's here now, though, I can tell."

"You should check the whole house."

"You mean maybe she came back and threw stage blood all over my bedspread again? I don't think she's going to do that. We've got a restraining order. And besides, she's getting what she wants. They're doing that TV show about the case. Whatever that is. God, I hate true crime shows. They're so boring."

"You're not worried about it? Those people coming here to look into it?"

"No," Darvelle said. "I've told you and told you, Kyle. Chester disappeared. He just disappeared. He was supposed to pick me up and drive me to school and he never showed up. And that's all there was to it. No matter what his mother thinks."

"You don't have to have evidence to — to suggest things, if you know what I mean. Those shows suggest things."

"And what are they going to suggest?" Darvelle asked. "That I killed him, why, exactly? Has anybody ever been able to come up with a motive? He was my boyfriend, yes, okay, but he wasn't my husband. I didn't have a life insurance policy out on him. And I wasn't worried about losing him. In fact —"

"In fact, you were already going out with me."

"Exactly. So I don't see the point here. I just wish that old bat would give it a rest. It's been twelve years."

"I've got something here," Kyle said. "We've got some kind of call."

"Really?" Darvelle said. "Crime in Mattatuck? Is it a homicide?"

"I don't think so," Kyle said. "I've got to go. I'll tell you about it later if there's anything to tell."

"It'll probably be another one of those convenience store robberies," Darvelle said. "I mean, how stupid can you possibly get, anyway? They go running into these places and they have to know there are security cameras. They have to know it. *The World's Dumbest Criminals.* That's a show I like. Except I don't like Tonya Harding, and they always have her on doing commentary."

"It's something out at the college," Kyle

said. "I have to go, really. If you find something in the rest of the house, call here and get somebody to come out. I don't like the way that woman behaves. I don't think she's safe."

"She just comes around and puts up hundreds of those damned flyers," Darvelle said. "She puts them up and I take them down."

"Even so. You said she put them up today."

"She did."

"So check the house and call if there's anything wrong," Kyle said. "I'll be over after shift. Leave something in the refrigerator I can microwave in case I'm late."

"Maybe she killed him," Darvelle said. "Wouldn't that be an absolute gas?"

"I'll see you later," Kyle said.

Darvelle put the phone on the end table near the lamp and got up to go down the hall to her bedroom. Her head hurt a little. She didn't think she was going to sell the Petrovski house to these people she'd brought out there today. She didn't think she was going to sell it to much of anybody until she convinced the Petrovskis to bring the price down by at least thirty thousand dollars. It was not the kind of market you could play games in, and the Petrovskis were playing games.

Darvelle stepped out of her shoes. She picked them up and walked down the hall to the master bedroom in her pantyhose. It wasn't much of a master bedroom. It didn't have a bathroom *en suite.* It was just the bigger bedroom of the two, and the one with the walk-in closet.

She stopped at the bathroom and looked in. Everything was what it should be. She went to the bedroom and opened the door and looked in there for a moment, too. There was nothing to see. There was no stage blood on the bedspread. There was no wadded mess of flyers on the carpet. There was no bright-red CHESTER written in lipstick on the vanity table mirror. Honest to God, Charlene Morton was some kind of lunatic.

Darvelle Haymes did not believe in being afraid of her own shadow. She didn't believe in being afraid of anything. She was certainly not afraid of the ghost of Chester Ray Morton, wherever he might be and whatever it was he was doing.

She sat down on the side of the bed and started stripping her pantyhose off.

It was a good question — just what it was Chester had been doing, and where it was he'd been doing it.

She'd been wondering that for twelve
years.

5

The flyers were lying on the counter next to
the sinks in the third floor women's bathroom in Frasier Hall, and that made Penny
London very nervous.

She put her two big tote bags on the floor
and picked up the flyers, one by one. There
were six of them, splayed out in a fan, as if
somebody had deliberately placed them for
maximum recognition value. She put the
flyers down again. It wasn't as if they were
anything unusual. HAVE YOU SEEN THIS
MAN? they read. Then there was that same
picture that was up on the billboard at the
front entrance to the college. It had to be a
dozen years since Chester Morton went
missing. Penny still remembered him.

She pushed her mop of gray hair out of
her face and bent down to the tote bags.
She found the one with the shampoo in it
and got it out. She didn't like those flyers.
Those flyers meant that somebody had
come up to this bathroom, and the reason
Penny had chosen it in the first place was
because she was sure nobody ever came up
here, except perhaps the cleaning staff. It
was hard to find bathrooms at Mattatuck–

Harvey Community College that nobody ever spent time in. There were too many students looking for places to get stoned.

Penny glanced toward the door. It would be better if she could lock it, but there was no lock on it. If there was an emergency, a hostage situation, one of those school shootings, anybody who came into the bathrooms in this place would be doomed.

She turned on the hot water in the left-hand sink full blast, then turned on the cold a third of the way. Then she bent over and put her head under the faucet. The cold water felt good on her scalp. It felt so good, Penny thought she might give in in a day or two and spend some of her money taking a motel room for a night. It would be wonderful to have a full-on shower for once. It would be even more wonderful to have a full-on bath. She'd promised herself she'd take a hotel room whenever it got to the point where she just couldn't stand it.

She put shampoo in her hair. She rubbed the soap deep down into her scalp with the tips of her fingers. She put her head back under the faucet and let the soap rinse out. When she was done with her hair, she'd risk taking some of her clothes off and washing the rest of herself. Then she'd change into the clothes she'd brought from the car. It was only twenty-five minutes before class. She would have to hurry.

It would be terrible if somebody walked in on her.

Maybe Chester Ray Morton's mother was still in the building somewhere. Maybe she would come back to see if her flyers had been thrown away by a janitor. Penny had met Chester Ray Morton's mother when all that had happened, and she was of the opinion that the woman was a stark raving loon.

Penny took off her shirt, and then her bra. She dressed very carefully for the days she took sponge baths in the Frasier Hall bathroom. She took the fresh shirt and the fresh bra out of her tote bag. She put them down on the counter next to the sink. She got out the Irish Spring soap and the Dove deodorant. She thought it was odd how she'd gone on buying all the familiar brands even after she'd lost her apartment.

Her cell phone rang. It played the theme music from *Looney Tunes.* Penny took it out of her other tote bag, the ones with the books in it, and stared at it.

It was a good little cell phone, nothing fancy, but with "features" to it, as her sons said. She could read and answer e-mail on it, for instance. She could instant message.

She could have a presence online just as if she still had a computer and a home to put it in.

She slid the phone open and put it to her ear. Her body felt oddly exposed, without the shirt. She bit her lip.

"Mom?" George said. His voice still sounded high, as if it had never changed with puberty. He was twenty-three now. "Mom, are you all right?"

"Of course I'm all right," Penny said. "I'm trying to get my act together for class. I've got a night class this term."

"I know. You told me. Are you sure you're all right?"

"I'm positive I'm all right. I've got at least three kids who are going to end the term without handing in a single paper, but that's par for the course. And I'm kind of in a hurry. I could call you back later."

There was a long, dead pause on the line. It was the thing Penny hated most about cell phones. With a landline, when the other person wasn't talking, you could still tell the line was open, that the call hadn't gone south. On a cell phone, when nobody was talking, the line just sounded dead.

Penny moved her things around on the counter. She looked at the flyer again. Chester Ray Morton hadn't been the kind of student who did nothing all term and then panicked about it during exam week. He'd come to every class.

"Mom?" George said.

"I'm still here," Penny said.

"I talked to Aunt Jenna this morning," George said.

Penny bit her lip. "Did you call her because you wanted to keep in touch? What? I thought you didn't like the woman."

"She called me."

Penny wondered if it would be easier if she just dropped the phone into some water. But that wouldn't do. That would only ruin the phone, and the phone was the one thing that made what she was doing possible.

"Well," she said. "That must have been interesting. What did she want?"

There was another long silence again. Penny looked at the soap and the shampoo. She wanted to get on with it. She hated going to class without washing up. Besides, in her position, it was important to stay washed up. If you started to stink, you'd find yourself without any options at all.

"She wanted," George said, "to tell me you were living in your car."

"Did she?" Penny said.

"She said she saw you in the parking lot of the Walmart in Mattatuck and you had

41

everything you owned in your car. She said she saw you changing your shirt."

"I've never changed my shirt in a parking lot in my life," Penny said. "And you know what your Aunt Jenna is like. I haven't really talked to her since your Uncle Zach died, and that was four years ago. She wouldn't know if I had all my stuff in my car to save her life. She wouldn't know my stuff."

"But she saw you at Walmart," George said. "That's true, isn't it?"

"Yes, George, she saw me at Walmart. In the parking lot. I saw her, too. We said hello."

"And that was all?"

"She stood around for awhile having one of those conversations. You know. What's George doing. What's Graham doing. Alison is going to be queen of the universe next week. That kind of thing."

"And that's all?"

"That's all we ever say when we see each other. She didn't like me when Zach was alive and she likes me even less now."

"And you're not living in your car?"

"I'm just fine. I've got two courses to teach here and one over at Pelham."

"Pelham doesn't pay anything."

"Pelham doesn't pay much, but it pays something. It doesn't hurt."

"You didn't get a summer course."

"No, I know I didn't," Penny said. "But the summer is over and we've started on fall term and I'm as booked up as I'm allowed to be. I'm fine."

"If Graham and I find out you're living in your car and you didn't tell us you needed money, we're both going to come out there and kill you. I mean it. There's no reason for you to be teaching at all anymore if you don't want to. We could support you. You could come out here and we could find a place big enough —"

"I'm not going to move out to California," Penny said. "And would you stop? I'm fine. I really am. And I'm going to be late if I don't get off this phone and do something. I really do have to get to class."

There was yet another long dead silence on the phone. Penny took a deep breath and counted to ten.

"All right," George said suddenly. "Call me when you're done. I'm going to call Graham."

"I really am all right," Penny said.

But George had hung up. That did not bode well.

Penny looked down at the shirt and the shampoo and the soap. Then she put her old shirt on and swept everything else back into the totebag.

She'd have to come back up here after class and wash up then. She didn't like the idea. She didn't like being up in this part of the building in the middle of the night. There just wasn't any help for it.

Maybe she'd postpone the idea of taking a night in a hotel. She was going to have to have enough money put by to get herself a place to stay when the weather got cold, because the weather got very cold in this part of New York state.

And it wasn't that far until October.

6

Charlene Morton knew she couldn't go out, not so close to night, not with half the family in the house. They watched her these days, her family did. They made sure she wasn't carrying anything but the usual leaflets and flyers and posters. They made sure she wasn't wandering around at odd hours that some judge might consider "harassment."

Still, she could come out to the greenhouse, and she had. Part of that was to be by herself for a while, to be away from them and on her own. Part of it was to look at the flowering Judas tree. It was the hardest thing she had ever undertaken to grow. It was tall and its purple flowers looked like

44

they were made of silk. She was proud of it, but worried about it, too. The dirt around the roots was chopped up and mounded here and there. She'd worked at it for half an hour and barely made it what she wanted it to be again.

Then she'd headed back to the house, because she knew they would be waiting for her. They were suspicious of her even when she was only tending to plants.

This was the truth of it — no matter how often Stew and Suzanne and the boys all said they cared about what happened to Chester, no matter how often they all said they wanted to bring him back home . . . well.

They all wanted a quiet life. That was what was going on. They wanted Chester back if it took no pain or suffering to get him back. If it meant lawsuits and stalking charges and nights in jail, that was something else again.

Charlene had heard Kenny leave for school, but she hadn't gone out to the hall to say good-bye. Kenny didn't want to be in school, and he didn't want to join the business, either. He wanted what Chester used to want, a place of his own and a life of his own. Charlene was not completely stupid. She knew that was a natural thing for young

men. They always wanted to be off somewhere.

But still.

Charlene was sitting at the big round table
in the kitchen. She had poured herself a cup
of coffee an hour ago. Now it sat, cold and
only halfdrunk, near her elbow. There was a
stack of the latest flyers in the middle of the
table. There was a stack of the latest posters
right next to it. The posters were not real
posters, the way they had been when Chester first went missing. These were just
ordinary pieces of typing paper with the
picture and information printed on them by
the printer Mark had downstairs. There
wasn't as much energy as there used to be
in the search for Chester Ray Morton.

Of course, it had been twelve years. Twelve
years was a long time.

The kitchen door swung open. Charlene
looked up. It was Stew standing in the
doorway. Charlene wondered what had happened to Mark.

"Kenny got off to school," Stew said.

Charlene nodded. She put her hand up to
touch Chester's face in the picture on the
poster. It was the same as the picture on the
flyer. She'd brought those flyers all the way
up to the third floor of Frasier Hall today.
She didn't even know if anybody ever went

to the third floor of Frasier Hall. At least the bathrooms were clean.

Stew came in and sat down on the other side of the table. He looked old. Charlene thought she probably looked older. She couldn't really see herself in the mirror anymore.

"I think we've got to at least consider the possibility that our boys are not cut out for school," Stew said.

Charlene took her hand away from the posters. She didn't like touching them. They didn't feel like Chester's skin. Nothing felt like Chester's skin.

"I've got to clean the house this week," she said. "We've got to send the curtains out. The ones in the living room."

"If you want."

"I don't want it to look like we live like pigs when we're on television."

"We don't look like we live like pigs."

"I wonder if it would have made a difference. If there had been television shows like this back when Chester was first missing. Maybe if we'd gotten on one of them, we'd have him back by now."

Stew got up. He checked the water in the electric percolator.

"Even if we just got his body back, he'd be back," Charlene said. "You think I expect him to come walking alive through the front door. Well, I don't. Chester is dead. I know he's dead. He's been dead all this time. And she killed him."

Stew was filling the percolator with water. He had his back to her. The water was running in the sink. "Don't start that again," he said.

"There's no 'again' about it," Charlene said. "She killed him. You know that as well as I do. Killed him and hid the body somewhere, just like she had her own baby killed."

Stew turned the water off. He brought the electric percolator pot back to the stand and began fiddling with it. He put in a fresh filter. He put in new coffee grounds. The silence went on and on and on. Charlene didn't care.

Then Stew said, finally, "You don't know any of that. And don't start in on me, Charlene. I know all your arguments. I know everything you're going to say."

"I took flyers out there this morning," Charlene said. "She'll have taken them down before she left for work. I've got to be more careful than that. I couldn't help it this morning, though. I couldn't go later. I had things to do."

Stew sat down at the table again. "You

shouldn't have gone at all. The judge said —"

"The judge was overruled by the federal district court," Charlene said. "I've got a free speech right to put my posters up, even in that little bitch's neighborhood. I can't go into her house without being arrested and I can't talk to her and I can't call her on the phone, but I can put my posters up. Because she killed him, Stew. You know she killed him."

"I don't know. And you don't know she killed a baby, either," he said. "There's no evidence —"

"There's no evidence because nobody went looking for evidence," Charlene said. "There are tests you can take for that, tests that can tell if you've ever been pregnant. There are tests that can tell if you've had an abortion, too, at least if you take them close to when you get the abortion. But she never took any of those tests. They never made her take any tests. They just 'talked' to her a few times and let her go on her way."

"There's no evidence —"

"Chester brought that girl to this house not four days before he died," Charlene said. "And she looked pregnant enough to me. She looked enormous —"

"But —"

"I know all that," Charlene said. "All those people she worked with, saying she never looked pregnant a day in her life, saying she never told them she was pregnant. Well, maybe she didn't. Maybe she was hiding it. Maybe she was getting ready to kill Chester even then. But she was pregnant the day she got here, and you know it."

Stew rubbed his face with his hands. "Maybe we just saw what we wanted to see," he said. "Maybe we were both so anxious to find a way out of the situation we'd caused that we took any lifeline we could get —"

"Chester wouldn't come to me and say his girlfriend was pregnant if it wasn't so," Charlene said. "She was pregnant. And then, four days later, Chester is gone and so is the baby. She's flat as a board and saying she was never pregnant in the first place."

"I don't think they let them have abortions that late," Stew said. "She was supposed to be, what, almost due? I don't think —"

"Oh, you can find an abortionist to kill a baby at any stage of the game, believe me. I know what goes on. I'll bet he got on to her. I'll bet he decided to ditch her, and she wanted to get back at him."

"Chester wouldn't ditch his own child."

"He wouldn't ditch the child, but he'd ditch the mother if he ever found out what she was. It's the only explanation that fits, Stew. She thought it was going to make everything all peachy keen, a baby, we'd never turn away from a baby, and it wouldn't matter that we didn't like her. Chester could marry her and he was the oldest. He'd get the business. And then he found out what she was and he walked out on her, and she got mad. And she killed him. And then she killed the baby out of spite."

"Charlene," Stew said.

"She killed him," Charlene said. "And that's all there is to it."

Stew got up. The percolator was making odd noises. It was probably finished, or something. Charlene had never gotten the hang of how to use it. She looked down at her hands. Her fingernails were cracked. She hadn't put polish on in years. If Chester were still alive, he'd come back to find her an old woman.

But Chester was not alive.

Charlene got up from the table.

"I'm going to watch television," she said, even though she never watched television, and Stew knew it.

Stew was getting a coffee cup down from

the cabinet. "There's no evidence," he said, for at least the third time. "You can't go calling people murderers when there's no evidence."

"You can call a murderer a murderer no matter what kind of evidence there is," she said.

Then she marched through the swinging double doors and away from him, and from the posters and the flyers and the endless reality of the last twelve years.

7

Althy Michaelman didn't give a rat's ass about . . . well, about anything, really. It was just that the goddamned empty trailer bothered her.

It didn't bother her all the time. Sometimes she had enough of a buzz on to forget all about it, sort of, unless she heard a noise over there. Then she got spooked, because of course the trailer was empty. The trailer had been empty for years, ever since Chester Fucking Morton had disappeared. Althy wasn't surprised he'd disappeared. He was the kind of person who disappeared. He was a fucking-A idiot.

Tonight, there was not enough of anything in the house to really get buzzed on, and Althy didn't like the idea of going out and stealing it. There was no advantage to stealing from liquor stores. They had cameras, and most of the ones around here knew who she was, anyway. The whole point of drinking instead of doing all the other stuff she used to do was that she couldn't go to prison for just having it around. Robbing a fucking-A liquor store therefore made no sense.

Therefore.

Althy thought it was funny as hell that she'd thought of a word like "therefore." Haydee would love that, if she ever heard it. Haydee wasn't even home. There was a fucking tragedy, there was. Haydee over there at the junior college, what was anybody supposed to think? The girl was a fucking-A idiot, and always had been.

And besides, who did she think she was?

The trailer over there was absolutely quiet. It was absolutely empty. Every once in a while, that crazy woman, Chester Morton's mother, came to look it over, but that was it. Althy thought it had to be nice, having enough money to rent something you weren't even going to use. Just rent it and leave it there. Leave it empty. Then every couple of months, kids would break in and the police would be out here and how was that good for anything?

Althy was lying on the bed in the bedroom at the back of the trailer, the one that spanned the whole width. The bed was full of dirty clothes and the floor was full of dirty clothes, too. You had to take clothes down the street all the way to Colonial Plaza to get to the laundromat. It was too long a walk carrying a bag of shit like that, and besides Althy didn't like Colonial Plaza anymore. It used to be a real shopping center. Now half the stores were empty and the place felt like there were vampires in it. Althy had seen a movie with vampires in it on TV. That was before they'd shut the cable off.

This time.

Althy sat up. Mike was somewhere around. Haydee was over at the college, going to class with that woman she couldn't stop talking about. Penelope London. What kind of a name was that? She was a snob. All the teachers Althy had ever met were snobs. You could tell the woman was a snob with a name like that.

Althy's head hurt. It was getting dark. It was always getting dark. Haydee had money in this trailer somewhere. It was a lot of money. Haydee squirreled away money in coffee cans and weird places trying to make it so that nobody could find it, but what sense did that make? If you had money, you spent it. Especially when there were things you needed. Althy didn't understand why she let Haydee live here anymore at all.

Besides, the money should be going to the rent on the trailer. It should be. Haydee threw in a little every month, but it wasn't enough. She had room and board here. That was going to cost you. She couldn't just stuff all her money away in coffee cans and expect it to be there when she went back to it.

Althy steadied herself against the side of the bed and got to her feet. She was swaying a little. This was the worst hangover she could remember in months. Everything glowed, and everything shimmered. She steadied herself against the dresser, next, and then against the wall. She pushed herself out into the narrow hall. Everything in this trailer was narrow. It was a single wide. There was that. No fancy double wides with cathedral ceilings and gourmet kitchens in this trailer park. It was just single wides and cinder block.

Althy inched down the hall and looked inside. Mike must have been here first. The room had been completely destroyed. There were clothes everywhere. There were books everywhere. That was something else about

Haydee. She was neat. She kept all her things in special places. Maybe Mike had found the money.

There was noise down the hall. It could be a burglar, but Althy didn't think so. She went back out into the hall and down it toward the "living room," which was full of dirty clothes, too. Dirty clothes traveled. They were everywhere.

Mike was sitting on the recliner. The recliner was broken. It showed raw wood at the joints. Mike had his head back and his eyes closed.

"Did you find the money?" Althy said.

"Of course I didn't find the goddamned money," Mike said. "Why would I find the fucking money? She's a bitch, that girl is. I'm going to beat the fucking crap out of her when she gets home."

Althy sat down on the metal folding chair. She couldn't remember where the chair had come from. It was just there in the trailer one morning, and it still was.

"Listen," she said. "You don't want to touch Haydee. She's not like other people."

"Beat the fucking crap out of her," Mike said.

"She'll call the police," Althy said, feeling anxious now. "She did last time. She'll get you locked up."

"You ought to learn to control the fucking bitch," Mike said. "She's your daughter."

"We don't want the police around here," Althy said. "Not again. It's one thing we find the money and we take it. We have a right to take it. She's living here. She's supposed to be contributing to the household. I read that in the papers. But you can't touch her. She'll call nine-one-one."

Mike was so still on the recliner, he looked dead. "I looked everywhere," he said after a while. "I took a knife to her fucking mattress. I couldn't find it. How much do you think she has?"

"Eight or nine hundred dollars," Althy said.

"What's the bitch want a car for anyway? Where does she think she's going? To work? Right. Some work. Quik-Go, for Christ's sake. And that school. What the fuck does she think she's doing going to school?"

Althy looked at her hands. "Did you dig up the ground? You know, out there? Haydee thinks you did. She thinks you were looking for the money."

"Of course I didn't dig anything the fuck up," Mike said. "Jesus. If she'd dug that thing down in the ground that way, somebody would have seen her. It would have been gone in a day. And she likes to look at it. I know she does. She hoards the fucking stuff. Like a miser. She hoards the fucking stuff."

"Somebody dug it all up," Althy said. She was pushing words past the haze in her brain. They were having a hard time coming out. "Somebody's going to come out from the company and have a fit. She thinks you dug it all up looking for the money."

"I didn't dig it all up."

"Don't you wonder who did dig it up? Don't you wonder? Under the circumstances."

"What the fuck's that supposed to mean? 'Under the' fucking 'circumstances'?"

Althy looked down at her hands again. It was hard to keep the times straight, sometimes. That had all happened so long ago. Haydee was only six. That was all. Haydee was sitting right here in this living room while Chester Ray Morton paced up and down and that girlfriend of his . . . that girlfriend of his . . .

It was hard to remember. There was nothing left of it but the trailer next door, and it was empty.

And haunted.

Maybe Haydee had put the money over there.

Althy closed her eyes and put her head in

her hands and waited for the headache spasm to pass. Then she opened up again and looked around the room.

If Haydee was hiding the money in Chester Ray Morton's empty trailer it was safe enough from Althy Michaelman.

She wouldn't go back into that place on a bet.

8

Kyle Holborn could have told Darvelle Haymes where he was going, and why he was going there, and what the dispatcher said the man on the phone said he'd thought he'd found out there at the building site — but it would have taken too long to explain, and much longer to handle. Kyle didn't know if he was handling it now. He wished he'd been the one to drive. It was always Jack who drove when they went out together. Kyle didn't know why.

Jack parked the cruiser as close as he could to where everybody was standing. That wasn't very close. Kyle could see them all through the darkening evening, a little clutch of men around some construction equipment, swaying back and forth, their hands in their pockets. One of them looked up and saw the patrol car. He broke away from the crowd and headed toward them.

"Crap," Jack said. He popped the driver's side door and got out.

Kyle got out, too. It was thick and muggy, still heavy summer even though it was this late in the year. He looked to the left and to the right. Everything was torn up. He didn't recognize the place.

"You remember what it was like before?" he asked Jack.

"Before what?"

"Before they started this building."

"Sure I remember what it was like before."

"Do you remember them digging it up the first time?"

"They dug it up before?"

"When Chester Ray Morton went missing. There was a rumor. Somebody said they saw him out here, or saw some guy out here, and we came and dug it up. We dug the whole thing."

"Wasn't that twelve years ago? You were on the force twelve years ago?"

"No," Kyle said. "I was at the college. But I remember it. I thought everybody remembered it."

"I'm from Kiratonic," Jack said. "I wasn't living here then."

The man walking toward them was beginning to look like something besides a blob in haze. Kyle recognized him. It was old

Tim Kika, except that his name wasn't really Tim. It was something complicated that sounded foreign. He just called himself Tim.

Shpetim Kika stopped in front of them. He looked bad. Kyle couldn't put a more precise word on it. He just looked bad.

"Well," Jack said.

"We left it alone," Shpetim said. "After we opened it, I mean. I mean, it was there, what were we supposed to do, it came out of the dirt. So we opened it."

"You opened it?" Kyle asked.

"One of the guys opened it," Shpetim said. "I was there. They pulled it out of the ground, and then they were worried about it. I mean, it's a yellow backpack. We should have thought not to touch it. But we opened it. And there it was."

"Have any of you touched it?" Kyle asked.

"I don't think so," Shpetim said. "Nderi, my son, came out here to look at it first. Before I did. Only, we didn't, you know, any of us, put our hands on it. We opened it, with a stick, because we wondered. You guys looked at this place already. You dug it all up. I remember."

"I remember, too," Kyle said. "I was just thinking about it. But I don't think we actually dug it all up. I think we just searched the place."

"Even so," Shpetim said. "Somebody dug a hole in the ground, you'd have noticed it. Wouldn't you? We thought you would."

"Maybe we better go take a look at it," Jack said.

Kyle looked at the sky over his head. There wasn't much to see. Everywhere it was getting dark. The air was thick and hard to breathe. He did remember police going over this whole field, inch by inch of it. And that was — what? Weeks later?

"It wasn't like it was wooded," Kyle said.

"What?" Jack said.

"I know what you mean," Shpetim said. He sounded relieved. "It wasn't wooded. It wasn't like there were trees that would make something hard to find. The police were here. They went all over it. If there was something dug in the ground just then, you'd have seen it. So we didn't think, you know, that this could be related to that. Except here we are."

"Here we are," Kyle said.

"I don't know what the hell you're all talking about," Jack said.

Kyle sighed. "He's talking about Chester Ray Morton. You know, the guy who went missing, the guy on all the billboards all over town? He had a yellow backpack the night he went missing. Bright yellow, L.L. Bean backpack."

"It's bright," Shpetim said. "It's been in the dirt. If it's even his. And not, you know, other kinds of trouble."

"They didn't search anything for weeks after he went missing," Kyle said, "because the police didn't think he was dead. They just thought he'd decided to disappear. But his mother kept pushing, and his mother kept pushing, and then somebody said they'd seen somebody in around here, and we went over the entire area. I remember it. I remember the day of the search. A bunch of us drove our cars up over there and got out and sat on them and watched. But they didn't find anything."

"Is this the guy whose mother is supposed to be crazy?" Jack said.

"If it was my son, I'd keep pushing," Shpetim said.

Then he looked back at the little crowd of men, and Kyle and Jack looked back with him.

"Well?" Shpetim said.

Jack was tired of waiting. He started across the building site, all torn up now, the grass mostly gone. Kyle and Tim looked at each other. Shpetim shrugged.

"I've seen it already," he said. "I'm not in

a hurry to see it again."

Kyle headed across the site himself. He wished it wasn't so close to dark. He wished the site didn't feel so much like a graveyard. He wished he'd told Darvelle something, or that he'd told somebody something. He should not be out here. He should not have anything to do with anything to do with anything about this case.

He got to the little group of men. Jack was standing there in the circle of them, looking down.

"Damn," he said, as Kyle walked up.

"If we thought there was anything important inside it, we would have left it alone. Still, no one actually put their hands on it," one of the men said. "It was just that we didn't know what to do. It was all zipped up when we found it. It wasn't like we could see anything."

"It wasn't like that guy's body could have fit in it," another man said.

"It made sense to open it," a third man said, and Kyle knew this one. It was Nderi Kika. It was funny the way things worked. Nderi had been born in Albania, but he was now so American nobody would think he hadn't been here forever.

The crowd of men stepped away a little, and Jack pointed at the ground.

"Look at that," he said.

At first, all Kyle saw was the yellow of the backpack. He took his flashlight out. He turned it on and aimed it down. It wasn't really dark. The flashlight helped but it almost didn't. Kyle ran the light up and down the now-open pack, up and down the bones half crushed and lying there, some of them bent, not quite the way they ought to be.

The tiny human skull was cracked in half.

9

The last person to see the body hanging from the billboard on Mattatuck Avenue was Chief of Police Howard Androcoelho, and he was paying more attention to it than he thought he could ever pay to anything.

By then it was almost full dark, and the lights across the top of the billboard were glowing. Traffic on Mattatuck Avenue had turned into a communal parking experience. Traffic in and out of the front entrance of Mattatuck–Harvey Community College had come to a halt. There were a good half-dozen patrol cars, a good thirty uniformed police officers, four plainclothes detectives, two EMT vans, the coroner's van, and seven mobile news trucks clustered around the bottom of the billboard. There were newspeople doing stand-up reports in the middle of the street.

Howard Androcoelho was sitting in his car, looking up at the body hanging there, twisting a little as three men did what they could to bring it down. They couldn't just cut the rope. It could fall. There was always a chance that the man was still alive. There was always that chance even if there wasn't one.

Howard's cell phone rang. He took it out of his pocket and opened up.

"Well?" the voice on the other end of the line said. The voice on the other end of the line belonged to Marianne Glew, the mayor of Mattatuck.

"We won't know for sure until we bring him down."

"Don't do this to me, Howard."

"I'm not doing anything to you. We won't know until we bring the body down and they can do the tests. DNA. Fingerprints. Dental records."

"He's dead?"

"Whoever is up there is definitely dead."

"You don't need to do tests for that one?"

"They'll do tests for it," Howard said. "I don't need tests to know. You ever seen the face of somebody's been hanged? Their tongue sticks out —"

"All right, yes, Howard. I was with you on the Keith Marbury case, for God's sake. It might have been a million years ago, but it's the kind of thing you remember."

"Yeah, well," Howard said.

There was that odd dead silence on the cell that happened whenever nobody was talking, or when somebody had hung up. Except that you couldn't really hang up a cell phone, not in the way you used to hang up the real phone. Howard thought of all those old Forties movies his wife liked to watched so much, the black-and-white ones where Fred MacMurray was a villain and the cops were all overweight. If he was in one of those movies right now, he'd be carrying a hip flask full of whiskey.

Which would not be a bad idea.

Marianne coughed. "Howard?"

"I'm still here," Howard said.

"It was all a million years ago," Marianne said. "But you've got to remember it. You've got to remember him. He's hanging off the billboard with the goddamned picture on it. Are you really telling me you can't tell if it's him or not?"

Howard considered his left hand. It looked the way it always looked. Then he looked out at the scene going on above him. Somebody had hold of the rope. They were pulling the body upward.

"I can't tell for sure," he said finally. "But I can guess."

"And you guess it's him?"

"I guess it's him."

"Then what does that mean, Howard? Is that good news? Has he been dead for twelve years? What do you think is going on here?"

"If he'd been dead for twelve years, he'd be a skeleton by now," Howard said. "Unless he was embalmed, of course. Somebody could have embalmed him and kept the body in a refrigerator all this time. He'd be pretty solid then."

"For God's sake, Howard, I mean it. I'm going to murder you."

"Marianne, for God's sake. What am I supposed to say? *I* mean it. What am I the hell supposed to say? He's up there. I'm pretty sure it's Chester Ray Morton. I don't know how long he's been up there. I know it hasn't been twelve years. I don't think it could have been all of twenty-four hours. There were day classes at the college today. Somebody would have seen him. After that, I haven't got a clue, and I'm not going to have a clue until the tech people get done with what they do. I'm not a clairvoyant. I don't know what happened here."

This time, the cell line was not silent. There was a *click, click, clicking* sound. Howard knew what that was. That was Marianne tapping the top of her pen on her desk. She used to do that when they were both detectives and she was his partner. It had always driven him crazy.

"Listen," Marianne said. "We're not going to be able to do it. We're not going to be able to say it was suicide."

"We don't know that it was suicide."

"His body hanging off the billboard? What would it be except suicide?"

"He could have been killed first," Howard said. "Somebody could have shot him, or strangled him, or stabbed him, and then bundled up the body and hung it off the billboard."

"And you think that's what happened? How could anybody have done that? That billboard is right out in front of everybody and everything. Somebody would have seen."

"Well, you'd think somebody would have seen if he hanged himself from it," Howard said, "but they didn't see that, either. There are people running all over here. As far as I know, they haven't found anybody who saw anything yet, except the security guard who called it in."

"I'll bet a dozen people saw it," Marianne said. "They just didn't bother to phone it in."

"People see things without seeing them," Howard said. "They see a vague thing and they're not sure what it is and their minds are on something else. You know how it goes."

"We're still not going to be able to say it's suicide," Marianne said. "I don't care if the guy left a video message saying he was going to off himself, we're not going to be able to go with that. We've going to have to investigate it as a murder whether it makes sense to do it or not. And you know that."

"I do know that," Howard said.

"That woman will be around any minute, if she isn't already. She'll be on CNN and MSNBC and Fox and all the local stations and she'll be screaming bloody murder."

"Yes," Howard said.

"She'll do that even though we were right," Marianne said. "He wasn't dead. We said that at the time. He wasn't dead. He'd gone off somewhere. And we were right. But it won't matter. Because he's dead now. Do you see?"

"Yes, yes, I see," Howard said. "You don't have to yell in my ear. I know what the ramifications of this are. I've always known what the ramifications of this would be. I knew as soon as they told me about the call. Give it up, Marianne."

"This could be big trouble," Marianne said.

"I know."

"This could be lethal trouble. For both of us."

"I know that, too."

"I think we need some help," Marianne said.

Howard leaned forward a little. The body was going up and up. There was a man on the ladder with a hook holding it from one side and what looked like two other men on another ladder pulling carefully upward. One of the men at the top had hold of the rope and was trying to saw through it. The weird lighting made everything look wrong.

Howard could still remember the day that he and Marianne had searched the trailer for the first time — the dust on all the surfaces, the bed made up with hospital corners, that small thin line of caking blood that had snaked across the top of the kitchen counter. They'd never been able to connect that blood to anybody.

"Damn," Howard said.

"What is it?" Marianne said.

The men trying to take the body down

had dropped it.

It seemed to hover in the air for a second all on its own.

Then it just fell, a dead weight, into the grass and bushes below.

■ ■ ■ ■

PART I

■ ■ ■ ■

Damnation is simple.

— Vladimir Nabokov

ONE

1

If anybody had asked Gregor Demarkian if it mattered to him to feel he had someplace settled to live, he would probably have said no. Why should it matter to him? Being homeless would not be good, but he'd never been the kind of person to care about the messiness of his kitchen or the view from his balcony. At the moment, he didn't even have a balcony, and he didn't want one. He wasn't sure what he did want. Not being liable to trip over stacked carpet samples in the hallway might be one thing. Not to find bathroom tile samples in the bathtub might be another. The bathroom tile "samples" were actually bathroom tiles, big ones, in all kinds of colors. There had to be hundreds of different colors, sizes, shapes, and materials for bathroom tiles. It was insane.

It was six o'clock on the first Monday in September. Labor Day. Gregor had managed to wrestle the bathroom tiles out of the bathtub so that he could take his shower, and now he was standing at the big window in his living room that overlooked Cavanaugh Street. Upstairs, Grace Feinmann was practicing, the faint sound of the harpsichord rippling up and down scales. Out on the street, nothing much was happening. It was a holiday. Donna Moradanyan Donahue had put up a big mural of Thirties-era workmen with big muscles outside Holy Trinity Armenian Christian Church, sort of in honor of somebody named Glenn Beck.

"No, she isn't honoring Glenn Beck," Bennis had tried to explain, a week ago, when Donna was first out there putting things up and getting her son Tommy to hammer nails. "It's kind of a joke. Glenn Beck is the sort of person who sees Communists in his soup, or, you know —"

But Gregor didn't know. He hadn't known then, and he didn't know now. Glenn Beck was somebody on television. He had tried to catch Glenn Beck on television. He'd never managed it.

He walked away from the window and headed toward the kitchen. Ever since Bennis had discovered coffee bags, he'd been able to make his own coffee in the morning.

This was a good thing, since it turned out that Bennis needed to do all kinds of things in the morning, and getting the coffee wasn't one of them.

He went through the swinging doors and found himself confronted by the kitchen table, which had cabinet façade samples stacked up on one side of it and handle samples stacked up on the other. Gregor was beginning to think you could put an entire house together from samples alone if you didn't care if things matched. He picked up one of the façade samples and looked at it. Then he picked up another. He was sure there were lots of differences between them. He just didn't understand why anybody would care. He really didn't understand why Bennis would care.

He filled the kettle and put it on to boil. He took a clean mug out of the cabinet and put a Folgers Coffee bag in it. He put the mug on the table between façades and handles. Then he took it off and put it back on the counter.

The Post-it Note with the information for today's meeting was stuck to the front of the refrigerator. It said: H. ANDROCOELHO, EIGHT. That was it. He had always been rather cavalier about the business part of what he did. He had a good pension from the Bureau and a solid wall of savings behind it. He didn't need to worry about the details as much as he might have. Still. It had gotten to the point where his professional life was like a poem by William Carlos Williams.

The kettle went off. He took it off the heat and poured water over the coffee bag. Bennis left her tea bags to steep for twenty minutes or more. If Gregor did that with a coffee bag, he'd have tachycardia in a minute and a half.

He looked at the handle samples again. Some of them were actually handles. Some of them were knobs. Some of them seemed to move. Some of them obviously didn't. How did anyone choose among all these things? Why would anyone want to put herself through this? Why not just let the contractor pick what he thought was practical and go with that?

Gregor came to again. He felt as if he were going in and out of fugue states. He took the coffee bag out of the coffee with a spoon. He threw the coffee bag into the garbage pail next to the sink. He wondered if, somewhere, Bennis had hundreds of samples of sinks that she'd gathered to look at before deciding which one would go into the kitchen of the new house.

Gregor took a sip of coffee. It didn't help. He took another sip of coffee. It still didn't help. He thought of H. Androcoelho, who was coming all the way out here from someplace in New York, on a holiday, to talk to him about something — and Gregor couldn't remember it.

Gregor took the coffee cup and went back through the living room and down the hall again, to the bathroom and the bedroom. Bennis was just coming out of the bath, wrapped in an enormous bathrobe, her wet hair falling down over her shoulders. The bathrobe was Gregor's bathrobe. Bennis had a dozen bathrobes of her own, including ones from special stores where everything cost as much as a small car, but she didn't wear them.

"Hey," she said, pushing the door to the bedroom open. "Are you okay? I left a note about your appointment on the refrigerator."

"I saw it. The kitchen table is full of — stuff."

"I know it's a pain, Gregor, but it's only for a little while. We should be into the new house by Thanksgiving. Or maybe Christmas. Anyway, it will be worth it when it's done. You'll see."

"I don't think I can go without sitting at

79

my kitchen table for four months."

"I don't see why. It's not like we ever eat here. I mean, really eat. We go to the Ararat. You're going there now. There's something we can do in the new house. Or I can do. I can cook."

"Do you cook?"

"Well enough when I was living on my own," Bennis said. "I could get Donna to teach me. It's going to be a really spectacular kitchen."

"I'm going to go downstairs and see if old George wants to pick up Tibor with me," Gregor said. "I wish you'd made more notes about that appointment. Don't you think it's odd, this guy coming out on a holiday?"

Bennis was putting clothes out on the bed. All the underwear matched. Bennis's underwear always matched. That was something odd to know about her.

"He's the chief of police in wherever this is," Bennis said. "Maybe this was the only time he could get away. And it's not really all that far from here. It's just New York. Maybe two hours or so north? Can't be much more than that. I forgot the name of the town. It's an Indian name."

"All right. I'd still feel better if you or I remembered exactly what it was he wanted to talk to me about."

Bennis had the hairbrush in her hand. She put it down on the bed. "It's a cold case — a missing persons cold case, except just a little while ago the guy turned up dead. And there were complications, but I don't remember those, because there are always complications. If there weren't complications, they wouldn't come to you."

"All right."

"Don't get all *sigh-y* on me, Gregor. I'm renovating an antique house and I've got a book due at the end of the month. Which is going to be late. And besides, I don't know. It's one of those things. It's been on television."

"The case?"

"Yes. Really, you've got to remember this. I told you. It was on one of those shows. *Disappeared,* that kind of thing. Or maybe it was only going to be on one. I'm sorry. The thing sounded garbled as hell to me when I took the call, and he said he'd come today, so I figured he'd tell you about it. He will tell you about it."

"He will," Gregor agreed. "I really am going to go down and see about old George. Are you coming out for breakfast?"

"Yes, and no," Bennis said. "I'm meeting Donna. I keep telling her I don't like wallpaper, I really much prefer paint, but

81

she has some samples for me to see. She's going to bring them and then if I hate them she'll bring them back. I'll probably hate them."

"We don't have room in this apartment for wallpaper samples," Gregor said.

"Go see about old George. I don't like the way he's been looking lately. He looks like kindergarten paste."

"What?"

"Go," Bennis said.

Gregor went.

2

Outside on the landing, Grace's playing was clear, not exercises now, but a recognizable piece. Gregor thought she had to have her door open up there. She did that sometimes when she was sure everybody in the building was awake. Gregor didn't mind. Bennis didn't mind. Old George was too far away to be bothered by it if he didn't want to be.

Gregor thought about going upstairs for a minute and asking her what she was playing. Then he decided that would be rude. Grace was always rehearsing for something, and besides, she might think he was actually bothered by her playing and being polite about it. It never ceased to amaze him how complicated people were, in their relationships with each other. Here they were, empowered by speech, and they were always looking for clues and hints and signs and omens. Maybe that was why so many people loved things like *The Da Vinci Code.*

The landing was clear of debris of any kind, which made him feel better. He went downstairs a flight and found that that landing was not. There were two tall stacks of what appeared to be plumbing fixtures — the faucets for a bathroom, maybe, or for a kitchen. Some of the faucets were brass, so Gregor opted for a bathroom. Or maybe many bathrooms. There were a lot of bathrooms in the house he and Bennis had bought at the other end of the street.

"It'll be fine," Bennis had said when they did it. "We'll fix it up a little and then we'll be practically next door to Donna and Rush."

"Right now we're right across the street from Lida and Tibor."

"We're not exactly moving to California, Gregor. We're still going to be on Cavanaugh Street."

Gregor went down another flight, and that was the ground floor. He could see the line of mailboxes in the little vestibule between the inner and outer doors. He could see the rub of faded paint against the blank wall that was on the far side of the stairway. That was the problem with condominiums. You needed everything to go right, or they didn't get kept up.

He thought about that sentence for a moment, and then decided that he wasn't ever really awake until he had made it to the Ararat. Then he went around behind the stairs and knocked on old George Tekemanian's door.

"It's open," old George said.

Gregor pushed at it. It wasn't only not locked. It was not latched.

Old George was sitting up in the enormous leather lounger chair that took up the middle of his living room, pounding away on a laptop he had placed on a tray table. The laptop, the lounge chair, and the table — all the way across the living room — that the laptop was supposed to go on had all been given to him by his nephew Martin, and they were all so expensive, they looked like if you scratched them, they would bleed money.

Old George looked up as Gregor walked in.

"You shouldn't leave your door unlocked like that," Gregor said. "I keep telling you, you only think it's perfectly safe here."

"It's perfectly safe here, Gregor. Nothing

ever happens on Cavanaugh Street, except when Sheila Kashinian has one of her fits and throws Howard out into the street, and then he goes over to the church and wants Father Tibor to give sermons on the sanctity of Christian marriage. I remember Howard Kashinian when he was a boy, just like I remember you. He was an idiot even then."

Gregor went around to the side of the chair and took a look at the screen of the laptop. Old George was on Facebook.

"What's 'Mafia Wars'?" Gregor said.

"Tcha," old George said. "You really have to keep up with the times. It's a game. I can go all day on games, lately. That's what happens when you get old. You drift."

"You're been drifting lately?"

"I think I've been bored," old George said. "It's all well and good for people to tell you you ought to keep busy, but the fact is you get to where your knees don't really work right. Then what do you do? I'm not going into one of those nursing homes Angela keeps talking about."

Angela was old George's nephew Martin's wife.

"I didn't know you and Angela were still fighting about nursing homes."

"She doesn't call them nursing homes," old George said. "She calls them 'assisted living facilities.' That's really what she calls them. Can you believe that?"

"I think she's only worried about your being here on your own."

"I've been here on my own since Maria died. Well, all right, Gregor, not in this apartment. I appreciate the apartment. I tell Martin that all the time. I appreciate all the things. I don't know what I did with myself before I got on the Internet."

"You balled socks in the mechanical sock baller and shot them across the room," Gregor said. "You broke lamps. I was here."

"I've got better aim now," old George said. "I wish everybody would just stop worrying about me. I can't see myself moving out to live with Martin and Angela, either. They're very nice, Gregor, but they've got small children. Family is a wonderful thing. But it ought to live in its own house."

"There was all that about Sophie Mgrdchian," Gregor said. "That wasn't even that long ago. She'd been living on her own, too."

Old George did something decisive on the keyboard and then began to shut the computer down. "Sophie Mgrdchian," he said, "was a damned fool. And I knew her since she was a child, too. We were children together. Well, no, all right, she was a child and I was, what do you call it these days. I was a teenager. But you know what I mean. She was always a damned fool. I'm not about to let somebody I don't even recognize come in here and stay in my house."

"That isn't what she did," Gregor said, but he could see it was time to give it up. "Tibor is going to meet us there this morning. He's got something or the other to do, I don't remember what. He's probably on Facebook."

"I'm on Facebook, Father Tibor is on Facebook, Bennis is on Facebook. You're not on Facebook, Gregor. You should do something about it. Social networking is a very good thing. At least it keeps you from being bored."

"I'm too busy trying to launch the space shuttle from my phone," Gregor said. "Do you want a coat? I know it's only the beginning of September, but it gets chilly in the mornings sometimes."

"Stop fussing about me," old George said. "Everybody fusses about me. It's Labor Day. It isn't raining. I'll be fine. Give me a minute to put this away."

Gregor gave him a minute. Martin and Angela had bought old George this apartment. They paid for a maid service to come in and clean twice a week. The place was spotless, but it looked oddly blank and impersonal. There was something different.

Old George came out from the back, carrying his wallet.

"I know what it is," Gregor said. "I know what's wrong with this room. You moved all the pictures."

"I didn't move them, Gregor. I put them away."

"All your pictures of Maria? And of Stepan before he died? All of them? Why?"

"I gave the pictures of Stepan to Martin," old George said. "He doesn't have a lot of pictures of his father. I gave him the old home movie film, too. He's having it converted to DVDs. Did you know they could do that?"

"Yes," Gregor said. "Bennis thinks you don't look well. Is she right? You look fine to me, but if there's something wrong —"

"There is nothing wrong, Gregor, except that I'm hungry, and at the rate you're going, we're never going to get to the Ararat."

3

Fr. Tibor Kasparian was already at the Ararat when they got there, hunched down on the window booth that was supposed to best resemble the way a restaurant table would be in Yerevan. Gregor doubted this. He didn't doubt that his Armenian ancestors had eaten in restaurants, and probably in their homes, by sitting nearly on the floor with their legs folded up underneath them. He did doubt that they were still doing it even in 1965, never mind all this time later, when Armenia was free and there was probably a McDonald's where the old family tavern used to be.

He let old George slide down the low bench first and then slid in after him. Father Tibor had coffee already, and there were places set out for all of them, but none for Bennis. Linda Melajian probably knew before they did who would be sitting at this table every morning.

"Bennis is the one not coming?" Tibor said.

"She's coming, she's just meeting Donna," Gregor said. "Something about the house. I'm learning all kinds of things about houses. Did you know there were over five hundred different varieties of bathroom tile?"

"I knew there were a lot, Krekor, yes," Father Tibor said. "They rebuilt my apartment, you remember when it was destroyed with the church. They were always coming over asking me what I wanted to have. I never knew what to say. I didn't care which one I had, as long as it was serviceable."

"They built bookshelves," old George said. "I remember that. They wanted you to put all your books on bookshelves."

"It would take the entire Philadelphia library system," Gregor said. "I don't know if you've been over there lately. He's got them stacked to the ceiling in the dining room."

"And the apartment upstairs is still empty," Tibor said. "I told them we would never get an assistant. There aren't enough priests in this country to serve the churches we have, and we can't always get somebody from Armenia. And it doesn't always work out."

"You're from Armenia," Gregor pointed out.

"Yes, Krekor, I know. But I wasn't sitting in Armenia and happy there when they wanted a priest over here. I came over on my own, because I wanted to. I lived in New York for years before I got a church. These men come here, they're used to there, and all the children now, they're third and fourth generation. They haven't got the patience. And I don't blame them."

"Father Tibor is standing up for the younger generation again," old George said.

"*Tcha,*" Tibor said. "What would you think if you were an eighteen-year-old American

90

girl, and you had some priest with an accent telling you you were going to go to hell because you didn't let your parents pick your husband? Never mind that the parents aren't interested in picking the husband. It's a mess."

"I'm going to have an American omelet," old George said. "The one with ham and cheese in it."

"A Western omelet," Tibor said.

"Say what you want," old George said. "I didn't try to pick a wife for Stepan, and he did fine on his own. And I called him Steve as soon as he wanted me to."

"All my teachers in school used to call me Gregory," Gregor said. "It used to drive me crazy. It happened in the Bureau, too. Is Linda actually around here anywhere?"

Gregor turned around and looked across the restaurant. It was slowly beginning to fill up. Almost nobody on the street cooked anymore, unless they were having a party or family was coming. Lida Arkmanian was sitting with Hannah Krekorian and Sheila Kashinian. Lida and Sheila had on their chinchilla coats — end of summer, muggy hot weather be damned.

The doors to the back opened then, and Linda Melajian came in, carrying the coffeepot in one hand. She breezed by at least four tables that wanted her attention and came over to them, flipping the coffee cups upright with her free hand.

"George will have a Western omelet, and Bennis is eating with Donna, so Gregor will have scrambled eggs with bacon and sausages and hash browns, plus buttered toast and nine-one-one on speed dial," she said. "How am I doing?"

"Perfectly," Gregor said. "But Bennis is going to be here, even if it's at another table, so maybe I ought to tone it down a little."

"Do what you want," Linda said. "But Bennis is picking Donna up at Donna's, and you know what that's going to be like. They won't be here for an hour. I'm supposed to tell you that hardwood floors are better in the master bedroom than a carpet is, and you can always buy an Oriental rug."

"Bennis told you to talk to me about hardwood floors in the master bedroom?" Gregor said.

"No," Linda said, "Lida did. She was talking to Bennis about it yesterday, I think. Really, Gregor, I don't see the point. Do you? I mean, there isn't really a master bedroom in that place, not like there would be in a modern house, with a bathroom and walk-in closets —"

"There will be by the time Bennis gets

through with it," old George said.

"You know what I mean," Linda said. "Let me go get you your food and find out what everybody else wants. There was some guy in here at opening, he was standing right outside the door when I came to unlock it. Anyway, he's looking for Gregor."

"Is he here now?" Gregor asked.

"Nope," Linda said. "He said he'd be back later. I've got no idea where he went. There isn't anything open around here at a quarter to six in the morning, and it's not like he could go home. I saw his car. It had New York plates."

"That will be your appointment," old George said. "Bennis said he was from New York."

"He's also not supposed to be here until eight," Gregor said.

"Whatever," Linda said. "He's probably around somewhere, wandering into bad neighborhoods and getting mugged. Not that he's the kind of person you'd think would get mugged. He's absolutely enormous. Taller than Gregor even. And he's fat. I don't know. Maybe they'd mug a fat guy. They don't usually like tall, though."

" 'They' is muggers?" Gregor asked.

"Exactly," Linda said. "But there's the fat, and then there's the — I don't know. Aura.

He was the most nervous person I've ever seen. He practically jumped out of his skin when I came up behind him. And he had a briefcase. One of the old-fashioned floppy kinds with straps that you buckle like a belt."

"This is supposed to make him more likely to be mugged?" Father Tibor said. "You're not making any sense."

"I didn't say I was making any sense," Linda said. "I was just telling you what I saw. Anyway, I put a RESERVED sign on one of the bigger tables against the wall. Anybody with a briefcase as big as that is going to have to have some room to spread out. I'll go get everybody's food. Have the sausages, Gregor. Bennis won't be here anytime soon. Maybe I'll accidentally hit Sheila Kashinian on the head with the coffeepot when I get there. Honestly, if that woman wants to know the calories of anything else ever again, I'm going to slit her throat."

"She's waving at you," Gregor pointed out.

"She waves at me every twenty seconds," Linda said. Then she straightened up a little. "There he is. The guy from this morning. He's just coming through the door."

Gregor, Tibor, and old George all looked up at once. There was indeed a strange man coming through the door. He was strange in the sense of not belonging to Cavanaugh Street, and strange in the sense of being very odd looking.

Linda had been right about the size. The man was very, very fat, but the first thing you noticed was the height. Gregor was almost six foot four himself. This man had to be closer to six eight. He was holding the briefcase up to his chest, keeping his arms clapped across it as if he were carrying nitroglycerin. He looked around the restaurant and then around again. Gregor thought his head was moving too quickly to actually see anything.

Then the man caught sight of Gregor, and the air came out of him as if somebody had punctured his tire.

He practically ran to the window booth and held out his hand.

"Mr. Demarkian?" he said. "I'm Howard Androcoelho."

Two

1

For some reason, Howard Androcoelho reminded Gregor Demarkian of Shrek — Shrek the character, and *Shrek* the movie. He did not look like the sort of man who should run. It wasn't just his size. He didn't look healthy. His face was pasty and the wrong kind of white, not like skin but like paper. The veins in his neck stood out on his neck even under all the fat. His hands were faintly trembling. Gregor took it all in and decided that the man was not on any kind of drug he knew the symptoms of. For one thing, the kind of drug that made your hands tremble also made you thinner.

Gregor took Howard Androcoelho's hand and shook it. Then he looked at the brief-case. Howard Androcoelho looked at the briefcase, too.

"Oh," he said. "Yes. I brought everything with me. Well, not everything. Copies of nearly everything, though. I got the permission of the mayor. I'm sorry to interrupt you. I've been driving for hours. I just thought, it was a restaurant, I thought I'd stop and get something to eat, you know, before our meeting. I didn't realize you'd be here, too."

"It's all right," Gregor said. "I think Linda reserved us a table so that we could spread out —"

"It's right here," Linda Melajian said, moving in quickly. "I just knew he was your appointment, Gregor. I mean, why else would anybody be in here at this time of the morning if he wasn't from the neighborhood? I've got a nice big table. You can empty that briefcase all over it, if you want."

"Oh," Howard Androcoelho said. "Well. Thank you. Thank you very much. I'm sorry. I really didn't meant to interrupt anything. It's just that I don't know Philadelphia, not really, and I was afraid I'd get lost, so I started out early. And then, it's like I said. I drove for hours and hours and hours. I should have stopped at McDonald's."

"Don't be ridiculous," Linda said, shooing Howard toward the appointed table. "We can do a lot better than McDonald's. Sit down and I'll get you a cup of coffee."

Howard Androcoelho sat down. Gregor wasn't entirely sure how they had managed to get across the restaurant to the big table, but they had. Howard sat down in a chair and looked around.

"You don't have to bother about me now," he said, looking back at the window booth. "We're not on till eight o'clock and that's an hour and a half from now. You go have your breakfast and I'll have mine, and then —"

Gregor sat down at the other chair at the big table. "That's all right," he said. "You're here, I'm here, we might as well get on with it. Are you sure you don't need some rest? You look —"

"Terrible?"

"Like you're about to have a stroke," Gregor said.

"I know," Howard said. "Maybe I am about to have a stroke. I haven't slept for — I don't know. It's Monday? Of course it's Monday. It's Labor Day. I haven't slept since last Monday, because last Tuesday evening —" He paused. He put the briefcase on the table and opened it. It was complicated. Straps had to be unbuckled. The leather of the flap was old and bent and wouldn't straighten out.

Gregor considered offering to help, but

thought better of it. He thought he'd only confuse Howard Androcoelho more. Linda Melajian brought over his cup of coffee and a menu. She put them down on the table.

Howard Androcoelho found what he was looking for, double checked to make sure, and then put it down on the table. It was a photograph, printed out on glossy paper, but — Gregor was sure — originally taken on somebody's phone. For a moment, Gregor thought it was in black and white. Then he looked closer, and it was a scene at night.

It was a very odd scene. In the background was what appeared to be a part of a billboard. In front of it, a body was hanging, the neck bent and obviously broken, the head obscured by what looked like a burlap sack.

"Well," Gregor said.

"That's how we found him," Howard Androcoelho said. "Just like that. As if he'd been executed."

"All right," Gregor said. "Had he been?"

Howard Androcoelho shook his head. "I don't know," he said. "I don't think so. The medical examiner wants to call it a suicide and get it over with. I don't think there's any physical evidence that anything else happened. Except for the hood on his head, or the hood-ish thing. It was just a feed bag. But suicides don't usually do that, do they? Put something over their heads like that."

"Not usually," Gregor said. "If the medical examiner thinks it's suicide, what makes you think it's not?"

"I don't think it's not," Howard Androcoelho said. "It's just that — the circumstances are kind of odd. We tried to work it out after we cut him down, you know. As far as we can tell, he'd been hanging there for hours, hanging off this billboard all lit up by the nightlamps, you know, the way billboards are. And nobody noticed."

"Was it in an out of the way place?"

"It was right on the corner of the entrance to Mattatuck–Harvey Community College," Howard Androcoelho said. "The place is huge, and it was evening. Students and teachers were going in and out all the time. The ones going out wouldn't have noticed anything necessarily, but the ones going in had to pass right by the thing. There are evening classes, starting at seven, all fall term. People were going in and out. Nobody saw him."

"Maybe he wasn't there," Gregor said. "Maybe he got there, I don't know, when did you find him —"

"We cut him down, it was a little after nine."

"So maybe he got there a little before nine."

"Not according to the forensics," Howard said. "Not that we've got the kind of forensics you people have down here. We don't. But we got a bunch of money from the Homeland Security people after 9/11, so we've got a mobile crime lab, and a lot better equipment than we used to have. Anyway, our guy says he'd been up there a minimum of two hours. Which means that people were passing back and forth in front of him for — well, forever."

Gregor looked at the picture again. The lights around the body seemed to turn it into a display, something you were supposed to look at, something calling attention to itself.

"I wonder if he expected it," Gregor said.

"Expected what?"

"Not to be found for at least two hours," Gregor said. "Not everybody who tries to commit suicide is trying to commit suicide. Some of them are just trying to get attention. Maybe he hanged himself there because he expected people to notice him right away, and then, when they didn't, he died."

"If he hanged himself there, that won't be the only reason he did it," Howard said. "And if somebody else hanged him there, that won't be the only reason they did it, either. Let me show you something else."

Howard reached back into the briefcase, shuffled more papers around, took more papers out and put them on the table, and shuffled other papers around. Gregor didn't think he'd ever seen a police officer this disorganized about his evidence. It was a wonder that this man had ever solved any case at all.

Howard finally found what he was looking for and pulled it out. It was another photograph, also of the body and the billboard behind it, but taken from farther out, so that the billboard was clear. It was an oversized photograph, too, so that the billboard was very clear.

CHESTER RAY MORTON ran across it in outsized capital letters. Gregor looked above those and saw the words HAVE YOU SEEN

Below that, there was a phone number, also in outsized letters, and then, underneath that:

AWARD FOR INFORMATION LEADING
TO DISCOVERY OF HIS WHEREABOUTS

Gregor sat back. "That's interesting," he said.

"It's more than interesting," Howard Androcoelho said. "That billboard? The guy they're looking for there? That's the guy that we found hanging."

2

When Linda Melajian came back to take Howard Androcoelho's order, he had it ready. Gregor listened in fascination as the man ordered a double stack of pancakes with butter, syrup, sausages, and hash browns, as if he were the star of a television commercial for IHOP. Linda did not bring Gregor's own order — which really wasn't much better — although everybody else at the window booth had been served. Maybe she was trying to do the professional thing and make sure Gregor and Howard ate together. Gregor had had a talk with Linda once about the professional side of waiting tables. There was a lot more to it than he would have suspected.

Gregor waited until Linda had refilled his coffee cup and bustled off toward the kitchen. Then he waved at the mess on the table and said, "Well?"

Howard Androcoelho sighed. "I was one of the detectives in charge," he said. "When this whole thing first started. When Chester went missing."

"He was somebody you knew? Somebody you'd call by his first name?"

"Well," Howard said. "It's not like Mattatuck is a small town anymore. We probably have fifty thousand people. But the Mortons are sort of, I don't know — what would the newspapers call it? — locally prominent. Like that."

"Locally prominent as what?"

"They run the largest trash collection company in the country," Howard said. "And don't laugh. They were the first, and they've got most of the business in town, and most of the business in all the towns around us. They're good, and they're cheap. You've got to have trash collection in Mattatuck. We're too big now not to insist on it, so we've got a city ordinance. But most of the towns around us let you do what you want. A lot of people just pile their garbage in the back of their truck and then haul it on out to the dump. Morton's is good enough and cheap enough so that a fair number of them pay to have them haul it instead."

"All right," Gregor said. "I assume they therefore have money."

"Hard to tell," Howard said, "but, yes, I'd

guess so, too. Best guesses in and around town are that they're worth about ten million dollars, between the business itself and investments. They've got a bunch of kids, and the kids are going into the business. Even the daughter is doing bookkeeping. Hell, okay. They insist that the kids go into the business."

"And the kids don't want to?"

Howard considered this. "It's hard to say. You'd have to know Charlene. That's the mother. The woman is a lunatic. It's like she had these children, they came with umbilical cords attached, and she's never going to cut them. If you know what I mean."

"Sort of," Gregor said. It sounded like half the Armenian immigrant women he'd known in his childhood.

"So," Howard said, "Chester didn't want to. Go into the business, I mean. And there's probably another one of those coming up, because the youngest one? Kenny? He's got two Internet businesses going, he's got his own business cards. I don't know how she's keeping him at home. He's got to be making more than she's willing to pay him already. Whatever. Chester didn't want to go into the business, and he didn't want to live at home."

"So did he do something about it?"

"He did," Howard said. "He wasn't any Kenny, that's for sure. He didn't have that kind of drive. But he did get an outside job, at some convenience store, I think, and he got himself a trailer at the most white trash trailer park in Mattatuck and he moved out. Oh, there was a girl. Did I tell you there was a girl?"

"A girl the mother didn't like, I take it," Gregor said.

"Exactly," Howard said. "Darvelle Haymes. I didn't make that up. That was really her name. There's a go-getter, if you're looking for one. And I think maybe that was the problem. Charlene thought Darvelle was only after Chester for the money."

"And was she?"

"Hard to tell," Howard said again. "I'm not good at motive, Mr. Demarkian, I never was. Darvelle got her associate's degree and then she got her real estate license and now she's something of a big deal. She does a lot of business. She's got her own house, and it's not a trailer. So, I don't know. Maybe she was. Maybe that was her first idea for making something of herself. Maybe it wasn't and she already knew she was going to do all right on her own. I can't tell you. Just that she and Chester were a thing, and when Charlene tried to put her foot down and break it off, Chester quit the family business and moved out. And that was that for about six months."

"What happened after six months?"

"That depends on who you want to believe," Howard said. "If you believe Charlene and Stew — that's the father — Chester and Darvelle showed up at the Morton house one Sunday afternoon with Darvelle visibly pregnant, saying they were having a baby and they were going to get married. If you believe Darvelle, she's never been pregnant and the only thing they went to the Morton house for was to tell the parents they were getting married, because Chester didn't just want to spring it on them. They were going down to elope to Vegas. According to Darvelle."

Gregor took a long sip of coffee. "This was your case? When there got to be a case? You were the detective who investigated it?"

"That's right," Howard said. "I was a detective then. My partner was Marianne Glew. Anyway, there wasn't much of a case for weeks. Because there isn't a case in cases like this, do you know what I mean?"

"No," Gregor said.

"Chester and Darvelle go over to the Mortons' house for whatever reason it was, take your pick. They leave. Chester drops Darvelle back at her place and goes home — that wasn't the house then, it was a place over on the East side of town. He drops her home, he wanders around being normal for a while. Then he just disappears into thin air. Except, you know what missing persons are. Charlene tried to call him the next day and didn't get an answer, and that's when she started hounding the department about his being murdered and Darvelle murdering him. But there wasn't any body. There wasn't any anything, at that point."

"So you made her wait — what? Three days? Two weeks? What's the standard?"

"Two weeks," Howard said. "When nobody had seen or heard from him in two weeks, we got a search warrant to look through his trailer. I thought we'd find the place emptied out and that would be the end of it. But we didn't. There were all of Chester's clothes and things, everything but his yellow backpack. Everything else was there. We talked to the teacher of the one course he was still taking. That's Charlene's other thing. She makes them all go to school. Anyway, the teacher, this Penny London woman, hadn't heard from him. We asked Darvelle and she let us in to search her place without a fuss. Nothing there, either, except for a spare toothbrush and set of shaving things."

"And that was it? It was that clean?"

"Not quite," Howard said. "There was a little counter in the kitchen, and on the counter was a little snaking line of dried blood. And you don't have to ask. We had it tested. It wasn't Chester's blood, and it wasn't Darvelle's. And a couple of years ago, with Charlene going nuts the way she was, we had it sent to DNA analysis. It's not only not Chester's, it's not anybody in any way blood related to the Morton family or to Darvelle. But it's human blood."

"And what about Vegas? If they were going to elope, there might have been something — reservations, plane tickets —"

"We checked. There were no reservations and no plane tickets. Chester was gone. Just like that. Nobody knew where. But nobody thought he'd been murdered, either, no matter what Charlene said. We had no reason to think he was murdered."

"Not even all the clothes and things left in the trailer?"

"No," Howard said. "You must know how missing persons cases go. Stuff like that happens all the time. And we were right, weren't we? Chester hadn't been murdered. He was alive and out there somewhere. He just didn't want to be found. Until now, I guess. I don't know what happened to make him come back. He just did."

"Did you check on the girl's pregnancy?"

"No. Let's face it. She didn't have to give us confidential medical records if she didn't want to, and there isn't a court in the state of New York that would have given an order to have her tested. Maybe she was pregnant. Maybe she wasn't pregnant. Maybe we'll never know. I will say I never saw her sticking out so that it was obvious, and I used to see her around quite a lot. But that may be perception. I wasn't looking for it. Charlene was."

Gregor reached out to pick up the stack of photographs Howard Androcoelho had laid out on the table. He wanted to see them all, not just the two Howard had shown him to start. The photograph on top of the stack was of what looked like a very messy, incredibly tiny living room, its two pieces of furniture both oddly orange colored. Gregor wondered if the people who rented the trailers brought their own furniture, or if furniture was part of what they paid for.

"Gregor?" old George Tekemanian said, very softly, into Gregor's ear.

Gregor looked up. Old George was standing right next to the table, swaying a little on his feet, the way he sometimes did these days when he stood up too long. It took Gregor another minute to realize that old George was no longer completely dead white. He was tinged with just a little blue.

"Gregor, I apologize," old George said. "But I'm afraid I can't help it."

Then the old man collapsed to the floor, unconscious.

3

It was the same hospital Tibor was in when he got mugged — or was it Bennis? Gregor found it hard to remember the exact sequence of anything as they pushed through the corridors, trying to follow the gurney to wherever it was it was going in the bowels of the hospital. An ambulance had taken old George, thankfully not dead, still not conscious. Bennis, Gregor, and Tibor had taken a cab, and Bennis had spent the entire drive getting in touch with Martin and Angela. She got Angela first. Angela had one of those jobs the wives of successful men often had, where she worked part time and took care of the children part time, even though the children were now old enough to take care of themselves. Martin had the kind of job where putting in ninety hours a week was considered slacking off. It was in banking, or law, or something. Gregor couldn't remember that, either.

At the hospital, they had to turn off their cell phones. For the first time, Gregor felt lost without the thing, cut off from the entire world. The hospital was oddly quiet. He had expected noise and things, bureaucrats, something. Instead, they were taken directly into the room where old George was hooked up to tubes and monitors and were asked to sit down.

"The doctor will be with you in a moment," the nurse said.

Then she disappeared. Gregor didn't like modern nurse's uniforms. He much preferred the old-fashioned white ones that were always dresses. He also preferred the caps with their little black ribbons. His brain was making absolutely no sense at all.

Bennis was standing over old George's bed. "It's really odd," she said. "He doesn't look bad. He looks better than he did this morning."

"I didn't even see you come into the Ararat," Gregor said.

"I told you Donna and I were having breakfast. He looked blue in the Ararat. Now he just looks like he's sleeping."

"We need to get Martin and Angela here,"

Gregor said. "We need to get Martin. He's got old George's health proxy. What does he do in that job of his? Is he going to be able to leave in the middle of the day?"

"I've gotten in touch with Martin and Angela," Bennis said, "and I gave Martin's number to the nurse. She'll give it to the doctor. They'll be able to get in touch with him if they need to. I'm just hoping they need to."

"Why?" Gregor said.

"Because if they don't," Bennis said, "there's no hope."

Tibor was sitting in a small folding chair in the corner. He looked up at them and shook his head.

"It's two weeks from Friday," he said.

"What?" Bennis and Gregor asked, almost simultaneously.

"His birthday," Tibor said. He looked as bad as Gregor had ever seen him look, and Gregor had seen him in the hospital, and after the church was bombed and he was left homeless. "It's his birthday, two weeks from Friday. He's going to be a hundred years old."

Old George moved on the bed. They all turned to look at him. They all made jokes about how old he was, and still living by himself, in his own apartment. Everybody on the street made those jokes. For the first time, Gregor thought old George actually looked one hundred.

The curtain to the cubicle rustled and they looked up to see a doctor walk in, or somebody they assumed was a doctor. He was wearing the regulation white coat. He was carrying a clipboard.

"Is there a Mr. — Mr. Demarkian here?" he asked.

"That's me," Gregor said.

"Ah. Thank you. I've talked to Mr. — ah, Mr. Tek—"

"Tekemanian," Bennis said.

"Yes," the doctor said. "I'm sorry. I'm new in this area. What kind of ethnicity is that?"

"Armenian," Tibor said.

The doctor nodded. "Well, at any rate, I've talked to the gentleman's nephew? Grand nephew? Another Mr., uh, Mr. Teke— Tekemanian, who has the health proxy. He says I can talk to Mr. Demarkian. In the meantime, he's on his way. Are you the Mr. Demarkian who's in the papers all the time?"

"Something like that," Gregor said.

"Well," the doctor said. "We're going to take the old gentleman for some tests. He's had what I think, looking at the information I have, and looking at him the way he is

114

now, is probably going to turn out to be a small heart attack. But even a small heart attack is serious, no matter who you are, and especially if you're elderly." He looked at his clipboard. "The gentleman is, uh, what? Ninety-something."

"Ninety-nine," Bennis said. "He's got a birthday in a couple of weeks. He'll be one hundred."

"Yes," the doctor said. "Can you tell me something about the circumstances? I mean, I assume he lives in a nursing home —"

"He lives in his own apartment," Gregor said, "on the ground floor of a townhouse building on Cavanaugh Street. The same building where we live, Bennis and I."

"I live at the rectory," Tibor put in politely.

"He lives by himself, but he has somebody who comes in every day to help him out and check on him and clean. And we look in. He didn't look well this morning, but he was well enough to walk two-and-a-half blocks to the restaurant where we all have breakfast every morning. He has breakfast there every morning."

"Really?" the doctor said. "That's remarkable. Even people whose minds are still sharp at that age usually have bone issues. He didn't have any bone issues?"

"He had a hip replacement about five years ago," Tibor said.

"Really? And you're used to seeing him aware and alert? There weren't any problems with dementia, or anything like that?"

"No," Bennis said.

Gregor shot her a look. She shot him one back.

"I'm not going to shut up," she said. "I'm really sick of it, the way so many people are around old people. They're old, for God's sake. They're not a different species. Phyllis A. Whitney was actually writing a book a year right into her nineties, did you know that?"

"Who's Phyllis A. Whitney?" Gregor asked.

Tibor started to answer, but Bennis was on a roll.

"It was the same with my grandmother," she said. "That's my mother's mother. She was a hateful old bat, but her mind was perfectly fine. Then she was down in Palm Beach and there was a hurricane and she wouldn't evacuate, and the hospital down there tried to say that that proved she was incompetent and should be in a nursing home whether she wanted to be there or not — and for what? For doing what she'd done in every hurricane for forty years? She wouldn't evacuate when she was thirty. It had nothing to do with her being addled, and —"

"I don't think anybody is trying to force the old gentleman here into a nursing home," the doctor said. "I'm just trying to understand what the benchmark is, what normal would be for him. If his mind was as clear as you say, then anything less than that would be a symptom. If he was usually a little vague, say, or forgetful — well, then if he got vague and forgetful here, it wouldn't be a symptom. It would just be himself."

"His mind is fine," somebody else said.

They looked up to see Martin Tekemanian standing in the open curtains, looking like a mess. Gregor thought he was on the verge of tears.

"His mind is fine," Martin said again. "It's better than mine, most of the time. And his memory is phenomenal. And we've been asking him to come and live with us for years, and he just wouldn't."

THREE

1

For Kenny Morton, the worst thing about the time since his brother Chester's body had been found — hanging up there, on their mother's billboard — had not been the questions, or the publicity, or even the bad temper everybody had been in at home. God only knew there were questions. Where had Chester been over twelve years? Why had he ended up hanging himself? Kenny was sure Chester had hanged himself. Kenny had gone right out to the billboard the day after the body was discovered, just to see for himself. There was no way somebody could have climbed up there, even from behind, and thrown the dead weight of a body over the top, or hanged it from the top, or however it was supposed to have been done. And if Chester had been alive and conscious before he got up there, then it really couldn't have been done. Chester would have struggled. Why would Chester go away somewhere, and then come back, and then hang himself out there on the highway where everybody could see him?

The other questions all had to do with the backpack, which had been found on the same night, buried in the ground over where they were putting up the new tech building. Kenny thought it was odd the way the backpack always seemed to come as an afterthought. The backpack was almost as strange as Chester. It was the only thing that had gone missing at the same time Chester did. Now it was back, and Kenny was pretty sure it hadn't been buried up on that piece of land all this time. He and his friends had ridden their bikes out there all the time when they were younger, and they'd been all over those woods. They weren't all that much in the way of woods. If the backpack had been up there all that time, Kenny was sure somebody would have found it.

No, it wasn't the questions that bothered Kenny. The questions felt natural. What bothered Kenny was that nobody at home was asking them, and their mother was pacing up and down, back and forth, from one end of the house to the other, pacing and pacing, wearing the look of a person who was about to blow her brains out with fever.

"They're going to try and cover it up," she kept saying, whenever she said anything. It wasn't often. "They're going to get that man in here to say it was a suicide, and they think that will put an end to it. But nothing is going to put an end to it. I'm not going to let it."

Then she would walk away again. Kenny didn't think she was getting any sleep. His father was getting very little. Kenny would find him sleeping on the couch when he came in at night.

"Just in case she passes out," he would tell Kenny, and then he wouldn't tell Kenny anymore.

Kenny didn't think it was natural.

Now he pulled his car into the Frasier Hall parking lot and turned the engine off. If there was anything good that had come of the last couple of weeks, it was definitely that this situation had turned him into a much more conscientious student. School was the only place he could go with a completely clear conscience, and the only place he could say he'd been without everybody at home being ready to kill him.

He got his books off the passenger seat and got out of the car. It was a good car, a BMW, and even if it was old, it ran well.

He'd bought it to resell about a year ago, and then he hadn't been able to let it go.

He locked up carefully when he got out, and as he did he saw two girls coming up the long walk that led to the building itself. There was a pretty one and an odd one. He was sure they were both in his English class. The odd one was very odd, but he liked the look of the pretty one. There was something — comforting — about her face.

Comforting was the wrong word.

"Hey," he said.

The girls stopped. They both looked exhausted, and the odd one looked like she was about to burst out of her clothes. They all seemed to be made of Spandex.

"You're in Dr. London's English class, aren't you?" he said. It sounded to him like he was trying too hard. Maybe it was just that he wasn't used to the sound of his own voice. He'd been trying really hard not to say anything his mother could hear.

"That's right," the odd one said. "Not that I would be if it wasn't for Haydee here. I mean, for God's sake, it took four years to get out of high school, and now we're here. Does that make any sense to you?"

"I'm Kenny," Kenny said.

"I'm Desiree," the odd one said. "This is Haydee. We've been walking for an hour.

I'm about to fall the fuck down —"

"Desiree," Haydee said.

"I'm not supposed to cuss anymore," Desiree said. "That's her idea. Dr. London doesn't cuss, so I'm not supposed to cuss anymore."

"Why have you been walking for an hour?" Kenny said.

Haydee took a deep breath. "We don't have a car, and there isn't a bus that's convenient. So we walk here."

"Walk here from where?"

"From Thomaston Avenue," Haydee said.

It took Kenny a minute to put it together. "From the trailer park there? You live in the trailer park? And you walk all the way here? That has to be five miles. What do you do when class gets out?"

"We walk back," Desiree said.

Haydee blushed. "I'm saving up for a car. I mean, I almost do have enough, for a used one, you know. But I want to be careful. I mean —"

"You walk back in the dark?" Kenny said.

"I know," Desiree said. "We're going to get mugged. Or murdered. Oh, wait. I mean, I'm sorry, you know, I didn't mean —"

Kenny sighed. They knew who he was. He should have expected that. On the other

122

hand, neither of them had brought it up, so maybe that was a good sign.

"We're not really going to get mugged," Haydee said. "If you ask me, it's more dangerous at the park than it is here. And it's good for us, walking. It keeps the weight off."

Kenny did not say that walking had not kept the weight off for the odd-looking one. "I think she's right," he said to Haydee. "I think it's dangerous. There isn't a bus or anything you could use instead?"

"It's not convenient," Haydee said.

"She means it costs a dollar and a half," Desiree said. "You wouldn't believe this girl. She won't spend money on anything."

"I'm saving up for a car." Haydee looked near tears. "And it really isn't dangerous. It really isn't. Not as long as we're together."

"So what if I get sick?" Desiree said. "What if I get sick and tired? What happens if I can't come? For God's sake, Haydee, I'm sick of this already and you know it."

Haydee looked one or two breaths from breaking down. Kenny watched her carefully. He didn't really believe that she was only shaken and out of breath because she'd just walked a long way. There was definitely something else happening. He knew all about something else happening.

"Listen," he said. "I'll take you home. Tonight, you know, and any other night I'm in class. I try to be in class, you know, so that would be all right."

"She won't miss classes at all," Desiree said. "She comes in when she hasn't had any sleep or she's just worked twenty hours straight or any of it. She's crazy."

"I don't miss classes much, either," Kenny said. He was lying. He missed classes as much as he could. He'd just try not to miss this one anymore. She was really very pretty. "Do you live by yourselves out there, at the trailer park?"

"I live with my mother," Haydee said. "And Desiree —"

"I live with my mother, too," Desiree said. "You forgot to tell him about your stepfather."

"He's not my stepfather," Haydee said. "He's just — around."

"He's around and he's trying to find her money," Desiree said. "He's a real prick, believe me. She had twelve hundred dollars saved up the last time and he found it and took it and spent it on beer or whatever. And he knows she's got money now and he's looking for it. She won't even tell me where it is."

"My money is safe this time, it really is,"

Haydee said. Now she wasn't on the verge of tears. She was just there. Kenny could see the glisten just under her lower eyelids

"I'll drive you home," Kenny said. "I will. I can do it after every class. At least you won't have to go back in the dark."

Haydee seemed to collect herself. "Thank you," she said. "Thank you. That would be very nice. I'd appreciate it."

"Listen to this bitch," Desiree said. "She's changing the whole way she talks. She's trying to sound like Dr. Penelope London. She thinks she's going to go get herself one of those PhDs when she's done here. I mean, as if."

"There's no reason she shouldn't get a PhD if that's what she wants," Kenny said. "I mean, people do, don't they? All the time. And she's smart. I've heard her talk in class."

"Thank you," Haydee said.

Kenny didn't say that he probably would have told her she looked like Jessica Simpson if he thought that that was what she wanted to hear. She really was very pretty. She got prettier the longer he looked at her. And there was that something else he couldn't put his finger on.

"Okay," he said. "Come on. We don't want to be late after you two walked all this way."

Haydee adjusted her pack on her back and started to walk toward the building beside him. Kenny didn't think she noticed that Desiree was trailing behind.

2

Shpetim Kika didn't know what he thought his life was going to be like after the crew had discovered that backpack and that little tiny skeleton, but he was sure it had nothing to do with sitting on a bench in the waiting area of The Elms, waiting for the hostess to seat him.

Of course, Shpetim was not alone. Lora was there, looking decked out for a wedding already. She'd even made him buy her a big white orchid to wear on her best blue dress, and another orchid that he was holding in a box, for when Nderi brought Anya in. Lora was fussing, too, the way she fussed when they were going to have a party. Every once in a while, she poked at him and asked him to stand up.

"You'll get your suit wrinkled," she said. "Is that the way you want to meet your future daughter-in-law? With a wrinkled suit?"

Shpetim got up. It was easier to get up than it was to fight with Lora. "I didn't know she was my future daughter-in-law

126

yet," he said. "I thought you wanted to look her over."

The hostess was advancing on them. She had too many teeth, and they were all too big. She smiled the way a shark did.

"Right this way," she said, grabbing a little pile of menus. "We'll seat the rest of your party as soon as they arrive."

Shpetim followed Lora down the long passageway to the big table at the back. Lora had made him call ahead special to reserve it. The table was right up against a window, but instead of looking out on the parking lot, like the other windows did, it looked out on grass and hills and trees. The Elms was the most expensive restaurant in Mattatuck. It was the only restaurant in Mattatuck that served what Lora called "real American food." By that, she seemed to mean steak and fries.

The hostess with the teeth held out a chair. Lora sat down in it. The hostess put the menus down. Then she said, "Your server will be with you shortly," and disappeared.

Lora did not pretend to look at the menu. "Of course she's our future daughter-in-law," she said. "She's Nderi's choice. That isn't the way we did it in Albania, but we're not in Albania anymore. And I asked around. She's a very nice girl."

"She doesn't have any family," Shpetim said.

"Her family was killed by Milošević. Does it matter that they were Greek Orthodox? She will become Muslim for Nderi, that's enough."

"I thought you'd have more of an objection," Shpetim said.

To tell the truth, he'd thought she was going to have a screaming fit. Now here they were, in this expensive place. She wasn't even leaving the first meeting to chance at home.

Lora picked up her menu. "See if you can't get me a Diet Coke," she said. "She's a registered nurse, this Anya Haseri. Did you know that? A registered nurse. That's a good job. It brings in good money. It teaches a woman things she needs to know as a mother. And you can go back and forth with it, to stay at home when your children are young. Also, it shows that she's intelligent, and ambitious. You have to care about these things."

Shpetim did care about those things. He just also cared about other things. And then there was the — irregularity of it. There should have been a meeting of families. Now there were no families, or only their own, which might be worse. If one of the pair wasn't going to have a family, it ought to be the groom.

The waitress arrived. She had too many teeth, too. Maybe they only hired women who had too many teeth. Shpetim asked for a Diet Coke for Lora and a mineral water for himself. Muslims were not supposed to drink, but he did have a beer now and then, sometimes with Nderi, usually after work. He couldn't do that now.

"Then there's this other thing," he said. "This thing with the police. Maybe this isn't the best time to plan a wedding."

Lora put the menu down and gave him what he thought of as "One of Those Looks." "What would make it not the best time?" she demanded.

Shpetim took a deep breath. "The thing," he said. "With the police. Because we found that. That thing."

"The skeleton of the baby."

"Lora," Shpetim said. "Somebody will hear you."

"Well, I don't see that it matters if they do," Lora said. "Everybody knows all about it. It's on the television stations. They're bringing that man here, that man we saw on *American Justice.* That's his problem. It isn't ours."

The waitress came back with the drinks. Shpetim wanted to look at his watch. How long were Nderi and Anya going to take?

"It's not that simple," he said.

"Shpetim, please, it's just that simple," Lora said. "What would make it complicated?"

Shpetim thought he really should have ordered a beer, no matter how bad it would look in front of Anya. He wished he had the nature to overthrow the ban entirely and have a whiskey. He looked at the back of his hand on the table. It looked old.

"It was an old skeleton," he said finally.

"What?"

"It was an old skeleton," he said again, getting his courage up. "It had been there a long time. It had — the skin and the flesh had rotted away from the bone, it had done that naturally. Do you see?"

"Of course I see," Lora said. "But I still don't see why I should care, or why you should. Of course it was an old skeleton. The television said it had been in that backpack for twelve years. Really, you have to wonder what goes on with these people, the way these people live. They have no morals."

Shpetim tried again. "It wasn't in the ground there, where we found it," he said.

"It wasn't there for twelve years."

"How do you know?"

"Because we're working that ground," Shpetim said. "I've been walking over it every day for months —"

"But it was buried. You wouldn't know if you walked over something buried."

"It wasn't buried deep," Shpetim said. "They found it — they didn't do anything, practically, and it was right there. And I walked over that ground just the week before. And —"

"And?"

"And it didn't smell," Shpetim said. "There. I've said it. I've been biting my tongue, not to say it to the police. But that backpack couldn't have been buried in the ground like that for twelve years. It couldn't have been there a week. And we're the only ones there. We're the ones who are on that ground every day. What if one of us put it there?"

"Put a skeleton of a baby?" Lora said.

"Yes."

"In a backpack that belonged to that man who went missing? That's what the television said. The backpack belonged to that man who went missing, that they found hanging from the billboard."

"The skeleton couldn't have been in the

backpack all that time," Shpetim said. "There would have been — I looked into the backpack and there was nothing in it. No . . . no —"

"Rot?"

'Yes."

"Would there have been rot after twelve years?"

"There would have been something," Shpetim said desperately. "It didn't make sense, I'm telling you. What if the skeleton didn't have anything to do with the man who was hanged? Or hanged himself? Or whatever it was? What if it's something else? Somebody put the skeleton of a baby in a backpack and then put the backpack in the ground on my building site, and I don't know that —"

"You don't know anything," Lora said. "You're jumping at shadows. This is our Nderi. That must be the girl. She's a very beautiful girl."

Shpetim Kika already knew that Anya Haseri was a beautiful girl. He just didn't think it was the point.

3

For almost the last week now, Darvelle Haymes's clients had not been clients. They had been people who wanted to get a look at — even to talk to — the woman who might have killed Chester Morton. Darvelle knew all about those particular kinds of people. She'd met a lot of them after Chester first disappeared. She'd met them everywhere. Once, she'd come home — that was to the old place, the bad place — and found one of them in her living room, crawling around on the carpet with a magnifying glass, like a goddamned Sherlock Holmes.

So far, this time, there hadn't been much in the way of that kind of thing. There had been the "clients" who weren't clients, but it had all been very civilized and oblique. She'd go out to show a few houses to somebody who said she was looking for a four bedroom ranch or something new with copper plumbing. Then the questions would start. They were never direct questions. The "clients" never came out and said they knew she was the one everybody had talked about when Chester went missing, or that that crazy Charlene Morton had been talking about on television and in newspapers ever since. They didn't say anything, just "My my," and "Oh, dear," and "Don't you wonder if it's getting so it's not safe to live here anymore."

Darvelle had gone out on the night they found the body. She'd driven all the way over to Mattatuck–Harvey Community college and parked her car on the grassy side of the road. She wasn't up near the billboard. By the time she'd got there, half the town had come up. There was no space up near the billboard. Still, she'd been close enough. She'd been able to see the body swaying back and forth in the wind and the guys climbing up to bring it down. Nothing about it had looked familiar to her. She didn't know why she had thought it would.

Now she turned off her engine and looked up into the rearview mirror to make sure Kyle was pulling in behind her. He had his red pickup truck and not the police cruiser, which was as it should be. He wasn't on duty, and even if he was, she would have insisted. She didn't want police cruisers parked at her place, not the way things were. She didn't want police cruisers anywhere near her place.

She got out of the car and looked around. There were no flyers taped to the telephone poles. The last of those had gone up the day Chester was finally found. There was no crazy old woman sitting on her doorstep. Darvelle kept expecting her to show up there. Threatening. Or something.

Kyle got out of his truck and looked around. "It looks quiet enough," he said.

"It is," Darvelle said. "Of course, we're not inside yet. Maybe she's in the kitchen waiting for me to come home. Maybe somebody else is. You have no idea what it was like twelve years ago."

"I was there."

Darvelle considered this. This was only half true. She had seen Kyle on the night Chester was supposed to have gone missing, but she hadn't seen him again for months after that. He hadn't even wanted to talk to her.

She went up to the front door, and opened it, and looked around. She flicked on the overhead lights and waved Kyle in. It had started to get dark earlier again. She didn't like it when it got dark earlier.

Kyle came in and sat down on the couch and said, "Well?"

Darvelle headed toward the kitchen. "Don't be like that," she said. "You don't know what that woman is like. I wouldn't put it past her to have this place bugged."

"She had to get a warrant to get this place bugged," Kyle said, raising his voice so that it carried to her. "And no judge is going to issue a warrant to a civilian, and nobody in the department has asked for a bug. I'd have heard about it if they had."

Darvelle got a couple of beers out of the

refrigerator. She got a glass for herself.

"People install illegal bugs," she said. "You hear about it all the time."

"It doesn't matter. Whatever those get, they're not admissible as evidence."

"They wouldn't have to be admissible as evidence for you to lose your job," Darvelle said. "You're not supposed to be talking to me about this, and you know it."

She went back into the living room and handed a can of beer to Kyle. He popped the top and drank it.

"You know," he said, "it's not like they don't know that we're together. They know that we're together. That's why they took me off the baby thing —"

"But you were on the baby thing," Darvelle said. "You went out there."

"I went out there, we didn't know what it was. Not really."

"They tell you it's the skeleton of a baby in a bright yellow backpack and you don't know what it is, not really?"

"Yeah, I didn't know what it was. You told me you'd never had a baby. You'd never had an abortion. You'd never been pregnant."

"And it's true," Darvelle said. "I've never been any of those things."

"I had no reason to think you'd have anything to do with the skeleton of a baby.

Anyway, I wasn't, you know, much of any-thing when all that happened. I was still liv-ing with my parents in Kiratonic."

"We were going out."

"And everybody knew about it," Kyle said. "That idiot woman told everybody on earth that you'd killed her son because — hell, I don't know why. Because you wanted to be with me? What sense did that make? We were all about eighteen. If you wanted to dump him and be with me, you didn't have to kill him. You just had to do it."

"I did do it."

"I know."

Darvelle poured beer into her glass. She didn't really like beer. She used to like it, but that was before she'd gotten her life together and grown up. These days, she only kept the stuff in the refrigerator for Kyle.

"So," she said. "What's going on?"

Kyle shrugged. "They've hired this guy. Gregor Demarkian."

"I know that. I looked him up on the Internet."

"Then you know as much as I do. They hired him to consult, whatever that means. That's what he is, a consultant. He's due up here tomorrow or the day after."

"And then what?"

"I don't know then what," Kyle said,

sounding irritated. "He'll consult, I guess. I don't know how he works. The clerks have been spending all their time making copies of all the files and sending him things. Every once in a while, we get a request for something from forensics. That's a joke. What does he think this is, *CSI: Miami*? Forensics, for God's sake."

"I thought you got a lot of new stuff for forensics. From the stimulus package, or whatever that was."

"We did. But we didn't get the guys to run it. You've got to have really good guys. They cost a lot of money. We didn't get money for that. We going to make something or go out to eat?" Kyle said. "I'm starving."

Darvelle didn't want to go out to eat. There would be people in restaurants. The people might not be as polite as the clients.

"I'll make something," she said, getting up. "I could use the distraction, anyway. Are you going to be able to spend the night?"

"I even brought a clean uniform."

Darvelle headed back toward the kitchen. She'd make pasta and garlic bread. It would be simple and it wouldn't take a lot of time. She would not think about that whole week after Chester was reported missing, after everybody had begun taking it all seriously. She would very definitely not think of the very night, and herself standing in the door of Chester's trailer while the rain poured down outside and she knew Kyle was waiting for her at the side of the road.

Four

1

Gregor Demarkian did not know what disoriented him more: the fact that he had a hired car and a driver named Tony Bolero, or the fact that the first thing he saw when he walked into the lobby of the Howard Johnson in Mattatuck, New York, was his own face on the front page of the local newspaper.

The car and the driver made him feel odd in the way that Bennis's ideas often made him feel odd. The woman had been born and raised rich, and it seemed that that made a more permanent impression than the ten years she'd spent poor and disinherited. She was rich again — richer than her brothers who had not been disinherited — given the fantasy novels and all that, and she spent money in a way that Gregor, who had been brought up poor in a tenement, never could.

He had no idea what the car and driver cost, just as he had no idea what the renovations on the townhouse were going to cost. There were things he thought it better not to ask about. It did occur to him that, if he had asked about the cost of the car and the driver, he might have been able to stage a fight and avoid this trip. It interested him that he had not thought of it until he was already here and past complaining.

His face on the front cover of the newspaper was less disturbing to think about. The newspaper was the Mattatuck *Republican American,* and the other person on the front page was Sarah Palin. Gregor bought a copy on his way through the lobby and looked it over as he waited at the reception desk. Tony Bolero followed behind with the bags, both Gregor's and his own. That was another thing about the expense of the car and the driver. The car and the driver had come up from Philadelphia. The driver had to be fed and housed for however long this was going to take.

The headline said: ANDROCOELHO CALLS IN EXPERT FROM PHILADELPHIA. It was a very bad headline. There ought to be some school newspaper editors could go to to learn to write headlines. Maybe there was, and Gregor didn't know about it.

Bennis had been very clear about her motives when she'd hired the car and the driver.

"George is stable," she'd said. "You heard the doctor say that himself. He's not going to die tonight, or tomorrow night. He's not going anywhere for awhile. You're not going to do anything for anybody hanging around here making the doctors nervous."

"He's old," Gregor said. "I wouldn't want to be away if he, if he —"

"Died? Gregor, for God's sake, you can usually get the word 'died' out of your mouth without flinching. George has got Martin here. He's got Angela. He's got the children. They don't need you hovering around, either. And no matter what you think, your presence in George's hospital is not going to be what will keep him alive, if he gets through this. You do not have magic powers."

"I know I don't have magic powers," he'd said — but then, of course, he'd only been half serious. It wasn't that he thought he had magic powers for good. It wasn't that he thought he could keep old George alive. It was that he thought he had magic powers against — not evil, exactly. Maybe "against ill." There was a part of his brain that was convinced that if he went away, the very fact

142

of his going away would cause all kinds of . . .

It was an idiotic way to think, and Gregor Demarkian knew it. He looked down at his face on the front page of the newspaper again. His face was above the fold. Sarah Palin's face was beneath it. That said something, but he wasn't sure what.

"I'm going to leave these here and go out and get the big suitcase," Tony Bolero said, waving at the pile he'd made of the luggage.

Gregor said, "Okay." Then he went over to the briefcase and picked it up. It was the briefcase Bennis had bought him for his birthday, or Christmas, or sometime, a few years ago. It was made by Coach in beautiful black leather, and he hadn't asked what it cost, either.

He put the briefcase on the reception desk and looked up to find a young woman there, looking very neat and professional and young. She was smiling in that way people did when they were required to smile all the time, for business purposes.

"Can I help you?" she asked him.

Gregor suddenly wished Tony would come back, or that he'd brought Bennis along with him. "Gregor Demarkian," he said. "I think I have a reservation. In fact, I think I have two."

The young woman did not stop smiling. "Two," she said, tapping away at a computer. "Let me look that up." She tapped and tapped. Gregor looked at the caption under his picture. It read:

GREGOR DEMARKIAN, NATIONALLY RENOWNED CRIME CONSULTANT, WILL AID MATTATUCK POLICE IN MORTON HANGING MYSTERY

Everything was capitalized, as if it were a headline instead of a caption. Gregor's head was beginning to hurt.

"Here it is," she said. "It's two rooms, connecting, but you don't want the connecting door unlocked? Is that right?"

"That's right."

"That's no problem, then. We have everything set up for you. If you'll just sign here," she passed along a registry book, "and let me have your credit card."

Gregor handed over his credit card just as Tony came back in with the big suitcase. It was the one Bennis had packed for him herself.

"You never know what to bring," she'd told him. "You pack six pairs of underwear and five pairs of socks and think you have everything you need. And don't forget, the driver does errands. He can run out to the laundry if you need him to."

The young woman came back with his credit card and a large manila envelope. In fact, it was a huge manila envelope, and one of the padded ones, as if somebody had shipped him something from Alaska. Instead, Gregor noticed, it hadn't even been put in the mail. There wasn't a postage stamp or postal marking on it.

The young woman handed the two things over. Her smile was in place. It never moved.

"You're that man," she said. Then she saw Gregor had the paper and pointed at it. "That man. I'm sorry. I don't mean to be rude. Everybody's been talking about it for a week, though — the fact that they were going to bring you in. It's really exciting to have you here at Howard Johnson."

"It's not really exciting to have me anywhere," Gregor said. "I mostly just read through papers and organize them."

"Oh, I'm sure you do more than that. You're famous. And everybody wants to know, of course, because everybody knows somebody in the family."

"You mean you knew Chester Morton?"

"Oh, no," the young woman said. "I was, I think, six when he went missing. Something like that. I don't even remember it happening. But he had two brothers and a sister, and the youngest brother was in my class in school. John Bishop High School. That's over on the West side, near Sherwood Forest. You probably think I sound crazy. Sherwood Forest is a part of town. A nice one. The Mortons live over there. So do I."

"I'm sure it's very nice," Gregor said. He wasn't sure what else he should say.

The young woman got the computer card keys out and put them on the counter. "And, of course, there are the billboards."

" 'Billboards'? Plural?"

"Oh, yes. Didn't you know there was more than one? His mother put them up everywhere. There's even one on the interstate near the exit to downtown Mattatuck. I grew up with those signs. My mother says the first thing I ever read out loud was one of those signs. You pass them all the time. Makes you wonder why he chose that one to hang himself from, or for somebody else to — well, you know what I mean. It makes you wonder."

"I suppose it does," Gregor said.

"She's been all over the news lately, too, you know. His mother, I mean. You have to admire her. She never gave up hope of finding him. It had to be awful, finding him like that, though. Don't you think? Oh, and the restaurant is open until ten. I hope you enjoy your stay."

2

There were messages for him, and the big manila envelope. Gregor took the messages and the manila envelope himself and let Tony Bolero bring the luggage upstairs.

"I feel like an idiot," he said, when they were both in the elevator. "I feel like I should be in one of those movies where everybody is a movie star."

"I don't see why," Tony Bolero said blandly. "Movie stars don't usually stay at the local HoJo."

This was true, but beside the point. Gregor let it go. They got to the floor and then down the wide, carpeted hall to the rooms. Gregor found himself wondering why hotel corridors always seemed to be not just empty, but dead empty, as if nothing lived there. They got into Gregor's room and Tony put the luggage at the bottom of the closer of the two enormous beds. Gregor threw the messages and the manila envelope on the little desk and thought about a friend of Bennis's who had come to visit for the first time from France, and who had been absolutely astounded at the size of the beds in ordinary American hotel rooms.

Tony Bolero looked around and nodded, Gregor didn't know at what. "That's okay for the moment," he said. "If you don't mind, I'm going to go to my room and get organized."

"I don't mind at all. You should get some rest. We've been driving for hours."

"Not even two," Tony Bolero said. "It's right over the state line. I didn't like those mountains, though, I can tell you that. And I hated that damned tunnel. But never mind. I just want to unpack."

"Go unpack," Gregor said.

"Don't forget I'm on your phone," Tony said. "Speed dial nine. Just press the nine and hold it down —"

"I really do know how to speed dial."

"Mrs. Demarkian seemed to think —"

"Don't worry about it," Gregor said. "I know what Mrs. Demarkian thinks. Go unpack. I'll call you when I need you."

Tony Bolero shrugged, and went back out into the hall, closing the door behind him with a soft *click*. Gregor spent half a second thinking that if this were a slasher movie, it would be Tony he'd be wise to be afraid of. Then he sat down at the desk and looked through the messages.

There were four of them. They were all

from Howard Androcoelho.

Gregor pushed them aside and opened the manila envelope. It was full of photographs, in garish color, of what appeared to be the body during the autopsy. Gregor shuffled through the first few: the lacerations on the neck; the left arm with scratches on it; the piercing holes for a ring in the right nipple.

He got his phone out and pushed 3. Three was Bennis's speed dial number. Two was Tibor's speed dial number. Bennis had programmed the phone herself, on the assumption — apparently — that he wouldn't be able to do it.

Gregor listened to the phone ring and looked at a few more photographs. He had no idea why anybody would have taken this many photographs of an autopsy. And they were such irrelevant photographs. Usually, photographs of an autopsy first covered the parts of the body in sequence so that a record existed of what was there, then covered a few specific details of special significance at close range. Whoever had taken these photographs had been intent on detailing every hair follicle anywhere one appeared. And more.

Bennis picked up her phone and said, "Hello, Gregor. Are you even there yet? You've barely left."

"I'm here and in the hotel. I haven't called Howard Androcoelho yet. I may not bother. I may turn right around and come right back. How's old George?"

Bennis sighed. "Old George is as well as can be expected. Honestly, Gregor, you weren't doing any good here. You were driving everybody crazy. You were getting in the way of the doctors. He's in the hospital with a bunch of tubes and monitors stuck in him. He's up and talking. There's no indication he's going to drop dead right this minute."

"Is he eating?"

There was a long pause on the line. "Not much," Bennis said finally. "But you can't expect him to be eating, can you? I mean, he's just had a, an event —"

"You know, it might be nice if we could all stop saying 'event' over and over again and put a name to this thing," Gregor said. "I might even be calmer. The man is ninety-nine years old and he's in a hospital where nobody seems to be able to come to a single straightforward diagnosis of what's wrong with him. And that makes me nervous, because what doctors do is decide that just being ninety-nine is enough to be wrong with him, and then —"

"Gregor, for God's sake. The doctor is not Jack Kevorkian."

"Do you know what I think of Jack Kevorkian? I think he was a serial killer who'd figured out how to get away with it. And I don't think he was alone. I think there are a lot of doctors and nurses and even orderlies in our system who —"

"Really," Bennis said. "Really. We don't disagree on doctor assisted suicide. We don't even disagree on old George. But you weren't being any help here, Gregor. You really weren't. You need to be out of the way and doing something. If anything looks like it's going to happen, I'll get right back to you. I've even got your driver primed to drive back on a moment's notice in case of an emergency."

"Does that driver look to you like the human shell of a Stephen King shape-shifting monster?"

"Gregor."

"I should never have let Tibor talk me into *It.* And who names a book *It,* anyway? This is a big toe."

"What?"

"I'm looking at autopsy photos," Gregor said, staring down at the one in his hand as if there was something there to find. "Howard Androcoelho sent them over. They were waiting at the desk when I got here. They're incredible. Somebody took detail pictures, close-ups, of every square half inch on this guy's body, and there's no point to any of them that I can see. The one I've got in front of me is of a big toe. There aren't any marks on it. There aren't any wounds. There's nothing to see. It's just a big toe."

"Don't they usually take photographs of the body during an autopsy?"

"They do," Gregor said, "but they don't go to this kind of trouble with them. You know what this is? It's that stimulus money. When I first talked to Howard Androcoelho, he told me they'd gotten a whole pile of stimulus money and they'd used it to get themselves a crime lab, or something like that. So now they've got a crime lab and they don't know what to do about it. I wonder where the nearest really professional lab is. Is there a state lab in New York?"

"How would I know?" Bennis said. "I know you don't want to admit it, but you sound better already. You're the kind of person who needs to get work done. That's all there is to it. Go put your mind to something you can get interested in —"

"This is the fingers of the left hand," Gregor said. "There's nothing on them. Nothing. There isn't even a ring, or indentations saying he usually wore a ring. Nothing. It's just the hand, sitting there, looking like a hand. Oh, except a little too white for comfort. Did I tell you the guy had piercings? So far, I've found the holes for a nipple ring and an actual penis ring, which was lovely. Oh, and he's got a Death Eater tattoo on the inside of his left arm. I'll have to thank Tibor for taking me to all those *Harry Potter* movies."

"Isn't that odd, that he had the piercings for a nipple ring and he didn't have the nipple ring? I mean don't you have to keep those up or they fill in or get infected or something?"

"I don't know," Gregor said. He flipped back through the pictures until he found the one of the right nipple. He tried to get a good look at the piercing holes. He held the picture up to the light. He turned it sideways. He put it down again.

"Gregor?" Bennis said.

"I'm here."

"What is it?"

"It's a tattoo," he said.

"You're not making any sense," Bennis said. "He got some messages written into his body in a tattoo? What?"

"No," Gregor said. "No, the first time I saw it, I thought it was — I mean, there aren't any other tattoos on the chest that I can see so far, and I wasn't really paying attention, and —"

"Good," Bennis said. "You sound interested in something. That's all I ask. I want you to be interested in something that isn't old George for a while."

3

If there was one thing Gregor Demarkian had learned in all his years of doing this kind of work, in the FBI and out of it, it was this: It wasn't a good thing to jump to conclusions, but it was usually the case that things were what they seemed. Either the master criminal was a myth, or he was never caught, and they knew nothing about him. Real-life criminals, the kind that got arrested every day, rarely found themselves thinking straight, even when they thought they were. He could think of maybe three ordinary murders in all his career where the answer hadn't been screamingly obvious from the first. Serial killers were harder, but only because they picked their victims quasi at random. Although that wasn't completely true, either. Most of the serial killers Gregor had run into over the years had ended up having a personal connection with one of their victims. The only real question had been which one.

He picked up the photograph again. He

held it under the light again. He pulled over the desk lamp so that the light was shining directly at what he wanted to see. There was no doubt about it. There was a tattoo. It was a very small tattoo. It was also a bright, vivid red. He put the photograph down.

Most things were what they seemed. Suicides were suicides. Murders were murders. People killed out of blind rage or jealousy or the need for money or just because it was Tuesday. They did not run around making evil plans to conquer the world. They did run around making plans to get away with what they were doing, but those plans almost never worked.

Gregor picked up his cell phone again, went through the contacts directory, and found the number for Howard Androcoelho. He liked this new cell phone better than the old iPhone, which he had never been able to figure out how to use properly. He wasn't sure he really knew how to use this Propel thing, but at least he could use it as a phone.

There were two numbers for Howard Androcoelho. One of them would be for the office. The other would be for the cell. Gregor had no idea which was which, so he clicked on the first one.

The phone rang and rang, and was picked

up by a woman with a nasal voice. "Mattatuck Police Department, central station," the voice said.

Gregor let that pass — *"Central station"? — Who had a central station?* — and said, "This is Gregor Demarkian. I'm returning Howard Androcoelho's call."

There was a little pause. There was talking in the background. Gregor was surprised he could hear it. One of the things he liked least about cell phones was that it was almost always impossible for him to hear what was going on in the background.

The background noise stopped. The nasal voice said, "I'll put you through."

Then Howard Androcoelho was suddenly on the line, sounding agitated. "Mr. Demarkian? Thank you for calling. Are you in town? Did you get here all right? Are you at the Howard Johnson?"

"Yes," Gregor said, feeling that he needed to be patient to a fault. "I'm at the Howard Johnson. I got your package."

"Oh, that's good," Howard Androcoelho said. "That's very good. They're usually really okay over there, but then I got worried that I was wrong about the motel, the hotel, I don't know what to call anything these days. Do you want to come in to the station? I could set you up with some people, some of us who were here when the disappearance happened, you know, and some of us who caught the stuff last week. I figure, the more people you talk to, the more you know about all this —"

"Yes," Gregor said. "But there's something. In the meantime. What do you do for forensics up here?"

"It's funny you should say 'up here,' " Howard said. "I always think of us as 'down.' You know. Because we're in the southern part of the state. We're practically in Pennsylvania. Of course, they're a lot more south than us in Westchester, but —"

"Forensics," Gregor said. "What do you do for forensics?"

"Oh, I told you," Howard said. "We've got a new mobile crime lab. Because of the stimulus money."

"And you've got a medical examiner? A coroner?"

"Oh, yeah, we do. Well, we've got somebody on call, if you know what I mean. We don't have much use for one most of the time. We don't get a lot of murders. And, you know, things."

"Is there a state medical examiner you can appeal to?" Gregor asked. "Does the state have something set up where you could send things that are a bit out of the ordinary, just in case? Some states do that, you know —"

"I don't know," Howard said. "I — it's not that. I mean, we don't have much call for —"

"Yes," Gregor said. "All right. There are a few things that need checking out. You need to look into the possibility that the state or the county has a professional forensics lab you could use, somebody who's used to doing autopsies on possible murder victims. There are some things, at least as far as I can tell from the photographs —"

"You mean he didn't commit suicide?" Howard Androcoelho sounded shocked. "You mean we were wrong all this time? But how could somebody have done something like that in broad daylight in the middle of a busy intersection?"

Gregor tried counting to ten and letting the words flow over him.

"Listen," he said finally. "It might help if I could see the body. What I think I'm seeing might just be a trick of the photograph. It might not be anything. You do still have the body, don't you? You haven't released it to the family?"

"Oh, no, I haven't released it to the family," Howard said. "We were waiting for you to get here to do that. We've been saying we needed to hold on to it as long as we were doing our investigation, but I didn't think, none of us thought —"

"None of you thought it was going to be anything but suicide?"

Howard Androcoelho sounded defensive. "You're wondering why we called you in, if we thought it was suicide all the time. Well, we can't just go calling it suicide. The family would have a fit, and they're good at having fits. Especially Charlene. And they're a big noise up here. And we've made enough mistakes with this already. So —"

"Never mind," Gregor said. "It would really, really, really help if I could see the body. And if I could talk to your medical examiner."

"Because you don't think he committed suicide," Howard said.

"I don't know if he committed suicide or not," Gregor said. "I do know he didn't commit suicide by hanging himself over that billboard. At least, I know that if this photograph is accurate, which I can't know unless I actually see the body. So if you would —"

"You saw something in a photograph that makes you think Chester didn't hang himself off that billboard? How could you know that? What could you see?"

Gregor looked down at the photograph. Again. "Well," he said. "I see a tattoo. On his chest."

"Chester had a million tattoos. He was decked out better than Lydia the Tattooed Lady."

"He didn't have them on his chest," Gregor said. "He has a very hairy chest, from what I can see. Maybe that was why. But there's one little tattoo there now, and it's bright red."

"So?"

"So it's next to the holes of a nipple piercing, and the holes are large. Meaning he was used to wearing something in there. But whatever that is, is gone, and the tattoo is bright red."

"So?" Howard said again.

"I'm going to come over to central station and see you," Gregor said, "right now. Get something going with the medical examiner or whoever you have to talk to to let me view the body. Because looking at this, I'm willing to bet that this thing was put on the body after it was dead. And I don't think anybody could have done that hanging off a billboard."

FIVE

1

Althy Michaelman would have listened to all the news about Gregor Demarkian, but by the time she got up that afternoon, the cable had been cut off again. Althy didn't think it was fair. Back when she was growing up, you didn't need a cable box and a lot of money to watch the television. There was an antenna on the roof, and that was it. Of course, sometimes the screen was full of snow, and sometimes the signals got so badly crossed you picked up a station in Cleveland, but at least it was free. Althy approved of free. She thought everything should be free.

There was a tear in the white plastic shade that covered the bedroom window. Light came streaming through it and hit Althy in the eyes. She rolled over a little. There were clothes in the bed with her: a pair of Mike's pants; a sock that smelled odd and not just dirty; a bra. She pushed them aside and sat up a little. Her cigarettes were next to the lamp that was next to the mattress. The lamp was on a popcorn can they'd had popcorn in one Christmas, Althy couldn't remember when. Christmases tended to come and go. The only good thing about them was that she could almost always get work, and if she did, she knew she wouldn't get fired until Christmas Eve.

She felt around the base of the lamp and found her Bic lighter. Mike had boosted a dozen of the things from a 7-Eleven just a couple of weeks ago, and come out with a six-pack of Molson's Ale and forty Slim Jims in the process. Mike was really good at boosting things, and he never got caught. He always looked around until he found a store that was empty and only being looked after by some kid who was on his own. The kids never paid attention to the security cameras.

"Someday I'm just going to go into one of these places and take the money," he kept saying, but Althy knew this wasn't true. Mike had already done one two-year jail sentence. He wasn't the kind of person to go looking for more.

Althy got the cigarette lit. It was some local bargain brand, and the tobacco was harsh against the inside of her throat. Here was something else she considered completely unfair. Cigarettes used to cost about a dollar, and then they jacked the prices up and now they cost almost ten for a single pack. That was crazy. She had to find somebody going to North Carolina, or buy what she could black market on the street, or give up having a sandwich for lunch just to get something to smoke that they wouldn't put her in jail for smoking.

Of course, sometimes she smoked the stuff they did put you in jail for smoking, but she didn't give a rat's ass about that. She'd stopped it for a while when those people from Children and Family Services — OCFS — were coming around, but they hadn't been around for years now, and they wouldn't be back. Haydee was over eighteen.

At the thought of Haydee, Althy thought she ought to get up. She did get up, stepping on even more clothes on the floor, a couple of T-shirts, a couple of pairs of boxer shorts. Mike wore boxer shorts when he wore anything at all. He said the other stuff cramped his balls and made him impotent.

Althy went down the hall into the living room. It was bright daylight out. Haydee would not be home. She would either be at school or working. Althy thought about the night before and then let it go. It wasn't fair, Haydee living here like this and not contributing anything to the household. That's all that was about. That's all any of this was about. Haydee ought to grow up and act like a person one of these days.

The light hurt her eyes. She tried the television set, but there was nothing on it but a blue screen. In the old days, the cable company used to have to come out and shut your cable off at the street. Now everything was "digital," whatever that was, and they could turn you off with a computer somewhere out in the middle of nowhere.

Althy went to the door and opened it a little. There were a bunch of women out there, standing around and smoking. There was fat old Krystal Holder with her hair in a net. What did the stupid cow need with her hair in a net? There was hardly any of it left, anyway. She'd dyed it so many times it was just falling out of her head.

Althy went out and down the two steps to the dirt, leaving the door swinging open behind her. It wasn't as if she was going anywhere. It wasn't as if she had anything to steal. They'd finished all the beer last night, and this was her last pack of cigarettes.

The women were all looking at the other trailer, the empty one that Charlene Morton paid for in case her darling son came home. That was a crock. The darling son had done a nice little disappearing act, and that after twelve years of making them all think he was dead at the bottom of a ditch. Althy should have known. People don't end up dead at the bottom of ditches unless they deserved to be.

Of course, Chester Morton was dead now. There was that.

Althy went out to the women. They were all smoking, too, and she was willing to bet they were smoking the same kind of bargain brand she was. There was a time when people like them could afford to have Marlboros and Winstons. That was before the prissy-cunts got into the business of telling everybody else how to live.

Krystal Holder was waving her cigarette in the air. The few hairs she had left on her head were bright red.

"I'm just telling you," she was saying. "It's been all over the news for days, and I've got Dwayne out there at the police department —"

Krystal's son Dwayne was a janitor at the police department. Krystal thought that was a big deal. Krystal thought any kind of regular job was a big deal. It didn't matter to her that Dwayne was barely better than a moron.

"I don't see what they'd want around here," Patti Floyd said. "I mean, he didn't die here, did he? He ran away. Not that I blame him. If I had that mother of his, I'd have been in Alaska before I was sixteen."

"Yeah, well, he's dead now," Althy said.

"Exactly," Krystal said. "He's dead, and it's been on all the television stations. It's been on CNN. And they've brought this guy in, this consultant. They're going to want to look at everything. Especially after today."

"What happened today?" Althy said.

"Shit," Patti said. "Don't you ever get up in the morning? You look like crap."

"I feel like crap," Althy said.

"Dwayne," Krystal said, "says the word at the police department is that this guy, the consultant, he figured out that Chester didn't commit suicide on that billboard like we thought. He was killed someplace else and just hung out there later. So they're going to want to find where the someplace else is. And that means here."

"They think he was killed in the trailer?" Kasey Werl sounded like she was going to cry. Kasey always sounded like she was going to cry. Sometimes she sat out on the

166

stoop of her trailer and cried for most of the day. "But he couldn't have been killed in the trailer. The trailer is right there. It's right across from me."

"Yeah, well," Althy said, "it's right next to me. I could put my hand out my bathroom window and into the bathroom window over there, if it was open. And it's not like I've been going anywhere. Somebody'd pulled shit like that right next to my head, I'd have heard something."

"You could have been passed out," Krystal said.

"Then Haydee would have heard something."

"They're going to come and search the trailer," Krystal said. "That's what Dwayne heard. They're going to search the trailer, and then maybe they're going to search the whole park. And they're going to get somebody in, some lab people, special ones. The lab people can do a lot these days."

"Like on *CSI*," Patti said.

"They can't do anything like on *CSI*," Althy said. "Somebody told me."

"If they search the park, they're going to search the trailers," Krystal said. "So I just thought. You know. The kind of shit that can come out of that. I don't want any of that. And sometimes, you know, there are people."

"Somebody ducking a fucking warrant again?" Althy said.

"How the fuck am I supposed to know?" Krystal said. "I don't mind anybody's business but my own. I'm just saying."

"Fuck," Patti said.

Althy sucked at her cigarette like it was a breath inhaler and she had asthma.

2

There was a point this morning when Penny London thought her head was going to explode. She'd called the automated service line at the bank first at four, then at five, then at six, and all those times there had been nothing. She'd been unhappy about waking up early. It was one of the real drawbacks of living in the car. She'd thought she'd be able to call the bank, and know everything was all right, and go back to sleep again. But everything had not been all right. She had her paychecks deposited directly into her bank by both her schools. The money usually showed up far earlier than four o'clock on the morning of the day. This morning, there had been nothing, and nothing, and nothing again. Penny had found herself sitting bolt upright behind the steering wheel, wondering what she was going to do if there had been some kind of screw up. Pelham University was her worst job as a job, but when they screwed up something like payroll they fixed it on the spot. The money this morning was supposed to come from Mattatuck–Harvey. That was the state of New York. If they'd screwed up, she'd have to wait another two week cycle before she got her money. Then the way the tax formula worked, they'd tax it as if she always made double the amount she usually did.

The money showed up at seven o'clock. Penny called the bank and listened to the run-through with her anxiety running so high, she almost didn't catch it. She called back and listened again. It was there. It had just shown up like that, out of the blue. She only wished she would get back the ability to breathe. It wasn't that she wouldn't have had the money to get through the two weeks. She'd been squirreling away money for months, because winter was coming, and winter was no joke in Mattatuck, New York. She'd never get through it living in her car. She needed enough for the first and last month's rent on a small apartment some-where. It would be easier if she could rent the cheapest apartment around. The cheap-est apartments were in neighborhoods that wouldn't have her. She wondered if there was something ironic about that. When she was growing up, the issue was always whether or not black people could rent apartments in white neighborhoods. Now there were black neighborhoods no white person could rent an apartment in, and the landlords didn't bother to pretend they were doing something other than what they were doing. They weren't crazy enough to want a dead tenant and a lot of attention from the police.

Since it was seven o'clock, it was all right for her to park at school. She drove in and put her car in the second best space in the Frasier Hall faculty lot. It was always empty when she got there in the mornings. Nobody ever got there earlier.

She got out and carried her tote bag up to the third floor to wash. The building was as close to empty as it ever got. It was more empty than it was at night. At night, it was full of cleaning crews.

She got undressed and washed everything and then washed her hair. It was hard to do with the faucet being this far down over the sink. She got the soap rinsed out only by turning her neck back and forth in a way that made her think she was going to break it. She got clean clothes out of the tote bag and put the dirty ones in the plastic bag she'd been given at the grocery store. She'd have to hit the laundromat this weekend, just to make sure. It was important to keep everything about herself as clean and neat as possible. It was too easy to let everything go, and then what would happen to her?

She left the third-floor bathroom, went down another floor and crossed the enclosed bridge to the Students Building. She had no idea why this was called the Students Building and nothing else was. Wasn't every building at a college a "students" building? Or most of them? She hadn't had enough sleep. She was making no sense, even to herself.

The Students Building had a cafeteria in it, right on the other side of the bridge. The cafeteria was subsidized by the state. That meant she could get a pretty decent breakfast for about three dollars. That was more than she would have had to pay for it if she'd had a kitchen to cook for herself, but she didn't have a kitchen, and under the present circumstances, three dollars was doing very well.

She got to the cafeteria to find that she was just a hair early enough to get breakfast at all. It was nearly nine-thirty. She must have taken forever to do what she was doing this morning. It hadn't felt like forever. She put a hand up to her hair and felt that it was still heavily wet. She didn't understand that, either.

She got waffles, sausage, syrup, orange juice, coffee, plastic utensils, and a big wad of paper napkins; paid out at the cashier's desk; and then found an empty table along the wall of windows between the two main eating rooms. She didn't like to be out in the middle of those rooms. It made her feel too exposed.

She put her tray down on the table and her tote bag on the chair closest to the wall. She sat down and rummaged through the tote bag for her correcting: folders full of student papers; grade book; red pen. She laid all these out next to her breakfast and got her good glasses so that she could see. She was starving. If there was one good thing about this living in the car business, it was definitely that it was helping her lose some weight.

She opened the plastic syrup pack and put the syrup all over her waffles. She mentally kicked herself for forgetting to get butter. Then she opened the first of the folders and looked down at the latest paper from Haydee Michaelman. It was a good three times as long as it was supposed to be, and it would be a chaotic mess of incoherent thoughts and angry declarations — but it would be readable, and one of the best in the class, and Penny was looking forward to it.

She sensed someone standing next to her and looked up. It was Gwendolyn Baird, holding a cop of coffee the size of a small inflatable pool and looking down at the waffles like they were diseased. Penny almost said something, but there was no point. Gwendolyn was twenty years younger than she was, and head of the Writing Program.

"God," Gwendolyn said. "I don't understand how you can eat that stuff."

"I fell asleep last night before dinner," Penny said mildly. It was a lie, but she lied a lot to Gwendolyn.

Gwendolyn put her cup on the table. "I thought you taught night courses this term," she said. "In fact, I'm sure you teach night courses this term."

"I teach late, yes," Penny said. "Is there something? I mean —"

"Oh," Gwendolyn sat. She sat down across the table. "There is. It's about Chester Morton. Do you remember Chester Morton?"

"Of course I do," Penny said. "It's not like

it happens every day, one of your students going missing in the middle of a term. At the beginning of one. You know what I mean. And I'd probably have remembered him anyway. You don't get that many of them tattooed up like that, and, you know, the hair."

"Yes, well," Gwen said. "What we hear is this — the police are going to want to talk to all of his teachers from the term he disappeared. To see if they know anything. They say that that man they called in, that consultant? They say he says that Chester could not have committed suicide."

"Already? Is he even here yet?"

"He got here first thing this morning," Gwen said. "They say he got here and looked through some pictures and knew immediately that it wasn't a suicide, it was a murder. So now there's going to be a murder investigation. Can you believe that? They're going to come over here and interview all the teachers. They figure whatever it is that got him murdered, it must have been something from back then. You know, whatever the something there that had made him disappear. It could have been anything, really. He could have been dealing drugs."

"I don't think so," Penny said.

"Really? Do you think you'd know if your

students were dealing drugs? I know they're taking them, sometimes, you know, because they come to class high and it's really impossible not to notice, but —"

"Chester Morton never came to class high as far as I remember," Penny said.

"But there must have been something strange about him at the time, don't you think? There must have been something off. I mean, if he'd been murdered back then, it could have been anything, really. It could just have been a mugging. But for him to disappear for twelve years, and nobody knowing where he was, and then to come back and be murdered after all this time. Well. There must have been something."

"Maybe there was."

"Maybe there was and you just don't realize it," Gwen said. She stood up again. "That's what this consultant will be for. He'll talk to all the witnesses and he'll be able to pinpoint what's important that they don't know is important."

"Witnesses to what?" Penny said.

"Well, you must be a witness to something," Gwendolyn said, "or nobody would be interested in talking to you. I've got to go prep for a class. Check your e-mail, all right? We'll get in touch as soon as we know when he wants to talk to you."

"All right," Penny said.

But there was no point. Gwendolyn was already off and away, stomping away in those skintight pants and those mile-high wedgies she always wore, her middle-aged ass bumping and grinding like a fully inflated beach ball being juggled on the top of two thin sticks.

Penny picked up her fork and started working her way through the waffles and sausage.

There was something, of course, from that term — there had been something that bothered her at the time, but nobody had been interested in listening to her.

It was too bad she didn't have a place anymore to keep her records.

3

If there was one thing that bothered Kyle Holborn about his relationship with Darvelle Haymes, it was that they weren't married yet, not even after all this time.

Except that that was not true, not exactly. It wasn't that they weren't married that bothered him, but the reason why they weren't married. Kyle was, he thought, a very steady person. He liked things to be simple and straightforward and sure. That was why he had joined the police force.

There were never a lot of layoffs in the police force. In bad economic times, there might even be increases in force. Bad economic times meant people without money, and people without money meant more police needed to find them when they robbed the local convenience store. Police work was good, and steady, and not anywhere near as dangerous as people thought. Most of the time, all you were dealing with were kids being stupid. Having been a stupid kid himself once, Kyle knew how to handle that.

Kyle liked everything in life steady and straightforward, not just his job. He wanted to buy a house someday, or to move in Darvelle's, but it was a house *like* Darvelle's he wanted, not one of those big new things in the subdivisions in Kiratonic and Lakewood and Shale. Darvelle wanted those, and Kyle sometimes thought she wanted even more than that. She was always talking to him about what a good "platform" police work was. If he got a few promotions, he could run for the state legislature, and after that, there was no telling where he could go.

The problem was, Kyle thought he could tell where he would go. He didn't want to be in the state legislature. He didn't want to run for something even bigger, where people from news stations would go chasing around to find out if he'd ever been caught smoking marijuana in high school. He just wanted a quiet life, with a house and a wife and a baby. He wanted to listen to Rush Limbaugh on the radio. He wanted to shop at Walmart on the weekend. He wanted to go to the movies and see Bruce Willis kick ass.

He did not want to be here, at the central station, wondering what his partner was doing with a temporary partner. Kyle thought it was both understandable and a little ridiculous that he had been pulled off patrol just because of the backpack.

"It's not like it was me that put that backpack in the field," he said out loud.

Across the desk, Sue Folger looked up. "Did you say something?"

Sue Folger was a clerk. She never went out on patrol. She never did anything but shuffle papers. Kyle thought she looked old.

"I was talking to myself," he said.

"You ever intend to get back in a patrol car, you'd better watch that," Sue said.

She was old, really old. She was probably over forty.

"It's not like I did anything wrong," Kyle said. "I mean, I didn't tamper with evidence, or anything. And I wasn't even a part of all that. All I did was answer a call, right there with Jack, because we were the closest ones to it."

Sue took her glasses off. Nobody ever wore glasses anymore. People wore contacts. "It's the Morton family," she said, sounding so infinitely patient Kyle wanted to punch her. "You know what Charlene Morton is like. She's screaming to high heaven. Not that I blame her. All this time, and now her son's here and he's dead like that."

"Murdered," Kyle said.

"That seems to be the word," Sue said. "Don't ask me what it's all about, though. The man hasn't even seen the body, and the next thing you know, he's on the telephone saying Chester couldn't have hung himself off that billboard. You have to ask yourself where that sort of thing comes from."

"They've got stuff," Kyle said vaguely. "You know, in bigger places. They've got stuff we don't have to help them figure things out. He's from Philadelphia."

"I still say you don't throw around things like that if you aren't sure about what you're saying, and I can't see how he's going to be sure about what he's saying. What if he gets here and sees the body and decides he was wrong? What then?"

"The body isn't here, is it?"

"No," Sue said. "It's over at Feldman's Funeral Home, locked in a freezer or something. I don't know. Howard was absolutely losing it this morning, running around, making sure of I don't know what. And Charlene's called three times. Why Howard thinks you can keep anything secret in this town is beyond me."

"Shouldn't the body be in, like, a morgue or something?" Kyle asked.

"We don't have a morgue," Sue said. "The last time we had a murder in this town was in 1948. We've had dead bodies before. All those kids drinking and driving in the springtime, you're going to have bodies. And Dade Warren committed suicide a couple of years back. Okay, maybe twenty. I forget how fast time goes. Didn't you ever hear about Dade Warren?"

"Twenty years ago, I was ten," Kyle said.

"Oh, well. It was famous around here for awhile. It wasn't like this. There wasn't any mystery to it. Dade Warren ran a drugstore, a little independent mom-and-pop drugstore. He'd gotten it from his parents when they died. Anyway, Rite Aid wanted to come in, and Dade fought like crazy at the zoning board, but you can't keep businesses out of a community just because somebody already living there doesn't want the competition. Dade took a bunch of sedatives from the pharmacy and drugged the hell out of his wife and children during dinner. Then he took his rifle and shot them all in the head. Then he shot himself. He left a note, but it was more like a letter. A really long thing. It's like I said, there wasn't any mystery about it."

"Damn," Kyle said. "You'd have thought I'd have heard something about that some-time."

"We don't talk about it around here," Sue said. "It was Howard's last case before he became a detective. It drives him crazy to talk about it. So we don't bother."

"Chester Morton was Howard's case, too," Kyle said. "That's got to be odd."

"Chester Morton wasn't anybody's case," Sue said. "Nobody but Charlene ever thought he'd been murdered, and as it turned out, nobody was right. I wonder where he's been all this time, don't you? Twelve years. He had to be somewhere."

"Yeah," Kyle said. "I don't think of it that way, though. It's like he vanished under an invisibility cloak, or something."

"People ask why I never let my children read *Harry Potter*," Sue said, "and there it is, that's it. It's not that *Harry Potter* encourages witchcraft. It's that it encourages nonsense. Don't you have work to do, or something?"

"Wait," Kyle said. "I think this is it."

All around the big room, people were sitting up, heads were turning to the door. It was too quiet. Then the door swung open and a man came in, tall without being as tall as Howard Androcoelho, slightly heavyset without being at all like Howard Androcoelho. Kyle was disappointed. He'd expected to recognize the man from the pictures he'd seen, and the pictures on television especially, but he could have passed this man on the street and not given him a second thought.

"Excuse me," the man said, leaning a little on the counter that divided Kyle's part of the room from the general public. "I have an appointment with Howard Androcoelho. I'm —"

"Mr. Demarkian! Mr. Demarkian!" Howard came barreling out of his office at the back, moving faster than Kyle had ever seen him before. "Mr. Demarkian! I'm glad you're here. If you could come back here for a moment —"

"He doesn't look all that impressive," Kyle said.

"No, he doesn't," Sue said. "Just you watch, all this crap will be wrong, and then we'll have a real mess on our hands. I'm surprised Charlene isn't with us as we speak."

Kyle sat back down a little. Gregor Demarkian was disappearing into Howard Androcoelho's office. People had started to talk again. The room was getting loud.

He thought of picking up the phone and calling Darvelle, and decided against it. He just wished that she'd calm down. He wished that everybody would calm down.

He bent over the paperwork he was supposed to be doing and tried to think about fishing. Fishing always took his mind off everything.

Six

1

Gregor Demarkian had seen dozens of small-town police departments in his life. He had seen them smaller than this, which was, after all, only the main of something like three stations. This was, in many ways, a good-sized community. The local community college was here. There was a solid little section of town with gridded streets and stoplights instead of stop signs. There were sidewalks.

Still, there was some kind of tipping point somewhere, that distinguished a small town from a small city, and it wasn't just population. There was a change in attitude, or maybe experience. It was a tipping point Mattatuck hadn't crossed.

Gregor passed through the big open room full of people working at desks on computers, ubiquitous now not only in police departments but in every other kind of organization. He went into Howard Andro-coelho's office, which was nothing like the office of somebody called a "police com-missioner" anywhere else. Gregor wondered who had thought up the title, and why. What Howard Androcoelho actually seemed to be was the local chief of police.

The office was small, but it did have windows. The windows looked out onto a small grassy area defined by a spiked wrought-iron fence. Howard Androcoelho's desk was regulation size and covered with papers. His computer was on a little wheeled "workstation" that Gregor was willing to bet was nearly impossible for such a large man to do anything at. There was a visitor's chair — a plain wooden one, without cush-ions.

Gregor sat down in the visitor's chair and looked around. Howard Androcoelho was bustling. He shut the door and then checked to make sure the air conditioning was work-ing. The air conditioning was an ordinary window unit. The building they were in had to be a hundred years old.

Howard Androcoelho hurried around to sit at the desk. Then he beamed, or tried to.

"Well," he said. "You really came. I wasn't sure, you know, with all that trouble the day I came to Philadelphia."

"I did say I would come."

"Yes, yes. I know you did. It was just — well, I hope that friend of yours came out all right. That was a terrible thing. Terrible. You don't expect that sort of thing to happen right in front of you."

"He's doing as well as can be expected," Gregor said. "Can I ask you something? Why are you called the police commissioner? Why aren't you just the chief of police?"

This time Howard Androcoelho did beam. "Oh, I am," he said. "There's not really much call for a police commissioner yet. Not here. But we're growing. We're growing so fast, we can hardly handle it. And Marianne and I thought —"

"Marianne?"

"Marianne Glew," Howard said. "She's the mayor these days. Funny how these things work out. She was my partner once. She was my partner on this, you know, when Chester Morton first went missing. We were both detectives then, and we thought — well, we thought being detectives was the most amazing thing we could be. That was only a few years after this town started hiring detectives. You really would be amazed at how fast this town has been growing."

"And police commissioner?"

"Well, we thought we'd get to police commissioner eventually," Howard said. "We've got almost fifty thousand people within the city limits these days, and that's almost ten thousand more than we had twelve years ago."

Gregor considered this. "You've got almost fifty thousand people, and you don't have a regular morgue?"

"We're getting people, Mr. Demarkian, not crime. This is only the second time we've felt any need for a morgue since I joined the force as a patrolman. Not a lot happens here."

"Drug overdoses?" Gregor suggested. "Domestic violence murders?"

"Oh," Howard said. "Yeah. We get some of that. But you don't need one of those fancy medical examiners for that sort of thing. And not much else has happened here. I told you when I came to see you, the last time there was a real murder in this town, it was 1948."

Gregor thought about it. He did remember Howard saying something like this, but at the time he had imagined that Mattatuck, New York, would be like Snow Hill, Pennsylvania — a little nothing of a place entirely out in the sticks, with more dirt roads than paved ones. From what he had seen of Mattatuck so far, however, it was a largish "small" town that was well on its way to becoming a small city. The crime statistics couldn't be what Howard Androcoelho said they were. Either he was deliberately downplaying the reality here, or he was spending most of his time looking the other way when bad things happen.

"We do have that mobile crime lab," he said suddenly. "I told you that, didn't I? We got it with the stimulus money."

"Yes," Gregor said.

He was still thinking. He looked at the walls of Howard's office. What wasn't obscured by old-fashioned filing cabinets was blank and painted that odd sick green that covered the insides of so many public buildings from the Thirties.

"You're still using filing cabinets? You're not putting your records on the computer?"

"Oh, we're putting all the new records on the computer," Howard said. "We've been doing that for fifteen years or so now, more or less. It's the old records we don't have on the computer."

"You don't have a storage space?"

"Sure we do. In the basement of this building, as a matter of fact. But you know how it is. You stack the stuff up here and there and forget all about it. I suppose I ought to clean out this office once in a while."

"What about the case we're talking about, Chester Morton? Is that on the computer, or in analog files?"

"Oh, most of that's in the computer," Howard said. "But we've also got files. You know, Mr. Demarkian, no matter how good these computers are supposed to be, in the end, you always end up with files. You have to. We've got all of Charlene's letters, for instance, and we've got them in files. She didn't send them on the computer. I don't even know if she had one back then."

Gregor looked around a little more. Howard Androcoelho cleared his throat.

"Well," Howard said. "You were saying, Mr. Demarkian, on the phone, that Chester Morton couldn't have committed suicide."

Gregor turned his attention back to Howard. "No," he said. "That's not what I said. I said that I could prove that Chester Morton didn't commit suicide by hanging himself off that billboard. That doesn't mean he didn't commit suicide somewhere else."

"Well — did he? Did he commit suicide somewhere else?"

"Even if he did," Gregor said, "it doesn't get you out of your problem. If he committed suicide someplace else, somebody still had to get the body and hang it off that billboard. And that person has to be guilty of half a dozen things, including tampering with a crime scene."

"Oh, well," Howard said. "Yes. But —"

"Here," Gregor said. He put the briefcase he had brought with him onto Howard's desk, opened it, and took the photograph that mattered right off the top. There was barely any room on Howard's desk to put a briefcase or even a cup of coffee, but the papers there didn't look particularly worked on. They just looked messy.

Gregor handed the photograph across to Howard Androcoelho. "There," he said. "What do you see?"

Howard Androcoelho frowned. "A bare torso," he said. "Holes that look like they're for a nipple ring. Some discoloration."

Gregor reached back into the briefcase and came up with his little magnifying glass. "Try this," he said. "Right over the nipple near the holes."

Howard took the magnifying glass and stared at it. "My God," he said. "It's just like Sherlock Holmes. I don't think I've used one of these since I was a Boy Scout."

"I got it for my birthday one year," Gregor said. "From a friend who was thinking of

Sherlock Holmes himself. Look at the area right around the nipple."

Howard Androcoelho looked. Then he sat back, puzzled. "That's — what is that? A tattoo?"

"A pinpoint tattoo, yes. The kind men give themselves and each other in prisons. Notice anything else about it?"

"It says MOM."

"Anything else?"

"If you can see something else here, you have better eyes than I do, Mr. Demarkian. And I don't understand what you're getting at. Was Chester Morton in prison? Is that why he disappeared for twelve years and nobody knew where he was? How does that have anything to do with whether he hanged himself off the billboard or not?"

Gregor sighed. "Well," he said, "it depends on what this looks like on the actual body. But assuming it looks the same, then it's fair to say that that tattoo was put on that body after death."

"What?"

"The red of the ink is far too bright," Gregor said. "In a living body, ink fades. It gets sucked deeper into the skin. It gets acted on by all kinds of bodily chemicals. New skin grows and old skin sloughs off, and it's a process that makes the ink look

191

duller. But that ink is bright red. It's like it was put on with red nail polish."

"Was it?" Howard said. "Put on with nail polish, I mean?"

"I don't think so. We can check that when we see the body. But there's something else. There's the hair."

"Hair," Howard said.

"The hair on the chest," Gregor said. "There's a reason why that's the only tattoo on the chest. Chester Morton had enough chest hair to be a werewolf. He's literally carpeted with it. But somebody shaved that one small space, and shaved it clean."

"Are you sure? I mean, couldn't it just be a bit of a bald spot?"

"No," Gregor said, "I don't think so. But again, I'd have to see the body. And then there are the holes for the nipple rings."

"So?"

"So, they're very wide. Which means Chester Morton was used to wearing a ring in that nipple. He wasn't used to leaving it out. So we have to ask where exactly that nipple ring has gone."

"I don't see how you can tell all that from a single photograph," Howard said.

"I don't, either," Gregor said. "But that's why I want you to take me to see the body. Let's make sure I'm not just overinterpreting some anomaly in a picture."

2

Feldman's Funeral Home was on East Main Street, and like the rest of Mattatuck, it was bigger and more impressive than he'd been led to expect. East Main Street itself was bigger and more impressive than he'd been led to expect. It not only had stoplights, it had a divider down the middle, running up to the town green. The green began at an enormous granite war monument dedicated to THE CITIZENS OF MATTATUCK WHO GAVE THEIR LIVES IN THE WAR FOR THE UNION. The monument was four-sided, though. Gregor expected he'd find the name of Mattatuck men lost in other wars on the other sides of it. The green was relatively substantial, too, with benches along the edges of it for people who were waiting for a bus. Gregor saw one of the buses come and stop and pick up a lone black woman with three overloaded tote bags.

Howard Androcoelho parked in a space clearly marked NO PARKING, which Gregor put down to police privilege. He got out and hurried around the car to Gregor's side of it, then stood back as Gregor got out on his own. Gregor hated having car doors opened for him.

"Parking's getting to be a problem," Howard said. "I've got to admit it. If there's one sign Mattatuck is getting to be bigger than we want it to be, it's the parking. It's hard to believe, do you know what I mean? Most places in this part of the country are falling apart. And here we are. Having a problem with parking."

Gregor looked up at the THE FELDMAN FUNERAL HOME, as the sign read. He was almost sorry Bennis wasn't here to see it. It was the kind of house she would have loved. It was two story, and Victorian, but on top of that it had enormous porches on both floors, and at the front right corner, where the corner of the intersection was, it had stacked built-on gazebos, too. It was the kind of house girls liked to play fairy princess in, when they were in grade school.

"It's something else, isn't it?" Howard said, flapping his arms at it. "They don't build houses like this anymore, do they? That one was built here in the nineteenth century sometime, before World War I, anyhow. Guy who built it had a big metal-working factory on the outskirts of town. That's long gone, of course. Nobody has metalwork factories in places like this anymore. Too expensive. Cheaper to build them down in Mexico where you can pay people a dollar a day. It's something else, let me tell you."

Gregor grunted something deliberately incomprehensible and followed Howard up the steps to the porch and the big double front doors. The door was opened moments later by a small, older man in a fussy suit, the kind of suit Gregor thought must be given away at every funeral director certification ceremony in the world. The man's hair was very thin and slicked back over his skull like the villain's in a silent movie. He was very nervous.

"Oh, it's you," he said, standing back and letting Howard and Gregor come inside. "I told you on the telephone. This isn't a very good time. We've got the Mollerton viewing starting up any minute now. I don't know what they're going to think about a police car parked right out front."

"You should build yourself a parking lot out back," Howard said.

The fussy little man rolled his eyes. "You know there's no room to build a parking lot out back. There's no room to build a parking lot anywhere. He still thinks we're back in 1950. Or even 1930. Or before that. I don't know."

"I'm sorry to bother you," Gregor said. "It's just —"

"Oh, I know what 'it's just,' " the fussy little man said. "I understand completely. I'm just about beside myself, though. This has been the biggest problem. And of course Charlene has been here. Several times. Last time I had to call Stew to come and get her out. She was howling like a dog, she really was. And of course, we had a wake. We almost always have a wake."

The fussy little man had been moving while he'd been talking, and he'd brought them to a door in a back hall.

"Charlene is the mother," Gregor said. "That's right, isn't it?"

"Charlene is definitely the mother," the fussy little man said. "And of course, we've done all the Morton funerals. I expect we'll go on doing all of them, in spite of the things she said. But she's not completely sane on this subject. She is really not."

The fussy little man opened the door and turned on a light with a switch at the bottom of the stairs. He started down the steps himself. They followed.

What was at the bottom of the steps was an enormous finished basement, fitted out to serve as an embalmer's studio. Along one wall there were three metal doors that Gregor recognized immediately as belonging to what the police in Philadelphia would probably call meat lockers — cold storage boxes for bodies.

The fussy little man went to the one on the far right and opened the door. Then he put both hands on the end rail and pulled the slab out.

"This has been a problem, let me tell you," he said. "I've got him as close to freezing as I can get him, and he'll keep, but I've only got the three. You can see that. And I've got business coming in all the time. It's been hard to handle."

Gregor went to the slab and looked down on the body. He was not a medical examiner, but he knew that purple tinge to the face, and the bugging of the eyes and tongue. The man had been alive when he'd been hanged, or hanged himself.

"He looks much better now than when he came in," the fussy little man said. "Then — well, you're supposed to be an expert on crime, aren't you, Mr. Demarkian? It's Mr. Demarkian, isn't it? We've all heard about you down here by now. The effects of a hanging recede over time. And of course we can make them recede a lot faster. But Howard said I wasn't supposed to do that. So I just put him in here and let nature run its course."

"That was probably a good idea," Gregor

said. The body had been left naked except for a pair of briefs. The briefs were not soiled, which meant they must have been put on after death.

"Did you put the briefs on him yourself?" Gregor asked.

"Oh," the fussy little man said. "Yes, yes I did. It just seemed wrong, somehow, leaving him in there with nothing — I mean with everything. Wasn't I supposed to do that?"

"I don't see why you shouldn't," Gregor said. "Did somebody keep the clothes he was wearing when he was found?"

"They're in evidence bags down at the station," Howard said.

Gregor bent over the chest. It was there, and it looked exactly as it had looked in the photograph. The letters were not large, but they were large enough so that they would not be missed, especially with the hair cut away the way it was. And they were bright red. Gregor put his finger down and ran it over the surface of the word MOM. Then he stood back and shook his head.

"It's a tattoo," he said.

"Oh, Chester had tattoos," the fussy little man said. "He was that kind. Terrible to say it, really, but there it is. The Mortons are probably the most prominent family in this town. They've built that business into a powerhouse. They've got a vacation house in Florida. They're good, hardworking people. But Chester was always Chester. He didn't like home. He didn't like the business. He was always trying to — I don't know what you'd call it. But he had a lot of tattoos. You can see for yourself. And then he had that girl. And that place out at the trailer park."

"He didn't have any other tattoos on his chest," Gregor said.

"It was probably too much trouble to keep up with the hair," Howard Androcoelho said. "God, he's got a lot of hair."

"And this hair," Gregor pointed to the MOM in red, "was shaved off after he was dead, and the tattoo was put there after death."

"Really?" the fussy little man said. "How could somebody do that? Doesn't it take hours and hours to put on a tattoo?"

"Depends on the tattoo," Gregor said. "This is just those three letters, they're not large, they're not fancy, they're all in the same color ink. They're the kind of thing prisoners put on each other, or even themselves. Something like that might take forty-five minutes. It would probably take less, even assuming whoever did it didn't have access to professional tools."

"But why would anybody put a tattoo on the body after the guy had died?" Howard said. "What would be the point of that?"

"I don't know," Gregor said.

"Well, whoever did it, didn't know Chester," the fussy little man said. "Chester would never have had that tattooed on him, anywhere. Chester hated that woman, he really did. The whole bunch of them hate her. And it's not hard to see why."

3

The fussy little man was named Jason Feldman, and as he stood on the sidewalk outside The Feldman Funeral Home watching Howard Androcoelho get himself back inside his car, he fussed even more.

"We're really not prepared for this kind of thing," he said to Gregor Demarkian, rubbing his hands together as if he were standing in front of a fire. It was nearly 80 degrees out, and it was already half past one.

"It used to be all right, you know, in my father's time," he said. "In those days, what did you get that you had to worry about? Hunting accidents? There are a lot fewer of those than you'd think. And they don't amount to much, if you know what I mean. No, what you'd get mostly was the wife beating, and that was terrible, but it wasn't as if they were our clientele anyway. The kind of people who come here either don't beat their wives, or they're very careful not to kill them when they do it."

"Ah," Gregor said.

"Well," Jason Feldman said, "there are the suicides, of course. We have surprising few of those, too. And mostly it's teenagers. That's the terrible thing. Are you going to be here long?"

"I don't know," Gregor said. "I suppose it will be as long as it takes."

"This town needs to wake up and see the changes," Jason Feldman said. "We're not a tiny little burg anymore. Things are going to happen." He stopped and looked thoughtful. "Not that things didn't happen before," he said. "I mean —"

It was hot, and Howard Androcoelho was in a rush. Gregor said good-bye and got into the car. Howard had the air conditioner blasting.

"Having an interesting talk?" he said. "Jason could tell you a lot of things. His father could tell you more, but his father's been dead now two or three years. There was a time, this was the only funeral home in the area. You'd have to go clean off to Binghamton to find another one. The Feldmans got all the business."

"Apparently, there was business they didn't want."

"Oh," Howard said, easing the car out into what was definitely downtown traffic. "Yeah, well. We've got an element. Any rural town has got an element. That's the trailer park I was telling you about. The one where Chester Morton had a trailer after he moved out of his mother's house. God, did that cause an explosion. She didn't want him moving out of that house. She doesn't want any of them moving out of that house."

"Not even when they've married?"

"Well, Suzanne's married. That's the eldest, I think. The girl. She's married, and she and her husband have a house in the next block, and the husband works in the business. I guess there are advantages to that kind of thing if you can stand putting up with it. Guaranteed job. Don't have to worry about unemployment. Don't have to worry about the down payment, either. As long as you're willing to stay tied to the umbilical cord, the money will be sitting there waiting. It would drive me nuts, let me tell you about that."

Gregor thought about it. "The trailer — didn't you say something about the trailer in the notes you gave me? Isn't the trailer empty, or something?"

"It's empty," Howard said. "It's been empty ever since Chester disappeared. Charlene pays the rent on it. Keep the home fires burning. Leave a light in the window. Whatever. Just in case he ever came home, she says."

"Do you know if he went to the trailer on the day he died?"

"Nope," Howard said, "and in case you're going to ask, yes, we did go over there. There was no sign of anybody having been around."

"Would he have been able to get in?"

"You mean, did he have a key he didn't have to ask Charlene for?" Howard shrugged. "I don't know. She's got a key, though. I half think she goes over there and just sits in the place, communing with spirits. Or what she thought was spirits. She was that convinced somebody had killed him. But then, I can't really see Charlene spending any time in that trailer park. It's not the kind of thing she'd put up with."

Gregor was thinking about it some more. "Can we go over and see the place?" he asked. "Would we have to get a warrant? Would Mrs. Morton let us in?"

"Charlene would let us in with bells on," Howard said, "but maybe she'll be busy.

Then we can get her to just give us the key. When do you want to go?"

"What about right now?"

"You mean drive over there right this minute?"

"Something like that. We should stop and call Mrs. Morton, if she's the one we need permission from, and the key —"

"Give me a second," Howard said.

He punched something on his dashboard, and Gregor suddenly realized that the car was set up to make it possible to dial, talk, and drive all at the same time when Howard Androcoehlo said, "Charlene Morton," very loudly, and the car was suddenly filled with touch-tone beeps.

"Neat, isn't it," Howard said.

"More of that stimulus money?"

"Absolutely," Howard said. "I loved that stimulus money, I really did. It had to go to law enforcement, we used it for law enforcement, but it's not like we needed more cops on the street or more clerks in the office. We even got ourselves a SWAT team, and I don't know what we're ever going to use it for. For terrorists, it's supposed to be. Any terrorist who finds himself in Mattatuck is lost."

What had been the vague background buzz of a ringing phone suddenly became a voice, a harsh and low voice. "Morton Rubbish Removal," the voice said.

"Hello, Kay," Howard said, "this is Howard Androcoelho. Is Charlene around somewhere I can talk to her?"

Gregor took another look at the road. It had moderate traffic. Howard seemed to be able to concentrate on it. Gregor told himself it would be all right — he needed to use Tony for these things; he didn't like the way Howard Androcoelho drove — and took his own cell phone out. He punched Bennis's speed dial number in and waited. He got the answering machine.

"Hey," he said. Then he wondered why he'd said it. He never said things like "hey." "Bennis, listen. I suppose you're out doing something with tiles or wallpaper. I've got a problem. Do you think you could find out for me if the New York State Police have some kind of service to provide autopsy help for small towns without their own full-time medical examiners? I don't know what to call this, but I remember Connecticut does it. It's just — we could use some serious forensics up here and I'm not going to get that kind of thing from the town of Mattatuck. Call me back and tell me what you find. And give me an update on old George."

Gregor slid his phone closed. He saw that Howard Andocoelho was staring at him.

"You want to bring the state police in on this?" he said, incredulous.

"Not really," Gregor said. "There are some states, Connecticut is one of them, where the state police provide help with things like forensics for towns too small to have their own permanent, full-time systems. I was hoping we could get a qualified pathologist to look at that body and explain a few things to me."

"And it's not like any doctor couldn't do that?"

"No, any doctor couldn't. I'm not insulting your people here, Mr. Androcoelho, I'm just hoping to get a little expert advice. There are things going on here that don't make any sense to me, starting with that tattoo. It was a small tattoo. Too small to be readily visible — well, not visible. It *was* visible. But you know what I mean. It wasn't the kind of thing that slaps you right in the face."

"The state police," Howard said. "If they come in here and do anything, they're going to charge us an arm and a leg. They really are. There's going to be hell to pay."

"There shouldn't be, if it helps you catch a murderer," Gregor said. "There shouldn't be even if it helps you establish that this was a suicide and somebody tampered with the body after death."

"You don't know Mattatuck," Howard Androcoelho said.

Then he turned down a long paved road called Watertown Avenue, a road that was oddly half-country and half-strip development. There were half-a-dozen fast-food restaurants, the low-slung crumbling brick of the Department of Social Services, three pawnshops, and intermittent overgrown vacant lots, all of them full of automobile parts. The Department of Social Services had a crowd of people in front of it, all of them looking deflated.

"The trailer park is up here," Howard said. "Charlene should be there waiting for us."

"She'll get there before we do?"

"Yeah," Howard said, "it's irony or something. Chester moved out to the trailer park, and it's far enough from their place out at Sherwood Forest, but it's right across the back from and maybe fifty feet down the road from the business. I mean, let's face it. If you had a trash business, where would you put it?"

Gregor had no idea what that question meant, but he didn't bother to ask. There was a faded, unreadable sign by the side of a dirt track driveway, and that was the beginning of the trailer park.

SEVEN

1

Charlene Morton was neither a fool nor a mental defective, and she didn't have time to waste. The office was only across the lot at the back of this place. All she had to do was wade through the mud, if that's what she wanted. It wasn't what she wanted. She'd done enough wading through the mud since this whole thing began. She'd put up with that little tramp from the trailer park — except, of course, the little tramp wasn't from the trailer park. The whole thing was just impossible. With a name like that, that girl should have been best friends with a biker gang, and there she was.

Charlene took her own car. It was against her better judgment, and against any judgment she'd ever had, even the bad kind. That's what you needed to do, to make your day complete, drive a nice shiny new Ford Fusion into that mess of tin and garbage.

Charlene could see it now, the faces hidden behind plastic blinds, looking out, making plans. She'd have the car stolen out from under her if she didn't have people coming to meet her, and that was a fact.

Of course, the people coming to meet her were Howard Androcoelho and that friend of his. That was going to be a joke. Charlene had watched a couple of television programs now that had Gregor Demarkian in them, and Mark had found her something on the Internet about a case in Philadelphia from a month or two ago. The man looked like — well, Charlene didn't know what he looked like. "The Armenian-American Hercule Poirot," the Web site had called him. Charlene remembered something about Hercule Poirot. He was a fussy little man with a mustache. They had movies about him on A&E.

She parked the car in front of Chester's old trailer and sat for a moment looking at it. The sky was clouding up. It was going to rain. She remembered the first time she ever saw this trailer, when Chester had come home happy as a clam to tell them all he was moving out. He expected her to let him go and wait around for an invitation. She wasn't like that. She'd gotten right into the car and come right over here, and then she'd sat just like she was sitting now, appalled.

There were other people in the trailer park, of course. It had inhabitants. Charlene didn't understand how anybody on earth could want to live in a place like this, but there were people who did. She thought about getting out and looking around on her own. She did that sometimes. More often, she sent Mark or Kenny to do it for her. She just wanted to be sure none of these people were getting into the trailer and stealing Chester's things.

Another car came up, Howard Androcoelho's unmarked special-expensive commissioner of police car, as if Mattatuck was the kind of town that needed a commissioner of anything. Charlene got her purse and got out. Sometimes when she came here, there were people sitting out on their steps, women mostly, smoking cigarettes and not doing much of anything. This was something Charlene really couldn't understand. There wasn't a moment in her life when she wasn't doing something.

Howard got out of his own car. The man Charlene assumed was Gregor Demarkian got out after him. Charlene held her purse on her arm and over her stomach, like a shield.

"Howard," she said.

"Charlene," Howard said. He turned to his side and sort of gestured in that vague direction. "This is Gregor Demarkian, Charlene. I told you all about him. Mr. Demarkian, this is Charlene Morton, Chester's mother."

"How do you do?" Gregor Demarkian held out his hand.

Charlene had no intention of taking it. She took her pocketbook off her arm instead and reached inside it for the keys. She'd had a special key ring made for those keys only a few weeks after Chester was gone. It had his picture in it in a plastic bubble.

She stuck the keys into the trailer's door and opened it. She didn't know why she bothered with the key. The whole damn thing was made of tin. Anybody who wanted to could get in with a can opener.

She stood back and let Gregor Demarkian go through first, but she went in before Howard. The last thing she was going to do was get formal and polite with Howard Androcoelho. When she got up the steps she saw that Gregor Demarkian was drawing his finger across a thick layer of dust on top of the half-high divider that separated the so-called "entry" from the living room. She cleared her throat.

"I've kept the place on, just in case he came home," she said. "I'm not a lunatic. I haven't been cleaning it."

"That's a good thing," Gregor Demarkian said. "It tells me the first thing I needed to know. Your son didn't come back here when he came back."

Charlene considered saying absolutely nothing. She didn't like giving Howard anymore ammunition than she had to. She decided that it would not be a good idea, in this circumstance.

"He couldn't have come back here without seeing me first," she said. "After he disappeared, I had the locks changed. Lock, I suppose it is. I had it changed, anyway, just in case that woman had a copy. He'd have had to come to me for the key."

"All right," Gregor said.

"I suppose you think I'm a suffocating mother," Charlene said. "I know the kind of thing Howard says about me. He's been saying it since we were all in school together. But I had good reason, in this case. Chester was gone, and no one would listen to me."

"There was no reason to listen to you," Howard said. "You were going on and on about how Chester was dead and Darvelle had murdered him. Well, Chester wasn't dead."

"He's dead now," Charlene said.

"That's not the same thing, is it?" Howard asked her.

Gregor Demarkian cleared his throat. "Did you see him when he came back?" he asked.

"No," Charlene said. "He didn't come to the house. I guess he didn't come here, either. Maybe he went to see Darvelle."

"She doesn't still live in the same place," Howard said. "How would he know where to go to find her?"

"Maybe they've been in touch all this time," Charlene said. "Maybe this was one of her bright ideas. She's got a lot of bright ideas."

"What about you?" Gregor Demarkian said. "Were you in contact with him at all during the twelve years he was gone."

"Of course I wasn't," Charlene said. "What do you take me for?"

"Do you have any idea where he might have been for twelve years?"

Charlene decided she was really beginning to hate this Gregor Demarkian. She hated the look on his face. It was the same look he had in all those television programs. It was supposed to be "thoughtful."

"Howard here thinks he's going to be able to blame all this on me," Charlene said.

"He's got you out here to back up his fool idea that he can call this a suicide and get away with it. Chester couldn't stand being on the run anymore and he couldn't stand the idea of coming back to me, so he killed himself. Well, he didn't kill himself. And I'm not going to let any of you say he did."

Gregor Demarkian was walking up and down the length of the trailer, looking at things. There wasn't much to see. The place was neat enough — Charlene had seen to that — but that thick layer of dust covered everything, half an inch thick at least and completely undisturbed. Charlene found herself wondering if the boys had really come in here and checked things out when she had asked them to. It didn't look like it.

Gregor Demarkian stopped in the middle of the living room, looked at the ceiling, looked at the windows, and shook his head. "This is where he was, twelve years ago, the last time anybody saw him?"

"Yes," Howard said. "Yes, Mr. Demarkian, that's it. Some people who lived in the park saw him walking around that last night, and then that was it."

"There are clothes back there in a closet. Did you go through those at the time? Was anything missing?"

"I went through everything in this trailer

piece by piece," Charlene said. "I did it no more than four days after Chester disappeared. Not that anybody was listening to me about Chester disappearing. Oh, no. They all thought he'd run out just to get away from me. But I went through everything, and there was nothing missing."

"Except the backpack," Howard said. "Don't forget about the backpack."

"Oh, for God's sake, Howard. Yes, the backpack was gone, but nobody goes missing with nothing but a backpack full of schoolbooks."

"Chester did," Howard said. "You can't say he didn't, Charlene. He did."

"Wait," Gregor said. "The last time anybody saw Chester was here, in this trailer park, when?"

"The night he went missing," Howard Androcoelho looked confused.

"I mean what time of day?" Gregor Demarkian asked.

"It was late," Charlene said. "Around ten o'clock. Which makes sense, because he'd been to class. The class started around seven or eight, I don't know. It only lasted about an hour and twenty minutes, but he and Darvelle liked to go eat at those fast-food places. She likes fast food, Darvelle does."

"Chester and Darvelle were in the same class?"

"Yes," Charlene said. "They were taking all their classes together. They were *in love*. Wasn't that sweet?"

"Oh, Charlene," Howard said. "Just can it."

"And of course," Charlene said, "Darvelle was supposed to be pregnant. And don't start in on me, Howard. She came to my house, no more than a week before Chester disappeared, and she was as big as a house. You can ask Stew, or Mark, or Suzanne. They were all there. She came into my living room and she was as big as a house. And if she wasn't when you went to talk to her, it's because she went somewhere and got rid of it."

"Charlene," Howard said. "I've told you a dozen times —"

Charlene wheeled around on Gregor Demarkian. It was hard to do in this small a space, but she managed it. "He's going to say it was proved positive that she was never pregnant," she said. "He's going to say dozens of people saw her all that same month and they didn't think she looked pregnant at all. Well, she was pregnant. I saw her. My whole family saw her. And if Chester did run away and hide for twelve years, I know why he did it."

"Why?" Gregor Demarkian asked.

"Because she went somewhere and aborted that child," Charlene said triumphantly. "She went somewhere they weren't particular about the trimester and had that child killed. That's how the skull got cracked, Mr. Demarkian. That was the skull you found in the backpack. That's how they do a partial birth abortion. They crack the skull and they haul the body out with forceps. Darvelle Haymes had that done and then she handed over that body to my son, and do you know why she did it? She did it because she knew she was never going to get hold of my money, even if she did marry Chester."

2

Howard Androcoelho wasn't really comfortable in his body, but he could usually tell himself there was nothing he could do about it. Men who were big the way he was big always ran to fat in middle age. Just look at all those football players. There were also other football players, but he chose not to think about that. The problem was, with Gregor Demarkian in the car, he could think about nothing else. Gregor Demarkian was tall. It was obvious that he had once been very muscular. You couldn't say that he was fat.

"Flabby, maybe," Howard said, out loud, getting the car to start.

"What?"

Howard looked across the car to the other seat. Gregor Demarkian was on the phone — text messaging. He had been on the phone and text messaging ever since they had left Chester Morton's trailer and sat down to watch Charlene sail off into the distance in her shiny new Fusion. Charlene always had a new car. She got one every two or three years.

"It's a miracle somebody didn't throw a rock at that windshield," Howard said.

"What?" Gregor Demarkian said again.

"The windshield," Howard said. "It's a miracle somebody didn't throw a rock at it. You don't want to bring a new car like that to a place like this. You don't want to bring it even if they don't know you here. And everybody here knows Charlene."

"And doesn't like her, I take it."

"Nobody likes Charlene," Howard said. "I don't think her own husband likes her. I really mean it. Well, you see how she was."

"She seems to want to control the lives of her children more than is really feasible."

"She does control the lives of her children," Howard said. "God, you should have seen her, you really should have, when Chester went missing. Of course, now I look like an idiot, not taking her seriously at the time. Or maybe I don't. I don't know whether it's a good thing or a bad thing, for my reputation, I mean, that I didn't take her seriously and he wasn't actually dead. Except that now he is. If you see what I mean."

"You came out and looked at the trailer," Gregor said. "You found that blood. I presume you got it tested."

"Oh, yeah, well, we did," Howard said. "The way you could get things tested at the time. It wasn't Chester's blood. It wasn't his type, anyway."

"Do you still have samples of it around somewhere?"

"I think so," Howard said. "You know what it is. We don't have room to store things like they do in the cities. But this has been an open case. Charlene has kept it an open case. So all the evidence is still on file somewhere."

Gregor's phone made that odd tinkling noise that announced a text message coming in. Howard sat still and watched while Gregor opened the message, read what was there, and then texted back again. He did not text-type as fast as Howard had seen the kids do it, but he wasn't a complete klutz, either. Gregor closed the phone.

"That's it," he said. "The New York State Police do have a service you can use if you don't have a proper medical examiner's office. I'll talk to them later on this afternoon and we'll arrange for them to pick up Chester Morton's body and do a more thorough autopsy. Then, if you don't mind, I'd like you to haul out all of that old evidence and let me go through it. In the end, we've got four questions that need to be answered before we can be sure that we know what really happened here. First, why did Chester Morton disappear? Second, why did Chester Morton come back? Third, where did Chester Morton die? And fourth, was Chester Morton murdered, or did he commit suicide? If you answer those four questions, you'll at least know what happened here. Whether you can make a case for it in court is another thing. That will have to be up to you."

Howard got the car started and pulled it slowly around in the dirt ruts until they were facing the exit and on their way out. A woman came out on the steps of the trailer that directly abutted the one they were just in, and Howard saluted her halfheartedly.

Then he got the car out onto Watertown Avenue and turned back toward the central station.

"I've never understood the people who live in that place," he said. "I mean, it's one thing if you don't have a choice, if you're disabled or something like that. Then you have to take what you can get. I don't understand people who could do something to get themselves out of there and don't."

"Can many of them do something to get themselves out of there?" Gregor asked.

"Some of them at least could have, once," Howard said. "See that woman I waved to back there? Althy Michaelman. *Althea* Michaelman. Her mother was like that, all these fancy names. She had a sister named Jael, from the Bible. The sister's long gone. Althy was in my class in high school."

"Intelligent?"

"I don't know what you mean by intelligent," Howard said. "She was bright enough until she got to be about sixteen. Then it was guys here and guys there. She never graduated. She got pregnant and got on welfare and moved out there. And she's been out there ever since, half drowned in beer. She's got four kids and none of them are worth a damn that I can see, except maybe the youngest one. The youngest one goes to the community college and she's got a job."

They were almost back, but the clouds had had enough. They were black and close to the ground, and now they opened up and started pouring rain over everything. It was big-dropped, soaking rain, the kind Howard liked least.

"Do you know everybody in town?" Gregor asked him. "Everyplace we go, you seem to have gone to high school with half the people in the room."

"It's a small town," Howard said, easing his car around to the back to park it. Gregor Demarkian's driver's car was there, with the driver still inside it. The driver was reading a book. "It was an even smaller town then," Howard went on. "There were only about a hundred and twenty people in my graduating class. It's odd to think of what happened to everybody. Charlene married to Stew Morton. Althy in the trailer park. Not that Charlene would have been surprised about that. She always thought Althy was a tramp, even in high school. But that might have had something to do with the fact that Althy was pretty, and Charlene was definitely not. Funny to think Althy was pretty once, isn't it?"

"I don't know," Gregor said.

Howard watched him get out of the car and then got out himself. He didn't have an umbrella with him and the rain poured down over his head like a shower that had been turned on too high. Gregor was getting wet, too, but he didn't seem to mind it. He went to his own car and tapped on the driver's window to get his attention.

"Well?" Howard said.

"I want to go back to the hotel and work on a couple of things," Gregor said. "It's getting late anyway. I'll talk to the state police and set up a time and place so that we can get that body properly examined. Are you going to be on your cell phone all evening?"

"I always keep the cell phone on," Howard said.

"Good. I'm going to get out of this rain. I'll talk to you later."

Howard thought he ought to get out of this rain, too, but he stood for a while watching Gregor Demarkian get into his car. When the car started up and began to ease out of its parking place, Howard turned toward the back door of central station and started walking across the lot. He did not feel very well at the moment. He wasn't really sure why. Maybe it was just that he was tense.

He got to the back door of the station and slipped into the back hall there, past the rain.

When he had first talked to Marianne Glew about calling in Gregor Demarkian, she had warned him that he was going to cause more trouble than he would fix. He thought now that this was probably true.

3

It was raining when Haydee Michaelman left the trailer that evening, raining in that way where water pours out of the sky in sheets. She was running late and it was going to take even longer to get to school than usual. She wouldn't be able to use the shortcuts now, both because of the wet — the ground out there got muddy as hell — and because of the dark. It was enough to make her want to scream. She wanted to scream all the louder because her wasted time had been so thoroughly wasted. It had been forty-five straight minutes of Mike whining about what she owed him and how he was going to get it.

"You're not so big I can't take my belt to you," he'd said.

Haydee hardly believed she'd heard it. It was like something out of a Lifetime movie.

"I might not be too big, but you're too

225

drunk," she'd said. "And I know how to dial nine-one-one and I've got nothing against filing charges when the police get here. If you want money, go get a job and make some for yourself."

"I can't get a job, you fucking cunt," Mike had said, except he wasn't "saying" things by then. He was more like spitting them. "I'm disabled. I'm sick. You know I'm sick."

"You drink too much beer, that's all that's sick about you. You've got a doctor that's willing to write you notes to the state. God, the two of you are a pair, you really are. Get off your butts and do something for once."

"You owe me," Mike had said. "You owe me. And if you don't fork over that cash, I'm going to throw you out of here right on your ass, and see how you like it. Fucking cunt."

Haydee picked her way down the rutted mud flat that served as a "road" inside the trailer park. She wasn't going to hand over her money to Mike Katowski, or to her mother, and she didn't think either one of them would ever throw her out. She was the only one who was working. She was the only one who was ever working. They were too sure they could get some money off her sometime to want her to leave.

On the other hand, leaving would be a

226

good idea. Someday Mike was going to actually come at her, and she was actually going to have to call 911. That would be all right as far as it went. She was more than happy to see Mike's ass in jail. The problem was that if he put her in the hospital, she could miss school and work for days.

Haydee got out to Watertown Avenue and started to cross it, when a car parked on the shoulder honked at her. She ignored it. Cars honked at women on Watertown Avenue, especially women coming out of the trailer park. They all figured that if women were coming out of the trailer park, they had to be willing to . . . well.

The car honked again. Haydee ignored it again. There was a lot of traffic and she was stuck having to wait. Then a voice she recognized said, "Haydee? Haydee, it's me. I thought you might need a ride."

It took a few seconds for her mind to adjust, but she really did recognize the voice. It was Kenny Morton from English class. She wondered for a second if he'd come out here to pick up hookers, but she didn't think so. She'd have seen him here before if he was in the habit of doing that.

Kenny had the window on his car rolled down. The rain was falling down on the length of his arm.

"You can't really be thinking of walking to school in this," he said. "You can't. It's a complete mess out there."

Haydee came over to the car. "You're going to school?"

"Well, I would be. We have English class. I just saw the weather and thought you'd like to have a ride. Then when you didn't come out, I wondered if I'd gotten it wrong. I mean, you know, that you were working. Do you want to get in so I can close this window and stop getting soaked?"

Haydee was already soaked. She was a little worried she would ruin the upholstery of the car. She was more than a little worried that somebody would see her getting in. She got in anyway, and slammed the door shut behind her.

Kenny rolled up his window. The heater was on, just a little, to keep the windows from fogging up. "You really were going to walk to school in this stuff," he said. "That's crazy. Why didn't you call me? You're going to get sick, acting like that."

"I don't have your number," Haydee said.

Kenny gave her a long look of exasperation, then reached into the pocket of his pants and came up with a little plastic case of business cards. "Take one of those," he said, throwing them down on her lap. "My cell phone number is on the top. Where's your friend Desiree?"

"I don't know. I haven't seen her around. She doesn't always come to class."

"So you walk back and forth to school by yourself.?" He eased out into traffic.

"If I have to," Haydee said. "I don't think Desiree really wants to be in school. She only goes because I do and I nag her about it. But you have to go to school, you know. If you don't go to school, you get stuck working at the Quik-Go for the rest of your life."

There were cars and people going by. Haydee could see he was going around by the reservoir, not the way she went through town. It was a nicer drive, but a much longer walk.

"Do you mind if I ask you something personal?"

"No," Haydee said. "I guess not. What is it?"

"Well," Kenny said, "the thing is. Well, are you all right? Because last class, you know, and now tonight, you don't look too good. You're shaking like a leaf. And okay, that could be the rain this time, but you were doing it last time, and it was a really nice day. So . . ."

Haydee thought about it for a minute, but

then it didn't seem important to hide anything. There was nothing about her life he couldn't guess just by knowing where she lived.

"I had a fight," she said. "Not a physical fight, you know. Just a screaming fight."

"With your mother?"

"With her boyfriend. He knows I've got money stashed away someplace. They both do. I don't know how they find out, but they always know. And last time I'd put away nearly twelve hundred dollars and they found it, and of course before I realized they'd found it it was gone. So this time I found a better hiding place. So he was screaming at me. And he was going through my room. Once a couple of weeks ago he actually dug up the dirt around the trailer looking for it. He says he didn't, but the dirt was dug up. He's crazy. But I want that money for a car, and he's not going to get it."

"Does he — hit you?"

"Not yet," Haydee said.

They had reached the DMV building, which always made Haydee think of an elementary school. It was that kind of building. On the other side of the road was the river.

"Why do you keep it around, if you don't

want him to find it?" Kenny sounded genuinely puzzled. "Why don't you just put it in the bank?"

"I looked into it for a while," Haydee said. "It costs money to have an account in a bank. The only way it doesn't is if you have a big amount you can leave there all the time, or if you can have where you work direct deposit your paycheck. And the Quik-Go wouldn't know direct deposit from a cucumber. I mean, you know, it's very nice people, the people who own it, but —"

"They're from China," Kenny said. "I know. Not all banks charge you, though. You could join the credit union. You're a student. Anybody who's a student or a teacher or on staff at Mattatuck–Harvey can join it. And they don't charge fees for a savings account. I could take you over there tomorrow if you have the time. I could — I could come with you to get your money, wherever you've put it, so this guy couldn't jump you, you know, and then I could take you out to the credit union and you could open an account. Then you could put your money in there when you got it. That has to be better than hiding it out at your mother's place. He couldn't get to it there."

"That's true," Haydee said.

They were at the reservoir now, going over

it to the other side of the river where everything was green and country. Haydee liked it out here, even in the rain.

"Thank you," she said finally. "I'm sorry if I seem abrupt, or something. I'm just a little tired. Thank you for this. I'd really like to do it, if you could."

"Tomorrow?"

"I could do it tomorrow in the morning," Haydee said. "I'm supposed to start work at one and be there until six, I think. I really need a car. If I had a car, I could get a job out at Walmart or maybe in one of the supermarkets. Someplace that paid more money and could give me better hours."

"So, okay, we'll get your money into the credit union, then we'll go looking for that car. I don't mean right away, I mean —"

"I know what you meant," Haydee said. "That's all right."

Kenny was silent for a long moment while they negotiated an intersection with a traffic light, but almost nothing built about around it to justify needing the light. Finally Kenny cleared his throat and said, "You know, I don't mean to be a jerk, or anything, but maybe you ought to consider finding someplace else to live. I don't like the sound of your mother's boyfriend. And 'not yet' doesn't sound like you're sure he's never going to beat you up."

"I know," Haydee said. "But it costs a bomb to get a place of your own, and I wouldn't want to stay in the trailer park. What would be the point in that? Besides, I think this is just, you know, stuff. That man was here, the one the police brought in to find out what happened to your brother."

"Gregor Demarkian? Really? He was at the trailer park?"

"Your mother was there, too. You'll probably hear about it at home. They were looking at your brother's old trailer. I can still hear the thumping."

"Thumping?"

"I was really little," Haydee said. "I was, I don't know, six years old, I think. When your brother disappeared, you know. And I had the small bedroom and it was right against the back of that trailer. And there was always thumping. My mother said she thought it was your brother and his girlfriend, you know . . ."

"Okay," Kenny said.

"And then, of course, he went missing, and the police came, and that was the first time I was taken into foster care. Not that it lasted long. It never lasted long. I never knew what the point of all that was."

They had come nearly full circle now, and

were headed up Straits Turnpike toward the Middlebury Road. It would be an impossibly long walk this way, but Haydee loved it. The green hung down on all sides of them. The yards looked painted on.

"Have you ever noticed that even the grass looks better in the richer parts of town?" Haydee asked. "I wonder how they get it that way."

"I was just thinking that my family keeps causing you an awful lot of trouble."

Haydee had no idea what Kenny was talking about, but she let it go. First she'd get a car, then she'd get a better job, then she'd get her associate's degree, then she'd go on to a four year and get a bachelor's degree, then . . .

But there were a lot of "thens", and now she wanted not to sound stupid in class.

EIGHT

For Gregor Demarkian, after Howard Androcoelho, Tony Bolero was something of a relief. The man didn't talk much, and he never said anything in clichés. The ride back to the Howard Johnson was peaceful, even though the bad rain started in the middle of it. The trip back up to his room was even more peaceful. Gregor closed the door behind himself and sat down on the bed to take a breath before he called Bennis and found out what was actually going on. He woke up five hours later because he had left the phone on the pillow next to his head and it was blaring out the *1812 Overture.*

The *1812 Overture* was the ring tone Bennis had picked out for him for "general" calls, meaning calls from people he either didn't know or didn't hear from often. The ring tone she had picked out for herself was that Disney song from *Mary Poppins* that was a word he could never pronounce right. For Tibor, she'd given him the theme music from *Star Wars.*

Gregor sat up a little and looked at the phone. The caller ID listed a number he'd never heard of — or might have, but didn't recognize. It was a Philadelphia number, at any rate. The area code was 215.

He put the phone to his ear and said, "Hello?"

"Oh, good," Bennis said, "I got you. I'm sorry, Gregor. I don't have my phone with me and I don't actually recognize anybody's phone number anymore. I've got it all stored."

"Where are you?"

"I'm at a pay phone in a Chinese restaurant on City Avenue. I couldn't believe it when I saw it. Does anybody have pay phones anymore? I thought they were phasing them out. Anyway, this is here, and I wanted to check in and make sure you were all right. Did you get all that information I sent you? Oh, and I talked to the guy, and if you don't call him, he's supposed to call you."

Gregor did not think he was actually awake. He tried sitting up a little straighter. Just on the other side of his windows, rain was coming down in sheets.

"Gregor?"

"I'm here."

"You were going to tell me if you got the information about the guy."

"If you mean the guy from the New York State Police, yes I did," Gregor said. "And I kept the text messages so that I wouldn't lose them. Thank you for all that. The people up here are driving me crazy."

"It must be a very small town."

"It's not as small as it thinks it is," Gregor said. "It doesn't matter. I just want somebody to look at this thing that I can trust to see whatever's there. What about you? What about George? What are you doing in a Chinese restaurant on City Avenue?"

Bennis sighed. "I was eating dinner," she said. "We went to see George, and then Donna took Tibor somewhere he had to go. Some meeting. So I decided to sit somewhere and have dinner and call you. That's when I looked through my bag and found I didn't have the phone. Which is just as well, I guess. They don't like phones in hospitals. It interferes with the equipment."

"What about George?"

"Resting comfortably and as well as can be expected."

"Which doesn't tell me anything."

Bennis sighed again. "Okay," she said.

"Try not to overreact. Liver cancer."

Gregor swung his feet off the side of the bed and stood all the way up. He had no idea why. He was not going to help himself, or George, pacing back and forth across a motel room in Mattatuck, New York.

"I'm coming home," he said.

"I told you not to overreact," Bennis said. "I knew you were going to overreact. There's no point in your coming back here right now. George is in no danger of dying anytime soon — well, you know, anytime in the next week or two, anyway. He's practically a hundred, so —"

"Why would I want to stay up here?" Gregor demanded. "I mean, what would be the point? I'm not all that interested in this case, the people are driving me crazy, I'm spending all my time worrying about what's going on down there —"

"And if you came down here right now, you'd only get in everybody's way, and you know it. Finish the case and get it over with. Then come back here."

"For the end."

"Gregor."

"Do you know any other way to put it?" Gregor asked. "Is there some other prognosis I don't know about?'

"No," Bennis said, "but for God's sake —"

"He's nearly a hundred years old," Gregor said. "He will be a hundred next week sometime. They're not going to operate on him. He probably wouldn't survive it. They're not going to put him on the transplant list. He wouldn't last long enough to get a new liver. If he did, he wouldn't survive the surgery, and if he did survive the surgery, he wouldn't survive it for long. So what we're talking about here is —"

"Look," Bennis said. "Stay where you are. Call him, if you really need to talk to him. He'd probably like the diversion. But stop acting like an idiot. I don't like this anymore than you do, but the man is very old, Gregor. Something like this was almost inevitable, one way or the other, eventually."

Gregor stopped pacing when he got to the windows. The rain really was coming down, down, and down. He'd hate to be out in it.

"I know," he said finally. "I do know. I'm not a complete idiot."

"Well, yes you are, a lot of the time," Bennis said, "but I love you for it. Look, I'm going to go find a cab and get back to Cavanaugh Street. George was asleep when I left, so you might want to wait until morning. But it's not a bad idea. Call him every once in a while. Talk to him. You'll feel better, and he'll like it."

"How is Martin holding up?" Gregor asked. "He was frantic, the last time I saw him."

"He's still frantic," Bennis said, "but Angela's keeping her head straight. They'll be all right. And there are grandchildren, did you know that? And great-grandchildren. They've been piling in from as far away as Colorado. For some reason, I thought the family was small."

"There was one son," Gregor said. "Anton. He died in the service. Vietnam, I think. He left, I think, three."

"Well, one of the other two must have had sextuplets. The kids are everywhere. It's really amazing. It makes me think I'm right, though, about not wanting to die in a hospital."

"People go to hospitals when they're sick," Gregor said. "Are you trying to tell me you want to be hit by a bus?"

"No, I'm saying that if I get to the end of my life and there isn't much anybody can do for me but lessen the pain, then I'd rather have them do it in my own bedroom. It would save on the amount of time nurses would have to run around telling everybody not to disturb the other patients."

"I think I'd rather get hit by a bus," Gregor said.

"I'm going to go back to Cavanaugh Street," Bennis said. "I'm tired and I'm depressed and I miss you, but that does not mean I want you to come right back home. There's no place to sit in the living room, anyway. I've got curtain samples on the couch."

"I don't understand why you're worrying about curtain samples when you say we've got to redo all the window treatments, whatever those are."

"It's the windows themselves we're redoing. A lot of them have to be recaulked. I'm going to go, Gregor."

"Call me when you get back to the apartment," Gregor said. "I don't like City Avenue in the dark."

Bennis hung up. Actually, she did the cell phone equivalent of hanging up, which was something like disappearing into thin air. Gregor missed real hanging up, where there was a *click* or a *bang* and you really knew where you were.

He walked back to the bed and put the phone down on the night table. There was a regular landline phone there. He wondered if anybody ever used it.

Then he walked over to his suitcase and

started looking through the things Bennis had packed for him so that he'd have something clean to put on after he took a shower.

2

Gregor Demarkian called the hospital as soon as he got out of the shower, only to be told that Mr. Tekemanian was sleeping. The nurse at the desk said this as if he should have known, as if there was something about — *What? Seven o'clock?* — that made it obvious that people in hospitals would be asleep, that anybody with any sense would be asleep. He got less information out of the nurse than he had gotten out of Bennis. He thought about calling Martin, but that seemed excessive. Martin and Angela probably had enough to do with all this already.

He wasn't really very good at walking around doing nothing. He was less good at doing what had to be done next when there was something else he wanted and couldn't have. He got dressed. He put on a tie. He sat down at the room's little desk and picked up the things on it one after the other, as if they could tell him what he ought to be doing. Finally, he had a thought that required some kind of action.

He was hungry.

There was a restaurant downstairs. Of course there was. When Gregor was growing up, Howard Johnson meant restaurants to him, not "motor inns." He left his room and went down the hall to the elevator. He went down the elevator to the lobby and then across the lobby to the restaurant. There was a hostess waiting at the door, which appeared to be necessary. The restaurant was nearly full.

The waitress showed him to a booth in a back corner, so far away from everything else that it was almost like being put in Siberia. Gregor didn't mind it. He had things to think about and he didn't really want to listen to people talk about their dogs or their relationships or the terrible things their mothers-in-law had done to them. The waitress brought a menu, and Gregor thought it would be a good time to indulge in something fried. Tibor wasn't here to rat him out to Bennis. Bennis wasn't here to give him the impression that, now that he was married, he had no right to try to commit suicide by saturated fat.

He had just about started on his enormous pile of fried clams when his telephone went off, the *1812 Overture* again, not a number he was supposed to recognize. He got the phone out and looked at the caller ID. It wasn't an area code he knew, which meant it wasn't likely to be Bennis or anybody else on Cavanaugh Street.

He put his fork down across his plate and said, "Yes?"

"Is this Gregor Demarkian?" a man said.

"This is Gregor Demarkian," Gregor said.

"Good. This is Ferris Cole. I'm with the New York State Police. I'm a medical examiner —"

"Oh," Gregor said. "I was going to call you in the morning. Isn't it late? Are you working late?"

"I'm always working late," Ferris Cole said. "Not that that's anything you have to worry about. Anyway, I saw the note and I decided to call right away. It isn't often we get a call from Mattatuck."

Gregor picked at a fried clam. "The chief of police, police commissioner, I don't know what I'm supposed to call him. He told me they don't have much in the way of violent death down here."

"Oh," Ferris Cole said, "they *have* it. They just pretend that they don't. It's Howard Androcoelho you've been talking to, I guess."

"That's the one," Gregor said.

"Well, it's not like it's just Howard," Ferris Cole said. "They're all like that down there. And it's not just police work, either. Couple of years in a row, they still hadn't passed a school budget. Teachers were working without getting paid. They won't vote the taxes for anything. They keep trying to pretend that it's thirty years ago. They've got fifty thousand people in that town these days. They need to face reality. I'm surprised they hired you. From what I hear, you're not particularly cheap."

"Not particularly."

"And you got them to call us in? You must be a miracle worker. Either that, or Charlene Morton has put the fear of God in them."

"Ah," Gregor said. "I was wondering if you knew what case I was calling about."

"There's only one case you could be calling about," Ferris Cole said. "It's been in all the papers anyway, and on television. Mrs. Morton even got in touch with us, although there was nothing we could do. It was a municipal matter. Of course, she also got in touch with the FBI. Maybe she did put the fear of God into Howard and Marianne. I wouldn't put it past her."

"Marianne?"

"Marianne Glew," Ferris Cole said. "She's the mayor down there. If you haven't met her yet, you will. She's at least as big a piece of work as Howard is. Maybe more."

Gregor thought about it. He was pretty sure he'd heard the name from Howard Androcoelho at least once.

Gregor played with another fried clam. "What I want," he said, "is to get a proper autopsy done, something that will give me some clue as to whether this was a murder or a suicide. I do know enough about dead bodies to know that the man was in fact hanged, while he was still alive. I also know that he wasn't hanged from the top of that billboard where he was found. What I'd like to know is if he hanged himself someplace else and then was moved to the billboard, or if he was hanged by somebody else somewhere else and then moved to the billboard. And in either case, I find it completely bizarre that he was moved to the billboard."

Ferris Cole sounded interested. "How do you know he was moved to the billboard? How do you know he didn't just —"

Gregor explained about the tattoo.

"So," Ferris Cole said, "somebody took the dead body, shaved a little hair off the right breast area near the nipple, and tattooed —"

"Don't forget the nipple ring," Gregor said. "I'm pretty sure there was a nipple ring in the ring holes and the ring was taken out."

"To facilitate the tattooing."

"Right. The holes were enlarged. They looked like they'd had something heavy in them recently."

"But why would anybody go to all that trouble?" Ferris Cole asked. "I mean, why bother? I mean, I can see the hanging part, if you wanted to make it look like suicide, but the rest of it makes no sense. Is there supposed to be a code here? Is somebody sending a message? What?"

"All of this would be better answered if I could just get the body properly autopsied," Gregor said, "which is why I called you. Do you think you could send somebody down tomorrow to do this, or to take the body back to where you need it to be? The longer we wait, the more we're likely to lose."

"Oh, I agree with you," Ferris Cole said. "Sure, I can arrange to have the body picked up in the morning. We can bring it back here and I can look at it myself. Seems odd, after all these years. We've been living with this case up here for a decade."

"Well, finding out how he died won't even begin to answer the questions," Gregor said, "but it bugs the hell out of me that, in this day and age, we don't have a rudimentary forensics finding — oh, never mind. It's just me. I've been riding around with Howard Androcoelho all day, and the town used the stimulus money to do things like install a hands-off cell phone system in his car. It's enough to make me lose my mind."

"We'll pick the body up in the morning," Ferris Cole said again. "And don't let Howard worry you. Or Marianne, either. That town won't vote money for anything. A couple of months ago, somebody figured out that the police radios didn't work in at least half the territory, and they couldn't get the town council to vote the money to get better ones. So then they held a referendum, and they couldn't get the people of the town to vote the money to get better ones. Police radios. Do you believe it?"

"The whole town thinks it doesn't have any crime when it actually does?"

"It's mostly the Mattatuck–Harvey Taxpayers Association. Older people, most of them on Social Security, who don't want taxes raised for any reason. They're not the majority of the town, but they are the majority of the people who will actually go out and vote in local elections. And it's like I said. They only think they don't have crime. I'm willing to bet that Howard gets four or five cases a year that are at least iffy, and then there are the domestics, of which Mattatuck always has a few. You've got to wonder about some people."

Gregor agreed that you had to wonder about some people. Then he said good-bye to Ferris Cole and went back to his mound of fried clams.

Somehow, it wasn't nearly as much fun eating them as it was when he had Bennis around to complain.

3

Back in the room, Gregor lay down on the bed — well, one of the beds, the one closest to the door — and considered his options. He called the hospital again, even though he knew it was useless. He got a different nurse from the one he'd had before, but with the same attitude. He thought about calling Bennis. That was something he wanted to do before he went to sleep, but right now it just felt wrong. He rarely discussed case problems with her. She understood them when he did, but her attitude to justice tended to be as direct as anything in a *Die Hard* movie. If she knew who the bad guys were, she wanted to blow them away.

Actually, Gregor couldn't imagine Bennis blowing anyone away. Giving them the kind of tongue lashing that reduced them to ribbons — yes, that he could see. Using a weapon was not really her style.

He got off the bed and went to the desk. He had left his little airplane bag there, the one Bennis packed what she called his "miscellaneous essentials" in. He rifled through it until he came up with his little L.L. Bean folding alarm clock. It was bright yellow, because Bennis thought something bright yellow would be hard for him to lose. He opened it. It was nine-twenty.

I'm losing all sense of time, he thought, and it was true. The day had started too early. He'd been moving through it too fast. He thought he'd gone down to dinner at seven, but maybe it had been earlier. He hadn't really checked. He put the alarm clock on the beside table next to where he expected to sleep and went back to pacing. Then he went to the window and looked out on the parking lot. The lights of Mattatuck were spread out before him, and there were many more lights than you'd expect to see in a "small town." Gregor wondered if the teachers were getting paid this year. Then he wondered if the police had working radios. Then he decided that he couldn't do this much longer without going insane, and headed out into the hall and down one room to get Tony Bolero.

Tony Bolero had not undressed to go to bed. If he had, Gregor might have changed his mind about what he wanted to do. Tony Bolero was still in his full driver's uniform, except for the hat. Gregor took that as an omen.

"Could you drive me somewhere?" Gregor asked. "I don't know what the arrangement is. If it's too late —"

"I can drive you anywhere you want," Tony Bolero said. "Where do you want to go?"

Gregor thought that in a murder mystery, Tony Bolero would definitely turn out to be the murderer. Since he was from Philadelphia, that was not likely to be the case here.

"I want to go to a place called Feldman's Funeral Home. Or The Feldman Funeral Home. I'm not sure how they phrase it. I was there earlier today, but not with you. It was when I was driving around with Howard Androcoelho."

"It's The Feldman Funeral Home," Tony Bolero said. "I know where it is. Give me a couple of minutes and I'll bring the car around to the lobby."

Gregor did not ask how Tony Bolero knew where The Feldman Funeral Home was. It felt like one of those better-kept secrets.

Maybe Bennis had hired this guy on purpose, because he seemed to her to be the kind of person who would fit in a murder investigation. Meaning, Gregor thought, that he seemed like the kind of person who could be a second lead on *The Sopranos.*

Gregor went back to his room, made sure he had things like his wallet and his phone, and went down to the lobby. There was a young man behind the desk this time instead of a young woman.

"Oh, Mr. Demarkian," the young man said. "I'm glad I've got the chance to meet you. Is what I heard really true? Are you really going to bring in one of those state medical examiners to look at Chester Morton's body?"

Gregor sucked in air. "That got around fast," he said.

"It's a small town," the man behind the desk said. He was much too young to have known Chester Morton before his disappearance. "And people talk."

Tony Bolero was pulling the car up under the big porte cochere. Gregor mumbled something noncommittal and went out into the warm September air. It was still raining, but the roof of the porte cochere kept that off his head, and the young man at the checkout desk kept him distracted.

"I don't care how small a town is," Gregor said, when he got into the car. "News doesn't travel that fast unless somebody is spreading gossip. Howard Androcoelho must have gone back to the station and announced it all over a bullhorn. And it's not all that small a town in the first place."

"All right," Tony Bolero said.

Gregor didn't impose on him any further. The Howard Johnson was on the edge of town. They turned into the lights and Gregor watched the buildings go by, first stretched out along thin strips of green, then coming closer together. When the buildings began to come close together, Gregor saw at least three pawnshops, and four convenience stores, and two bars. More than size distinguished a small town from a larger one. These were the kinds of places that asked for trouble.

They made a turn and then another turn, and they were suddenly on the green, with the tall Civil War monument looking like a miniature pyramid displaced from the Middle East. It didn't look that way in good light. Tony went down one side of the green, turned left at the end of it, then came down the other. The Feldman Funeral Home was just beyond it.

"Here we are," Tony said, parking at the

curb. "Do you need me to come inside?"

"No," Gregor said. "I may need to talk to you, later. Is that part of this arrangement? Can I sit you down someplace and run ideas by you?"

"You can," Tony said, "but I don't know what good it would do. I've never investigated anything in my life."

Gregor gave a noncommittal grunt. Then he got out of the car and walked up to the funeral home's front door. There was something going on in the front room. It was all lit up, and Gregor could see people moving around. He rang the doorbell and waited. At least he wasn't going to get the Feldmans out of bed.

The man who came to the door was Jason Feldman himself, and he looked surprised.

"Mr. Demarkian," he said. "Did we have an appointment? Was Howard supposed to call? Howard really is completely irresponsible in some ways. I don't know why he gets to head up the police department. I really would like to accommodate you, but as you can see, we have a wake going on and —"

"I just need to go downstairs and take a look at the body for a minute," Gregor said.

"Now? Right now? Why do you have to do that right now?"

"I won't be long," Gregor was in the foyer now. It wasn't that hard to get past Jason Feldman. "I don't need to disturb anything you're doing. I just want to check something out."

"But it's the middle of the night!"

"I couldn't settle down to sleep," Gregor said, moving slowly but inexorably toward the basement door he remembered from earlier. "It really is just one small thing. So if you —"

Jason Feldman rushed to get to the basement door before Gregor did, but he didn't block the way. It was as if what mattered to him was that no guest in the funeral home should ever open his own doors. Jason Feldman flung the basement door open, turned on the light, and stepped back.

"Really," he said. "Really. This is not the way I expect things to be done here. We're not a morgue. We've got a business to run."

Gregor went down the steps. Jason Feldman closed the basement door behind them and followed.

"Really," he said. "Really. We can't have things like this here. Bereaved families are very fragile. They're in a very delicate position. We can't have their mourning interrupted by police nonsense and all kinds of other things —"

Gregor had reached the room with the cold lockers built into the wall. He turned on the light there and looked at the lockers one by one. They looked exactly as he remembered them from earlier. The room looked exactly as he remembered it from earlier, too, although it was a messy room. A lot can happen in a messy room without anyone noticing.

Gregor went to the locker where Chester Morton's body was kept and opened it. Then he pulled out the slab.

"Really," Jason Feldman was saying. "I mean, really, you can't —"

Jason Feldman stopped dead. Gregor had to force himself not to laugh.

The slab was empty.

■ ■ ■ ■

PART II

■ ■ ■ ■

In a football match, everything is complicated by the presence of the other team.
— Jean-Paul Sartre

ONE

1

It was like watching a movie, the wrong kind of movie, a Keystone Kops exercise that Gregor was sure was staged for his benefit. He let it unfold without interference. At this time of night, there was very little else he could do. He needed to get someplace and sit down to think. He needed to wake Bennis or Tibor out of a sound sleep and rail at them. He needed something. What he got was Howard Androcoelho puffing up and down the stairs giving every indication that he was about to have a heart attack while the new mobile crime unit did things with brushes and vials that Gregor wasn't sure they knew how to use.

It was nearly eleven o'clock when they were all finished, and nothing had been discovered or decided that Gregor could tell. He had done his once-over of the area while they were waiting for the police to show up, so he knew all that was available to know. Jason Feldman kept pacing around the room and up and down the cellar stairs, moaning over and over again that it was all impossible, the funeral home was going to get sued, you couldn't have the police crawling all over the place during a wake. The family wouldn't stand for it.

Out in the car again, with Tony Bolero at the wheel, Gregor considered his options.

"We going back to the motel?" Tony asked.

Gregor shook his head. "I don't know," he said. "I take it you don't know this area any better than I do. You wouldn't know where there might be an all-night diner somewhere, or a McDonald's that stayed open twenty-four-seven, or something like that. Except, not in Mattatuck. I want to be at least two towns over."

Tony Bolero cleared his throat. "Give me a minute," he said. Strange clicking noises came from the front seat. Tony grunted. Then he said, "There's a place called Five Brothers Fast Food. It's about twenty miles from here. They're supposed to be open all night. Will that do?"

"How did you know that?"

"I looked it up on the GPS."

Gregor wasn't sure what a GPS was — he'd thought it was a way to find routes to where you were going, but to do that you would almost surely need to know where you were going already. This would be something else digital he hadn't heard about.

He filed the information away and said, "Yes, all right. That will be fine. When we get there, would you mind very much coming in with me and listening to me talk?"

"This is the bouncing-ideas-off-me-thing you were mentioning before?"

"Exactly."

"I wouldn't mind at all. It sounds kind of exciting. I've never had much to do with crime, you know, except watching it on TV. You know what I've learned from the TV? If your wife takes out an insurance policy on your life, run like hell."

Gregor thought this made a great deal of sense. He sat back and watched the scenery go by, such as there was of it, and such as there was that he could see in the dark. The lights of Mattatuck lasted a little while, first as the town itself, then as the long stretches of strip malls and one-story buildings, then as houses that got farther and farther apart the longer they drove. A few miles after the last of these, Tony Bolero got onto a highway. After that, there was nothing to see by the big arched safety lights over their heads, and other cars, all of which seemed to be on the other side of the meridian and going in the opposite direction.

The exits were far apart and, for Gregor, hard to see. Tony Bolero got off at the third of them, swung around the curve to a stoplight, and turned right. A few seconds later, he was pulling into the parking lot of Five Brothers Fast Food — but it wasn't a fast-food place, it was an old-fashioned diner, the kind that had been made out of an aluminum-sided dining car. The aluminum was polished to a high shine. The windows were lit up as if it were noon.

"This is wonderful," Gregor said.

Tony got out and opened the passenger door. "It looks pretty empty," he said. "I mean, there's waitresses, but there doesn't look like much of anybody else. That what you wanted?"

"It's just what I wanted."

The two of them went up a steep set of steps to the glass door and went in. There was one guy sitting at the counter on a stool with a revolving seat. There were waitresses. There was nobody else. Gregor and Tony went to a booth way in the back and sat down, Gregor in the seat that allowed him to see anybody coming in the front door. The menus were sitting in the clutch spring of a metal carrier for sugar, salt, and pepper. There was one of those little wall jukeboxes screwed into the wall. Gregor checked the music and found Patsy Cline, Conrad Twitty, and Frank Sinatra, but nothing from after 1963.

"If this were a *Twilight Zone* episode, we'd do ourselves a favor by running like hell," Gregor said.

The waitress came by with her pad. Gregor ordered coffee. Tony Bolero ordered coffee and a hamburger club sandwich.

"Sorry," he said. "I never got around to eating earlier."

"That's all right."

"I figured what you wanted was someplace out of the way where it didn't matter if you were overheard," Tony said. "I figured twenty miles ought to do it for you."

"I don't know how much it matters if I'm overheard," Gregor said, "because I'm fairly well convinced that anything I might have to say is already common knowledge among half of Mattatuck, or at least among those people in Mattatuck that I don't want to know. So there's that. But yes, at least trying to be discreet was what I had in mind."

"I take it from what I heard that there's a body missing," Tony said.

Gregor sighed. The waitress had come

back with the cups and the coffeepot. She set up the cups, poured coffee in them, and left little plastic packets of cream. Gregor tried his coffee and decided that it was not quite as good as the Ararat's, but that that was to be expected.

"It's not that the body is missing," he said, "it's that I knew it was going to be missing. I knew who was going to have had to make it missing, and I just can't see the point. I mean, yes, I do see the point in some ways. Howard Androcoelho doesn't want that body autopsied. Not by a real medical examiner, at any rate."

"Howard Andro—"

"Androcoelho," Gregor said. "The guy who got me up here. The man I went to see this morning. The chief of police, except he calls himself the police commissioner, which is so ridiculous I can barely stand it. Anyway, I was sitting there at dinner tonight, thinking that now that I had a way to get the body autopsied, it was going to disappear. And it's Howard Androcoelho who has to be responsible for it, one way or the other, because not anybody could just wander down to The Feldman Funeral Home basement and take a body out of there. I wonder where they put it."

"I saw the police searching the grounds,"

Tony said. "They'd have found it if it were there."

"Oh, I'm sure it left the premises in somebody's trunk," Gregor said. "It would be easy enough to get the thing out of there and into a car, because there's that cellar door that opens right onto the service entrance lot. Just pull your car up there, go down the basement stairs, get the body out, and bring it back up."

"But couldn't anybody have done that?" Tony said.

"I suppose they might have," Gregor said. "But I'd still be willing to bet anything that it was either Howard Androcoelho himself or Howard and an accomplice. He's the only one I know of with a direct concern about the body — anybody else would have been willing to let the thing go once we'd figured out that Chester Morton didn't die on that billboard. After that, if the issue was just the murder of Chester Morton, nothing mattered. Getting rid of the body is not going to change the finding or even put it in doubt. We've got the pictures from the first autopsy that show clearly that that little tattoo was applied after death. It's not the murder-finding somebody wants to avoid, it's the autopsy, specifically. Which leaves a lot of questions and not a lot of answers."

"It doesn't make a lot of sense to me."

"It doesn't make a lot of sense to me, either," Gregor said. "What could possibly be in that body, or on it, that didn't come out in the first autopsy that might come out if a second and more professional autopsy was done? I was concerned about whether or not Chester Morton had been sedated so that somebody could hang him up and make him look like a suicide — but then we come back to the same thing I was talking about before. That's a murder-finding, and we'd have that even if there was no second autopsy to confirm it. Assuming it even happened. Even an amateur autopsy isn't going to miss a load of drugs stuffed into his stomach or his ass. It makes no sense."

The waitress came with Tony's sandwich. The sandwich came with a huge pile of french fries. Tony picked up the bottle of ketchup and opened it.

"So what do we do now?" Tony asked. "If you're right and it's the police who are hiding the body, it doesn't make much sense to ask the police to go find it."

"I know," Gregor said. "I wish I knew why Chester Morton disappeared. I wish I knew why he came back. And then there's the skeleton of the baby. There's something. If Chester Morton was female, a second autopsy might have caught signs of a former pregnancy the first autopsy missed. But Chester Morton isn't female."

"Is detecting things always this hard?" Tony Bolero said. "It looks a lot easier on *Law and Order*."

Gregor looked at Tony's immense, exploding sandwich. "I'm not going to ask why Howard Androcoelho brought me in," he said. "That was to cover his ass with the Morton family. The question now is whether he's going to try to get me out. And it still comes down to why he'd want to stop a second autopsy, and that is still a question I have no answer to."

"Maybe you should go out on your own," Tony Bolero said. "That's the way Bruce Willis does it in the movies."

Gregor didn't want to know what Bruce Willis did in the movies. He did want one of those sandwiches, but after the fried clams a few hours ago, it would probably kill him.

2

Gregor reached old George Tekemanian, finally, in the morning. The crisp, bouncy voice of the nurse said, "Put him through to the room," and he heard old George complaining about the food.

"I don't understand why they think it's better for sick people not to eat," he said. "I tried to get Martin and Angela to bring me something from the Ararat, but they're not listening to me. Nobody is listening to me. What do they expect, if they're just careful enough, I'll live another hundred years?"

"I think the food is made to nutritionists' standards," Gregor said. "The right amount of protein, the right amount of carbohydrates, the right amount of salt."

"Well, Gregor, if this is what is healthy for me, I'll be unhealthy. I never liked those hamburger places, but after three days of this, I'm ready for a Big Mac."

Gregor put down the phone and thought that old George sounded better than he had expected him to. He sounded almost better than he had on that day at the Ararat. Gregor wondered when that had happened. He was beginning to feel like one of those comedians who annoyed him so much. He wanted to complain that nobody ever told him anything.

He phoned Ferris Cole's office to warn him against coming down to look at a body nobody could find for the moment. Then he called Bennis and explained to her, as well as he could, what was going on.

"I don't like these situations," he said. "I

don't like it when I'm called in not to do a job, but to cover somebody's ass, and especially not when the person who wants to cover his ass doesn't want me to do the job. I told you back in Philadelphia that I shouldn't have touched this one."

"But if they're covering up a murder," Bennis said, "isn't it a good thing that you're there? If it's the police who committed it, especially . . ."

"I've got no evidence that a murder occurred," Gregor said. "At best, I've got a dead body that was moved sometime between the time the man died and the time he was found. And I've got a lot of garbage. A huge amount of garbage. Somebody shaved a bit of hair off the man's chest and tattooed MOM on it in capital red letters —"

"I don't get that part. Wouldn't that take a long time?"

"No, not necessarily. Half an hour. Forty-five minutes. Tops. And that's assuming that whoever it was that did it didn't have professional tools. It really was a tiny thing. But it's garbage, Bennis. It's not a real clue —"

"Oh, you mean it's a red herring."

"Yes, all right, maybe," Gregor said. "But I prefer to think of this kind of thing as garbage. It's meaningless. It's a distraction.

I'd be willing to bet you anything you want, that whoever tattooed that word on Chester Morton's chest wasn't his mother, wasn't his siblings, didn't really have any point at all except to get us thinking about it. Assuming we ever noticed it to think about in the first place."

"But wouldn't he want you to notice it?" Bennis asked. "I mean, what would be the point if you didn't notice it?"

"Backup, maybe," Gregor said. "In case the original plan didn't work."

"What was the original plan?"

"To make everybody think that Chester Morton had committed suicide by hanging himself from the top of that billboard," Gregor said. "And I think that the second half of that sentence is just as important as the first."

"What second half?"

"From that billboard," Gregor said. "Whoever put the body there didn't *just* want people to think that Chester Morton had committed suicide, but that he'd committed suicide by hanging himself there. Since we know Chester Morton was hanged, either by his own hand or otherwise, then the point must be to make sure we don't find out that he was hanged somewhere else. Which brings up all kinds of issues."

"Like what?" Bennis asked. "Maybe somebody just didn't want the publicity."

"There's that," Gregor agreed. "But then there are other things. The most obvious one is murder. Maybe somebody drugged the man and then hanged him, then moved the body to be hanged again on the billboard. But even if Chester Morton really did commit suicide, the place he chose to commit it might have been . . . inconvenient for somebody. Who was doing something else *unconnected* with Chester Morton that he doesn't want looked into?"

"I think you're tying yourself in knots for no good reason," Bennis said. "If Chester Morton committed suicide, wouldn't he be connected to any place he did it in? People who commit suicide don't just pick random places to do it in, do they? They pick some place with significance to them. I mean, I suppose there must be people with mental illnesses, you know, that kind of thing, who pick places you'd never be able to figure out why. But people who aren't like that pick places they think have meaning."

"True," Gregor said.

"And most of them leave notes," Bennis said.

"Half true," Gregor said.

"You really can be enormously annoying

271

sometimes," Bennis said. "I'm just saying that wherever Chester Morton died, it had to be someplace that had something to do with him. Either he was murdered, so you have to ask where he'd go and who he'd go to and why, and all those things would matter to him. Or he committed suicide, and then —"

"Yes, I got that part. I'm just trying to figure out how I'm going to go about doing this when the police are going to be more hindrance than help. Are you sorting through tiles or something today?"

"I'm going to look at sinks. It will all be over by the time you get back. Don't worry."

"I'm not a hundred percent convinced that I'm not going to be back today," Gregor told her. "Don't forget. One way situations like this work out is that the local police change their minds and send me home. It's not the kind of thing I'd fight at the moment."

"Go do something sensible and let me go do something sensible, too," Bennis said. "Tommy Donahue says, 'Hi'. Try not to eat yourself to death when I'm not there to watch you."

Gregor thought about the fried clams, but didn't report them. There was time to get into that particular argument — *never.*

A few minutes later, he was in his clothes and down the hall, knocking on Tony Bolero's door. Tony came out looking as if he'd never gone to sleep late. His hair was still wet from a shower.

"Are you in any shape to go running around?" Gregor asked. "Could we maybe get some breakfast to take out and take a little ride? There's something I want to see before I make up my mind what to do next."

"Sure," Tony said.

Gregor's cell phone went off. He took it out of his pocket and looked at the caller ID. It was a local number, which meant it was either Howard Androcoelho on yet another line — how many lines could any one person have access to? — or somebody connected to the case somehow trying to get in touch with him. Gregor thought of Charlene Morton and shuddered. He rejected the call and put the phone back in his pocket.

"I'll talk to people when I've seen what I want to see," he said. "I want to go out to that place and get a look at that billboard. It's supposed to be at the entrance to Mattatuck–Harvey Community College. Do you think you can find where that is?"

"Sure," Tony said again. "Give me five minutes."

"I'll go down and order some food. Or coffee, or something."

Tony made a noncommittal noise and retreated into his room to get ready.

Gregor went down the hall to the elevators, and then to the lobby. The lobby was deserted except for one young woman sitting on a couch in the middle of everything, holding a large tote-bag-sized purse on her lap and looking around as if she were lost. Gregor noted the off-the-rack business suit and the shoes that matched, asked for messages at the desk, got the answer that there weren't any, and headed for the dining room.

He was almost at the hostess's station when the young woman with the purse suddenly scooted up beside him, breathless, and said:

"Gregor Demarkian? I'm Darvelle Haymes. I have to talk to you."

3

The first thing Gregor thought was that this was not what he had expected of somebody named Darvelle Haymes, and then he felt a little exasperated with himself. Forget the social sin of indulging in stereotypes. It was unprofessional of somebody who called himself a detective to jump to conclusions the way he had. The woman couldn't help her name. The picture he'd had in his mind might have been more appropriate to her mother than it would ever be to her.

Or it might have been wrong about both of them. There was that.

Tony was just coming in to the lobby from the elevators. Gregor caught his eye and shook his head slightly. Tony looked at Darvelle Haymes and nodded.

"I was just going to have a cup of coffee," Gregor said. "Why don't you join me?"

Darvelle Haymes looked into the dining room and then back at the reception desk, and sighed. "I suppose I might as well," she said. "It's not like everybody in town hasn't seen me here already."

"Everybody in town?"

Darvelle jerked her head back toward the reception desk. "The girl on this morning is Molly Dankowski. Her sister Mary Beth goes to school with the head of my agency. The guy is Eddie Berman. He lives across the street from me and his mother is the worst gossip in town. They'll have me grilled under a heat lamp and carted off in handcuffs before the day is out."

The hostess came by with a little stack of menus and gestured them toward a table near the windows. Gregor followed her, and

Darvelle followed him.

"Is it always like that around here?" he asked, when they two of them had been seated. "Does everybody talk about everybody else all the time?"

"Sort of," Darvelle said. "Oh, I know it's not the way it was when I was growing up. It's not that small anymore. There are probably plenty of people you never even hear about. But people are going to hear about me. For the last twelve years, half of them have been thinking that I killed Chester Morton and hid his body somewhere. Now they think I killed Chester Morton and hung his body off that billboard last week. I just killed my baby twelve years ago."

"Did you have a baby twelve years ago?" Gregor asked.

"No," Darvelle said. "I've never been pregnant. I hear there are tests for that kind of thing, and if you want me to, I'll take one, I don't care how embarrassing it is. I'm sick of this. I really am. I'm sick of it even though I know for certain it's my own fault that the rumors are there. Or, you know, mine or Chester's."

The waitress came by. Gregor asked for coffee, and so did Darvelle Haymes, but they didn't need to. The waitress had a pot at the ready, just like Linda at the Ararat.

"I'll leave you two to make up your minds," she said.

Gregor waited until she was well and truly gone. "So," he said. "Why is it your fault, or yours and Chester's, that people think you were pregnant twelve years ago."

Darvelle looked into her cup of coffee. "Here's the thing," she said. "You have to understand, Chester isn't the kind of guy I usually dated. He wasn't then. He isn't now. I've been working almost all my life. I've had to work. And even back then, I sort of had my whole life mapped out, what I'd work at, how much money I'd save, when I'd be able to buy my own house — I did buy my own house, by the way, and I'm in no danger of foreclosure. I work hard. I don't spend money on silly crap. I make a plan and I stick to it."

"That's very admirable."

"Yes, well, thank you, I guess. But the thing is, back around twelve-and-a-half years ago, I met Chester. I was going to Mattatuck–Harvey Community College to get my associate's degree. At the time, I thought my best bet would be going into some kind of human resources work with a corporation somewhere. That's before I found out that human resources is the great corporate sinkhole, where they put people they'll never let within a mile of top management. But I didn't know that then and I was getting this degree, and so was Chester, and we met."

"In a class?"

"In the cafeteria. We had a class, but we were just sitting in the same room. We didn't get to talking until we met up in the cafeteria. Anyway, it's like I said. He wasn't what I was used to. His family had money. Still does. It might not be a lot of money compared to people in Philadelphia and New York, but around here it's what passed for rich. And Chester had moved out of his family's house and into the trailer because they were just driving him crazy. They'd drive anybody crazy. I don't know if you've met Charlene yet, but she's a loon."

"I've met Mrs. Morton once," Gregor said. "It wasn't for very long."

"Well, trust me, she's a loon. And one of those women who want to hang on to their children until death, if you know what I mean. So Chester had moved out. But even though he'd moved out physically, he hadn't really moved out mentally. He wasn't used to taking care of himself. He didn't really like it. He didn't like the trailer park or the people there. He didn't like the trailer. He didn't like not having the cash to throw around the way he was used to. I think, if he hadn't met me, he might have moved back home sooner rather than later. But he did meet me, and Charlene hated me."

"Did she have reason to?" Gregor asked.

Darvelle shrugged. "She thought I was low class. I was low class. Nobody in my family had ever had anything, and nobody was ever going to have anything unless it was me. But she didn't like me, and she did one of her stupid Charlene things and tried to say that Chester had to give me up if he wanted — I don't know what, exactly. If he wanted to come home. If he didn't want his family to disown him. Except that I can't see Charlene disowning any of her children. She's more the stainless-steel umbilical cord type."

"That's an image," Gregor said.

"Yeah, well," Darvelle said again. "Anyway, Chester thought he was madly in love with me, but he didn't want to be separated from his family. That would be understandable, you know, if he loved them, but he didn't seem to. He seemed to just be worried that he'd never get back with the money. So he came up with this idea that we should get married."

"And he thought that would help him out with his mother? When his mother didn't like you?"

"He thought his mother would never give up a grandchild," Darvelle said. "So his idea was that we should say I was pregnant and that we had to get married, and then even if Charlene didn't like me, she'd put up with me, because she'd want to be near her grandchild. The problem was that I wasn't pregnant and I wasn't going to get pregnant. That was one of the big rules of my life. I didn't just practice safe sex, I damn near married it. That's what happened to most of the girls I went to high school with, do you know what I mean? Knocked up and knocked out. I had no intention of having it happen to me."

"But you told Charlene Morton you were pregnant? What did you think was going to happen when the months went by and you didn't have a baby?"

"Chester said we'd be married by then and we could just say I'd had a miscarriage," Darvelle said. "Oh, I know. It's completely ridiculous. But I was eighteen and I was being stupid, and I went along with it. Chester gave his family the whole story, and then we were invited over for dinner. I kept joking that Charlene was going to poison my soup, but I don't know if I really was joking. Anyway, we went over there. And I — um, I — well. I wore a little costuming, if you know what I mean."

"Something under your dress to make you look pregnant?"

"Exactly. And I went over there, and it didn't work out the way Chester had expected. Charlene was not warming up to the idea of a grandchild. Or at least she wasn't warming up to the idea of me and a pregnancy wasn't going to change that. So we had this really uncomfortable dinner and then we left and that would have been the end of it. Except Chester had a better idea."

"What idea was that?"

"Chester thought that the pregnancy wasn't going to be enough, but an actual child would be. So at first he tried to convince me to get pregnant for real. And, like I said, I wasn't having any. Especially not in that situation. I mean, God, can't you see it? First he talks me into getting pregnant, then I get pregnant, then Charlene wears me down, then he dumps me, then there I am, in exactly the same position my mother was in when she was my age."

"All right," Gregor said. "Not the best scenario."

"No, it wasn't. And when he finally accepted the fact that I wouldn't do it, he came up with something else. He said he knew where we could buy a baby."

"What?"

"I know. It sounds crazy, doesn't it? But that's what he said. He said he knew where we could buy a baby, and that it wouldn't be cheap, but it wouldn't be as expensive as I'd think. And I just blew up. I mean, being pregnant would have been a disaster, but he was talking about jail time — I mean, it's not legal to sell babies, right? I thought he was out of his mind. So we had this huge enormous fight. And that was the last time I really talked to him."

"This was what," Gregor said, "right after the dinner? The next day?"

"Maybe two or three days later."

"And was that the last time you saw him?"

"Oh, no," Darvelle said. "We didn't go out or meet up or anything after that, but we were taking a class together again. English Composition. The one they make everybody take. So I saw him in class toward the end of the week. That was the last time I saw him before he disappeared."

"Did you talk to him?"

"No, not really. He came up and tried to talk to me before class, but I didn't want to and finally he went away. I don't know what happened to him after that. I know Charlene is always saying that he disappeared on whatever date it was, but we don't really know that, none of us. That was the last time I saw him. I think Charlene talked with him on the phone the next night. And that was it."

"Was it, really?"

"As far as I'm concerned it was," Darvelle said. "I don't care what people say, it was an ordinary college thing except for that stupid charade about the pregnancy, and I didn't go anywhere with that after we had that dinner. If Chester decided to disappear for twelve years after that, I'll bet anything it had nothing to do with me."

Two

1

Shpetim Kika sometimes spent all evening worrying about the skeleton of the baby in the backpack — not worrying about it, exactly, but brooding about the way it seemed to have disappeared from public view. Maybe it was because he had seen it face-to-face, so to speak — but that made no sense. It really didn't. In Shpetim's mind, everybody should be concerned about the skeleton of a baby in a backpack. It should be on everyone's mind, all the time, instead of a side issue that might as well not have happened. Shpetim got up every morning and checked the television news on all three of the local stations. Never once did he hear a single word about the baby. That news had come and gone in a day after Chester Morton's body was found hanging from that billboard.

"Listen," he told Lora sometimes, at

night. "It's a terrible thing. You should have seen it. No, all right, nobody should have seen it. But somebody should be caring about it. A baby is dead. That's not a small thing. A baby is dead and nobody knows who it was, or why it died. There should be an outcry."

Public outcries were one of the things on Shpetim's long list of confusing facts about America. He loved America. He really did. He was overjoyed to have had a chance to come here, and he'd done very well since he'd set up shop, too. He would not have been able to build a business like this back in Albania. He would not have a son who had been to college and was about to be married to a girl whose wedding would be something out of a fairy tale. He did truly love America. He just thought Americans were crazy a lot of the time. The news would give you day after day and week after week about some politician who wasn't even in office anymore, or running for anything, making a sex tape with his mistress — and not say a single thing about the skeleton of a baby in a backpack.

Right now, Shpetim was sitting in the little construction shed, watching men walking along girders on the second floor of the new tech building. It was going to be a beautiful building when it was done. That was something else he liked about America. They talked and talked, back home, when the Soviets were still in power, about how they were doing everything for the people, and how in America the people were left to fend for themselves. Well, it was in America that there would be this beautiful new tech building and anybody who wanted to study in it could just come in and sign up, no approval necessary except for a high school diploma. And if you didn't have the money, there was financial aid.

Nderi was walking back across the site to the shed. Shpetim straightened up a little. He knew it was silly, but he wanted Nderi to be proud of him. He didn't want to be the kind of ignorant immigrant parent whose children couldn't wait to leave home.

Nderi made a pretense of knocking at the side of the shed door and poked his head inside. "We're going to get the shell on the south end of the second floor done today," he said. "We're going a lot faster than I expected. I think we can be sure we'll have the whole thing enclosed before the really bad weather hits. Then we'll have to deal with the electricians."

Shpetim nodded. There was an English word he had truly learned to hate. It was "subcontractors."

"I thought that would cheer you up," Nderi said. "I thought you were all worried we were getting behind."

"I wasn't worried about getting behind," Shpetim said. "Construction projects are always behind. I was worried about impossible."

"Well, there's nothing impossible about this. I've been feeling really good about it. First really huge project we've had, and we're going to do a spectacular job. And that's sure to mean more big projects. So, you know, if everything works out all right —"

"I want to go out for awhile."

"What?"

"I just — I want to go out. I want to take a drive. I'll be gone about an hour, I think. Could you look after things here?"

"I look after things here all the time," Nderi said. "I did it for three days last spring when you had the flu. But you don't just go places. Where do you want to go?"

Shpetim took his keys off his belt and handed them over. "I'll be about an hour. Maybe two. I'll be right back."

"You're making absolutely no sense," Nderi said.

Out on the road, Shpetim thought that he

wasn't making sense. He was bumping along in the downtown traffic in Mattatuck, and he had no idea what he was going to do when he got where he was going. He passed The Feldman Funeral Home and noticed the crime tape up along the sidewalk. That was where the body of Chester Morton had disappeared from just last night. Maybe the problem was that they weren't paying attention to anything. Shpetim was not entirely clear in his mind who "they" were. "They" were definitely the police, but "they" were also the television news reporters, and the people at the newspaper, and that kind of thing.

He got to the central station of the Mattatuck Police Department and pulled around the back to park. He sat for a moment behind the wheel of the truck and tried to think of what he wanted to say. He didn't know. He didn't even know who he wanted to talk to.

He got out of the truck and went around the front to enter the building by the door there. The door at the back was labeled OFFICIAL PERSONNEL ONLY, which was just another way of saying, "Keep Out." This was a beautiful building, too, near new and very well kept. The town of Mattatuck might not know what it was doing in a lot of ways, but it did know what it was doing with buildings.

There was a counter just inside the door, and past the counter were dozens of people in uniform doing things at computers. Shpetim walked up to the counter and waited. A middle-aged woman in a police uniform came up to greet him, holding a clipboard in her hand.

"Yes?" she said.

Communism or capitalism, Shpetim thought, *public officials were rude.*

"I'd like to talk to somebody," he said.

It sounded lame even as it was coming out of his mouth. He looked around the big area full of people in uniforms. All of a sudden, he was frantic. He was here, and he had no idea why he was here. Then he saw a young man he recognized, and felt better immediately.

"I want to talk to him," he said, pointing. "That one over there."

The middle-aged woman turned around. "Which one?"

"That one. The one with the — the young man. He's got a folder that he's carrying."

"They've all got folders that they're carrying," the middle-aged woman said. "Do you mean that one over near the cooler? Officer Holborn?"

Shpetim tried desperately to remember the names of the officers who had come to the building site when they'd called about the baby in the backpack, but he couldn't. He was still willing to bet that the young man with the folder was one of them.

"All right," he said. "Yes. Officer Holborn."

The middle-aged woman gave him a look. Then she turned around and shouted, "Hey, Kyle. Somebody here to see you."

Shpetim waited patiently while Kyle Holborn came up to the counter. He didn't look glad to have been called. There was something else about public officials — communist or capitalist, they didn't like being called on to do any work.

"Yes?" Kyle Holborn said, stopping at the counter.

The middle-aged woman seemed to have disappeared. Shpetim straightened up a little.

"I am Shpetim Kika," he said. "I remember you. It is my company that is building the new tech building for the community college. You came to the building site with another policeman on the night we found a yellow backpack with a skeleton in it."

"Oh," Kyle said. "Yes, yes I did. But I'm not on that case anymore."

Shpetim had no idea how to interpret this. "I have come to find out what is happening about the baby in the backpack," he said. "You came to the building site and took away the backpack and the skeleton, and then there was a mention in the news the next day, and after that there was nothing. Nothing. A baby is dead, and it seems to me nobody is doing nothing."

"I'm sure people are doing something," Kyle said. "We don't tell the newspeople everything. But I'm not on that case anymore."

"I want to know what is being done about the baby in the backpack," Shpetim said again. "Do you know what a horrible thing it was, to find it like that? Maybe you're a policeman, you see things like that every day, it doesn't bother you. I don't see things like that every day. There were the tiny bones. There was the tiny head, cracked in half like you do with eggs. And all of it lying there on top of schoolbooks. I can still see those school books. *Current Issues,* that was one of them. And *The Everyday Writer.* I know *The Everyday Writer.* My son, Nderi, had that book when he was in the community college."

"Right," Kyle Holborn said. "I remember. I mean, I don't remember the titles of the books, but that's in the report, and —"

"I want to know what is being done about the baby in the backpack," Shpetim said. "Something should be done. You people should be taking it seriously."

"But I'm not on that case anymore," Kyle said. "I really can't help you."

Shpetim Kika leaned against the counter, and folded his arms in front of his chest, and frowned.

"I'm willing to stay here all day," he said. "But I want to know what's being done."

2

The screaming had started early, almost at midnight, when the first calls had started to come in saying that Chester's body had gone missing from The Feldman Funeral Home. *Except that the screaming wasn't really screaming,* Kenny thought. If it had been, he'd have had less of a problem with it. His mother didn't get right in there and make loud noises so that the neighbors could hear. She sat in a chair with her arms folded over her chest and talked in a voice that sounded like it was coming from something made of metal. It sounded — Kenny didn't know how it sounded. He only knew he was going to have to get out of there, sooner rather than later. He was not an idiot about Chester. He knew Chester had not been a saint. He also knew why Chester had had to get out of this house. It was as if the walls were closing in, sometimes. It was as if the walls had already closed in and were starting to crush him.

His mother was in the living room when he left, sitting in the overstuffed armchair next to the hearth.

"It was Howard Androcoelho who did this," she said, as Kenny opened the front door. "He's afraid of a real autopsy. He's afraid of what it will show."

Kenny had no idea if this was true or not. He didn't know Howard Androcoelho, except as the object of his mother's enduring and very terrible wrath. He thought his mother could be one of those Viking women in the movies, the kind who could wield a broadsword with precision.

Kenny did have an idea of where he wanted to go, but he wasn't sure how he was going to get there. One of the difficult things about falling in love with a girl before you really knew her was that you didn't have all her habits and routines down to where you wanted them. You didn't know where she was supposed to be when.

He drove over to the trailer park and sat for a while at the entrance. Then he remem-

bered what Haydee had said about the drug
dealers parking in that place and moved the
truck inside. He got out and asked a woman
sitting on a stoop if she knew where Haydee
Michaelman lived. The woman pointed to
the trailer right next to Chester's trailer and
Kenny felt like an idiot. He had known that.
He really had. He had talked to Haydee
about it.

Kenny knocked on the door of Haydee's
mother's trailer. A woman came to the door
with half her clothes on and a cigarette in
her mouth and asked him what the fuck he
wanted. He asked her where Haydee was.

"How the fuck am I supposed to know
where Haydee is?" the woman said. "Get
the fuck out of here."

Kenny went back to sit in the truck and
think. If that was really Haydee's mother,
he thought he loved Haydee even more than
he thought. He'd never heard a single
person use the "F" word that many times in
that few sentences. Even in junior high
school, when half the boys he knew seemed
to be working on using it as often as it could
be used, nobody had done it like that.

The next obvious place to look for Haydee was the Quik-Go. He knew which one
she worked at, and he knew she worked as
often as she could. He didn't want to go

there, though, because he didn't want to get her into trouble at work. He had a good idea that if he ended up getting Haydee fired, she'd dump him faster than garbage.

He pulled the truck back out onto Watertown Avenue and started driving through town. It took him a while to realize that he knew where he was going. He was heading out to school. This made a certain amount of sense. Haydee was taking a full academic load as well as working full time, so she'd be just as likely to be at school as at work. Kenny just wished he'd gotten her schedule.

He was pulling up to the main entrance and thinking about how to look for her — maybe start at the cafeteria first, keep a lookout for that friend of hers — when he realized there was something going on around the sign. There was a car parked there, and two men. One of the men was leaning up against the car. The other, the taller one, was walking back and forth from the front of the sign to the grassy area behind it, looking up.

Kenny pulled the truck around, through the entrance. Then, when he got to the roundabout at the top, he pulled through the circle so that he was going back the other way. The school roads were busy this time of day. He had to watch out for a Volkswagen and two more trucks when he made his way around. Then he got a violent honking from a little Chevy Cavalier when he pulled off into the grass where the billboard was. As soon as he did, the man who had been leaning against the car stood all the way up, and the man who had been walking around the sign walked toward him.

Kenny cut the engine and got out. The man who had been leaning up against the car came up to him.

"Can we help you?" the man said.

Kenny suddenly felt really stupid. His family didn't own this billboard, and they certainly didn't own the land underneath it.

The taller man came closer, and Kenny suddenly realized who he as. "Oh," he said. "Mr. Demarkian. I'm sorry, I thought it was, I don't know, reporters, or people just screwing around, or something —"

"Who are you?" the shorter man said. Kenny thought he sounded faintly belligerent, but he didn't know why.

"I'm Kenny Morton," Kenny said. "Chester Morton was my brother. I mean, I'm sorry I bothered you. I didn't mean to get in the way of anything. I just thought —"

Kenny didn't know what he thought. He decided it would be a good idea to shut up.

Gregor Demarkian's suit looked dusty and

worse. There was brown dirt on the knees. There was a little tear in the jacket. He put his hand out and Kenny took it, although Kenny never felt entirely comfortable when he had to shake somebody's hand.

"I met your mother," Gregor Demarkian said. "I'm probably going to go see if she'll talk to me again this afternoon."

"She's loaded for bear," Kenny said. "She thinks Howard Androcoelho stole Chester's body because he was afraid of a new autopsy that would show he was really murdered."

"Well," Gregor Demarkian said. "That's not necessarily a crazy way to think. I'd say that thought could have occurred to anybody."

Kenny looked away. Traffic on the road and at the entrance had begun to slow down. People were staring at them.

"Listen," Kenny said, turning back to Gregor Demarkian. "I know, you know, that the body is gone and that that's weird. But you don't get it. It's not that my mother thinks that guy stole the body so nobody could prove a murder happened *now,* it's like she thinks the body could prove that a murder happened *then.* Am I making any sense here? It's like she's lost the time frame. The body turns up now and it's like she's been vindicated for twelve years of thinking that Chester was dead all along. But Chester couldn't have been dead all along. Do you see?"

"I do see," Gregor Demarkian said. "How old were you when your brother disappeared?"

"I was ten," Kenny said. "And before you ask, I do remember it. I remember it perfectly. And I remember Chester, too. My mom talks like he was some saint who would never do anything like just take off on his own or do something criminal or something, but that wasn't true. He was — well. He was weird."

"Weird?"

Kenny shrugged. "He gave me my first marijuana joint." He flushed. "Not that I smoke anymore, you know, I mean —"

"It's all right," Gregor Demarkian said. "I'm a police consultant, not the police."

"Right," Kenny said. "Anyway, you know what I mean. He had an earring. A great big one that he wore in his right ear. And he had a tattoo. And he did other drugs besides marijuana. And —"

"Yes?"

Kenny shook his head. "I don't know," he said. "I was only ten. But I think there was something going on with my parents, and not just Darvelle. I remember when Chester moved out, it was before he met Darvelle, I'm almost sure of it. Anyway, there were screaming fights, fights like you wouldn't believe. Fights with my parents and fights with my brother Mark. The first thing I noticed when Chester left was how quiet it got."

"Do you remember what the fights were about?"

"Money," Kenny said. "And responsibility. Well, at my house, my mother is always talking about responsibility. But this wasn't like those. This was real crazy stuff. And then Chester left, you know, and got the trailer. And then he went missing. Wherever he went."

"Do you know where he might have gone?" Demarkian asked.

Kenny brightened up. "Not exactly," he said, "but I just remembered. I know where he always said he'd go if he could ever get good and away from here."

"Where was that?"

"Caspar, Wyoming. He had pictures of it, posters of it, up in his room. And he took the posters to the trailer when he moved there. He had them up on a wall there, and more on the refrigerator. Maybe they're still there, if you look."

Darvelle Haymes thought she'd done the right thing by talking to Gregor Demarkian, but it was the kind of "done the right thing" that made her nervous and upset, and it didn't help that every single one of her buyers this morning had wanted to talk about nothing else.

"I don't want you to think it's in any way your fault," Mrs. Castleton had said, over the phone, while she was canceling her appointment for the afternoon. "Of course, you had nothing to do with it. It's just that you have to be so careful these days, when you're looking for a place to raise your children. It isn't like it used to be. We didn't have all these sexual predators hanging around when I was growing up."

Darvelle had wanted to scream at that point. Sexual predators? Who was talking about sexual predators? Chester Morton had never been anything like a sexual predator. He hadn't even liked sex all that much. Or did this woman mean that she thought that sexual predators went around stealing bodies from funeral homes?

At least Mrs. Castleton didn't know that Darvelle was in some way "involved" in the situation. A lot of the others did know. Darvelle was sure that some of them had chosen her because of it. That was something she had Charlene Morton to thank for. Darvelle would never have done that interview with *Disappeared* if she'd realized they were going to make her sound like Lizzie Borden reincarnated.

Of course, when all this started, she hadn't even known who Lizzie Borden was. She learned that from one of her buyers who liked to gossip.

The buyer who liked to gossip was not Mrs. Lord, but Mrs. Lord was the buyer for the late morning, and Darvelle was stuck with her.

"It must be so painful for you," Mrs. Lord kept saying, as they drove from one house to the other across the length of Sherwood Forest. "I mean, he was a young man you knew, wasn't he, and you had a relationship with him? And you were only eighteen. That might have been your very first love."

"I don't think it was that serious," Darvelle said. "And it was a long time ago."

"Of course it was, dear. But time doesn't really mean much when you're in the grip of strong emotion. And then to have him disappear like that, and everybody thinking he was dead."

"Actually," Darvelle said. "I never did think he was dead."

"And then to have it on all those television shows," Mrs. Lord said. "I feel sorry for you. I really do. It must have been horrible, to have that brought back to you over and over and over again, when you probably just wanted to forget about it. And those billboards. Mrs. Morton must be such a *dedicated* mother. But I know how she feels. I'd do the same if something ever happened to one of my little children."

Mrs. Lord's little children were twenty-four and twenty-six, with wives and children of their own. They lived on the West Coast. When Mrs. Lord wasn't obsessing about Chester Morton, she was telling Darvelle all about the wonderful things her grandchildren did and where they were all going to go to college when they got big enough.

Darvelle pulled into the driveway of the last house they were scheduled to see. It was a Tudor split-level, and it was blessedly empty. It was also directly across the street from the Morton's house. Darvelle had debated with herself long and hard about showing it today at all.

She cut the engine and put her car keys in her purse. "Well," she said. "Here we are. This is absolutely the best section of Mattatuck. And this is a beautiful house. It was custom built. It has all hardwood floors. It's got a brand new kitchen and brand new baths, everything updated within the last year. It's the best buy on the market, if you ask me."

Mrs. Lord beamed. "And now," she said. "Now with all of this. He comes back, but he comes back only so that somebody can murder him. And steal his body. It must be terrible for you, dear. It must break your heart."

"Actually," Darvelle said again, "at the moment, the word is that it's more likely that he committed suicide than that he was murdered."

"Is it?" Mrs. Lord said. "But they don't bring that Mr. Demarkian in to investigate suicides, I don't think. I hear he's very expensive, and very picky about the jobs he takes. It has to be something really mysterious and complicated before he gets interested. Oh, I've heard a lot about him. And of course, I've seen him on television. It's really exciting to have him here, I must say. Have you met him? I'll admit I've sometimes wanted to just find a way to run across him in the street, you know, just so I could say hello."

"I think," Darvelle said slowly, "that it was because of Mrs. Morton that they brought Gregor Demarkian in. The police think

Chester committed suicide, but Mrs. Morton doesn't, and they wanted an independent evaluation. Just so nobody could say they hadn't done everything they could."

"Well, then," Mrs. Lord said, "there's the matter of the disappearing body. Bodies don't disappear on their own. I tell you, when I heard that on the morning news, I nearly passed right out. I nearly did. Can you imagine something like that in Mattatuck? Really. And I was thinking. It had to be at least two people involved, don't you think? I mean, a single person couldn't carry a dead weight like that out of the basement of Feldman's without being seen by somebody. I'm surprised the two of them weren't seen by somebody. Feldman's is a busy place. Oh, no, dear. I'm sure there's nothing like suicide involved in this thing. I'm sure it was murder, and the police know it. You just have to ask yourself who you know who's likely to do a thing like that."

Darvelle didn't have to ask herself who was likely to do a thing like that. She could think of a dozen people she'd be perfectly willing to murder herself, starting with Mrs. Lord. She sat behind the wheel and counted to ten in her head. She wished the muscles in her arms and back didn't feel as if they had all the plasticity of petrified wood. Then she popped the driver's side door and got out onto the driveway.

"It's an excellent value in a house," she said firmly. "And they aren't building split-levels anymore, so this is a very rare chance to get something in a style I know you like. And unlike most split-levels, this is especially large, over three thousand square feet, so you'll have more than enough room for anything you want to do. And it's designed for entertaining, with an L-shaped living-dining room space that allows a free flow of traffic for really large groups of people. Think of your annual Christmas party, the one you were telling me about —"

Mrs. Lord stepped out of the car and looked around, but Darvelle didn't see her. She was looking at the end of the driveway. That was Charlene Morton standing there. Yes, of course, Charlene lived across the street, but Darvelle hadn't expected her to actually show up. Or even to know that Darvelle was there.

On the other hand, she should have expected it. Charlene always knew where she was and what she was doing. It had been that way for twelve years. Charlene had known the house Darvelle was buying before she bought it. Charlene had known every car Darvelle bought before she bought it. Darvelle sometimes thought Charlene lived inside her head.

Mrs. Lord looked at the end of the driveway and brightened up. "Oh, that's Mrs. Morton, isn't it? Does she live around here? I mean, I knew she lived in Mattatuck, of course, that's been on the news, but I never realized she was right in the neighborhood. Oh, the poor thing! Look how distraught she is!"

Distraught my ass, Darvelle thought. She slammed the car door shut and turned her back on Charlene, as if Charlene weren't really there, as if she was one of those hallucinations from the *Beautiful Mind* movie.

"The foyer," she said firmly, "is really entirely unlike anything else I've shown you so far. It's one of those custom touches I was talking about. It's got a cathedral effect, and skylights. You feel like you're walking into a palace instead of a split-level."

"I'm not going to let you get away with it," Charlene said.

Charlene wasn't shouting, but it sounded like a shout. Maybe the street was unusually quite. It was a very quiet day. There was no traffic. Of course, there wouldn't be a lot of traffic on a residential street in Sherwood Forest. She started up the cobblestone walk to the front door.

"Look at this walk," she told Mrs. Lord, just as if Mrs. Lord was following her. "I really like the cobblestone effect, don't you? A lot of care and planning was put into this house."

"Oh," Mrs. Lord said, "aren't you going to —"

"I'm not going to let you get away with it," Charlene said again. "Do you think you can just walk off and pretend you don't hear me? You hear me. I don't know what you did with my son's body, but I'm going to find out. I'm going to find out how you murdered him, too. Don't think you're going to get away with it."

Darvelle could feel the strength of whatever it was that maintained her self control snapping inside her, like ropes tying down a beast whose wildness was beyond their capacity. Her brain felt as if it were pulsing inside her skull, hard enough to crack the bone. She wheeled around and looked Charlene in the face. Then she marched to the end of the drive and forced Charlene into the street.

"For God's sake!" she said. She was screeching. She could hear herself. "For God's sake, Charlene, I didn't murder him. Nobody murdered him. He ran away from here to get away from you and he stayed

307

away for twelve years. And when he came back, when he got home, well, then what, Charlene? Then he killed himself rather than get stuck with you again. And I don't blame him. I don't blame him. If you were my mother, I'd have murdered myself at birth."

THREE

1

The most important thing to understand, in situations like this, was why it was that the people who had hired you didn't want you to do the job they had supposedly hired you to do. Gregor Demarkian knew, from experience, that there was more than one possible answer to this. There was even more than one possible answer when the local police called in the FBI. If anything, being a consultant had reduced the amount of friction between himself and local law enforcement agencies. A local law enforcement agency could be pressured by public opinion or the state government to ask in Feds it wanted no part of, but it didn't usually ask in a consultant unless it had come to its own decision to do it. Of course, it didn't always come to its own decision willingly.

One of the reasons a local police department might ask in a consultant when it didn't want to was that it might otherwise be required to ask in the FBI, which it *really* didn't want to.

Gregor considered all of this sitting in the backseat of his hired car, feeling like something of an idiot being driven around like a debutante in the wilds of western New York state. He looked at the back of Tony Bolero's head and wondered if the man shaved it. He thought about calling Bennis, or Tibor, or even the hospital. Then he got out his notebook and looked at the notes he had made about the billboard.

They'd gone a meandering half a mile when he couldn't stand it anymore.

"Could you pull over?" he asked Tony Bolero.

Tony Bolero looked curious, but he pulled over. "Is there something you need to see, Mr. Demarkian? I've got to admit, I didn't notice a thing, but if there's something you think is important, you just tell me where you want me to stop."

"Stop as soon as it's safe," Gregor said. "Stop anywhere at all."

Tony Bolero pulled the car over to the soft shoulder of the road and cut the engine. Gregor got out and came around to the front. Then he got into the front passenger seat and slammed the door. Then he grabbed the seat belt.

"That feels better."

Tony Bolero frowned. "I don't know," he said. "I don't know if I'm supposed to —"

"Look," Gregor said. "My wife grew up on the Philadelphia Main Line in a house that could be turned into a boarding school if her brother ever felt like it. I grew up in a tenement slum area that's gotten a little better over the years."

"Oh, Cavanaugh Street is more than a little better, Mr. Demarkian. I'd say it's one of the nicest streets actually in the city. As nice as anything on the Main Line, if you ask me."

"Yes, well. It wasn't when I was growing up. The thing is, I feel like an idiot sitting back there like that, as if I'm some sort of — I don't know what. And then there's talking to you. I do have to talk to you. I have to talk to somebody, and right now I can't talk to Howard Androcoelho. And I don't want to be shouting things from the backseat and having to explain them three times before you understand them."

Tony Bolero considered this. "All right," he said. "Mrs. Demarkian did say I should give you any assistance you needed."

"That'll do it," Gregor said. "And we

don't have to tell her anything about me sitting up front if it would make you feel better. Right now, I *think* I want to go to the police department. I'm not sure. So, in the meantime, do you think you could drive me around the long way, give me about half an hour to think?"

"You mean take the scenic route? Sure."

"Good," Gregor said.

Tony pulled the car back onto the road, and Gregor began flipping through page after page of his notebook, the same kind of spiral stenographer's notebook he'd been using since his first days as a Federal agent. He didn't even know if there were stenographers anymore. Certainly, fewer people had secretaries. Everybody had cubicles now, with their own computers in them.

Computers.

He had a computer with him. He had one that could connect to the Internet, if he found something called a "Wi-Fi" connection.

He put the notebook down on his lap.

"Something wrong, Mr. Demarkian?"

Gregor looked up. "You have to keep all the questions separate, that's the problem," he said. "The natural inclination is to see them all as connected. That's the way the human brain is built to run. That's why there are so many conspiracy theorists. But you have to keep the questions separate, or you could end up making an idiot out of yourself."

"What questions, Mr. Demarkian?"

"Didn't I do this for you before? I might have been doing it for Howard Androcoelho. It doesn't matter. The more I go over it, the better off I am. Well, first, there's why Chester Morton left. Because we know now, of course, that he did leave. He wasn't murdered twelve years ago. And I have two pieces of information I didn't have yesterday. The first is that there were fights between Chester Morton and his family, and especially his mother, which led to his moving out of the family home and into the trailer park."

"Fights about what?"

"We don't know that," Gregor said. "I'll ask Charlene Morton, but I'm not sure I'll get anything like an accurate answer. But there were fights, not just Chester's need for independence, that led him to move out. In fact, I wonder if there was anything going on about independence at all, because the other thing I know that I didn't before is that Chester wanted to reconcile with his family, at least enough to get some financial support." Gregor tapped his fingers against his knees. "You know, that doesn't make any sense."

"What doesn't?" Tony Bolero asked. "I mean, it makes sense to me, you know. Kid's used to picking up pretty good change from not much work, doesn't have to kiss the butt of a boss, doesn't like being out on his own where things are different."

"Oh, I agree," Gregor said. "But the story, from everybody — from Howard Androcoelho, from Darvelle Haymes, even from Kenny and Charlene Morton — has been that Chester had a mind of his own, he was independent, he was going to move out if he wanted to, and he was going to date the girl he wanted to and he didn't give a damn about the family. But is that really the case? Does he sound like somebody who would do that?"

"Well, he did it, didn't he?" Tony Bolero said.

"I don't know," Gregor said. "There were fights, and he moved out of the house. He wasn't forced out. That is, they didn't tell him he had to leave. Everybody agrees on that. And yet — And what is it with Darvelle Haymes? Supposedly he was so in love with Darvelle Haymes, he was willing to do anything not to give her up. Even go through with that ridiculous plan of buying a baby so that he could have his cake and eat it, too. But maybe that's wrong. Maybe he didn't give a damn about Darvelle Haymes at all, except that she was the kind of person he thought he could talk into the things he wanted to talk a girl into."

"You've gone to the moon, Mr. Demarkian."

"No, I haven't," Gregor said. "The impression I got from Howard Androcoelho was that Chester Morton moved out of his family's house because he wanted to date Darvelle Haymes without getting a lot of hassle about it. But that isn't true. He started dating Darvelle after he moved out. The arguments at home were about something else. What if he started dating Darvelle because he thought she was the kind of girl he could get to go along with, say, getting royally pregnant out of wedlock and then keeping the baby?"

"You mean he was looking to knock somebody up."

"I mean I think he was looking for somebody to have his baby because he thought the baby would bring his mother around on — on whatever it actually was that the problem was. Which brings me right back to the problem I had when I started talking to you. If Chester Morton's primary motiva-

315

tion in the months between the time he left his family's house and the time he disappeared was to make some kind of peace with his family and get taken back into the fold — presumably on his own terms, there was something he wanted a concession for, I don't know what — but anyway, if that was his primary motivation, why did he leave at all? Well, okay, that was always the question. Why did he leave at all. And if he cared so much about being in his family's good graces, or good enough graces, maybe I should say, then why disappear?"

"If I keep going the way I'm going, I'm going to be at the police station in a minute or two. Do you want me to circle around some more? Or are you ready to go in?"

"No," Gregor said. "Find me one of those places — you know, where they let me plug the computer in and get on the Internet."

2

Tony Bolero's GPS found a coffee shop one town over with unlimited Wi-Fi access. Gregor didn't know if he'd gone out of his way to pick something away from Mattatuck proper, or if this was just the closest place that had what they needed. Gregor didn't think it was the closest place. He was pretty sure there was a Barnes & Noble in Mattatuck, and pretty sure that Barnes & Nobles had coffee shops that let you plug into the Internet.

"They don't let you plug in," Tony said, as he helped Gregor set up at a table along the back wall. "So, you know, your battery runs out and that's it. Of course, we could have just stayed at the hotel, but I figured you had to have some reason. So we came here."

"Here" was nice enough. Gregor hadn't asked to go back to the hotel because he hadn't thought of it. You got up, you got dressed, you got out of the house — there seemed like there was something essentially wrong with going back again, as if you weren't really working. He looked at the big menu over the counter where coffee was being ordered and being served.

"I don't suppose they have actual coffee in this place," he said. "You know, no caramel, no whipped cream, no chocolate sprinkles. Why do people drink this stuff, anyway? It isn't coffee. It's a milk shake. Milk shakes. Whatever."

"You just sit and I'll find you something," Tony Bolero said. "You care if it's fair trade or not?"

"There's a politics of coffee?"

Tony shook his head and went off over to the counter where he was third in line. The two people ahead of him were both women in their forties with their hair pulled back off their faces and Coach bags.

Gregor opened up and turned the laptop on. He was much more comfortable with the computer now than he used to be, and the more he got used to doing searches, the better he liked using the thing. He opened Internet Explorer and got online. Then he went to Google and typed in "Chester Morton." The first link that came up was "Justice for Chester," the Morton family's official Web site on Chester and what might have happened to him.

Gregor looked at the big picture of Chester that was the first thing under the site's title. It was the same picture that appeared on the billboard near Mattatuck–Harvey Community College. He scrolled down a little and found a page of more pictures: Chester with Charlene Morton and a little crowd of other people that Gregor thought must be the Morton family; Chester on a lifeguard's chair at a beach somewhere; Chester with a jacket and tie at somebody's wedding. Gregor moved around from page to page. There were no other pictures. The first picture, the one from the billboard, kept appearing over and over again.

Gregor found a link that said, "About

Chester," and tried that. It turned out to lead to a page with long paragraphs of type, all presented on a slightly beige background with pictures of leaves scattered across it, red and orange leaves, the kind that fell in the fall. Gregor had no idea why somebody would choose to use a background like this for a page like this. He wondered who had designed the site. He wondered when it had been designed.

He read down the page about Chester, but found out very little. There was a line or two about Chester Morton's fascination with the state of Wyoming, and with Montana, and with living near really tall mountains. This was a fascination he was supposed to have picked up when the family went on vacation to Wyoming when he was eight. There were references to other things Chester was supposed to have liked. Some were the names of bands Gregor had never heard of. Some were obvious things for a young man of that age: Harley-Davidson motorcycles; pumpkin pie with whipped cream; the World Wrestling Federation; NASCAR.

Gregor went back to the Google search page. There was a link to the episode of *Disappeared* that was going to tell his story — that wasn't going to air for another month.

There were links to a couple of amateur sites that used the Chester Morton case as an item of interest for conspiracy nuts of various kinds.

Tony came back with two coffees and put a big one down next to Gregor's laptop. Gregor opened the inevitable plastic top — why they did that when they knew you were going to drink the stuff in the car, he didn't know — and stared down into what looked like plain black coffee.

"Not bad," he said.

Tony settled himself across the table. He had a tall pink-looking thing with a straw in it. Gregor didn't ask.

"So," Tony said, "have you found anything out?"

"Not really," Gregor said. "The case has been a minor item on a couple of the true crime shows, but there hasn't been anything major. Until just about now. There's going to be an episode of *Disappeared* about it. But maybe not, now that he's been found."

"Yeah, well," Tony said. "There's going to be some interest now from some of those shows, don't you think?"

"Probably, but hardly to the point." Gregor tried the coffee. It wasn't bad. In fact, it was better than not bad. "It's frustrating, though. I can't get any real sense of this man. Darvelle Haymes says he wanted her to help him buy a baby. His brother Kenny says he remembers Chester as someone who did drugs and drank alcohol at least some of the time. That MOM tattoo on his chest was put on after death, but he had other tattoos, on his arms, that had been there for years. There was a snake, I think. And there were piercings. The holes for that nipple ring. The penis ring. I'd think anybody willing to get a penis ring would have to be fairly hard-core something. Hard-core crazy, if nothing else."

"What're you getting at?"

"I don't know," Gregor said. "I guess that it just doesn't sound, to me, like the description of a guy who was enthralled by the outdoors, a guy who wanted to go live in a state with nearly nobody in it and spend his time looking at mountains. First he went away, and then he came back. Why?"

"I keep telling you not to ask me," Tony said. "I'm not even Watson. I'm just a fly on the wall."

Gregor got out his cell phone. He thought cell phone address books had to be one of the greatest inventions ever. They not only kept your numbers for you. They let you dial them with a single punch of a button.

He found the number he was looking for,

punched it in, and waited. Kurt Delano picked up his own phone and said, "Delano speaking, Federal Bureau of Investigation."

"God, you sound official," Gregor said.

"Gregor! I can't believe it! It must have been a year! How are you?"

"I'm fine. But this is something in the nature of a business call."

"Of course it's a business call. You called my office. I'm going to be in Philly in a month, though. We've got some kind of regional conference. More of the *happy-crappy* that comes with having a desk job. You had a desk job. How did you stand it?"

"I reminded myself every day that it could have been worse and they could have made me the director. Listen, what do you know about Chester Ray Morton?"

"Oh *that*." Kurt Delano laughed. "Okay, I knew you were doing that. I heard it on television. I'm the wrong person to ask. The bureau was about to start looking into it, but it wasn't on my desk. And now it doesn't matter at all, I guess. It's a local murder. Or do you think it isn't local?"

"No, I think it's local enough. It's just — did you ever hear about Chester Morton having a fascination with Wyoming?"

"No, but like I said, that wasn't on my desk. And I'm still not sure it should have been on anybody's desk. As far as I know, it was mostly the result of the mother just not taking no for an answer, so after a while — well, you know what I mean. I could put you in touch with the agent who was set to handle it."

"Could you? That would be helpful. Or I think it would."

"Her name's Rhonda Alvarez. Give me your number and I'll ask her to call. Don't worry. She's not one of your protecting-the-turf types. I used to think we'd have less of that once we got enough women in the Bureau, but sometimes I think it's been worse."

3

The next place Gregor needed to go was the Mattatuck Police Department, but he didn't want to go there, and he wasn't sure he was at the place where he couldn't do anything else. He looked at his notes a few more times. Then he picked up his cell phone and called Bennis.

"I'm in some kind of coffee shop," he said. "It's not Starbucks, but then Starbucks is less fey. You can get coffee to drink here that's pink."

"How do they make coffee that's pink?"

"I don't know, but I've seen it. How's old

George."

There was a sigh on the other end of the line — except, Gregor reminded himself, it wasn't a line, and that was why it went disturbingly blank-silent when nobody was talking. He didn't understand why he got himself so tangled up with the technology, but he did. There was a point where he just wanted to do more than turn back the clock. He wanted to turn back the world. Or maybe he didn't. If he turned back the world, he might be back at a place where nothing could be done for old George but wait for him to die.

"Gregor?" Bennis said.

"Never mind," Gregor said. "I was obsessing about technology again. It doesn't matter. How's old George."

"I think the proper terminology is 'resting comfortably.' There's just not much anybody can do with him. He's not in pain. He's reasonably alert most of the time —"

"Oh, I know. I actually got to talk to him once."

"And he's nearly a hundred years old," Bennis said. "It's hard to complain, really. He's nearly a hundred and he's been living on his own and ambulatory until last week, no nursing homes, no dementia. If I get to live to be a hundred, this is what I want it to be."

"Isn't there a prognosis?"

"The prognosis is that he's a hundred years old," Bennis said, "and don't tell me the medical system gives up on old people. I know it does. But I don't think anybody is giving up on old George. The nurses love him. The doctors admire him. I think Martin would keep him alive by feeding him his own blood if that was what it took. But the man is a hundred years old. There just gets to be a point."

"I know."

"Are you all right? This case was supposed to take your mind off things. It doesn't sound like it has."

"I've just got my mind on other things," Gregor said. "I'm sorry. I forget if I've discussed things with you or only discussed them with Tony here. Tony was a brilliant choice, even if he does drink pink coffee."

"It's red coffee," Tony said. "It's got cinnamon hearts in it."

"Is he right there?" Bennis said.

"Absolutely," Gregor said. "I've got to go do something. I'll talk to you later."

"Do that," Bennis said. "And don't worry so much, Gregor. If something looks like a crisis, I'll call you immediately. Tony will drive you back home."

"Right," Gregor said.

He put the phone down on the table. The problem, of course, was that with somebody of old George Tekemanian's age, crises could come up without notice and be over before anybody had a chance to call anybody.

Gregor got up. "Let's go," he said. "We might as well go over to the police station and see what happens. I really hate being in situations of this kind."

Going back, they did not take the scenic route. Tony cut across one small crumbling neighborhood after the other, the houses triple-deckers and close together. Mattatuck looked like any one of a hundred dying industrial towns of the Northeast — but it looked like an industrial town, not like a rural hamlet. They turned onto a slightly wider-than-average two-lane blacktop, and Gregor began to recognize some of the scenery. There was the welfare office. There were the pawnshops. There was the trailer park.

"Wait," Gregor said.

Tony slowed, but he didn't park. "You want me to pull over somewhere?"

"I don't know," Gregor said. "That's the trailer park Howard Androcoelho and I were at when I met Chester Morton's mother. I'm sure of it. I recognize the neighborhood."

"Okay. Is that important?"

"I don't know," Gregor said. "Could you maybe go around back to the trailer park, then turn around and head in this direction again, and go directly to The Feldman Funeral Home? Maybe that's not what I mean. Let's go to the trailer park and then go to The Feldman Funeral Home in the most direct way possible. How about that?"

"Okay."

Tony swung the car around and brought it back to the entrance to the trailer park. It was the same trailer park. Gregor was sure of it. He looked up the road and down again. There was nothing on this stretch that would be of any help to anybody, as far as he could see. He looked into the distance. The main offices of the Morton's garbage business were supposed to be right there, past the trailers and through the trees. Somebody could walk if they didn't mind smashing their way through the brambles.

"You want to sit here for a while?" Tony asked.

"No," Gregor said. "Drive to The Feldman Funeral Home on the most direct route possible. I expect that's going to be main streets, right?"

"Probably. There isn't much around here except main streets."

"I know. Drive to The Feldman Funeral Home. Pull into that parking lot around the back."

"Fine with me," Tony said.

They got back out onto the road. They were heading in the direction they had been heading in originally. Gregor had been right about that. He was beginning to get some kind of bearings in this place. They passed a huge strip-mall-like shopping center where more than half the stores seemed to be empty. Then they turned left at an intersection with three different gas stations and a Kentucky Fried Chicken. Then they went under a trestle and they were at the green. Gregor remembered the Civil War monument.

"It's right over there," Tony said, pointing across the street. "It's closer than it seems, but we have to go around the green to get there."

"Right," Gregor said.

They pulled around the green, then down the road to The Feldman Funeral Home, then down the side street to the entrance to the parking lot in the back. Tony parked, and waited.

"What would you say?" Gregor asked him. "Starting from here, are we in walking distance to that trailer park?"

"It's less than a mile," Tony said. "And it's on your way from here. Turn right at the end of the little street this parking lot is on and you don't have to go around the green. You can go straight back to the KFC and then right again and then you're there."

"I thought so."

Gregor got out his cell phone, looked quickly through his notes for the number he wanted, and punched it in. A chipper little voice said, "Morton's." Gregor identified himself, asked for Charlene Morton, and waited.

"I need to get into the trailer again," he said, when the woman got on the line. "Do you think you can meet me there in — well, as quickly as possible? I'm at The Feldman Funeral Home, so I'm not far."

"I'll be over there in a minute and a half," Charlene Morton said. "But I hope you know what you're doing. I've had about enough of the whole crapload bunch of you."

"I'm sorry to bother you," Gregor said. "It won't take long."

Gregor put his cell phone back in his pocket and nodded at Tony. "Let's go," he said. "Let's see where we're going here."

Tony got the car out of the parking lot, down the side street, and back onto East Main. Seconds later, they were at the intersection with the Kentucky Fried Chicken. Seconds after that, they were passing the nearly deserted shopping center. Barely a hiccup after that, they were at the trailer park. Tony turned the car into the dirt drive and let it bump along against the ruts as women came out of their trailers one by one, just to look at them.

"Want to go to where that green trailer is," Gregor said, "and then just around it to the trailer on the other side."

Tony moved slowly. Gregor caught sight of Charlene Morton standing at the door of Chester Morton's trailer, her Fusion parked in the dust and mud just a few feet away. Gregor tapped Tony on the shoulder and the car eased to a stop.

"Thanks," Gregor said.

He popped the passenger side door and got out. It was hot today, hot and muggy. The air felt full of rain that hadn't happened yet. Gregor walked up to the trailer and looked it over. It did not seem changed in any way.

"I hope you know what you're doing," Charlene Morton said. "I really do hope that. Because I've been put through enough by you people."

"As far as I know, you haven't been put through anything by me," Gregor said. "You didn't think to go inside while you were waiting for me?"

"I told you the last time we did this," Charlene said. "I don't go inside. I don't clean up. I just keep the place. And I'm not going to be keeping it any longer, now that I'm not waiting for Chester to come back anymore."

"If you'll let me," Gregor said, taking the keys.

Charlene Morton gave up the keys reluctantly, but she gave them up. Gregor took them and opened the door. He did not hesitate. He did step in front and go through the door first.

Chester Morton's body was sitting up in the ancient armchair in the far corner of the minuscule living room.

It was the first thing anybody would see when they walked through the door.

Four

1

Althy Michaelman would have slept all day if she could have managed it. She had been out until two in the morning, and she'd been drinking that sweet heavy stuff that gave her a headache that lasted all day. All she wanted to do was to lie down some- where soft and black out until she didn't have to give a shit anymore, but that was impossible with Haydee home and slam- ming around the trailer as if she were in a bowling alley. Haydee wasn't usually home in the middle of the day. She had work at the Quik-Go, and school, and now she was talking about working somewhere else. It was enough to make Althy tired. It was enough to make her *furious.*

It was the police sirens that put an end to it. Once those police sirens got going, there was no way to sleep unless you were dead. Or better than dead. Althy tried to remember what they'd done last night to get the liquor, whether they'd finished the bottles, whether they'd brought anything home. She might as well have been trying to remember the fall of Rome. They'd been out near the reservoir, that was all she remembered. They'd started a bonfire, and Dickie Klemm had fallen in.

The police sirens were very loud, and the police lights were very bright, and they were all practically on her doorstep. Althy got up far enough to look through the little window, but there was nothing there to tell her what was going on. It was the middle of the day. People were mostly not coming out of their trailers to find out what was going on.

She hauled herself up on her feet and then out into the little hall. Haydee was not moving around in the living room anymore. Maybe she'd left without delivering her customary lecture. Other people's daughters said good-bye. Althy's told her what a fucking piece of trash she was.

Althy went down the hall. It was so narrow she could bump into it from side to side without falling over. She got to the living room and saw Haydee standing very still, looking out the picture window at whatever was happening outside. *Christ,* Althy thought. *Who the hell ever thought to call that fucking thing a picture window?*

Althy banged on the wall. It rattled a little, but Haydee must have heard her coming. She didn't turn around.

"You want to let me in on what the fuck is going on?" Althy said.

This time, Haydee did turn. "The police are over at the empty trailer. The police and Mrs. Morton and that guy they've got here helping to investigate."

"Yeah?" Althy said. "Well, so what? What's that got to do with us?"

"I don't know so what. I don't know what's going on. There are a lot of police cars over there. They've got that mobile crime unit, you know, that they bought last year. It was on the news."

"I don't watch the fucking news."

"I know you don't," Haydee said.

Althy wondered where Mike had gone — but then again, it was just as well. The last thing she wanted was Mike around when the police were here. She wondered if Mike had come home with her the night before, but she didn't remember that, either. All she really remembered was Dickie Klemm with his ass on fire.

There was a little table built into the floor with a curving bench built around it. Althy sat down on the bench, got a pack of cigarettes, and lit up. Haydee turned around at the sound of the match and wrinkled her nose.

"Dickie Klemm got his ass on fire last night," Althy said. "He had to jump in the reservoir to put himself out. I laughed so hard I pissed my pants."

Haydee didn't respond. She was still watching what was going on outside. Then she turned away from the window and went back to what she had been doing before. She was packing up her backpack with her school stuff.

Althy took a deep, sucking draw on the cigarette, as if it were a joint. She wished she had a joint. She wished she had something.

"Aren't you supposed to be at work right now? You're always at work in the middle of the day. Fucking idiot."

"I worked a bit and then they sent me home," Haydee said. "I've got class now. Then I'm going to work again tonight. They took me on the dinner shift to waitress over at Pat and Carol's."

"Shit," Althy said.

"It's a good waitressing place," Haydee said. "I talked to one of the girls who already works there. You get a lot of people for dinner and they're good with tips. The woman whose place I'm taking worked there for forty years and raised a whole family on what she got, and raised them right, too. They all of them went to college. Now she's retired and they're taking care of her."

"Pat Nickerby went to high school with me," Althy said. "He grew up right here in this trailer park. He's a little shit."

"Well, it just goes to prove it."

"To prove what, for fuck's sake?"

"To prove that you don't have to stay in a place like this, just because you were born in it," Haydee said. "If you work hard, and you do right, and you don't stop, you can end up in a ranch house in Sherwood Forest."

"Go fuck yourself," Althy said.

"You shouldn't cuss all the time," Haydee said. "People who don't live in places like this don't cuss all the time. Did you know I didn't know that? I didn't know it until I went to college. When you cuss all the time, you sound like an absolute idiot."

"You sound like a prissy little fuck," Althy said. "That's what you are. Won't even support your family. Just as happy to let your mother starve if it means you can keep a fucking dime for yourself. Fuck, fuck, fuck. Do you hear me? You'd let me fucking starve."

Haydee zipped her backpack closed and threw it over her shoulder. "You're not starving. You're just short the money for another drink. You know it, and I know it, and the only thing new about today is that Mike isn't around. Maybe he got arrested. He's not even a good thief."

"Oh, well," Althy said. "Look the fuck at you."

Haydee turned away and left the living room, went out to the little vestibule, and down the stairs to the door. Althy wouldn't usually let herself go wandering around when there was a fucking police convention going on outside, but she couldn't help herself. Sometimes Haydee made her fucking head want to explode.

"Fucking A," Althy said, going out of the door herself.

It really was a police convention out here. There had to be six police cars, plus the mobile crime unit, plus Charlene "Fucking" Morton, and that crime consultant person, plus a wagon from Feldman's. The sirens were off, but the police cars all had their top lights pulsing in that way that made Althy feel dizzy. Maybe she ought to fall down right here and have a fit and see what happened with it. You could get some money that way if people thought they'd given you a seizure. She looked around. It probably wouldn't work, not right here, right now. There were too many professional people around. There might even be a doctor. When you pulled the thing with the seizure, you wanted to be one on one with some idiot who was scared of his own shadow and didn't want anybody to know he was in that particular parking lot at that time of night.

Haydee was talking to the crime consultant, leaning over close to him and nodding while he wrote something down. Wasn't that just fucking precious? It sure the fuck was. Haydee the saint and Haydee the model citizen.

Haydee turned around and pointed at her. Althy nearly spit.

"Listen," Haydee said, coming up to her with the crime consultant in tow. "Ma, this is Gregor Demarkian. He's helping with the Chester Morton investigation —"

"I know who the fuck he is," Althy said. "I've seen him before."

"Fine." Haydee closed her eyes. "I was just telling him I wasn't home all day. I only got home about an hour ago. He needs to talk to somebody who was home all day."

"I wasn't the fuck home," Althy said. "I was the fuck asleep."

"And it's not just today," Gregor Demarkian said. "It could have been last
night."

"I wasn't the fuck here last night," Althy
said. "What do you take me for? I was out
till two at least and then when I came the
fuck home I just passed out. I'm not some
fucking plaster saint."

"I was telling Mr. Demarkian that I heard
a lot of vehicles before I went to sleep, but
there are always a lot of vehicles around
here."

"All the fucking time," Althy said. "Somebody must have brought a fucking truck."

Gregor Demarkian leaned in, interested.
"A truck? You saw a truck?"

"No, I didn't see a fucking truck," Althy
said. "What do you take me for? I tripped
on the rut, that's all. We came home and I
came down this path and there was a fucking rut the size of a whale right here in front
of my door, and I tripped on it. I fell flat on
my face. Hurt like fucking hell."

"It was an old rut?" Gregor Demarkian
asked. "It was dry?"

"No, it wasn't the fuck dry," Althy said,
her voice at maximum volume, as if she
were talking to somebody who couldn't
speak English. "There's mud everywhere.
What the fuck is wrong with your fucking

eyes? It was just a big rut, is all. Deep and wide. And I fell the fuck into it. Fuck, if there'd been a truck the size of that rut around, I'd have seen it. I'm right in the fucking middle of the park. I'd have seen it even if it were black as shit and had its lights off."

"Yes," Gregor Demarkian said. "Yes, I see."

"I don't see why you have to shout," Haydee said.

"Go fuck yourself," Althy said.

Then she turned to look at the whole mess of them out there milling around doing nothing useful, and headed back to the trailer.

There was more than one way to make sure you had enough money to have a good time, and Althy Michaelman knew all of them.

2

Kyle Holborn was on the desk when the call came in, and for the next half hour all he did was make little notes in the margins of the call sheet to make sure there was a record of who was going out there and why. Well, maybe not why. There was no why to this thing besides panic, and just as it was with all panic, it made a lot of noise. What

Kyle couldn't get his head past was just how much he resented it. He resented being at this desk. He resented the incredible fuss this was causing. He resented Mr. Gregor "Great Detective" Demarkian, who had waltzed in here and acted like none of them knew what they were doing.

It was the kind of gossip that got around town very fast. He didn't expect to be the first to tell anybody about it. He really didn't expect to be the first to tell Darvelle, who spent her day with women who lived for the moment when they could impart shocking information to somebody. He called Darvelle anyway. So many of the other people in the station were either on their way over to the scene or huddled into tight little groups to discuss it, he thought he was probably safe no matter what he said.

Darvelle's cell phone rang so many times, Kyle thought he was going to get that message that told him to stop trying. Then Darvelle picked up, and she sounded angry.

"Darvelle Haymes," she said, as if she hadn't seen his name on the caller ID.

Kyle took a deep breath and let the air out very slowly. He imagined himself as a plastic blow-up clown, deflating.

"It's me," he said. "You had to know it was me."

"Oh," Darvelle said. "Oh. I'm sorry. I wasn't looking. Things are a little tense here."

"Are you out with a buyer? I didn't mean to get you in the middle of something."

"I'm back at the shop. But there are buyers here, and I don't know who else, and the whole place is going crazy. If you called to tell me they found Chester Morton's body sitting up in a chair, stark naked, in his old trailer, I already know. Mice at the town dump already know."

"I wish people would stop getting so worked up about the stark naked," Kyle said. "I mean, of course he was stark naked. He was in a cold locker at Feldman's. You don't put clothes on a body in a cold locker. At least, you don't until you want to put him in a casket. And what did they expect? That whoever took the thing was going to dress it up before he put it somewhere?"

There was a long pause on the line. Kyle knew that Darvelle was thinking it through. Then she said, very cautiously, "All right. I can see how that would work."

"I'd think the real problem would be the time," Kyle said. "I mean, the body disappeared from Feldman's last night, we know the approximate time, sort of, you see what I mean? And now the body is in the trailer. So the question is, did the body go directly to the trailer, or did it get there later. You know, did someone hang on to it for a while."

Darvelle did some more considering. "And that's one of those things they can figure out?"

"Maybe," Kyle said. "It depends on where the body was when it wasn't in the trailer."

"Why?"

Kyle shrugged. He knew she couldn't see his shrug, but, he didn't care. "Bodies leave things behind. You never get them away completely clean. They leave fibers, and blood, and DNA, and stuff. Except I don't think there would be any blood in this case. But they leave things. Forensics."

"I thought you said that was all a lot of bunk," Darvelle said. "*CSI* and all that stuff. I thought you said it was all a lot of crap."

"It is a lot of crap," Kyle said. "I mean, they make up half the stuff they do on *CSI*. But forensics isn't a lot of crap. There really are forensics. So, you know, if somebody had the body someplace for a while before they put it in the trailer, there'd be stuff left behind. And that stuff lasts. It can last a really long time."

"What's a really long time?"

"Months," Kyle said. "Years, sometimes.

Fibers. That kind of thing."

"Crap," Darvelle said again.

Kyle looked up and around the station. There was still nobody near the front desk. They were all huddled in the back, telling each other stories. There was nobody coming through the front door. He might as well have been alone.

"If I was the person who moved the body," he said, "the best thing I could do would be just get rid of whatever I moved it in. Sell the car or the truck or whatever. Junk it if I had to. But that's not as easy as you'd think. Everybody keeps records these days. So the next best thing would be to clean out the space with something strong. Lye, maybe."

"Wouldn't the police be able to detect the lye?" Darvelle said. "I mean, for God's sake, Kyle. Detecting blood with some chemical that lights up purple in the right kind of light sounds like science fiction, but detecting lye is a job I could give to a cat."

"They'd be able to detect the lye," Kyle said, "but they wouldn't be able to detect anything else."

The pause this time was even longer. Kyle looked down at his fingernails. His fingernails looked awful. There was dirt under them, and the edges were ragged.

"You're out of your mind," Darvelle said finally. "You really are. I don't know what it is you think you're thinking."

"I'm thinking that I'm sick of Gregor Demarkian," Kyle said. "I'm sick of everybody running around acting as if he's God. Sometimes I wonder if he doesn't cause this stuff he runs into. Maybe he moved the body himself. Maybe this is some big plot to turn this into a sensational case that will make all the magazines and get him on television again. Maybe there are a lot of reasons for people to want to move that body that have nothing to do with whether they murdered Chester 'Goddamned' Morton."

"You're out of your mind," Darvelle said again. "I'm going to get off the phone now. I'm going to go get some work done."

"That Albanian guy who owns the construction company was in here this morning," Kyle said. "He was asking about the baby."

This time, Darvelle was angry. "I told you what I was going to do about that, and I did it. I talked to Gregor Demarkian this morning. And no body of any baby has anything to do with me, and you know it. You are not going to get me worked up over this again."

"I'm not trying to get you worked up over anything."

"Yes, you are, Kyle, yes you are. And I've had enough. And if you don't leave it the hell alone, I'll ambush Demarkian at breakfast again tomorrow and give him chapter and verse of my suspicions about everything. Because if you think I don't know what's going on, you're even stupider than I think you are."

The phone went dead silent. Kyle looked at the receiver in his hand and then replaced it in the cradle. It had started to feel a little odd to him, using landlines. He pushed the heavy black phone away from him. The women were still in the back, yammering. Almost every one of the patrol cars was over at the trailer park, creating more upset and confusion in the middle of a genuine crisis. If you wanted to rob a bank in Mattatuck, this was definitely the time to do it.

He got off his seat and wandered back toward the hall with the restrooms, not because he needed to use one, but because he was just tired of sitting there doing nothing. He caught Sue Folger's eye as he went, and she nodded to him. Then she went to take his place at the front desk. Kyle thought he could ask her anything he needed to know about what was going on and she would tell him, with additions.

In the men's room, Kyle walked into a stall and bolted the door. He put the lid of the toilet down and sat, stretching his legs out in front of him. There was no other man left in the station as far as he knew. He still felt as if he needed protection from something or somebody.

He put his head back and closed his eyes. He had well and truly hated Chester Morton, back in the days when he had known the man. He had hated Chester Morton because Chester had been Darvelle's main squeeze, and he was in love with Darvelle himself. He had hated Chester Morton because Chester was loud and obnoxious and a regular pain in the ass whenever they had classes together. But mostly, he had hated Chester Morton because Chester always seemed to be standing between him and wherever it was he wanted to go. It was as if he and Chester had lived parallel lives, always going in the same direction, but Chester always got there first.

Of course, that wasn't the direction Kyle was going in any more, but he didn't know if that mattered.

3

Howard Androcoelho was willing to admit
that he'd done the wrong thing in bringing
Gregor Demarkian into this case. He was
willing to bet that there were small town
heads of police from one end of America to
the other who had felt the same. The problem was that it was impossible to bring in
any outside investigator and be sure of getting what you wanted. In this case, Howard
had only wanted someone to come in and
tell him that of course Chester Morton had
committed suicide. There was no other way
Chester Morton could have gotten up on
that billboard. Nobody could have dragged
him up there to throw him over the billboard
either as a squirming murder victim or a
dead weight. The whole idea was ridiculous.
Now it was bad enough that it turned out
somebody had thrown him up there, and as
a dead weight. It was worse that things were
happening that seemed to be totally insane,
as if people were deliberately doing things
to make the situation more complicated.
That was the real problem with bringing in
a "Great Detective." A Great Detective was
a focal point for cameras and the press.
Where cameras and the press congregated,
nutcases went to work to make themselves
famous.

Howard reminded himself that he did not know for sure that anybody was out there trying to make himself famous. Then he pulled his car into his marked space behind city hall and cut the engine. He was not ready to go back to central station yet. He was not ready to deal with police work. He was really not ready to talk to Gregor Demarkian. Demarkian was beginning to sound as if he were out of patience, and Howard thought that was more than a little outrageous.

He got out of the car and stood for a while, catching his breath. He was so heavy now he had trouble breathing except when he was sitting down. It was hot, too, ridiculously hot for any time in September. Little pinpoint rivulets of sweat kept starting under his chin and making their way down his neck. Beyond the City Hall parking lot, the town of Mattatuck was mostly loud. Too many people were leaning on their horns. Too many people were revving their engines.

Howard went around to the front of the building and in the front door. He could get in the back — he was an authorized person — but he didn't feel like ringing the bell and waiting for somebody to come and get him. He didn't feel like making this visit. He went across the foyer to the elevator, got in, and pressed the button for the second floor. City Hall was a pretty building, built back in the Thirties when everybody seemed to be trying to do something about Public Works. They cared about what they built in those days. They wanted to make the government majestic.

On the second floor, Howard got out of the elevator and walked down the long corridor to the mayor's office. He let himself into the anteroom and said hello to the receptionist there. She was not somebody he knew. Marianne seemed to go through receptionists the way Howard went through Philly cheese steak sandwiches. He gave the girl his name and waited until she'd announced him. He thanked her when she told him he could go in.

He was, he thought, keeping his manners glued on, which was a good thing. There had to be something wrong with letting the people at large know that their police commissioner was panicking.

Howard opened the door to Marianne's office and found her sitting behind her desk, dressed in one of those perky pastel suits she thought was "professional" for a woman in an important political position. Howard was a little surprised that she was still mayor of Mattatuck. He'd expected her to run for the state legislature, and then maybe run for Congress, or for lieutenant governor, or something like that. The Marianne who had been his partner all those years ago had always had ambition.

He closed the door, got the spare chair from against the wall, and sat down. Marianne kept the spare chair just for him. It had no arms, so there were no issues about whether or not he'd fit.

Marianne was waiting for him to get settled. He got settled. It bought him a little time.

"Well?" she said finally.

Howard gave her a long look and then shrugged. "I don't know," he said. "It's hard to tell what's going on."

"Well, something must be going on," Marianne said. "This sort of thing doesn't happen naturally. Or maybe I mean habitually. For God's sake, Howard. Somebody's treating that body like a prize piece in 'Hide-the-Treasure.' There's got to be a reason for it."

"I was thinking maybe the only reason for it might be Gregor Demarkian," Howard said. "Maybe he attracts this sort of thing. People who want to see themselves on *American Justice* or *City Confidential* or one of those shows, so they do crazy stuff to make the case seem more interesting."

"You can't tell me you think it's not interesting," Marianne said. "You can't tell me you still think Chester Morton committed suicide."

"I still think that's what makes the most sense," Howard said. "And Demarkian doesn't think that's completely crazy, either. He said that one of the possible explanations would be that Chester Morton committed suicide someplace where he'd get somebody's attention, and then that somebody decided to get out from under. The psychology of it works, too. It wouldn't be crazy to think that people would be so traumatized by finding the body there that they wouldn't think to look into it any farther."

"You don't think it would be crazy to think that?"

"No, it wouldn't be," Howard insisted. "I mean, Marianne, for God's sake, it's just what we all did. We didn't ask Gregor Demarkian in here because we thought there was more to this case than Chester acting like the punk ass he was. We called him in because Charlene wouldn't shut up. And all we expected him to do was come on to the scene, declare the thing an obvious suicide, and get us out from under."

"But we're not out from under."

"No, Marianne. I know that."

"And there are things," Marianne said. "There's that stupid tattoo, for one thing. And then the body going missing from Feldman's and turning up in that goddamned trailer. Didn't your people search the trailer last night?"

"We sent somebody out to look, yeah," Howard said. "There wasn't anything there. And somebody would have seen something, anyway. You know what that place is like. It's more alive in the middle of the night than it is in the morning. Nobody could just waltz up there and drag a body into a trailer without being seen. Somebody would have noticed something."

"But nobody did notice anything."

"Not that they're telling us," Howard said. "But you know how that is. We'll keep asking. There may be at least one person in that place that doesn't hate cops on general principles. Or maybe it was one of them that did it. Maybe it was somebody from the trailer park that moved the body."

"And you don't think he'd be noticed, dragging the body into that trailer?"

"He'd be noticed, but nobody would tell us about it," Howard said. "They don't like to talk to us. You know that."

"I know that they don't think twice about running their mouths about their neighbors if they think it's going to cause trouble," Marianne said. "And you know that, too. They clam up about themselves, but they're more than happy to get the guy next door landed in jail. If they'd seen one of their own dragging a body into that trailer, you'd have heard about it."

"I didn't hear about it."

"I know."

"And the body was definitely in the trailer," Howard said. "I just saw it, sitting up in an armchair stark naked and going a little to seed after all this time. Gregor Demarkian thinks I put it there."

"What?"

"Gregor Demarkian thinks I put it there," Howard repeated. "He won't come out and say it in so many words, but that's what he thinks. He thinks I'm trying to avoid having the state do an autopsy."

"Well," Marianne said.

"Yeah, well," Howard said. "But Christ Almighty, Marianne, if that's what I wanted I could get it done without dragging the body all over hell and gone. Whoever's doing that has got to be some kind of idiot. Maybe he's an alien and he has a teleportation device. At least that would explain how somebody got that body into that trailer without anybody noticing anything. I think I'm going to have a migraine."

"Well," Marianne said again.

Howard looked away from her. There were two windows in the far wall. They looked out on West Main Street.

"Well," Marianne said again.

"Don't tell me," Howard said. "It was a bad idea to bring Gregor Demarkian into this case. I've already come to that conclusion. But damn it, Marianne. There's absolutely no reason why things should be turning out like this."

FIVE

1

Gregor Demarkian did not spend all night standing watch by the body of Chester Morton — although he thought about it, and he probably would have done it, if he hadn't been able to hear Bennis's voice in his head telling him what an idiot he was. Instead, he went back to his hotel room, set up his laptop, and started running the only kind of searches he knew how to run that might be some help in finding a missing person.

It was Tony Bolero he sent to keep watch over the body of Chester Morton, and he was shocked nearly speechless when he got no interference from Howard Androcoelho.

"They must be embarrassed," he told Tony. "If I was in Howard Androcoelho's shoes, I'd have screamed bloody murder if anybody had suggested anything like that. Never mind. Go. Sit. I'll get a cab over there in the morning, and then I'm meeting Ferris Cole. I can't imagine that a new autopsy is going to give us any more information than we already have, but by now I want it done just because somebody doesn't."

Tony had made noncommittal grunting noises and gone off, and Gregor had sat down to his computer again. Then he had taken out his cell phone and called Bennis. Sometimes, these days, he felt as if he'd entered an old-fashioned science fiction movie.

"There's no change," Bennis said, when he was finally able to make her sit down and talk. "Unless you count a request as change."

"What request?"

"Well, we finally got his dates straightened out," Bennis said. "He is about to be a hundred, but not the day after tomorrow, the way we originally thought. It's a week from tomorrow. He wanted to know if you'd be finished with the case by a week from tomorrow."

"If I'm not, I'll finish it myself by shooting half the people I've met here," Gregor said. "He wants me to be there on his birthday?"

"He wants a cake. Lida and Angela are arguing about who gets to bake it. I figure that's preliminary to whoever wins arguing with Hannah and Sheila about who gets to bake it. But you get the picture."

"He wants a birthday party."

"A hundredth birthday party, yes."

"Even if he's still in the hospital?"

"The impression I got was especially if he's still in the hospital. But that's been it. He wants a birthday party. But he actually seems fairly well, Gregor, considering. I mean, he's very old, and he's very frail, but he's — himself. If you know what I mean."

"I know what you mean, yes. All right. I'll make a point of being back for his birthday, if not earlier. Whether I've finished the case or not."

"Really?"

"Really."

"That's not like you," Bennis said. "You like to finish things."

"I'm getting old," Gregor said. "I'm running out of patience. And besides. There's nothing to say that I can't come down there for the birthday and then come back up, if I have to. I like Tony Bolero. He does what I tell him to. He's a good listener. And you're paying for him."

"Right."

"I'm going to go back to playing with this computer. I'll talk to you later."

Gregor put the phone down next to the laptop and thought that this was one of the very odd things about his second marriage. In his first, he and Elizabeth never said good-bye to each other without saying, "I love you." He and Bennis never said, "I love you," or barely ever. And yet, Gregor was as sure that Bennis loved him as he had been that Elizabeth had. And he was sure that he loved Bennis as much as he had Elizabeth. Maybe that was age, too, along with the lack of patience. He'd only been half kidding when he'd told Bennis he was getting old.

He applied himself to the laptop. First, he did a Google search for anything and everything having to do with Chester Ray Morton. This time he got a "sponsored link" with a picture from some magazine somewhere. Apparently, the case was beginning to attract some media attention. Gregor wondered if they'd made the "Oddball" segment on Keith Olbermann's show yet. He checked out the magazine and found absolutely nothing he didn't know already.

He tried again, this time searching for "Chester Morton WY," as if Chester were a town in the mountains. He got a small flurry of hits, most of them the same hits he'd had before, but targetted to the parts of them that mentioned that Chester had always loved Wyoming. He tried the Wyoming Citizen's Crime Watch, and got nothing. He tried the New York Citizen's Crime Watch and got a long lead story about a woman who had robbed a bank wearing a burka. Except that nobody was sure it really was a woman. The burka covered too much.

Gregor got up and moved away from his laptop. He went to stand at the windows that looked out onto the parking lot. He pulled the curtains back and stared at the darkening evening, the lights going on in the town of Mattatuck, the cars in their parking spaces. At the edge of the parking lot, there were grass and trees and what looked like a dirt access road — except that it might not have been dirt. It might just have been dusty from lack of use.

If you eliminate the impossible, Sherlock Holmes used to say, whatever is left, no matter how improbable, must be the truth. Gregor had no idea if he was quoting that correctly. But he got the general idea, and the general idea was right. The problem was that everything in this case was improbable, and nothing was really impossible. What felt impossible were the really massive improbabilities — that body wandering all over creation like it was still ambulatory; the complete lack of anything like professional police work in a town that was large enough to qualify as a small city; the entire story of Chester Morton, which was half like a fairy tale and half like the kind of pulp novel that had been popular in the Forties.

One day, twelve years ago, Chester Morton had decided to leave. One day, a couple of weeks ago, Chester Morton had decided to come back and had brought with him a baby's skeleton in a yellow backpack. There was no rhyme or reason to it. None. Maybe, twelve years ago, he'd left town because he'd killed the baby. Maybe that was the baby Darvelle had said he'd wanted to buy. But, what baby? There was nothing in any of the material Howard Androcoelho had sent him to indicate that there was a baby that had gone missing at the same time Chester Morton had. There was nothing to indicate that a woman had gone missing around the same time, either.

Gregor walked back across the room to the door, then back again to the window. He leaned his forehead against the glass. He counted to ten. Nothing shook itself loose.

He opened his eyes again, and looked out.

And that was when he saw it.

Out on the access road, half hidden by the trees and the grass and the puddled darkness beyond the security lights, a car had come to a stop. The light from the headlights hung in the air for a while and then went out. The interior light went on and stayed on for longer than it had any right to. Then that light went out and another light went on in the interior, as if somebody were using a flashlight.

It didn't look right at all, and it didn't feel right.

And Gregor Demarkian didn't trust anything that happened in Mattatuck to be about anything but the Chester Morton case.

2

Gregor Demarkian didn't think for a moment about what he was doing until he got past the parking lot and into the grass. Then it occurred to him that he was behaving like an idiot. It had been years since he'd done any kind of field work, and even that had required him to spend time sitting in a car, not thrashing through the underbrush. He wasn't dressed for this. The slick soles of his wing-tip shoes kept threatening to slide out from underneath him. The landscape around him was too dark. The security lights in the parking lot were aimed inward, toward the hotel. The access road in front of him had no lights at all.

Whoever was in the car still had the flashlight going, though, and Gregor thought that was interesting. Batteries didn't have all that long to run before they conked out on you, and whoever was using these was behaving as if that didn't matter. Gregor tried to see what the person in the car was doing. The impression he got was that the person was . . . reading a book. But that made no sense.

After the tall grass, there was a stretch of marshy stuff and brush, and then some small trees. Gregor made himself move slowly. He didn't want to be heard, but mostly he didn't want to fall. The closer he got, the more obvious it was that the person in the car was a woman, and that the woman was at least middle-aged, if not edging toward elderly. It wasn't anybody he recognized. It certainly wasn't Charlene Morton. Whatever could she be doing here sitting alone on an access road with her engine off in the middle of the night?

Suddenly, the woman's head went up. She looked around, from one of the car's windows to the next. Gregor stood very still, he wasn't sure why. He must not have stood still enough. The woman put a stiff plastic card into the book she was reading and then put the book down on the dashboard. Then she leaned over and got something out of the glove compartment.

What happened next happened so fast that Gregor was never able to remember it properly, never mind explain it to anybody else. One moment, he was standing still next to a weak tree, thinking he was entirely invisible. The next, the door of the car popped open, the woman inside jumped out, and there was the clear backfire of a bullet going off in the air. Less than a second later, the bullet hit the ground near his feet, and he jumped.

"Damn," he said.

"Who are you?" the woman said. "Come out of there. Come out where I can see you."

Gregor thought that if he really had been a mugger, or a crazed homicidal maniac combing the bushes for his next serial kill, this woman would never have made it off this access road alive. She was holding the gun as if it were a Popsicle stick.

"Come out of there," she said again. "Who are you? What do you want?"

Gregor swore under his breath, for real this time. "For God's sake, stop shooting that thing," he said, moving closer to her through what was still very tall grass. "You don't know what you're doing."

"Who are you?" the woman demanded again.

By now, Gregor was out on the access road proper. The woman had to be able to see that he was nearly as old as she was, and probably in far less good physical shape. She was squinting at him through the darkness.

"My name is Gregor Demarkian," Gregor said, "and —"

"Oh," the woman said, letting the gun drop to her side. "Oh, my God. You are Gregor Demarkian. I'm so sorry. I could have hurt you. I didn't mean to. It's just that I have to be so careful, I mean out here, you know, you can never tell who's going to come along, that's why I got this thing, but I've never actually used it before, so —"

"I could tell you'd never actually used it before."

"Oh, well. Actually. I did use it once. I took it to a firing range. You know. To see how it was. I fired it there."

"Did you hit anything?"

"I think I hit the floor. I hurt my wrist."

"Of course you did," Gregor said. He got closer to the car and looked inside. Even without any lights at all, it was obvious that the car was loaded down with stuff. Clothes were piled high in the backseat. Books were everywhere. "My God," Gregor said. "You're living in this car."

The woman was quiet for a long time. "Only temporarily," she said finally. "Only until the cold weather hits. I've got almost enough money to rent a place for the entire winter. I only need a couple of more weeks."

"A couple of more weeks," Gregor said. "You've got a job?"

"Of course I've got a job," the woman said. "I've got two of them. If I've got any luck, I'll have three for the fall term. I teach English."

"At a high school?"

"At Mattatuck–Harvey Community College," the woman said. "Also at Pelham University. That's a private place, down the road. It doesn't pay nearly so well."

"You're a college teacher and you can't afford to rent an apartment?"

"I'm an adjunct," the woman said. "That means I'm only part time. Except with teaching it isn't like part time in most places. They don't divide your hours by the hours for full time and give you that percentage of a full-time salary. I get paid forty-one hundred dollars to teach each course at Mattatuck–Harvey, and nineteen hundred to teach each course at Pelham —"

"That's what? A week? A month?"

"That's the *course*," the woman said. "The entire course."

"This Pelham University place pays you less than two thousand dollars to teach an entire course?" Gregor said. "Over, what is that, three months?"

"Fourteen weeks," the woman said. "Three classes a week of an hour each, plus office hours every week, plus whatever it takes to do prep and correcting. At Mattatuck–Harvey, it's sixteen weeks. It used to be all right, though, because I used to be able to teach three courses at Mattatuck–Harvey every term, and with the two at Pelham I'd just about make it. But there's a union at Mattatuck–Harvey, and they got a rule passed that nobody can teach more than two classes a term in the entire community college system, so I can't even drive out to Binghamton and teach there. So I'm making some accommodations."

"That's insane," Gregor said. "How do they ever get anybody to work for them? Are you the only — what did you call it? Adjunct?"

"Better than three quarters of all the teachers at Mattatuck–Harvey are adjuncts," the woman said. "And the percentage is higher at Pelham. And the reason why I do it is that it's the only job I could get. I've got a doctorate. I'm almost sixty. Put the combination together and you're not going to get hired full time at much of anything. All the people they've hired full time at Mattatuck–Harvey over the last ten years have been under forty."

The woman held out the hand with the gun in it, then dropped that hand to her side. Gregor swore he could see her blush, even in the darkness. "Sorry," she said. "I've never had any cause to take it out before. And it's a good coincidence you found me here, really, because I've been meaning to come and talk to you. My name is Penelope London. I was Chester Morton's English teacher at the time he disappeared."

Gregor thought about it. "London," he said. "That name's in my notes somewhere."

"Oh, it should be," Penny said. "When they actually bothered to start investigating Chester's disappearance they did get around to me. Howard Androcoelho and Marianne Glew came and interviewed me for nearly an hour. And Marianne took notes. I knew both of them, though, before that, because they'd both been at Mattatuck–Harvey for a while. That's what people do around here. If they go away to college, they don't come back. If they're going to stick around, they go to Mattatuck–Harvey."

Gregor looked at the woman standing there, and then the car, and then back at the lights in the parking lot of the hotel. He'd come through all that tall grass, and as far as he knew, there were snakes in it.

"Come on," he said. "You can give me a ride back to the hotel. Then we can go sit someplace and talk."

3

It took less time than Gregor thought it would to talk her into it, just the assurance that there was an entirely separate room, with nobody in it for the night, and nobody likely ever to sleep in the second of the big queen-sized beds.

"It seems a shame that the man has to spend the entire night sitting up with a corpse," Penny London said. "And what for? Because Howard Androcoelho can't get his act together. Howard's always a big fave with the Mattatuck–Harvey Taxpayers Association. They're the ones who don't want to pay for anything. They're the reason the police radios don't work for half the town."

"Excuse me?" Gregor said.

"Oh, I'm not making that up," Penny said. "Mattatuck's a huge place, really, considering just land mass, and there are dead areas for the radios in at least half of it. So we had a referendum a few months ago, to vote on getting a new system put in and a new service provider, but it was going to cost five million dollars, and that was that. I suppose none of them live out in the middle of nowhere where the radios wouldn't work if they were in trouble. I mean, for God's sake. Really."

Gregor let her go into Tony Bolero's room to shower and change. He heard the shower go on immediately, and when he did he called down to the restaurant and ordered takeout. He ordered a lot of takeout. He had no idea what Penny London liked to eat. She could be a vegetarian. She was a middle-aged professional woman with a doctorate. She could even be a vegan. He ordered four entrees — everything from the vegetarian stir-fry to a pair of very thick steaks — and slipped out to pick them up. This kind of thing was easier to do in places that had real room service.

When he got back to the room with his bags of food, the room next door was quiet. Penny London had finished taking her shower. Gregor knocked on the connecting door.

"Are you all right for company? Come on in. I brought us some dinner."

"Oh," Penny London said, from behind

the door. Then the door opened and she stuck her head into Gregor's room. Her hair was wet and sleeked back. She was wearing a pair of loose cotton pants and a sweatshirt. "Oh," she said again, looking at the food Gregor was spreading out on the table near the windows. "You know, I'm really not poor. I do eat."

"You're living in your car, and dinner is on me. Come on in and have something and tell me about Chester Morton in your English class."

"Just a minute." Penny London disappeared for a second. When she came back, she was holding a manila file folder. She left the connecting door open and came in to sit at the table in front of the food. "This is incredible," she said. "Do you normally eat this much?"

"I didn't know what you liked. I like steak, so I got two of those, in case you wanted one. Is that folder about Chester Morton?"

"I do want a steak," Penny London said. She sat down in front of the food, pulled a styrofoam box toward her and then fished a set of plastic tableware out of the bag Gregor had left at the center of the table. "This folder is definitely about Chester Morton," she said. "Except 'about' may not be the right term. It *belongs* to Chester

Morton, sort of. It's things he wrote in my class and never picked up."

Penny waved the folder in the air. Gregor took it. Then he sat down in front of the food and got a steak for himself.

"So this is what?" he asked. "English papers? Compare and contrast Jane Austen's *Emma* with Erica Jong's *Fear of Flying?*"

"Very good," Penny London said. "But nobody takes that kind of English course these days, at least not in a community college. We don't read Jane Austen or anything else except essays that are supposed to be models for student writing. They're boring as hell, mostly. We had a pretty good textbook Chester's year, though. *Current Issues and Enduring Questions.* It even had something by Rush Limbaugh. That shut up the ones you always get telling you how they're not going to be brainwashed by liberal academia."

"Is that what you do? Brainwash students for liberal academia?"

"Hell, I wish they had brains to wash," Penny London said. "But that folder you've got there is interesting. And I've been holding on to it for twelve years."

"And it's what?"

"It's papers, some of it, but most of it is

the fifteen-minute writing exercise we do at the beginning of every class. Come in, sit down, write three paragraphs in fifteen minutes on whatever topic I give you."

"And?"

"And," Penny London said, "that is the first interesting thing. When Chester went missing, there was all this stuff in the paper — well, there was eventually. Charlene Morton had to kick and scream pretty hard to get anything done. But anyway, when they finally got around to it, there was some publicity, and part of it was all about how much Chester loved Wyoming and Montana and places like that — wide open spaces, big sky country, mountains, and wildlife."

"And?"

"And," Penny London said, "I think it's full of crap. I don't know. Maybe Charlene had lost touch after Chester moved out, although you wouldn't think it would be time enough. But by the time he was in my class, Chester wasn't interested in hunting and fishing and breathing the clean mountain air. Considering the tattoos and the piercings and the attitude, I'd think he hadn't been interested in anything like that for years."

"What was he interested in?"

"Urban everything," Penny London said

definitively. "And he spent a lot of time fantasizing about where he'd like to be, too. Los Angeles. Las Vegas. Lots of lights. Lots of urban grit. Lots of gambling."

"Gambling," Gregor said.

Penny London nodded. By then, she had calmly polished off a steak, a baked potato with butter, a pile of green beans, and most of the vegetarian stir-fry. She waved her fork at the folder Gregor was holding. "It's all in there," she said. "Just read through it for a while. Chester Morton loved to gamble. He wrote about it nearly all the time. Going out to Vegas was his big dream, going out there and breaking the bank, as he used to put it. He wasn't all that bright. Which is interesting, you know, because I've got his brother this term, and the brother is very bright. Kenny. And you'd guess that Charlene, lunatic that she is, has to be very bright herself. It's hard for a truly stupid woman to be that consistently bitchy."

"Oh, I don't know," Gregor said. "I've met a few. But is that it — that Chester Morton liked to gamble and that he wasn't likely to take off for a rural area? Was there something about his gambling? Was he in trouble?"

"With the gambling? I don't know," Penny said. "But the other thing has to do with the last night I saw him. I've looked at the reports, and I think it might be the last night anybody saw him. It was after class. Chester and Darvelle Haymes were both in that class, and so was this other kid who had a thing for Darvelle, named Kyle Holborn."

"For some reason, that name is vaguely familiar," Gregor said. "I don't know why."

"Well," Penny said reasonably, "if you got police reports about what happened when Chester was found, you probably saw his name. He's a police officer now. But at the time, you know, he was just a kid. And Chester and Darvelle were inseparable. Except that night —"

"It was a night class?"

"It started at seven. We don't usually make a big difference between day and night classes here. It's all one schedule. Anyway, Chester and Darvelle were inseparable, until that class. And then they ended up sitting on opposite sides of the classroom glaring at each other. It was so bad, I nearly threw one of them out just so I could get something done. But we got through class, and the students left, and I sat behind for a bit to get myself organized."

"Were you living in your car then, too?"

Penny gave him a look. "No," she said. "Twelve years ago, the union hadn't negotiated a contract that restricted adjuncts to only two courses in the system per term. I could afford an apartment all year round in those days. But here's the thing. I waited a couple of minutes. I got my tote bag packed up. Then I went downstairs to the Frasier Hall parking lot. Students aren't allowed to park there before five o'clock, but after five, it's fair game. And there the three of them were, Darvelle and Chester and Kyle. Darvelle was kind of hanging back. Chester and Kyle were fighting."

"Fist fighting?"

"Well, I don't know about Chester's fists," Penny London said, "but Kyle was using his. I stood there and watched while he pulled back his arm and hit Chester so hard in the jaw that Chester went down flat on the ground. If I'd had a cell phone then, I would have called security."

"Did Chester get up?"

"Oh, yes, he definitely got up. He took that bright yellow backpack of his and slammed it into the truck next to him hard enough to cause a dent. I saw the dent. I have to assume it was Kyle's truck or Darvelle's or even Chester's own, because as far as I know there was no trouble about the dent. It was too bad, too, because that truck was mint new and shiny black. It looked like something out of a rock video about the devil."

"Did you ever see it again?"

"The truck?" Penny asked. "No, not that I remember. But I wasn't really looking for it."

"And you never saw Chester again?"

"No, never."

"How about Darvelle and this Kyle person?"

"Oh, they were in class every week. Darvelle always got A's in everything she took. She pushed herself. I think Kyle just stuck with it because of her. It was that kind of a relationship. It still is, as far as I know. I see them around town together quite a lot. I asked some people I know, and they don't seem to be married, but — well, you know. They always seem to be together."

"Interesting," Gregor said.

Penny London opened one of the smaller styrofoam boxes and discovered the first of the three desserts Gregor had brought in. She opened the other two and then took the big piece of chocolate cake.

"Do you always eat like this?" she asked him. "I'm surprised you're not the size of Howard Androcoelho."

SIX

1

Haydee Michaelman had to admit it. She had come to rely on Kenny Morton showing up out of the blue whenever she needed a ride, and she got a little depressed when she was hoping to find him and he wasn't there. This was a very bad sign. She'd only met him at the very start of this term, and she'd only talked to him face-to-face just after Labor Day. It wasn't all that long from then to now. Any minute now, she'd start mooning around, unable to concentrate on anything that was really important. She'd seen it happen too many time to too many girls. They started out with ambition. They started out with plans. They started out with a clear idea of who they wanted to be when they hit thirty.

Then they got pregnant.

Haydee rolled over in the unfamiliar bed with its massive wads of quilts and pillows and told herself not to be stupid. She and Kenny hadn't even been out on a date yet, never mind done it. She wasn't going to get pregnant just because she let some boy keep her out of the rain when she didn't have an umbrella.

Haydee sat up and looked around. The door to the bedroom was open, and she could hear the sound of somebody messing around in a kitchen from the other end of the trailer. Trailers, Haydee thought, were all alike. In fact, the trailers in this particular park were identical. Somebody must mass produce trailers somewhere, tooling them up on a conveyer belt, dumping them onto big flatbed trucks at the end of the line.

Haydee looked at her watch. It was only six. The light outside the window was only pale and promising, not full-bore morning.

Haydee got up from the bed and went to the door. She could see down the hall to where Desiree was cooking something on the tiny kitchen stove. The door to the other bedroom was shut tight.

"Dez?" Haydee said, moving through the hall toward the smell of coffee.

Desiree looked up. *"Shh,"* she said. "You don't want to wake my mother up."

Haydee went down the rest of the hall and through the living room and sat down on the built-in bench behind the kitchen table. All these trailers were, in fact, exactly alike. The bedrooms were all the same. The living rooms were all the same. There were the same built-in tables and built-in benches.

Desiree was making bacon. She kept turning it over and over and over in the frying pan, using a fork instead of a spatula.

"I didn't actually tell her you were staying here last night," Desiree said. "I mean, she was close to passed out anyway, and I didn't want to cause any trouble. She doesn't like you staying here."

"She doesn't like Mike coming over and busting up the place," Haydee said. "Mike didn't know where I went. Doesn't know where I am. You know."

"He could guess," Desiree said reasonably. "You always come over here, Haydee. He knows that. I'm surprised he didn't land in our laps in the middle of the night. He was mad enough yesterday afternoon. Do you think he found your money?"

"Nope," Haydee said. "He can't find my money. It isn't around anymore."

"You mean you spent it? Did you buy a car?"

"I didn't spend it and I didn't buy a car, because I don't have enough money to buy a car yet. I put it in the credit union."

"The Mattatuck–Harvey Credit Union? That one? I don't get it. Did you get a credit card?"

"No," Haydee said. She took a strip of bacon from the paper plate where Desiree was letting them pile up. She took one of the ones that had been there the longest, so that it had the least grease. "As it turns out," she said, "a credit union is sort of the same thing as a bank, except that it's supposed to be owned by the people who have accounts there instead of some big corporation. Okay, I'm not sure I get that quite yet. But what it comes down to is that you can have an account there and they don't charge you money the way a regular bank does. So I can keep my money there where Mike can't get it and it doesn't cost me anything. Kenny told me about it."

"Kenny," Desiree said. Then she giggled. "Does he have a place to go? Because I really can't see you doing it over there with Mike hanging around to watch."

"We're not doing it," Haydee said. "We're not even sort of doing it. He hasn't even kissed me good-bye. He told me about the credit union, though, and he took me over there, and now when I get paid at the Quik-Go I can walk to the credit union and deposit the check, and there won't be any money around for Mike to find."

"Yeah, well," Desiree said. "You've got to worry about that, don't you? He's going to beat you to a pulp someday if he can't find it. I still can't believe you found someplace to hide it where he wouldn't look."

"Don't you know where I hid it?"

"No, I don't. And maybe you shouldn't tell me. Maybe you're going to want to hide money there again. I don't do too well when people are threatening me."

"I hid it over in the ghost trailer."

"What?"

"Oh, I didn't go all the way in," Haydee said. "I mean, I did, sort of. I went through the door and into the vestibule, you know, but I didn't go any farther than that. The place was full of dust and it smelled weird. I just put the money in a little roll in a space where there was a crack in the wall of the front closet. There were bugs there, but I didn't see why I should mind. It's not like bugs eat money."

"But I thought that trailer was locked."

"Please," Haydee said. "Anybody could get past one of these locks. And Mike wasn't going to go over there and look, because he thinks the place is haunted. Really haunted. The man's an idiot."

"Does your mother think it's haunted, too?"

Haydee shrugged. "I have no idea. She hates the place. She wasn't going to go looking around in it anymore than Mike was. Which is odd, now that I come to think of it."

"Why?" Desiree asked. "I wouldn't want to go into that thing. Maybe the ghost of Chester Morton is in there somewhere, just waiting to pounce on the first person who walks in."

"And do what?" Haydee said. "Don't be ridiculous. And Chester Morton didn't die there anyway. He didn't die twelve years ago at all. But, you know, it's like I said. It's a little strange."

"What is?"

"The way my mother is with that trailer," Haydee said. "I was thinking about it the other day, because Kenny said something to me about it. That Demarkian person is going around talking to everybody who had anything at all to do with Chester Morton when he disappeared. Kenny was saying we should expect he'd want to talk to us, because, you know, we lived right next door. But I was thinking about it. It was more than that. He used to come over to our trailer, and my mother used to go over to his. I remember it."

"How can you remember it? You must have been two."

"I was six," Haydee said. "And I do remember it. But then, you know, when the cops came looking for Chester Morton there was that one who called DCS and then I went into foster care for a while. I remember that, too."

"I remember all the times I've been in foster care," Desiree said. "That was a load of frigging crud. I can't believe they think that helps people."

"Yeah, well, whatever. There it is. I'd better go back to my place and have a shower. I've got two classes and work. Sometimes I think I'm going to get so tired, I'm going to fall over."

"What if Mike is back there waiting for you? Maybe you could take your shower here. If you were quiet, you know what I mean."

"I need clean clothes," Haydee said, yawning. "Besides, I don't think it's going to matter. I saw them go out after I came over here. They actually looked pretty happy. Mike was singing."

"That must have been interesting."

"It was. Anyway, they must have gotten some money from someplace, because they went out. Maybe Mike robbed a liquor store. That would be hysterical. But my money's in the credit union, and Mike can't get at it, and that's all I really care."

2

Darvelle Haymes knew women who liked to say, "I told you so," and sometimes she was one of them, but this was not one of those times. "I told you so" was only fun if you were saying it about somebody else. You told Sheila she'd get fat if she kept eating those doughnuts and she got fat? I told you so! You told your mother-in-law that she'd end in a car wreck if she kept running the stop sign at that intersection? I told you so! You told your boyfriend that the coming of this Gregor Demarkian was going to be a disaster for the both of you? I told you — wait. No, it wasn't fun anymore. It wasn't even funny.

Darvelle propped herself up on one elbow and looked down at Kyle sleeping on the other side of the bed. He was dead to the world, and she had no idea how. If she had rotating shifts like that, morning one week, afternoons the next week, evenings the week after that, she'd be losing her mind. She'd need pills just to sleep at all. Kyle had sex, then he rolled over and crashed, and he never moved until the alarm went off.

Darvelle got the alarm clock from the bedside table and turned the alarm off before it could ring. She wasn't going to get back to sleep no matter what she did, and she had a full day ahead of her.

Or she didn't. She went into the bathroom, shut the door behind her, and turned on the shower. Last night, two of her clients had called to cancel their appointments for today. She still had three more that she knew of, but the trend was unsettling. Maybe there got to be a point where murders were not interesting but only frightening, or where knowing a potential murderer — what?

She stepped under the showerhead and closed her eyes. Did anybody really think she might have murdered Chester Morton? And then what? Hauled his body all over Mattatuck? That great big body, that lardass body, that — but that was ridiculous. She didn't have the upper body strength to throw Chester Morton's corpse over that billboard, and anybody who looked at her had to know that. And what was she supposed to have done at the trailer park? Driven her car in there, dragged Chester's body out of the trunk or the backseat, dragged it some more into the trailer — her head hurt just thinking about it. She was pretty sure people were suspecting her nonetheless.

She got her hair washed and stepped out. The bathroom was steamed up. The effect was uncomfortable. It was getting on into September, but it was not that hot.

She went back into the bedroom for some underwear and a robe, and found that Kyle was up, up and moving around somewhere in the house. She put on the underwear and the robe and wandered out into the kitchen.

"Hey," she said. "What are you doing?"

"I'm making us breakfast. You got up."

"I thought you didn't have to. I thought you didn't work until afternoon or something today."

"I go in at three. I'm awake."

Darvelle sat down at the kitchen table. "Well?" she said.

Kyle was making an omelet. It had mushrooms and cheese in it. Darvelle could see the scraps on the cutting board next to the sink.

"Well?" she said again.

"If you want to start saying, 'I told you so,' I suppose you've got the right," Kyle said. "This is getting to be a bigger mess by the minute."

"We didn't kill anybody," Darvelle said. "I

don't care what kind of a mess this is, it can't be that kind of a mess."

"But it can," Kyle said. "You've got no idea. It doesn't matter if we didn't kill anybody. It only matters if they think we did."

"And do they think we did?"

"I don't think so. I think if they did, they'd have gotten me out of the station by now. Hell, I don't even know if they suspect us, one way or the other."

"Do they suspect me?"

"Well, you're on Howard's hot list," Kyle said. "I don't know about Gregor Demarkian. He's calling in the state, if I haven't told you that already. There's a rumor around that he's been in contact with the FBI."

"Charlene talked to the FBI," Darvelle said. "It didn't seem to make much difference."

"Charlene was just the pain in the ass mother of a missing person with a background that sounded halfway to organized crime," Kyle said. "Gregor Demarkian used to work there. They're going to take him seriously."

"Yes, I know," Darvelle said, "but I still come back to the same thing. We didn't kill anybody. We didn't. We had no reason to kill anybody. Why would they think of us at all."

Kyle picked up the frying pan and slammed it down again, hard, against the top of the stove.

"Because people kill other people for a lot less reason than you'd think," he said, finally angry. "Because you just don't get it. A prosecutor doesn't even have to prove motive at a trial. Motive is irrelevant. People kill other people over a pair of shoes, or because she dissed her husband one too many times, or because it's Tuesday. It doesn't matter if we had no reason, even if we had no reason. And as things stand, I can think of a really good one."

Darvelle put her face in her hands. "The baby."

"Bingo."

"But it wasn't my baby," Darvelle said. "I had nothing to do with it. He told me we were going to buy a baby and I told him to pack up and get lost. I didn't want any part of it. I didn't help him buy it. And you had nothing to do with it at all. For God's sake, Kyle, what else were we supposed to do? What else would anybody have done in that situation?"

"Call the cops, that would be one thing."

"But we couldn't have done that, and you

know it. You know what Chester was like. It would have been a matter of he said, we said, and we'd have gotten screwed, because you know what he'd have said. He'd have said that we were in on it. And even if we'd gotten it straightened out eventually, there'd have been a nice long meantime when they'd all have run around believing him, because he was a Morton and we were just trailer trash."

"You were just trailer trash," Kyle said. "I grew up in a split-level in Kiratonic."

"Thanks a lot."

Kyle was finished with the omelet. He got a knife out of the drawer next to the stove and cut it in half in the pan. Then he got the spatula and put one half of the thing on a plate. The house was suddenly much too quiet.

"There's the other thing, of course," Kyle said. "There's the fight in the parking lot."

"It wasn't much of a fight. Chester made a remark and you decked him. He must have been flying higher than Venus that night."

"I knocked him over. He fell on his back."

"So?"

"Maybe he had the baby in the backpack then," Kyle said. "Maybe that's what killed it. Maybe I knocked him over, and he fell on it, and that cracked its skull."

Darvelle got up off the chair she'd been sitting in and marched back toward the bedroom.

"If that baby was in that backpack that last night in Miss London's class, it was dead already. If it hadn't been, it would have made a noise. It would have made a lot of noise."

Darvelle was sure this was true, but she didn't want to talk to Kyle anymore anyway. She didn't want to talk to anyone.

3

If there was one thing Shpetim Kika was sure of, it was that somebody had to take this seriously, and nobody was. The problem had kept him up all night. Part of it was that he didn't know what to do next. Most of it was a slow burning fury at all the members of the Mattatuck Police Department. Shpetim Kika was a law-abiding man. Since coming to America, he had never once entertained the idea that the local police were incompetents, or fools, or corrupt to the core. That was the kind of problem you had back in Albania, before the Communists left, because all the Communists could do was to produce incompetents and fools and thieves. This was

America. In America, the policeman was your friend.

Shpetim got up at five o'clock in the morning — sort of. What he really did was decide there was no point lying there staring at the ceiling any longer, especially not when Lora was sound asleep beside him, and snoring. He got up and went to his kitchen. He made the first of several pots of coffee. He sat at the kitchen table and tried to think it out.

The most promising possibility — the one he wanted to be true — was that the young police officer he had talked to had been the wrong police officer to talk to. Maybe there was somebody assigned to the case he was supposed to direct his questions to, and instead he had spoken to a desk clerk who didn't know anything about what was going on. The probability of this possibility was a weak one, Shpetim had to admit. The police officer he had talked to yesterday had been one of the same two who had come out to the construction site in a patrol car the night the skeleton of the baby had been found. Surely he had to know something about the case. Maybe it was the partner Shpetim should have talked to. Shpetim hadn't seen the partner anywhere in the station when he went in.

Could it really be this hard to find the right person to talk to when you had information about a crime? On television, it looked easy. You walked into the police station and told the first person you met that you had information on the homicidal clown case. You were whisked away to an interrogation room and everything you said was taken down on a yellow legal pad.

The next possibility — and the one Shpetim thought was most likely — was that the police wanted to be competent and helpful, but that they were under too much pressure to "do something" about the whole Chester Morton mess. Shpetim Kika had met Charlene Morton on a couple of occasions. He wouldn't be surprised to find that she'd intimidated the entire police department. He wouldn't be surprised to find that she had intimidated the entire United States Congress. That's what you needed when you had a problem with officialdom — not a lawyer, not the media, but one of these women who was used to getting her own way and deaf to any arguments to the contrary. They were always mothers, too, those women. It was as if the pain of childbirth altered something in their brains. Shpetim had known a few of those women in his life. He had an uncomfortable feeling that his Lora might be one of them.

The last possibility was, of course, that the police were corrupt, that they had been bribed, that there was a secret baby-killing conspiracy going on that was being run out of the basement of central station. This seemed silly, to say the least. Shpetim couldn't imagine Howard Androcoelho running a conspiracy of any kind. Babies had to come from somewhere. Shpetim was pretty sure that if babies were going missing all the time, no conspiracy would be wide enough to keep it out of the local media. He watched too much television, that was the problem. He always thought of things as they would work out on one of the various versions of *Law & Order.*

The other question was what to do about all this. He had already gone to the police. He wouldn't know how to go to the media. There was only one thing left for him to do, and he wasn't sure how to go about that, either.

He went to Nderi's bedroom, turned on the overhead light, and waited. Nderi couldn't sleep in light. He had to have darkness, or he came right awake. This could be very useful.

Nderi turned over in bed. "What?" he said.

"Come to the kitchen," Shpetim said.

"There's something we have to do."

"If this has something to do with the wedding, I'm going to knock you over the head."

Shpetim went back to the kitchen and sat down. There were big pads of paper in one of the drawers near the refrigerator. He got up and got one, then got a pen from the collection in the pencil cup next to the microwave. He sat down again and tried to think. It was important to go about this rationally. You had to know what you wanted to say, but you also had to know what order you wanted to say it in. Things didn't make sense when they were out of order. When things didn't make sense, people didn't take you seriously.

By the time Nderi came into the kitchen, Shpetim had two full pages of legal pad filled up with writing. He had all his points numbered. He had a couple of them starred. Nderi looked down at the pad with all the writing on it when he came into the kitchen. Then he went to the coffeepot on the counter and poured himself some.

"Well," he said, "what is it that couldn't wait until six-thirty?"

"I need you to come with me to the Howard Johnson," Shpetim said. "I need you to go with me to see this Gregor Demarkian."

"At ten minutes after six."

"Right away. Before he gets up and goes about his business for the day. If we wait for that, we won't know where to find him."

"If you don't wait until he's up, he'll probably throw you out on your ear. And what about the project? If we're both chasing Gregor Demarkian, who'll run the crews this morning?"

Shpetim shrugged this away. "Andor can take over for a hour. He won't kill anybody. But a baby is dead. A baby has to be dead because there was that skeleton. You don't agree."

"Of course I agree."

"And something has to have happened to the baby, because the skull was cracked," Shpetim said. "I saw it as clearly as you did. Cracked right down the side. And yes, I know, you told me. That could have happened after the baby died. But the baby died. And somebody put its body somewhere for the skin to fall off the bones, and then he put the bones in that backpack. And somebody has to do something about that."

"I know they do," Nderi said patiently, "but that person doesn't necessarily have to be you. If I thought you really knew anything, it would be different, but we told the police all we knew and it wasn't much. The thing just showed up at the site."

"We didn't tell them everything we knew," Shpetim said "We didn't tell them the things we thought were obvious. When something is obvious, you expect everybody to see it, just the way you do. But they don't see it. Or I can't see any evidence that they've seen it."

"Seen what?"

"Two things," Shpetim said. "First is the timing. The backpack has to have been put there just the night before, and no earlier, because if it had been there even an extra day, we would have found it earlier."

"I don't think that's something they don't know and we do," Nderi said. "We came right out and told them that. Twice. That isn't something new."

"Yes, yes," Shpetim said. "But then there's the new. I really mean new. The backpack was new and so was everything else in it."

"I don't see what you're getting at."

Shpetim tapped his fingers on the table. "All along, everything we've heard, Chester Morton always carried a bright yellow backpack. The backpack was the only thing that disappeared when he did. The baby's skeleton is found in the bright yellow backpack, there was a baby or a pregnancy or something in the Chester Morton case, the backpack must be Chester Morton's and so it turns out there really was a baby. But, Nderi, that can't be true."

"Why not?"

"Because," Shpetim said, "the backpack was new. Brand new. That wasn't something Chester Morton had had for twelve years. It wasn't something he had had for twelve days. There were smudges on it because it had been in the dirt all day, but anyplace you could see the canvas was bright, bright yellow. Brand new. And that wasn't the only thing that was brand new."

"It wasn't?"

"The books," Shpetim said. "There were the books. The ones you had, too, when you went to Mattatuck–Harvey. *Current Issues and Enduring Questions. The Everyday Writer.* They were there, in the backpack. And they were new."

"Can you really tell if a book is new just by looking at it?"

"There were no creases in the cover. There were no stains. Nothing was bent back or — or even rifled. It looked like they'd never been opened."

"You can't really know that."

"Yes, I can," Shpetim said. "I really can. And if I'm wrong, it will only take a moment or two to prove it. They only have to go look at the backpack again. But nobody is looking at the backpack. Nobody is paying any attention to it. It isn't the baby they're investigating. It's the death of Chester Morton. So I think we should tell someone, and the someone I think we should tell is Gregor Demarkian."

"Just get in the truck and go tell Gregor Demarkian."

"Yes," Shpetim said. "Right now. Before it gets away from us."

SEVEN

1

For Gregor Demarkian, the really odd thing about Shpetim Kika was not that he'd arrived at Gregor's hotel room at a quarter to seven in the morning, unannounced and apparently knowing the way and room number without having to ask at the desk. By now, that kind of thing was beginning to seem par for the course in Mattatuck. Everybody knew everybody. Everybody knew everything. And everybody went barging around into other people's private spaces without thinking twice.

What got to Gregor about Shpetim Kika was how much he looked like Fr. Tibor Kasparian, and how much he sounded like him, too. That was odd because Gregor had just gotten off the phone with Tibor, knowing he'd already be at the Ararat and hoping to get more detailed information about what was happening with old George.

"No, Krekor," Tibor had said. "Bennis is not holding out on you. Nobody is holding out on you. There is nothing to tell. Yorgi is resting. He's comfortable. He turns down a lot of the pain medication, I think because he wants to be clear. He is not getting worse. He is not getting better. They are afraid to release him from the hospital. And that is all."

Gregor didn't think that really was all, but he did think it might be all they knew. He wanted to understand what was going on with that. He didn't know how to try. It was easier investigating crime. Nobody was trying to spare your feelings with that.

With his son standing beside him, Shpetim Kika sat on the chair next to the desk holding a hat in his hand. It was an ancient, battered hat, and Gregor had the impression that he didn't wear it often. The suit looked a little more lived-in, but Gregor was sure it was something that came out only on "Occasions." He wasn't used to being an Occasion all by himself.

The son was wearing work clothes. He looked too embarrassed to breathe.

"So," Shpetim Kika was saying, "you see what I am trying to say. It is a baby that is dead, yes? There is the tiny skeleton. I saw it myself. The skeleton's skull had a crack in it, a crack all along one side. Somebody cracked a long break in the skull. Something bad must have happened to the baby. Even if the crack in the skull didn't happen until after the baby died, the baby still died. It's important to know who the baby was and how it died. Am I right?"

"I think so," Gregor said.

"I have been trying to tell Nderi here," Shpetim said. "You can't let a thing like this go. It isn't right. You do not just let babies die and throw their skeletons away like trash. And then there is the thing that the skeleton was in a place I am responsible for. I do not want it being said in Mattatuck that the Albanians are murderers."

"They're not going to say the Albanians are anything," Nderi said. "They say that kind of thing about the Hispanics, but not about us. I don't think there are enough of us."

"Albania is a very messed up country," Shpetim said. "It has many political problems. It has not much money. But Albanians are good people."

"Pop, if you keep this up, you're going to start singing —"

"Albanians are good people," Shpetim said. He sounded positive.

Gregor was seated on the edge of the bed.

He was having a hard time clearing his head. He'd gotten to bed fairly late. He'd gotten up very early. He'd showered and dressed and talked to Tibor. He still hadn't had any coffee. His head was full of cotton wool.

"Let me see if I've got this straight," he said. "You dug up the backpack on this construction site of yours —"

"Yes. No. I did not dig it up myself. I was in the shed doing paperwork. My men dug it up. And Nderi was with me. He didn't dig it up."

"All right. Your men dug it up. And then what?"

"They called us over and we went," Shpetim said. "Nderi and I went across the site to where the men were all standing around in a circle. Nderi and I were talking about his engagement. He is engaged now, to a very fine Albanian girl, a Muslim. Her family was all killed by the Communists, but she is not what you would expect a girl to be living on her own. She has great modesty. And great sense."

"Is that what you said at the time?" Nderi demanded.

Shpetim waved him away. Gregor tried not to laugh.

"Let's get back to it," Gregor said. "You

walked over to where the men were standing. Where was the backpack? Was somebody holding it?"

"No, no," Shpetim said. "They had left it in the ground. They hadn't touched it."

"It was because it was famous," Nderi said. "We'd been hearing about that backpack for years. The bright yellow backpack. The only thing Chester Morton had on him when he disappeared. The only thing missing from his things. That kind of thing."

"Okay," Gregor said. "So they found the backpack and called you over, and then what?"

"The flap was partially open," Nderi said, "and somebody had pulled it back. With a stick, I think, not their hands."

"And the skeleton was right there," Shpetim said. "You could see it, with the crack in its skull. It was all right there to see. And the skeleton was white. Bright white, like it had been cleaned. Everything looked as if it had been cleaned."

"But it was lying on the ground," Gregor said. "Or in the ground. In a hole."

"It wasn't much of a hole," Nderi said. "It was —" He shrugged.

"Everything looked as if it had been cleaned," Shpetim insisted. "Or better than it had been cleaned. Like it was new. It was a bright yellow backpack, it was so bright, it could have been bought from the store the same day. It was blazing yellow. There were little pieces of dirt on it from being in the ground, but it wasn't dirty. And nothing inside it was dirty. There were books. *Current Issues and Enduring Questions,* that was one of them. And *The Everyday Writer.* I recognized them because Nderi had them when he was in school."

"For English Composition," Nderi said. "They're the textbooks for that course. Or they used to be, when I was in school, and that was about the same time Chester Morton was in school. I think somebody may have said it, that he was taking English Composition."

"Of course somebody said it," Shpetim said. "Everybody said it. Last seen in his English class. But, Mr. Demarkian. The books were new, too, just like the backpack. They were clean, white, and stiff. You could have sold them in a bookstore. They didn't look like they'd been carried around for even a day. They couldn't have been stuffed in a backpack with a skeleton for twelve years. And nothing could have rotted on them for twelve years."

"Well," Gregor said, "the official findings were that the skeleton hadn't been in the backpack. I mean, the body hadn't decomposed in the backpack. It had decomposed somewhere else and then the skeleton had been put in the backpack."

"Even without the skeleton," Shpetim said, "those books could not have been carried around. They were new. They were brand new. And the backpack also. And that is a problem. I think all the police, everyone, they are trying to solve the death of Chester Morton. They think the baby is part of the death of Chester Morton. What if it isn't? What if someone went out and bought all those things, bought them new, to make the baby look like it had something to do with Chester Morton, and now nobody is thinking about the baby because they are all thinking about Chester Morton."

"All right," Gregor said. "You mean you think the baby's skeleton has nothing to do with Chester Morton at all?"

"That's right," Shpetim said. "It is, I think, a — a frame."

"You think somebody is trying to frame the dead Chester Morton for the death of this baby?"

"Exactly," Shpetim said.

"I think that somebody must have brought that backpack to the construction site with ghosts," Nderi said. "That's what I can't get over. I heard on the news that the police think it was buried out there in the middle of the night, but that isn't possible. I mean, not without somebody seeing. We've got security cameras out there. We have to. People steal material and equipment. But I've looked at those tapes, and the police have, too, and there's nothing on them except the usual patrol cars checking up every once in a while to make sure nobody's doing something they shouldn't."

"Here, the police guard your property," Shpetim said. "In Albania, you have to worry they're going to take it."

"I thought you didn't want people to think that the Albanians were bad people," Nderi said.

"The Albanians are not bad people," Shpetim said. "Only their government is bad. Maybe you can come out to the site with us now, and we can show you. We can show you where the backpack was. We can even show you the security tapes. We have them on the computer."

Gregor blinked. "I've got to be at The Feldman Funeral Home at nine," he said. "And I need a taxi. The desk says that if you call a taxi it takes a while for him to get here. So —"

"We can take you to Feldman's," Nderi

said. "And you don't have to hang around watching hours of tapes if you don't want to. I can e-mail them to you and you can watch them on your own computer. It's better to have lots of copies anyway. That way, they won't all disappear."

"That's it, then," Shpetim stood up. "You'll come with us to the site, and you will look around, and then Nderi will take you to your appointment. I don't envy you. I don't like any appointment in a funeral home."

2

Gregor called Tony Bolero while he was being driven down to "the site," as the Kika men both called it. He found it hard to listen to a cell phone while he was being squished between the two men in the middle of the bench-like only seat of a pickup truck cab. He didn't even know they made trucks with bench seats anymore. It worried him to think that the truck might be as old as it looked. It had a logo on the side that read: MATTATUCK VALLEY CONSTRUCTION. Gregor supposed it sounded better than "Kika Construction," but he thought that any Armenian-American he knew would have gone with "Kika" and been done with it. The name was very important.

Tony Bolero had gotten some sleep, but not much. He'd had to settle for the off hours when the man from Feldman's had been willing to stay awake.

"I checked as soon as I woke up," he told Gregor. "The body is still there. There's nothing wrong with it that I can see. Nobody has lopped off a foot, or anything like that."

"You had any visitors last night? Anybody try to get in to see it?"

"Nobody came down here at all except the guys from the funeral home. The guy who runs it is a real nervous Nellie. If he wrung his hands one more time, I was going to offer to chop them off for him."

"Probably not a good idea, considering," Gregor said. "I'm going to check this place out and come over to you. One of the people here is going to give me a ride. Don't leave the body, even to go to the bathroom."

"I'll get nervous Nellie to watch if I have to use the john. Don't worry about me, Mr. Demarkian. I have your back."

Gregor shut the cell phone and stared at it a little. Nervous Nellie. Use the john. Got your back. Why was it that so many people, faced with an actual detective, started to sound like they were speaking dialogue from a Mickey Spillane novel.

The truck was turning in to what Gregor supposed must be the back end of the Mattatuck–Harvey Community College campus. He could see the rising girders of the new tech building as they drove. As they got closer, he could see the site itself. And that was interesting.

"Huh," he said, moving forward in his seat to get a better look.

"I wouldn't do that, Mr. Demarkian," Nderi Kika said. "If the truck stops quickly, you'll go right through the windshield. You don't have a seat belt."

"Oh." Gregor sat back.

"Seat belts," Shpetim Kika said. "Stupid things. Are we riding in a jet plane? No. Are we driving in some little car that could be run over by the first delivery van it gets next to? No. I do not need seat belts."

"It's against the law not to wear your seat belt if you're traveling in the front seat of a vehicle," Nderi recited, sounding resigned.

Shpetim flipped his right hand into the air. "That's what I think of the law," he said. "What kind of law is that? It's Communism, that's what it is. Did I come all the way here from Albania just to live under the laws of Communism?"

The truck came to a stop near a small shed whose roof barely reached as high as the truck's. Nderi gave Gregor a look.

"My father," he said, "got five tickets for not wearing his seat belt last month alone. Cost him nearly three hundred dollars."

"Communism," Shpetim said again.

Then he popped the driver's side door and got out. Nderi got out the other side, and waited for Gregor to follow.

It was an interesting place, the construction site. There was a wide area of raw ground, not so much dug up and trampled over again and again. There was the building itself, which was larger than Gregor had expected it would be. There was a small stand of trees way to the back, so far back that Gregor wondered if the trees were part of the site at all.

"So," he said. "You found the backpack, where? In those trees?"

"No," Nderi said. "If the backpack had been in those trees, we would never have found it. Well, maybe not never. But it would have been days. The trees are technically part of the site, but they're not really part of the site, if you know what I mean."

"No," Gregor said.

"We were given a specified area to work in," Nderi said, "and that included that little stand of trees. But they're just a cushion. We're not doing anything over there. We're just leaving them alone."

"So where did you find the backpack?"

"Over here," Nderi said.

He started walking off over the rough ground. Gregor and Shpetim followed him. They got closer and closer to the building itself, then, just as they were about to run into it, veered off a little to the right. There were gigantic concrete tubes stacked in pyramids, idle pieces of construction equipment with tarps thrown over them, big square stacks of concrete block. Nderi stopped in the middle of it all and pointed at the ground.

"Right there," he said. "You can see the depression in the ground. It was right there."

Gregor looked to where Nderi was pointing. It took him a while to find the depression, but it was there. It did not amount to much.

"That's a very shallow hole," he said.

"That isn't a hole at all," Nderi said. "I'm sorry, Mr. Demarkian. Maybe I'm stupid. And I know I haven't trained as a detective. But I can't believe anybody thought he was going to hide something in that. It's a little dent in the ground that somebody threw some dirt on top of. We'd have discovered it first thing in the morning except we were working on the other side most of the day."

Gregor got down on his haunches. It had been a couple of weeks, and anything could happen in a couple of weeks, but he didn't think anybody had done any digging here. It was more like somebody had scuffed at the ground with a shoe or a boot, gotten some dirt out of the way, then dumped the backpack and covered it — he stopped.

"Was the backpack completely covered?" he said, standing up.

"You'd have to ask Andor to be completely sure," Nderi said. "That's Andor Kulla. He's one of the crew. He was the one who found it. He was over here digging a run off, I think. We were having water problems when it rained. Anyway, he's the one who actually found it."

"I'd like to know if it was covered," Gregor said. "And if it was covered, what it was covered with. I don't suppose you have pictures of this, do you?"

"No, but the police took pictures," Nderi said. "They took lots of them."

"All right," Gregor said. "I'll see if those are in my file. Where are your security cameras?"

Nderi pointed to four places in a semicircle around the site. Gregor found them. They were closer than he had expected them to be. One of them was pointed straight at the place where he stood.

"They were working the day you found the backpack?"

"Yes," Nderi said. "And they were working the night before, which is more to the point. Look around, Mr. Demarkian. See for yourself. If our men were working over there, on the other end of the building, and going back and forth to the shed every once in a while, nobody on earth could have been here hiding a backpack in the ground. If he was a stranger, we'd have noticed him and chased him off. We're constantly having to do that. If he was one of us — well, somebody would have noticed he was where he wasn't supposed to be for work and asked him about it. But I can't see he was one of us."

"Why would one of us do such a thing?" Shpetim asked. "What do we have to do with this Chester Morton? And as for the baby. We would never have killed a baby. We have babies that die, but we don't crack their skulls open. And we bury our dead."

Gregor looked around again. The construction site remained open and flat. There were no real hiding places here. He looked back at the cameras.

"So," he said, "you have some copies of

the security film I can see?"

"Right now?" Shpetim said. "If you want to. We can go to the shed —"

"He doesn't want to see them now," Nderi said. "He has someplace to go. I'll send copies to his computer. He just has to give me his e-mail address. That's right, isn't it, Mr. Demarkian?"

Gregor took his pen and little notepad out of the inside pocket of his suit jacket, wrote down his e-mail address, and passed the paper to Nderi. "That's exactly right," he said.

"But you can see," Shpetim Kika said. "You can see, can't you? It is ridiculous, that this is the baby from the Chester Morton case, that Chester Morton buried the baby here, all of it. I do not know what this is, but it is not that Chester Morton came here and dumped his backpack with the baby skeleton in it. That is not what happened here."

"No," Gregor agreed, looking around again. "That isn't."

3

Nderi Kika dropped Gregor at The Feldman Funeral Home on East Main Street, instead of around the back in the parking lot. Gregor went in the front door, into a foyer that was, today, entirely empty, as if Jason Feldman had deliberately refused to schedule any more memorial services as long as Chester Morton's body was in his basement. Jason Feldman was both absolutely furious and just exasperated, alternately. He kept turning on and off like a defective light bulb.

"There are dozens of people in my basement," he told Gregor when he was ushering him to the stairs. "*Dozens.* And not the kind of people we want here. You people just don't seem to understand. A funeral home is in a very delicate position. The families who come to us are bereaved. They've lost the people they love. They don't want to be confronted with policemen, and they most certainly don't want to be confronted with coroners. Not even if you call them medical examiners. Coroners. Autopsy. The departed cut up like meat in a butcher shop. It isn't acceptable."

Gregor wanted to say that Jason Feldman had volunteered his services as Mattatuck's morgue, but then it occurred to him that it might not be true. Feldman could have been dragooned into this business by a city council with the ability to influence a zoning board. All city councils had influence with their zoning boards.

Gregor allowed himself to be shown downstairs, but he was relieved that Jason Feldman disappeared immediately afterward.

"Mr. Demarkian," Tony Bolero said. He looked exhausted. "It's still here. Safe and sound."

"And I'm Ferris Cole," a tall, thin, aggressively bald man said, coming out of the shadows to hold out his hand. "I'm a little early, I know, but I thought that, under the circumstances, it might be a good idea."

"Thank you," Gregor said. "It was a good idea. I take it there were no disturbances at all last night?"

"Not a thing," Tony Bolero said. "I'd say it was as quiet as the grave, but you'd probably hit me."

"What about Howard Androcoelho?" Gregor said. "Isn't he supposed to be here."

"He called," Tony said. "He's running late. He'll be here about half past nine. He didn't sound like he was running late. He didn't sound like he was rushed, if you know what I mean."

"I know what you mean," Gregor said.

Ferris Cole laughed. "Howard never sounds rushed. And I mean not ever. It doesn't matter what kind of an emergency there is. But you have to wonder how long they're going to be able to go on with this.

It's not 1950 any more. It's not even 1980. Some nasty things happen in Mattatuck these days."

"They got a slum," Tony Bolero put in helpfully. "Jason Feldman told me."

Ferris Cole brushed this off. "Every town has a slum," he said. "Even the smallest one. There's always someplace where the houses are small, or they're trailers, and the people who live there don't bother to pick up their own garbage, and they're always out of work, and there are too many mind-altering substances. Alcohol, mostly, around here."

"There was a meth lab a couple of years ago," Tony said. "It blew up."

"Yes, well," Ferris Cole said. "That's what happens when people who couldn't pass high school chemistry try to do high school chemistry. I've given the body a quick look over, if you're interested. I don't think I'm going to be able to get you what you want."

The body was still in the cold locker. Gregor went to it and pulled it out. Chester Morton looked very much as he had looked when Gregor first saw him, much as he had looked in the big stack of photographs Howard Androcoelho had sent him, except that now he seemed a little worse for wear. There wasn't anything definite Gregor could put a finger on, but there it was. The body looked older — older as a body.

Gregor stepped back. "Well," he said.

"We'll take him off your hands and give him a good thorough autopsy," Ferris Cole said, "but if you ask me, we're going to end up finding that suicide is just as likely as murder, and maybe more likely. And yes, I know, he didn't hang himself off that billboard. But my guess is that he was dead when somebody else hung him. A toxicology screen might be interesting. If he was drugged before he was hanged, that might prove murder for you. It's going to be touch and go, though."

"That's all right," Gregor said. "What about the tattoo?"

"You mean the MOM thing? I think after death is a good guess, and definitely not much before. That's a hairy chest and the area of the tattoo is absolutely clean. Someone either shaved him and tattooed him after he died, or he got that within a few hours of dying. Weird thing to find there, don't you think? It's like one of those ones the guys do to themselves and each other in prison. You know, no proper equipment. Ink and safety pins or sewing needles or whatever they can get their hands on."

"If somebody did tattoo him after he died, maybe the somebody wasn't a professional,"

Gregor said. "Or even if he was, maybe he wasn't within reach of his equipment."

"True enough," Ferris Cole said. "Do you really think you have a murder here? I don't know. Usually I'm crazy about getting Howard to ask for help. You have no idea what kind of trouble he's caused for himself over the years, what kind of trouble they've both caused for themselves —"

"Both?"

"Howard and Marianne Glew. The mayor. Haven't you met the mayor, yet? She almost certainly had to okay your coming here. Nobody spends money in Mattatuck without Marianne having her say about it. Which is largely why nobody spends money in Mattatuck. I can complain about Howard, but it's Marianne who's running the show. It always was. Even back when they were partners."

"Partners?"

"Howard Androcoelho and Marianne Glew," Ferris Cole said. "Didn't you know that? They both used to be on the police force. Well, Howard still is, I suppose. But they were partners, detectives and partners. They were the ones who originally investi-gated —"

"Chester Morton's disappearance," Gregor said. "I did know it was Howard Androcoelho who did that investigation."

"Well, but it was Marianne who really did the investigation," Ferris Cole said. "She's light years smarter than he is. Which doesn't take much, I'll admit, but she is. They caught a couple of big cases in their time, and it was always Marianne who made it work. If it hadn't been for Marianne on the Warren case, Howard would have botched the thing from start to finish."

"The Warren case?"

"Biggest thing to happen in Mattatuck before Chester Morton went missing and Charlene Morton went ballistic. Still the biggest thing to happen in Mattatuck, if you ask me. Local pharmacist by the name of Dade Warren. He had a wife and three kids. He drugged them all with Thorazine, then shot them all, and propped them up against the couch in the living room. Then he wrote the suicide note to end all suicide notes and shot himself in the head. It was an absolute, utter, and bloody mess. You really have no idea."

"It sounds like it," Gregor said.

"Anyway," Ferris Cole said, "it was almost something of a police scandal. Howard was the first one into the house, and he got spooked. He ended up discharging his firearm all over the place when there were

421

nothing but dead bodies in the room. Marianne had to haul his ass out of that one. She had to haul his ass out of a lot of things over the years."

"Interesting," Gregor said.

Ferris Cole seemed to shake himself out of a reverie. "Well," he said, "let me get my people in here and we'll take this guy out and give him a going over. Like I said, I don't know if it's going to do you any good, but at least you'll have tried. Howard and Marianne are just going to have to accept the fact that Mattutuck needs a thoroughly professional morgue these days. They can't go on pretending it's thirty years ago forever."

Ferris Cole ran up the basement steps, meaning to call for help in moving the body. He was stopped halfway up by a frantic Jason Feldman rushing down. Of course, Jason Feldman was always frantic, but this time he was really beside himself.

"Mr. Demarkian, Mr. Demarkian," he kept saying sounding as if he'd empty his lungs of breath minutes ago. "Mr. Demarkian, it's Howard Androcoelho on the phone and he says you have to come. You have to come right away because there are two bodies, two of them, and there's blood everywhere —"

■ ■ ■ ■

PART III

■ ■ ■ ■

Hypocrisy and dissimulation are what keeps social systems strong; it is intellectual honesty that destroys them.
— Theodore Dalrymple

ONE

1

The location of the emergency was not possible to find on Tony Bolero's GPS. "At the fork near the dam" was not something the GPS understood, and even "the dam" proved difficult to find.

"There have to be six dams within a twenty-five-mile radius of this place," Tony said. "There are two in the Mattatuck town limits. Can that be right? I thought dams were big things and you had one for an entire region. Unless, you know, we're talking about beaver dams."

Gregor wouldn't have put it past Mattatuck to have special designations for its beaver dams, but he didn't say so. He allowed a patrol car to lead the way. The officer in the patrol car obviously wanted Gregor to come along with him, but Gregor wasn't having any of that. Even dead tired, Tony Bolero meant independence, and

Gregor needed as much independence as he could get. It was even one of those times when he wished he could drive himself.

On their way out of town, Gregor put in another call to Rhonda Alvarez at the FBI, but still got nothing but her voice mail. This annoyed him only slightly. She was, after all, a working agent with a caseload. He'd had those himself once. Still, there were things he wanted to know. They were things he thought he did know, but he wanted to be sure.

The route to the dam turned out to be familiar. It went past the Kentucky Fried Chicken, the McDonald's, the Burger King, and the nearly empty shopping center. It went past the trailer park and the low brick building with the Department of Social Services in it. Gregor found himself wondering about that name. Social Services. Everybody used it. Everybody knew what it meant. It was still very odd. What was "social" about welfare?

On the other side of the little cluster of depressed-looking buildings — even the fast-food places looked depressed, Gregor had no idea why — there was semi-open country, and what looked like a river. Gregor was sure it had been there before. He just hadn't paid much attention to it.

Side roads went off to their right, but not, obviously, to their left, where the river was. They passed a big roadhouse place with a deep parking lot fronting the street and bright yellow awnings all across its single-story storefront façade. There was a sign close to the road, hand lettered in bright red marker against a white background. It read: BIKERS WELCOME.

"Has that always been there?" Gregor asked.

"It was there the last time we came through here," Tony said. "You don't pay attention much, do you?"

Gregor wanted to say he didn't pay much attention in the dark, or couldn't see in it, or something, but he let it go. This was not the time to start worrying about getting old. The dam was not too far ahead of them. In the sunlight and good weather, it was easy enough to see. The police cars were lined up along a little road that went off to the right just past it.

Gregor leaned forward. There were a lot of police cars. There was an EMT vehicle. There was a fire engine. Why was there a fire engine?

Tony Bolero slowed down and began to glide into the choked side road. He was stopped almost immediately by a uniformed patrol officer.

"Oh," the officer said, looking into the front seat. "It's Mr. Demarkian. Come right in and try to park out of the way so that we've got a clear shot at getting some of these vehicles out. Commissioner Androcoelho wants to see you right away."

Tony pulled off to the side and parked. Gregor got out of the front passenger seat and looked around. The center of activity was across the road and in the direction of the water, just on the other side of the dam from town. Gregor saw a lot of uniforms milling around, and the top of what looked like a big black pickup truck.

He left Tony with the car and walked across the road, looking around as he went. A hundred feet or so further down the road there was a derelict building, its paint almost entirely sheared off by wind and weather, its windows broken. He wondered what had been there once, and why it wasn't there anymore.

Gregor got to the other side of the road. The big black pickup truck was in a deep ditch, sitting sideways precariously on the grass. There were so many uniformed officers around it, it was impossible to see what was going on.

Gregor went down the embankment.

Howard Androcoelho was there, pacing back and forth on the other side of the vehicle, near the water. He was talking on a cell phone.

Gregor caught his eye. Howard Androcoelho said something else and then snapped the cell phone closed.

"Mr. Demarkian, Mr. Demarkian. I'm glad you got here."

"What happened?"

Howard Androcoelho waved toward the pickup truck. "Both dead," he said, "and really dead. Shot through three or four times apiece."

Gregor looked back at the truck. Now that he knew what to look for, he could see that there were people in it, people sitting at odd angles, one slumped against a side door, the other collapsed forward onto the dashboard.

He left Howard Androcoelho and moved toward the truck. The closer he got, the more obvious it was that the two people inside it were dead. Officers moved out of the way for him. Gregor got right up next to the windshield and looked inside.

"It's awful," Howard Androcoelho said, right at his elbow, causing Gregor to nearly jump out of his skin. "It's awful. Nothing like this ever happens in Mattatuck. It's not a Mattatuck kind of thing."

Gregor thought about the story about the pharmacist who had killed his wife and children and then himself. Then he looked back through the windshield again. There was a man and a woman. He was sure he'd never seen the man before. The woman looked vaguely familiar.

"Who are they?" he asked.

"Althy Michaelman and the current boyfriend," Howard said. "Mike something. We'll look it up. Althy always has boyfriends. She always did. We went to high school together. Her mother had ambitions, before she got pregnant. That's why Althy was Althy. Althea."

Gregor stared at her a little longer. She didn't look like an Althea. She didn't look like a woman who always "had boyfriends."

"She looks familiar," he said. "Have I met her?"

"I think so, once or twice," Howard said. "She has the trailer next to the Morton trailer out at the trailer park. She was there the first day we went out to look it over."

"Was she," Gregor said. "What about the man? Did he live there, too?"

"Oh, yeah," Howard said. "He has, now, two or three years. He wasn't going anywhere unless Althy threw him out. I don't think he's kept a job six weeks running in

430

the last ten years. He likes his beer. He shoplifts a little. He used to have some scam going about disability, but Social Services got wise to him."

"And they didn't have him arrested?"

"You have to prove something to have somebody arrested," Howard said. "Then you've got to go through all the rigamarole with paperwork and hearings. Easier just to declare him fit to work. That just takes a doctor. They got a doctor. Didn't hurt that nobody but Althy could stand him."

"Huh," Gregor said.

He backed up a little and went around to the front of the truck. There was a blank space where the license plate was supposed to go. He went around to the back and found the same thing. Then he came back to Howard Androcoelho.

"No plates," he said. "Did the truck belong to them? To Althy Michaelman and whatever his name was?"

"A nice truck like that?" Howard said. "Hell, no. Althy and Mike would never put away enough money to buy a truck like that. Or any truck at all. I don't think Althy's ever had a car of her own since I've known her. Nah, they'd get a little money in hand and they'd go drink with it. Beer, usually, because it was cheap. They had more money on them than that last night, though. The hospital guys say they smell like serious liquor, Scotch or whiskey or something like that. That probably means they found Haydee's stash."

"Who's Haydee?"

"Althy's daughter. The only one who lived, that is. Althy got pregnant a lot, but she got stillbirths a lot. Well, that was years ago. It's what happens when you drink like a fish when you're pregnant. But Haydee is something else. Goes to school. Works her butt off at two jobs. Saves her money. Problem is, Mike is pretty good at figuring out where she's stashing it. He got away with over twelve hundred dollars about a year and a half ago. Haydee came in to the police station to accuse him of stealing it, but the problem is, if it's not in a bank account or anything, there's no way to prove you ever had it. And by the time Haydee found out the money was gone, the two of them had pissed it all away. Literally. So there was nothing we could do."

"Do you think that's what happened here? That the two of them took this Haydee's money and she murdered them for it?"

"Nah," Howard said. "Haydee isn't going to murder anybody. Though I don't think I'd blame her if she tried. Is that what you think happened, that Haydee did it? I was going for they ran into one of those bikers down the road and they were flashing cash, and, you know."

"And the biker had a big black pickup truck?"

"Lots of bikers have other vehicles," Howard Androcoelho said.

"It's an expensive truck," Gregor said, "and nearly new. You think the biker just shot them in it and left them there? He took the plates and wrote off the vehicle?"

"I don't know," Howard Androcoelho said.

"Well, I do," Gregor said. "Run the serial number through the national databases. You'll come up with a Jersey registration. I'd like to know the name listed on it. What about the gun? Did you find that?"

"There was a gun on the ground next to the truck when we got here," Howard said. "Is that going to be registered in New Jersey, too?"

"No," Gregor said. "It isn't going to be registered at all. Can you get me in touch with this Haydee person?"

"Sure. We have to get in touch with her anyway."

"Good. I have to make a phone call. I'll talk to you in twenty minutes."

Gregor left Howard Androcoelho standing where he was and marched back across the road to Tony Bolero and the car.

2

Gregor Demarkian got himself back into the front seat of Tony Bolero's car and told himself that it did no good for him to lose his temper. What was worse, he knew why he wanted to lose it. He hadn't expected this. Every part of the analysis he had made up until now said that this was not the kind of thing that was likely to happen. That meant that exactly one part of his analysis had been wrong, and it was the one part he should not have made a mistake about.

He got out his cell phone and dialed Rhonda Alvarez's number at the FBI, once again. He was beginning to wonder if her phone was programmed to go directly to voice mail. He reminded himself not to sound annoyed, or impatient. He wasn't an agent anymore. The Bureau had only taken an interest in this case in the last week or two, or something like that — at the moment, Gregor couldn't remember how that particular sequence of events had gone. He looked up and across the scene at the top of the pickup truck. The big black pickup truck. Althy Michaelman had mentioned a big black pickup truck only yesterday. He had heard her.

Of course, there was only one big black pickup truck. There could only be one big black pickup truck.

The call was picked up, and Gregor prepared himself to hear Rhonda Alvarez's standard canned message. Instead, a very soft female voice with a back-of-the-throat nasal Ohio twang said, "Federal Bureau of Investigation, Alvarez speaking."

"Oh," Gregor Demarkian said. "I'm sorry. I wasn't expecting to actually get you. This is Gregor Demarkian. I —"

"I know who you are, Mr. Demarkian. Everybody knows who you are. The man who started the Behavioral Sciences Unit."

"Ah," Gregor said. "That was a long time ago. I don't do work like that anymore."

"You don't work on serial killers?"

"Not if I can help it. They're enormously depressing and enormously trite."

"Excuse me?"

"It's always the same story," Gregor said. "Haven't you noticed that? A true serial killer, what we mean when we say a serial killer — not some woman who's murdered her last four husbands for the insurance money, but the guys with signatures and sexual sadism. They all have the same story.

435

Over and over and over again. You start on one of those cases and you know the beginning, the middle, and the end. The only thing you don't know is the particular kink, and the kinks are all essentially boring, just gross. If you see what I mean."

"Oh," Rhonda Alvarez said. She obviously did not see what he meant. She cleared her throat. "Kurt Delano said you wanted to know about the Chester Morton case. There isn't much to know, not really. I mean, we did run a couple of checks, but we didn't find much. And that was about it."

"I know," Gregor said. "One of those cases where it took a while to accept that a missing person might be more than a missing person. Except that in this case, your instincts were right. He was just a missing person."

"A grown man can go missing if he wants to," Rhonda Alvarez said. "If he doesn't leave a lot of debts behind, or abandon a family, and if he isn't wanted by the police — well, there's nothing illegal about him just taking off. There's nothing illegal about it even if he does abandon a family. Adults get to decide where they want to be."

"Yes," Gregor said, "I totally agree with you. At the moment, however, the man showed up and was no longer missing, but was also no longer alive. And I'm sitting not fifty yards from two more bodies, each of them shot at least three times. So I'd really like to know anything you can tell me, and I'd really appreciate it if you could run a check for me."

"A personal check."

"That's the kind."

"On who?"

"On Chester Morton. Except he wouldn't have been calling himself that. The name isn't going to be much use. I may have something better than a name in half an hour or so. I'm pretty sure we just found his truck."

"Ah," Rhonda Alvarez said.

"It had the two bodies in it," Gregor said.

"But Chester Morton couldn't have killed them, because he's dead. He's *been* dead for, what?"

"Close to a month, I think. Did you ever check out any of those leads the Morton family gave you?"

"Just a minute." There was a great rustling of papers in the background and the sound of a door being opened and shut. Then Rhonda Alvarez said, "Here it is. I was looking at this yesterday because I knew you were going to call. We don't seem to have a contact from the Morton family here —

well, no, wait a minute. There was a contact about a month and a half ago. But they didn't contact us. We contacted them. Because of the television show."

"I heard there was a television show."

"*Disappeared.* It's pretty new. All about missing persons. Anyway, somebody from their staff called here, we talked to them, then we did a little looking on our own. Then we called the Morton family and talked to them. The only contact we had before that was with a police officer down there, a Howard Andro—"

"Androcoelho," Gregor said. "He made the initial call? Twelve years ago?"

There was more rustling of papers. "No," she said. "At the very beginning, the first call we got, was from a Marianne Glew. After that, it was Howard Whatshisname. It looks like they were partners."

"They were."

"It also looks like they weren't taking it very seriously at the time," Rhonda Alvarez said. "The general line seems to have been that they all thought the guy had done a bunk, but the family was frantic and they had to check it out. There were some inconsistencies, though."

"Like what?"

"Well, the guy had left all his stuff behind.

Didn't you say something about a black truck? He'd left the black truck behind. His mother had it in her garage. The cops said the mother didn't think he'd leave without it. He loved it like a wife. He didn't take anything else, either, except a bright yellow L.L. Bean backpack that he carried his books around in. He was in college."

"So somebody checked it out?" Gregor said.

"Sure, as far as we were able without anything much to go on. The cops said the guy had a thing about the West — Wyoming, Montana, like that, so we did a little looking. We never found anything."

"Did you check Las Vegas?"

"Absolutely," Rhonda Alvarez said. "I wasn't working on this then, but I'd be willing to bet whoever was checked Vegas *first*. Mothers always think of their children as absolute little angels who just want to commune with nature and the good clean air, but around here we tend to think most people who disappear like to commune with casinos."

"There was no luck in Vegas, I take it."

"No," Rhonda Alvarez said, "but you know, Mr. Demarkian, we wouldn't have been doing a full-charge check. It wasn't our case, and from the way these notes read, we didn't think it was ever going to be our case. We didn't have any reason to suspect a murder, or a kidnapping, not the way things were then."

"And they changed?"

"Well, there was all that stuff he left behind," Rhonda Alvarez said. "When the guys from the television program kept stressing that, it got people around here thinking. So we decided to give it a good go. You know how these things work. If the police had been more insistent at the time, or if the family had been bugging us — but it wasn't like that, so we didn't really start looking into it until about two months ago."

"And did you find anything?"

"No," Rhonda Alvarez said. "Not a thing. 'Somewhere out in the West' is not exactly the best tip we ever got on anybody."

"Well, I've got a better one. Try Atlantic City, New Jersey."

"Really? Why?"

"Let's call it a hunch, for a moment. I'm going to have the registration number and the engine number for a big black truck in a few minutes. It's in a ditch without plates. But I'm pretty sure the plates that were on it were Jersey plates, and if we can find the name of the person who registered that truck, we'll know what name Chester Morton has been using for the past twelve years."

"But I don't get it," Rhonda Alvarez said. "I've got a note here that says he didn't take the truck. His mother was keeping it for him. In her garage."

"I know," Gregor said. "Don't worry about it. Could you check Atlantic City for me, and call me back sometime this evening? Am I ruining your schedule? It's just that I might not be in a position to talk until around seven."

"I don't go home before seven," Rhonda Alvarez said. "Atlantic City, New Jersey."

"If I were you, I'd check the gambling addiction groups, although I think you're going to come up blank. And check the casinos for people they have recently, anytime in the last year, say, barred from play."

"You've practically got to murder your mother on the craps table to get barred from play."

"I know. But check it anyway. Something must have happened in the last few months to shake this all loose. I've got some pretty decent guesses as to what it was, but I'd like to know for sure."

"Right," Rhonda Alvarez said. "I'll get on it. If he did something bad enough to get barred from a casino, it shouldn't be hard to find."

By the time Gregor got back to the crime scene, there was a small, thin, frail young girl there, shaking as if she were about to freeze to death. Somebody had thrown a windbreaker over her shoulders, but it was a thin nylon thing. It wasn't going to keep her warm. Howard Androcoelho was towering over her, looking like a fat dragon menacing a damsel in distress.

"You shouldn't have come out here," he was saying. "And they shouldn't have let you come over here. There's a reason we don't let relatives wander around crime scenes. I didn't even have to go to the law enforcement seminar to know that one."

The girl didn't seem to be listening to him. She was staring straight ahead and still shaking. A little ways off, a boy was getting sick in the grass.

Howard Androcoelho looked up as Gregor crossed to the yellow tape. "Mr. Demarkian," he said. "I'm glad you're back. This is Haydee Michaelman."

The girl looked up. She looked interested for the first time since Gregor came upon her and Howard. The boy who had been sick in the grass started back toward them. The closer he came, the more familiar he looked, and Gregor finally realized it was

Kenny Morton.

The girl looked at Kenny Morton and said, "I'm sorry. I'm so sorry I put you through all this. You were just giving me a ride —"

"Don't be stupid," Kenny Morton said. "You can't think I'm going to be mad at you over this."

"It doesn't make any sense," the girl said. "They drank too much and they went out and partied but they didn't — they didn't —"

"Haydee Michaelman," Howard Androcoelho said firmly. "Gregor Demarkian."

"I know," Gregor said.

Haydee Michaelman looked up and straight at him, and Gregor reached out a hand to pull her a little farther from the scene. The forensics people were still working. Gregor doubted if they were competent. It was the stimulus package mobile crime unit at work again. It didn't matter. He didn't want the girl standing right there when they brought out the body bags.

"She's in shock," Gregor said to Howard Androcoelho. "She needs something —"

"It's supposed to be brandy, isn't it?" Kenny Morton said. "I can go get some brandy. There's a liquor store right up the road."

"Let's not go bringing liquor into this," Howard Androcoelho said.

"Why not?" Kenny Morton said. "I'm over twenty-one. And you can't say she can't have brandy if she's in shock. Mr. Demarkian said she was in shock."

"I was just comng home," Haydee said. "I had a class, and Kenny was driving me home, because it's a long walk, and I don't have a car. And we pulled in and Kenny was about to drop me off, because I didn't want to ask him in. The trailer is always a mess. They leave clothes and garbage everywhere. So I didn't want to ask him in, but he was walking me down there, and then Krystal Holder came out and said — said that — that they were here — that they were dead —"

"I'm going to go get brandy," Kenny Morton said.

He didn't actually move to go. Everybody else ignored him.

"Didn't you notice that they hadn't come home last night?" Gregor asked. "I'm assuming you lived with your mother, and with —"

"With Mike?" Haydee said. "I do. More or less. I sleep there. I spend most of my time at school or at work or somewhere. I just can't stand the whole thing there. It's not just that eveything's a mess, you know, or that kind of thing. It's the whole attitude. The whole 'there's no use doing nothing about nothing.' Anything about anything. It's just the way they were, you know. Just the way they wanted to be."

"And you didn't notice that they hadn't come home last night?" Gregor asked again.

Haydee shook her head. "I didn't go home myself last night. I stayed with Desiree, my friend. Desiree Skarm. She lives way in the back of the park. They were really crazy, yesterday. They had money, I don't know where they got it —"

"I thought it must have been yours," Howard Androcoelho said. "You know, like last time."

"Oh, no," Haydee said. "I put my money in the credit union. Well, I did that yesterday. Before that I had it hidden. But Kenny," she looked over at Kenny, still standing half-poised to go for brandy, "Kenny told me about the credit union. Where there aren't fees or anything for keeping your money in the bank. So he took me there and I put my money in. For my car. You know. I want to buy a car."

"She should have a car," Kenny said.

"Anyway," Haydee said. "I didn't want to be around it. Mike can be really crazy when he drinks. Especially when he drinks for serious, and they had some serious stuff. A bottle of, I don't remember what it was called. Johnnie Walker. That was it. They had that and they were really working themselves up. And they were going out, and I knew it was only going to get worse."

"Did you know where they were going?" Gregor asked.

Haydee looked up and nodded in the direction of the main road and the dam. "There's a place down there. It's supposed to be a biker bar, but it isn't really. It's just a lot of pathetic people pretending they're some kind of hip. Older people, mostly. Kids go into Mattatuck to the clubs. They're pathetic, too."

"So you don't know when they went out last night?" Gregor asked.

"Oh, I know that," Haydee said. "I was home for that. It was about, I don't know, eight o'clock. They had to walk to get to the bar. They didn't have a car, either. Half of everybody at the park doesn't have a car. They get all their food at the convenience stores. Going the other way, you know, toward Mattatuck. They get all their stuff there. And at Kentucky Fried Chicken. There isn't a real grocery store in two-and-a-half miles, and what would they do if they got there? How would they get anything home? All the frozen stuff would melt. But that's not why, you know. There used to be a grocery store. All anybody bought was potato chips and beer, so it moved out and went to Sherwood Forest."

Gregor let all this flow over him. "So you think they left about eight."

"Eight or eight-thirty."

"And what did you do?"

"I went over to Desiree's place," Haydee said. "Her mother was at work. Her mother doesn't like me hanging around. She thinks Mike is going to come and bust up the place someday, because I'm there, you know, and he's mad at me. But she was at work, so I just stayed there and then I went to sleep in Desiree's room. I didn't want to be back at my place when they got home. I thought they'd be, that they'd be —"

"Violent?" Gregor suggested.

"They're never really violent," Haydee said. "They're just sort of — sort of crazy. And Mike punches things. Not usually people. You know. He breaks walls. He's always angry about something. But last night he wasn't angry, he was just nuts. And they had money. They had money to get the Johnnie Walker bottle, and they had money to go to the bar. Even though it's the wrong time of the month for it."

"The wrong time of the month?" Gregor asked.

"Disability," Howard Androcoelho put in. "That pays on the third."

"And it's gone on the fourth," Haydee said. "But they had money last night. They had a lot of it, for them."

"Do you know where they got it?" Gregor said.

Haydee shook her head. "I thought they might've gotten lucky on a scratch ticket. That happens sometimes. But they didn't say so. They usually tell me when they get lucky on a scratch ticket."

"But they didn't this time?"

"No," Haydee said. "They didn't. They didn't say anything at all. They just kept flashing money around, and the bottle, and then they took off for the bar. And I didn't think anything of it. I really didn't. I just — I don't know. And then it's so strange, because I was telling Desiree about Chester Morton. And Chester Morton is dead."

"For God's sake," Kenny said. "You don't have to worry about Chester. You really don't. Not at a time like this."

"What about Chester?" Gregor Demarkian asked.

Haydee shrugged. "It was just that I was

telling Desiree about it. Chester Morton used to spend a lot of time at our place. I don't know how much, really, you know, I was only six. But he used to come over and sit around with my mother, and my mother would go over there. And I remember the day he disappeared, or when everybody finally decided he'd disappeared, or whatever, because that was the first time I was ever taken into foster care."

"Foster care," Gregor said slowly.

"I was always getting taken into foster care when I was little," Haydee said. "Social services would show up at our door and I'd be taken away, and then in a few weeks I'd be brought back and the place would've been cleaned up. I used to sort of like it when that happened, to tell you the truth. I didn't like the foster places, but when I got back home it would always smell of Pine-Sol and soap. It was kind of nice."

"And the mess in the trailer, that was the reason you were taken into foster care?" Gregor asked.

"I don't know," Haydee said. "I suppose so. I was too little to really understand it, if you know what I mean. I just knew Chester was there all the time, and then I went away and he wasn't anymore, and later people told me he had disappeared. Oh, and then there weren't anymore fights from the other trailer."

"There were fights from the other trailer?" Gregor asked.

Haydee flushed. "Really, Mr. Demarkian. I was too little. I didn't understand anything that was going on, and I probably got a lot of it wrong. I don't even know if my memories are right. But, yes, there were fights from the other trailer. It's so close up against ours. There were people yelling a lot. And sometimes one of those people was my mother. But I couldn't tell you who the other one was. I don't even know if the other one was Chester Morton. It was just a lot of yelling through the walls, and it scared me to death."

Two

1

Charlene Morton knew that they would be coming — Gregor Demarkian, certainly, but almost just as certainly, Howard Androcoelho. She'd heard about the bodies near the dam almost before the police had. Mattatuck was that kind of place. The guy who found the bodies called his brother-in-law before he called 911. His brother-in-law told his wife, his wife told her sister-in-law, her sister-in-law worked in Morton's front office. Yes, Charlene knew they would be coming. It was the way these people think.

There were two cars parked behind the family cars in the driveway, and two young men waiting behind the steering wheels. Why should it surprise her that Gregor Demarkian came with his own driver? Maybe the town was paying for that. That would be something to bring up at the next town council meeting.

Actually, Charlene missed the old town government, where everybody got together at a town meeting and voted on every little thing. You could do a lot with town meetings if you knew how to negotiate them.

The doorbell rang. Charlene pushed her hair back into place. She should have gone in to work today. She always did go in to work. It was just that, over the last few weeks, she had been feeling more and more tired.

The doorbell rang again. Charlene went out into the foyer and opened it. It was Howard Androcoelho who was standing right there in front, as if having someone she'd known forever come and talk to her about these things would make them better.

She stepped back and let Howard and Gregor Demarkian come inside.

"We checked for you over at the office," Howard said, "they said you weren't feeling well and you'd stayed home. Mr. Demarkian here wants to talk to you."

"I know," Charlene said.

She turned her back to them and marched into the living room. She sat down in the big wingback chair that was always called hers in the family, and folded her hands in her lap. The two men came in. Howard looked around vaguely and then sat down on the couch. Gregor Demarkian remained standing.

"Well?" Charlene said.

"Well." Howard cleared his throat. "We've had a murder," he said finally. "We've had two murders, actually. Althea Michaelman and Mike Katowski. You remember Althy, Charlene. She went to school with us."

"Of course I remember Althy," she said. "Not that she was ever a friend of mine. Or of yours, from what I remember. What does any of this have to do with me?"

"Ah," Howard said. "Well. For one thing, it was right over in the back there, near the dam, you could walk to the Morton offices from it. We're looking at everybody and everyplace in the area, you know, to see if anybody saw anything."

"To see if 'anybody saw anything'? Our offices close at five o'clock and they don't open again until eight."

"Yes, I know, Charlene, but you know how it is. Just in case somebody saw something. Just in case somebody was working late."

"Don't be a fool," Charlene said. "Nobody works that kind of late."

"Yes. Well." Howard was looking more uncomfortable by the second. Charlene wanted to laugh out loud. "We have to check, you know," he said. "It's not good police work if we don't check. And if any-body is going to know what's going on in the neighborhood, it's going to be you, Charlene. You know that."

"I don't know what's going on in that neighborhood at one o'clock in the morn-ing. I'm home in bed at one o'clock in the morning."

"Yes, well. I know, Charlene, I know, but there's more to it. Mr. Demarkian here had an idea. And I've got to admit, it's kind of an interesting idea."

"What idea was that?" Charlene said.

Gregor Demarkian seemed to have been looking out the window. Now he turned back to them. Charlene didn't like Gregor Demarkian. She didn't like him one bit. He had bad eyes.

"Well?" she said.

"There were two bodies," Demarkian said. "They were both found, shot, in the front seat of a black pickup truck. A black Ford pickup truck."

"So?" Charlene said.

"Your son, I believe, had a black Ford pickup truck."

"So?" Charlene said again. "That was twelve years ago. And he didn't take it with him. There are a lot of black Ford pickup trucks."

"I agree, but the age of this one looks to be about right," Gregor said. "You say Chester didn't take the truck with him when he left. What happened to it?"

"I kept it," Charlene said.

"Are you still keeping it?" Gregor asked.

"No," Charlene said. "No. After a while, I don't remember how long, after a while I got rid of it. I hated looking at it."

"The truck was here?" Demarkian asked.

"It was after a while," Charlene said. "It was parked over there at the trailer park, and I couldn't stand it. I really couldn't. Those people over there. They've got no respect for property. They've got no respect for anything. I went over one afternoon and somebody had spray painted on it. So I got my son Mark to drive it back here, and I got it cleaned up. After that, it just stayed in the garage."

"For how long?"

"Like I said. For a while."

"A month, two months, a year?"

"I don't *know*," Charlene said. "A couple of months, I guess. Something like that. I had other things on my mind."

"What did you do with it?"

"I sold it," Charlene said. "What else do you do with a car you don't want?"

"There are a number of things," Gregor

Demarkian said. "You can give it to charity. You can junk it. Did you sell it to a car dealership?"

"No," Charlene said. "We put up notices, you know, on those bulletin boards in the grocery store, and we put a notice in the paper. It didn't take that long. I wasn't selling it for all that much."

"So, let me get this straight," Gregor Demarkian said. "You put out ads to sell the truck only a couple of months after your son disappeared —"

"Well, I didn't think he'd disappeared," Charlene said. "I thought he was dead. I had every reason to think he was dead. He loved that truck. He worshipped it. I didn't think he'd go anywhere without it. And then I just wanted it out of the garage, out of my life, where I didn't have to look at it anymore. I wanted it away."

"Do you remember the person you sold it to?"

Charlene shrugged. "Just some kid. Some college kid, Chester's own age or younger, I'd guess."

"You don't remember his name?"

"No."

"Did he pay you by cash or check?"

"Cash."

"How much?"

"Twenty-five hundred dollars."

"Twenty-five hundred dollars for a pickup truck that was, at that point, nearly brand new?" Gregor Demarkian looked surprised. "Was it banged up in some way I haven't been told? That has to be significantly below book value."

"It wasn't banged up in any way," Charlene said, "and of course that was significantly below book value. I told you. I wanted to get rid of it."

"Do you have paperwork from that transaction?" Gregor asked. "A bill of sale, or a receipt, anything?"

"No, of course not. The buyer gets all that kind of thing. And it was years ago. It's not the kind of thing you keep."

"And you don't remember this kid's name?"

"No, really, I don't."

"It's all right," Howard Androcoelho put in quickly. "The kid would have had to register the truck. If we know the approximate date, and we've got anything at all — we could look up Chester's own registration. Then we could use the computer, and we'd find it eventually. Who the kid was, I mean."

"Good," Charlene said. "You do that."

Demarkian rubbed his hand against the

side of his face. "Did you see or speak to your son between the time he came back to Mattatuck and the time the body was discovered?"

"You mean did he show up on my doorstep and try to offer me an explanation?" Charlene said. "No. I had no idea he was in town. I had no idea he was even thinking of coming back to town."

"All right," Gregor Demarkian said. "Thank you."

"That's it?" Howard Androcoelho said. "That's all? I'm sorry, Charlene, I didn't realize it was going to be so —"

"Oh, for God's sake, Howard," Charlene said. "Go to hell. Get out of my house and go to hell. I've got nothing to do with two strange people being shot dead just because they had a pickup truck the same color as the one Chester used to have, and you know it."

2

Penny London woke up for the second time because her phone was ringing. When she sat up in bed and looked around, she wasn't sure where she was.

It got clearer when her eyes were finally able to focus. She was in a hotel room, at the Howard Johnson, that belonged to Mr.

Demarkian's driver, who was named Tony. She remembered all that from the night before. She was sleeping in a little, since Tony would not be coming back to the room until the end of the day. Mr. Demarkian had had to go out. He had woken her up and told her that . . .

She checked the clock at the side of the bed. Hours ago. It must have been hours ago since he left. It was nearly noon.

The phone stopped ringing. She picked it up and it started ringing again. She saw Graham's picture in the little ID window. She made a face at it. Then she picked it up.

"Graham," she said. "How are you? Aren't you supposed to be at work? Isn't this the middle of the workday?"

"I am at work," Graham said. "I'm a goddamned lawyer. I can talk on the phone in the middle of the day if I want to."

"You're an associate in a big firm," Penny said. "You know how hard it is to make partner. You can't afford to let your bosses think that you're taking care of personal business in the middle of the day."

"And you're damned near sixty years old. You can't afford to sleep in your car."

Penny's mouth felt bad. She needed to get up and brush her teeth. Her vision was fuzzy, on and off. She needed her eyes to focus on a more consistent basis.

"I'm not sleeping in my car," she said. "I'm sleeping in a perfectly wonderful bed, complete with quilts, and I'm sleeping in."

"You're sleeping in a room at the Howard Johnson that actually belongs to this Gregor Demarkian person," Graham said. "You're there because he found you sleeping in your car and he didn't want to leave you there. Don't try to put this on with me. He called me. And he called George."

Penny sat forward and bent over her knees. "He doesn't even know you exist. Where would he have gotten your number?"

"Off your phone. He said you left it in his room when you went to bed."

"I never leave my phone anywhere."

"Then maybe he lifted it."

"It was right here next to the bed this morning. You woke me up with it."

"Then maybe he lifted it and put it back. Would you stop this? What's wrong with you? You were sleeping in your goddamned car. You could have frozen to death —"

"Well, I wasn't sleeping there in the winter," Penny said. "What do you take me for?"

"Winter will be coming around again," Graham said, "and if you didn't freeze to death, you could have been mugged. You could have been murdered. And don't tell me nobody gets murdered in Mattatuck. There were two murders there just last night. It's been all over CNN."

"I wouldn't have been sleeping in the car when winter came around again," Penny said. "I'd have had enough for an apartment by then. It was just a temporary —"

"It's going to be a lot more temporary than you know. We're coming out there. We're going to be there by tomorrow morning."

"What?" Penny was now wide awake. "But you can't do that. You've got work. And all those college loans. You can't just —"

"The plane tickets are already bought. George will call you in a minute about what you're going to do tonight. We're getting all three of us rooms at that Holiday Inn of yours —"

"Howard Johnson."

"Whatever. It doesn't matter. We're getting them for tonight and you can go to bed in your room like a sane person. And you better be there and be ready for us when we get there, because when we say tomorrow morning, we mean it."

"It depends on whether or not I have to teach," Penny said. "I can't just cancel a class —"

"You don't teach at four o'clock in the morning. That's when our plane gets in. And you don't teach at six, which will probably be when we show up. And if we're late in any way, you'd damned better be sure you've left a note telling us where you've gone, because if you don't, we're going to hunt you down and wring your neck."

"But," Penny said.

The phone was dead.

Penny swung her legs off the bed and sat there, holding her hair in her hands. The remote was right there on the night table. She picked it up and turned the television on. The first channel she got was some kind of cooking network. She flipped around a little and settled on one of the local stations. It was broadcasting a talk show where everybody was much too cheery, but it had a news feed running underneath.

The two dead bodies discovered at Stephenson Dam this morning have been identified as belonging to Althea Marie Michaelman, 52, and Michael Robert Katowski, 48.

The names meant absolutely nothing to her. She had no idea what was going on.

The phone rang again, and she picked it up again. The face in the window this time belonged to George. Penny sighed.

"Yes," she said.

"Are you proud of yourself?" George said. "I mean, really? Are you just peachy keen proud of yourself? Because you've pulled a lot of stunts in your day, and I've even helped with some of them, but this really tears it. This really tears. it. What the hell did you think you were doing?"

"I was just trying to get through a couple of months," Penny said. "This really isn't as big a thing as you're making it. It was just for a few months and then in the fall I was going to rent a regular place. I just needed to save up —"

"Are you out of your mind?" George said. "Are you crazy? Seriously, Mom, listen to yourself. You had to get through a couple of months? Why? You've got two grown children and we're both working —"

"You've got your own lives to lead," Penny said. "You've got those college loans to repay. And you can't let those default. It ruins your credit rating. And you need a credit rating these days if you want a new job or anything like that. So you can't —"

"I can afford to keep you in an apartment in Mattatuck. What does that cost these days, maybe five hundred a month?"

"Five hundred a month is a lot of money."

"Oh, please. Between Graham and me, we could afford twice that, plus your utilities. Why didn't you tell us? That's what bugs me. Why didn't you tell us? You made such a point of it, after Dad died, when we were all growing up, about how we'd be all right as long as we remained a family and we all stuck together. Well, where's the 'sticking together,' Mom? Where is it? Was that only supposed to apply to you, and Graham and I were allowed to be self-absorbed little asses."

"You're not self-absorbed little asses."

"You can bet your butt we're not," George said. "You'd better get a pen and a piece of paper. I've got stuff you need to write down."

"I really don't want the two of you to tear up your lives just because I can't get my act together," Penny said. "I'm a grown woman. I can take care of myself. I'm supposed to take care of myself."

"We're supposed to take care of you," George said. "Take this down. We got two rooms. They've always got those big double beds. Graham and I shared a room for years when we were at home. Go to the front desk. Say you're Penelope London and you want to check in. We put it all on credit cards. It's all paid for. Check in, move in, order a bunch of room service —"

"I don't know if there is room service," Penny said. "And you can't do that. Room service is ridiculously expensive —"

"I'll call the restaurant and order you lunch. It'll cost more than an arm and a leg because it will be dinner for six and you'd damned better eat it."

"No, don't do that."

"Do you have any money on you at all?"

"I have money on me and I have money in the bank," Penny said. "You don't understand. This isn't what you think it is."

"I know what it is," George said. "We'll talk about what it's going to be when we get there. Go check in. I'm ready to kill you."

The phone went dead again. She closed her eyes. When she opened them again, the news feed had come around.

The two dead bodies discovered at Stephenson Dam this morning have been identified as belonging to Althea Marie Michaelman, 52, and Michael Robert Katowski, 48.

She had a girl in her class named Michaelman. Haydee Michaelman. Maybe this was her mother?

Penny shook her head. If anything, at that age, it would be Haydee's grandmother. Haydee had written about her mother, and her mother had gotten pregnant and had to drop out of school at sixteen.

3

Kenny Morton had been half-waiting for the call all morning — half-waiting and half-worrying about Haydee. The worrying would not leave him. Haydee was something beyond distraught. She cried for hours after they were done with the police. Then she'd let him drive her out to The Elms on Straits Turnpike, ordered a hamburger, and cried there. The Elms sounded fancy, but it wasn't. It was an ordinary old-fashioned offers-everything-American-kind-of restaurant with large portions and the kind of thing your mother made at home. You could get meatloaf there, and Brussels sprouts.

"It's kinda funny to think of it," Kenny said, by way of making neutral conversation. "Restaurants all used to be like this. You know, not Italian or Chinese or Mexican, just American. Ordinary stuff."

"I guess," Haydee said.

Haydee's hamburger was the size of a

small bowling ball. The fries were piled up like a pick-em-up sticks mountain. Kenny was willing to bet that nobody at The Elms had thought of replacing the good beef fat deep-fry for something more nutritional.

"I'm sorry about this," Haydee said. "I really am sorry about this."

"You don't have to be sorry," Kenny said. "Your mother died. You're upset. You're supposed to be upset."

"But that's the thing," Haydee said. "I'm not upset that way. I mean, I am, a little, but not mostly. I think a lot of it is guilt."

"Guilt? About what? She was shot. They were. You didn't go out and shoot them."

"No, no, of course I didn't. But I'm — I don't know. I never liked Mike at all. He could have disappeared any time and I wouldn't have cared. I'd have been glad. I'm glad now. I'm never going to have to see his stupid face again and that's good."

"That's nothing to feel guilty about," Kenny said. "That's understandable."

"I know it is. But I don't feel much differently about her. My mother. She was my mother. And I never liked her. I haven't liked her in years. Most of the kids I knew who went into foster care when I did, you know, on and off over the years, most of them hated foster care, they hated the social workers, they ran away, they did anything they could to get back to their families. But I knew what she was. Even when I was six that first time. I could see it. I knew what she was and I knew it was her fault."

"What?"

"I knew it was her fault," Haydee insisted. "I knew that it wasn't bad luck or men who were irresponsible or any of the rest of it. I mean, she did have all that, that was true, but I knew she didn't have to just sit down and let it drown her. I *knew.* I hated the social workers, too, but it was mostly because they had sort of the same attitude. Not that stuff just happened to people and there was nothing they could do. Not that exactly. More like, if you were the kind of person that stuff happened to you, then you were kind of sick, and you had to have treatment. Therapy. I didn't mind foster care, but I hated therapy. I think I lied my way through every therapy session they made me sit through."

"If somebody had made me sit through a therapy session, I'd probably kick them," Kenny said.

Haydee smiled a little and actually drank some Coke. "It's just guilt," she said. "All I wanted was to get the hell out of there and never see her again. Never see any of them again. Any of those people. I wanted to get out and go live with people who get their asses in gear and get things done in their lives. And now here I am."

Kenny's cell phone went off. He got it out of his pocket and saw his mother's picture in the screen. He knew it was his mother before he looked, though. He had given her a ring tone. He didn't know what the music was, but it sounded like explosions going off between the notes.

"Excuse me," he said. "I'm going to go out to the parking lot for a minute."

"It's important?" Haydee said. "I can go to the ladies room if you need privacy."

"I'll go to the parking lot," Kenny said. "Sit still and eat lunch."

He wanted to say she hadn't really eaten any lunch yet. He slid out of the booth and picked up. He said, "Hello," as he was walking to the restaurant's front door. When his mother spoke, she was loud. Kenny thought she could be heard all the way into the kitchen.

"Where are you?" she asked him. "What the hell are you doing? Do you know what's going on around here?"

Kenny was out in the parking lot. It was a big parking lot in the front of the restaurant. He could look right down on the street. The street was empty. This was not the middle of town.

"I'm having lunch," he said finally.

"You're having lunch," his mother said. "Isn't that wonderful? Isn't that just fine! I'm being persecuted, and you're having lunch."

"You're being persecuted about what?" Kenny said. "Who's persecuting you?"

"Well, you wouldn't know, would you? You wouldn't have any idea. You're having lunch."

"For God's sake, Ma. I went to class. I — ran some errands. Then I stopped to have lunch. Can you tell me what's wrong with any of that? School was your idea, not mine. I'm just doing what you told me to do."

"I want you back here right away. I want a united family. I want to make sure those idiots understand what they're dealing with."

"A united family about what? What the hell is going on?"

"He was here this morning," his mother said. "Gregor Demarkian. And Howard Androcoelho, of course, but Howard doesn't count. He never counted. I don't care what kind of fancy title he's giving himself these days."

"Okay. Mr. Demarkian and Mr. Androcoelho were over there this morning. About what? Do they know more about what happened to Chester?"

"They were here to tell me I'm a suspect in that murder case. The two people out by the dam. Don't tell me you've been in class and at lunch so long you don't know two people were killed out by the dam."

"Everybody knows two people were killed out by the dam," Kenny said. "What does that have to do with you?"

"They were in a black pickup truck," his mother said. "They've decided it must be Chester's pickup truck. I haven't had it for twelve years. I sold it ages ago. It doesn't matter. It's the way that Demarkian's mind works. He's decided it's Chester's truck and I killed those two people, and he isn't going to be satisfied until he puts me right in jail."

"I don't believe that," Kenny said. "I really don't. He wouldn't have the kind of reputation he has if he behaved like that."

"What do you know about reputations?" his mother said. "What do you know about anything? You're a traitor, just like Chester was, and you know it. You try to hide it better, but I know what you are. I've always known what you are. If you stood on the ground next to the tree, you'd turn the flowers red."

"What?"

"Judas," she said. "Except you're worse than Judas. You and Chester both. At least Judas got his money from Christ's enemies. You want to get it from Christ."

"Did you just compare yourself to Christ?" Kenny said. "I can't believe that. What's wrong with you?"

"Judas," his mother said again.

"I'll be back as soon as I can get there," Kenny said.

Then he hung up the phone, quickly. He had not lied. He would get back as soon as he could get there. The trick was in defining "as soon as he *could* get."

He flicked through the phone menu and found the REJECT list. He pushed a few more buttons and put his mother's number on it. Then he added the landline number at home, the numbers of his brother and his sister, and all three of the lines at the business. Then he put the phone back in his pocket.

When he got back to the table, Haydee was carefully dipping the world's longest French fry into ketchup.

Kenny slid into the booth and said, "Do you know what a flowering Judas it?"

"A flowering Judas? Do you mean Judas like in the Bible?"

"Yeah, sort of," Kenny said. "A flowering Judas is a plant. A tree, kind of. It doesn't grow up here except in a greenhouse. Anyway, it's got sort of red-purple flowers. The legend is that it used to have white flowers. Then Judas took the thirty pieces of silver and then he felt guilty, and he threw the silver on the ground and hanged himself. From this tree. And when he did that, hanged himself from the tree, I mean, the flowers turned from white to red. It's a legend. We got a little piece of paper with the legend on it when we got the tree."

"You've got one of these trees?" Haydee asked.

"My mother does," Kenny said. "In the greenhouse."

THREE

1

Going back across town to central station next to Tony Bolero in his own car, Gregor Demarkian tried to count the cases he'd been on that had left him in a situation like this. There had been a lot of them, lately. That wasn't a good sign. There were too many of these small and medium-sized towns out there that only thought about law enforcement when there was an emergency — or maybe not too many. Maybe *that* was a very good sign, both because there were so many places that had so few emergencies and because so many towns used their common sense about individual drug use. Or something.

Gregor's head hurt, and he thought it was going to get worse as the day went on. It wasn't the lack of crime in American small towns that he minded. He never minded a lack of crime. It was the attitude that by pretending that nothing ever changed, you could prevent crime from happening, or make it disappear when it did. It was the making it disappear that was the problem, because there could always be more behind it if that was what you were trying to do. The question here was just how much was behind this.

He got Ferris Cole on the phone as soon as he was on the road. Ferris Cole was also on the road, but Gregor didn't care. He explained the two bodies by the dam. Ferris Cole had heard of the dam.

"I've got them sitting out there waiting for you," Gregor said. "I've told them all to stay put, and they'll do it. I've done enough yelling so that Howard Androcoelho isn't going to get in my way for a while. Do you think you could see your way to getting out there and picking them up, or sending somebody out there to pick them up?"

"Of course I can," Ferris Cole said. "That's what we do. We wish the locals would call us in right at the start more often. But I don't understand. This is a different case?"

"I don't think so."

"All right. It doesn't sound the same as the other one. Shootings, this time."

"What other one?"

"The murder of Chester Morton," Ferris Cole said.

"That's not the other one."

"What?"

"It's a long story, and I don't have time to go into it now. There is another murder connected to these murders, and that murder is part of the Chester Morton case, but the murder in question is not the murder of Chester Morton. Unless I'm very badly mistaken about the people in this thing, and I don't think I am."

"But why would you think this had anything to do with the Chester Morton case at all? Did these people know Chester Morton."

"One of them did. One of them lived in the tailer that directly abutted Chester Morton's trailer in that trailer park."

"All right," Ferris Cole said. "That's interesting."

"In more ways than I can begin to tell you," Gregor said. "But even if that hadn't been the case, I'd have suspected that the two events were connected. There's the matter of the truck."

"The truck?"

"Chester Morton's black Ford pickup truck. From all the accounts of people who knew him at the time, Chester Morton was in love with his truck. Like some bad parody of a country song. Really in love with his truck."

"And?"

"And he left it behind when he disappeared."

"I don't get it," Ferris Cole said.

"It was one of the prime pieces of evidence for Chester Morton being dead or worse, instead of just some guy who took off," Gregor said. "He left his truck. He loved the truck. He never would have left the truck behind. Therefore, if the truck was left behind, he must have been killed and the police were being idiots for not following up on it. And it wasn't a bad argument. Even if he hadn't loved the truck, he would have needed transportation to get wherever it was he wanted to go."

"That makes sense," Ferris Cole said.

"Most of these guys, the ones who take off, take off in their own cars if they have them. Every once in a while, you'd get a guy with a particular kind of problem. He knows the car is about to be repossessed anyway, say, or there's some reason why he's really worried about being followed. But most of them take their cars and trade them in for another used one later."

"Makes sense."

"It does make sense," Gregor said, "but in this case, it doesn't, because in this case, Chester Morton really was missing. So here's this guy who's taking off, and he's out here in the middle of nowhere, at least relatively. He leaves the truck and does what? Walks? Hitchhikes? We'd have heard something if he'd been hitchhiking. Somebody would have come forward years ago. Okay, that's only about ninety percent sure. But it is ninety percent sure."

"All right," Ferris Cole said, "so he left the truck. I still don't see how that means his disappearance connects to two bodies by a dam —"

"They're in a black Ford pickup truck."

"The same one?"

"I don't know yet."

"So you're saying that somebody had the truck — his family, what? Somebody had the truck and then . . . I don't know what you're saying."

"I'm not sure of what I'm saying, either," Gregor said. "But I'm pretty sure it's the same truck. And it's one of those things. If anybody had been paying attention twelve years ago, they should have paid attention to the truck."

"Did his family keep it? Did the police impound it as evidence? What?"

"His mother had it in her garage and then she sold it," Gregor said. "At least, that's what she says. She sold it to some kid, she can't remember his name, it was a long time ago. But there's a black pickup truck sitting down there by the water with two bodies in it, and it's around the right vintage and, though the plates were removed, it was registered in New Jersey."

"All right," Ferris Cole said. "You've finally lost me."

"I'll tell you some other time when I'm not racing against time to stop a pack of idiots from mucking up the evidence enough to shoot their own case in the foot. Just get those bodies for me, if you can, and give them a thorough going over that won't get blown to pieces in court. And thank you."

"Don't mention it," Ferris Cole said. "This is very interesting. My life doesn't usually run like an episode of *Law and Order.*"

Gregor wanted to say that everybody's life ran like an episode of *Law & Order* these days, because there were so many episodes of *Law & Order* that they must have covered the known universe of contemporary American situations by now. He hung up the phone instead and called Rhonda Alvarez. He had her cell phone number now. She picked up immediately.

"I'm glad you called," she said. "I ran those numbers you gave me."

"And?"

"Absolutely right, Atlantic City. We've got an address. Are you going to want somebody to go over there?"

"Yes, of course."

"You're going to have to get local co-operation for that," Rhonda said. "I mean, officially, we're not actually in this at the moment, if you know what I mean. There are problems with jurisdiction. But we get along with the cops around here. I could talk to them beforehand."

"I'd appreciate it," Gregor said. "Can you do me one more favor? Can you text message from that phone?"

"Sure."

"Send me a text with the names and numbers of the people we have to contact," he said. "It'll be easier that way. I can just put the phone down on a desk somewhere and let them have at it. I'm in a moving car at the moment. Writing things down would be difficult."

"All right, I can do that."

"Thank you," Gregor said. "I'll talk to you later. We seem to be coming up on our destination. Or something."

"Right," Rhonda Alvarez said.

The phone went dead in Gregor's ear. He closed it up and put it in his pocket. They were curving around to the parking lot now. Howard Androcoelho was waiting for him by the back door, shifting nervously from foot to foot. There was a middle-aged woman with him, looking angry.

2

The middle-aged woman turned out to be Marianne Glew. Marianne Glew turned out to be one of those women who smile too much, too often, and with too little reason. Gregor gave her as much of a smile as he could manage, and let himself drift through her opening monologue.

"Mr. Demarkian!" she said. "I should have met you before now. I should have had Howard bring you to my office as soon as you got here. I didn't think. There's been so much going on. And not just in the police department. I don't have to tell you, I'm sure. A town like this is a gigantic time suck. It really is. There's no end to the kind of things we have to do just to keep going. And of course, the public is the public. It wants lots of services and low taxes at the same time, and if it doesn't get them it never stops complaining. It's quite a balancing act. We were so glad you were able to come in and help us out. Of course, I always knew nobody had murdered Chester Morton — not then, at any rate — but you know what people are like. Charlene wouldn't give up. Maybe I wouldn't, either, if I were somebody's mother. At any rate, you're here. That's the thing. And we're very glad to have you!"

Somewhere down the block, there were wind chimes. Gregor could hear them as the wind blew. It was too hot for this time of year. Gregor was tired.

"Well?" Marianne Glew said.

"Mr. Demarkian wants to look at some of the evidence we've collected," Howard Androcoelho said. "He wants to look at the backpack. I don't know if he wants to see the skeleton of the baby, but I've told him we don't have it. Not here in the station, at any rate. It's over there at Feldman's, and they're not very happy about it. It's not like a regular body. Nobody's going to come forward to claim it. They don't know what they're going to do with it. And I don't, either."

They both looked at him. Gregor took an enormous, deep, cleansing breath and counted to ten in his head.

"I don't need to see the skeleton," he said.

"Not right away. I want to look at the backpack and the contents of the backpack."

"Well," Howard said, "then you come this way. I mean, right through here and down the hall. The other way from the main office. You just come through here."

Howard was moving them into the building as he talked. Gregor and Marianne Glew followed him. The halls were just as dingy and uninspiring as Gregor remembered them. He had never understood why police departments always wanted to paint their hallways vomit-pea-soup green and very-vomit-yellow beige.

But they all did, half and half, every time.

Howard Androcoelho got them down to the end of a long corridor. There was a door there. He opened it and stepped back to let them pass.

"This is our evidence room," he said. "It isn't very big, but we don't usually have much use for it. We don't usually have much evidence, I mean. There's not that much crime in Mattatuck."

"No," Marianne Glew said positively. "There isn't. It's one of the great virtues of a small town. Not much crime, and too much gossip."

There was a big wooden table in the middle of the room with chairs all around it. The chairs were the metal and wood kind found in a lot of high school cafeterias. Gregor looked around.

"You don't keep somebody on duty here?" he asked.

"On duty?" Howard said. "What would somebody do here on duty?"

"Well," Gregor said, "he, or maybe she, might watch over the place and make sure nobody comes in and tampers with evidence."

"Oh, we know about tampering with evidence," Howard said. "We keep the room locked. It was locked right now. I mean, before we came in. I had to use my key to open it."

"How many keys are there?" Gregor said.

"Just three," Howard said. "I've got one. The town prosecutor's office has one. And there's one upstairs in the main office."

"Where upstairs?"

"In the drawer at the front desk, I think."

"So, in a drawer, out where anybody could pick it up," Gregor said.

"I don't know who you expect is going to pick it up," Howard Androcoelho said. "I mean, it's where the officers can get it. They have to be able to get it. They have to put things in here. You can't tell me that big city police departments keep their own officers out of their own evidence rooms."

"No," Gregor said. "Big city police departments have staff running their evidence rooms, so that everything is filed and everytime anybody comes to look at it the visit is noted, and a lot of other things get marked down to make sure that nobody can tamper with anything."

"But who would tamper with anything here?" Howard said. "Why would anybody want to tamper with the evidence?"

Gregor sat down at the table. "You're going to have evidence from that double murder coming in here any minute, aren't you?"

"Of course we are," Marianne Glew said. "We have a brand new mobile crime unit. We got it with the stimulus money. And —"

"You need to keep somebody down here at all times," Gregor said. "As soon as that evidence comes in. You're going to need to be able to prove that nothing has happened to it while it's been in your possession. Now, let me see the backpack, and whatever it was that was in it."

"Except the skeleton," Howard said quickly. "I told you we don't have the skeleton."

"I know you don't have the skeleton," Gregor said.

Marianne Glew sat down, too. "Howard was telling me that you think the murders of these two people are connected with what happened to Chester Morton, whatever that was. But I don't understand it. Oh, I mean, I know Chester lived at the trailer park, and this woman, this Michaelman woman —"

"Althy Michaelman, Marianne, you really do remember her. We all went to high school together."

"Yes, of course, Howard, but I didn't really know her know her, did I? It's not like we were friends. You'd think that in a small town like this one everybody would know everybody just because there aren't that many people to know, but it wasn't like that. We all had our groups. And Althy Michaelman. Well."

Howard came back from where he had been rummaging in the shelves and dropped a big, heavy cardboard box in the middle of the table.

"There it is," he said. "That's everything we found out at the construction site, except for the skeleton. The backpack and everything that was in it. And it's a bright yellow backpack, just like the one Chester took with him, and it had books in it —"

"Was the backpack dusted for prints when it was found?" Gregor asked.

"I don't know," Howard Androcoelho said, "but it doesn't really matter, does it? By the time we got to it, the guys at the construction site had been all over it —"

"No, they hadn't," Gregor said. "Both Shpetim and Nderi Kika told me that nobody touched the thing as soon as they saw what it was. I take it your officers did touch it?"

"Well, they must have, mustn't they? I mean, they brought it here," Howard said.

Gregor stood up a little and looked into the box. The yellow backpack was indeed very yellow. He could see what the Kikas had meant about it looking brand new.

He took the backpack out of the box and put it on the table. It was empty. Its contents had been dumped out into the cardboard box and left there.

Gregor turned the backpack over once, twice, a third time. There were no worn spots or frayed spots anywhere. There were no faded places in the yellow canvas.

"Back in the car," he said, "I've got a briefcase full of notes you sent me on the Chester Morton case. Several of them mention that when he disappeared the only possession that disappeared with him was his bright yellow backpack. His bright yellow L.L. Bean backpack."

"Yeah," Howard said. "That's right. So?"

Gregor pointed at the backpack. "That's not an L.L. Bean backpack. It doesn't have the L.L. Bean logo on it."

"L.L. Bean doesn't sell backpacks with other people's logos on them?" Marianne asked.

"No," Gregor said.

"Ah," Howard said.

Gregor reached into the box and came up with the copy of *Current Issues and Enduring Questions.* He turned the book over and over in his hands. The cover was very white. There were no marks on it. The pages were very stiff. They crackled in that odd way very thin pages do when they've never been turned.

Gregor looked at the spine and said, "Shrink-wrap."

"What do you mean?" Howard Androcoelho asked.

"Shrink-wrap," Gregor said again. He pointed to the spine, to the minute little piece of plastic still attached to it. "It's just come out of its shrink-wrap. You can see a bit of the plaster there."

"You mean — I don't know what you mean," Howard said.

"Can you get in touch with the two officers who picked this up?" Gregor asked him. "I'd like to talk to both of them. And I do mean both of them."

3

Kyle Holborn came up first. He was in the main office overhead. Jack DeVito had to come in from patrol. Gregor motioned Kyle to a seat and went back to making a list of what he wanted the Mattatuck Police Department to do.

"Go to Walmart," he said, "assuming there's one close. Go to every store that sells backpacks, the big chains, the little local things. That," he pointed to the yellow backpack, "will have been bought there sometime on the day Chester Morton's body was found hanging from that billboard, or maybe the day before. I don't think it could be longer than that, but be safe. Ask back at least a week, just in case. The big chains have a few things going for them. They're cheap, they tend to carry wide varieties in color and style. They've also got some drawbacks. They're usually out on the road somewhere. The little local places are close, but they don't always carry a lot of variety in color and they're expensive. It all depends on what was most important to our people, speed or price. But the color was nonnegotiable."

Kyle Holborn looked at the ceiling. Then he looked at the floor. Gregor ignored him.

"Paydirt is finding somebody who remembers the backpack being bought," Gregor said. "You've got a better chance of that at the local places. At the big stores, you're going to have to track some people down. And then, my guess is that they won't remember unless the person who bought it was a man."

"Why a man?" Howard asked.

"Because yellow is more likely to be bought by women," Gregor said.

"But Chester Morton was a man," Marianne Glew said.

"I know he was," Gregor said. "But you'll notice everybody remembered that backpack. There were probably half-a-dozen girls in school with him who also had yellow, and nobody thought twice about it. If you don't come up with anything, you need to check the second ring, the next set of big-box stores just a bit farther away. Just in case the most important thing was making sure they wouldn't be noticed."

"They?" Howard Androcoelho said.

"Probably," Gregor said.

There was a clatter on the stairs. They all looked up to see a uniformed patrolman coming through the door, his hat tucked under his arm the way officers did it in the army. Gregor looked from him, to Kyle Holborn, and back again.

"Officer DeVito?" he said.

The man nodded. "Jack DeVito," he said. "They told me to come down here. They pulled me right off patrol. What's going on?"

"Take a seat," Gregor said.

Jack DeVito sat down. He did not look happy about it.

Gregor went back to his list for the Mattatuck Police department. What he did not put on it was anything about the security tapes for the construction site for the night before the backpack was discovered. Shpetim and Nderi Kika had told him that the tapes were available, and that they had been sent to the police department. Gregor thought he'd just let them do what they wanted with them while he looked through his own copies. If he was right about what was on those tapes, and what wasn't, it would be all that much easier to do the thing he had to do after this.

Kyle Holborn and Jack DeVito were both sitting down, looking at him expectantly. Gregor finished his list and passed it over to Howard.

"That's it," he said. "It would be a good idea if most of that got done in the next couple of hours."

"You can't go asking in all those places and hunting down clerks in a couple of hours," Howard said.

"I know. There are other things on there. Do those. Get started on the clerks. These are the two men who were called to the construction site when the backpack was discovered?"

"Yes," Howard said.

"We were," Jack DeVito said. "Kyle and me, we're partners. Usually, you know. It's just that, with all this, you know —"

"I really don't think it's fair," Kyle said. "I mean, for God's sake, all that was twelve years ago, and it didn't have anything to do with me anyway. And don't tell me that it had to do with Darvelle, because Darvelle never killed Chester Morton and we all know it. He came back. He wasn't even dead."

"You had a fight with him, though, didn't you?" Gregor asked. "The last night he was in class, an English class, that you and he and Darvelle Haymes all attended?"

Kyle looked away. "I punched him out in the parking lot. He was being a jerk. Darvelle had dumped him on his ass, which she had every right to do, and he was harassing her. So when he wouldn't leave her alone, I punched him. And that was it. It's no reason to keep me off patrol and sitting in the station doing paperwork for two weeks."

"All right," Gregor said. It was actually a pretty good reason, but he was not here to argue. He wondered a little about Kyle Holborn, that telltale, sullen "It isn't fair." This was a grown man he was looking at. At what age do you expect a grown man to stop protesting that life isn't fair?

He filed it away for later. "You two went out to the construction site," he said, stating the already obvious. "Why?"

"We got the call," Jack DeVito said. "Somebody there phoned nine-one-one, and the dispatcher called us because we were closest."

"That's part of your regular patrol?"

"In the afternoons it is," Jack DeVito said. "And on the night shift, too. We swing through the site at night just to make sure nothing's being boosted. You'd be amazed at what people will take. Copper tubing? You can sell copper tubing, if you can believe it. People sell it to buy drugs."

"Not that we have a big drug problem in Mattatuck," Marianne Glew said.

Jack DeVito, Kyle Holborn, and Gregor Demarkian all gave her a disbelieving stare.

"Morning shift," Jack DeVito said, "we go by there, but we don't go in. We get in the way when they're just gearing up for work."

"All right," Gregor said. "So, you got the call and you drove on out there. What did you find when you arrived?"

"There were a lot of people standing around," Kyle said. "All the work had stopped. There weren't any machines going or anything like that. And the guys were all standing around. So we parked the car and got out and went to see what was going on."

"And what did you see?" Gregor asked.

"It was the backpack," Jack DeVito said. "The yellow backpack. The one everybody had been looking for. Or, you know, at least one like it. Everybody knew about that backpack. Charlene Morton must have been on the local news a dozen times talking about that backpack. So there was a yellow backpack, and there was a skeleton inside it."

"I thought it was fake," Kyle Holborn said. "When I first saw it. It looked fake, like it was made of plastic. Like it was from one of those places, you know. Those Halloween places. It was absolutely clean. Like somebody had washed it."

"Did you touch it?" Gregor asked.

"Of course I didn't," Jack DeVito said.

"What do you take me for?"

"I touched it," Kyle Holborn said. "Just for a second. It just didn't look real. I want to see, you know. I wanted to see if it was bone or plastic or what. I couldn't believe it."

"I didn't see you touch it," Jack said.

"I touched it," Kyle said. "I don't know what you were looking at."

"You touched it, Mr. DeVito didn't. I've got it," Gregor said. "What about the position of it. It was buried in a hole in the ground?"

"Not really," Jack DeVito said. "I don't think anybody ever bothered to dig anything. It was in the middle of all this stuff that was stacked up, serious big stuff but also a lot of small stuff that was probably going in the garbage, but nobody had gotten around to it yet. It looked like somebody had dumped the thing on the ground where it sort of dipped down a little and then kicked a bunch of the small stuff over it. It didn't actually look like anybody had been trying to hide it. Not for serious, if you know what I mean. And if whoever meant for us to think the backpack had been buried there for twelve years, well, that wasn't going to happen. People had been working at that site for months. It was in a

495

part of the site people didn't go to much *now,* but when they started work over there, people had to move all that material in. If it had been there then, somebody would have tripped over it."

Kyle Holborn was staring at his shoes. He looked not only sullen now, but angry.

Gregor looked at the top of his head. "You both knew there was a baby connected to the Chester Morton case?"

"I'd heard stories about a baby," Jack said. "But they were just stories, you know. I mean, I knew Chester when I was in high school. Kyle here didn't, because he lived a couple of towns away. And Chester was older than I was. He was a junior when I was a freshman. But I knew him. And I knew of him. Everybody did. It's not like anybody paid much attention to stories about Chester. Half of them were true and half of them ought to have been, if you get my drift."

"I knew he told Darvelle that he was going to buy a baby," Kyle said. "That's all I knew. What kind of sense does that make, anyway? Buying a baby. Who can buy a baby? Who's gonna sell one?"

"Oh, Christ," Jack DeVito said. "Any of those loons out at the trailer park. Those people will do anything."

"Not everybody who lives in a trailer park is trash," Kyle said. "Good people live in trailer parks sometimes. They just don't have the money to live anywhere else. Or, you know, it's their families."

"I still say they'd sell a baby in that trailer park," Jack said. "Honest to God, those people are crazy."

Gregor shook his head. "Were the two of you on the night shift the night before?"

"Nope," Jack said. "We've got afternoons this entire rotation. We won't be back on nights until October."

"There would have been other police officers checking the area out that night?"

"Absolutely," Howard said. "That's valuable equipment there. We have to be careful."

"Fine," Gregor said. "Then the next thing I need is the name of the officers patroling that area at night, and I need to talk to them, too. I think we can let these two go."

"Really?" Jack DeVito said. "But this was nothing at all. You could have asked us all this on the phone."

FOUR

1

Haydee Michaelman was not sure what she was doing. She was not sure what she wanted to do. She was not sure what she could do. The day seemed to stretch in front of her endlessly, and there were so many things in it that she couldn't refuse to do. She had to go to work. She had to go to school. She had to go through the routine of her day as she always did, because that was the key to everything. You could not give yourself excuses to not do the things you were supposed to do. That was how people ended up in the trailer park.

The day was bright and clear and still. It was the first day that had felt like September yet this year. She was miles and miles away from the dam, all the way on the other side of town. They did not have to go back that way to get to school.

"You're sure you want to do this," Kenny

said, holding the door open for her as she climbed into his truck. "You're sure? You don't have to go to class on a day like this. There isn't a professor on the planet who's going to mark you down for not coming to class right after your mother was — after she died."

Haydee climbed into the passenger seat and pulled the seat belt across her chest. "I'm not going to make excuses," she said. "Everybody always makes excuses. There was a kid in my biology class senior year who made up that his grandmother died. Twice."

"But you're not making anything up," Kenny said, climbing up into the cab beside her. "And he's going to know you're not making it up. It's probably all over the Internet already. It's at least on Channel 8."

"When that kid died in the crash out in Middlebury last year, *dozens* of people skipped class and said they couldn't face it because they knew him. You don't do things like this. You don't get it. I can't make excuses. I can walk if you don't want to take me. It's all right. I've walked longer than it is from here."

"Of course I want to take you," Kenny said. "Don't be an idiot. I'm just saying that you don't have to do this. It's all right to let it go just this once. And I don't know what good you're going to be in class in the shape you're in. You're not going to understand a thing."

"I'll be fine," Haydee said.

This was true. She would be fine, one way or the other. She would sit still. She would face the professor. She would take notes. She was not really worried about having the wrong answers if she was called on in class. This was math class. She always had the wrong answers.

She wondered why that was. She could remember kids in high school, kids she had very few classes with, at the end. The ones who did AP everything. The ones who sat around at lunch, looking through thick college brochures of places with famous names. Harvard. Vassar. Yale. The University of Michigan. Notre Dame.

Some of those kids had not been much different than she was herself, but some of them had been very different. It didn't matter what was said in class, they always understood it. It didn't matter what question they were asked, they always knew the answer.

Haydee wondered what that would be like, to be like that, to just know it, all the time. It was not a matter of work. She worked as hard as anybody else in school, and probably harder. She couldn't do that. She couldn't get through algebra except by staying up nights until she was ready to fall over, and then she'd only managed a C. She'd had to nearly kill herself to pass geometry at all. She had no idea what went on in the heads of people who not only got A's in algebra and geometry, but went all the way up to calculus and got A's in that, too.

They were coming up to the intersection where the signs were. That's how Haydee thought of it. For a long time there was a sign that read: MATTATUCK DESERVES WORKING POLICE RADIOS. Haydee looked. It was still there.

They were stopped at the light. Kenny looked at the sign and said, "Gives you a lot of confidence, doesn't it? The Mattatuck police are coming to your rescue, but their radios don't work, so if you're out in the country somewhere, you're screwed."

"There was a referendum," Haydee said. "The whole town voted about it. To have the system upgraded so that the radios would work all over town. But they didn't vote it in."

"I know," Kenny said.

"I'm sorry," Haydee said. "I'm feeling sort

of distracted."

"For God's sake," Kenny said. "Of course you're feeling sort of distracted. Haydee, you're not making any sense here. You're really not. I ought to be taking you to the emergency room instead of to school. I think you're in shock."

"Do you ever think about smart people?" Haydee said.

"What?"

"Do you ever think about smart people?" Haydee repeated. "You know, those kids at school. They take AP classes and they go away to famous colleges. Except not all of them. Some of them are just like everybody else, but they work harder. Except not exactly. I worked as hard as I could and I couldn't get into an AP class. And I couldn't do math. Some of them were just smarter than me."

"You're plenty smart," Kenny said. "And you're dedicated, and you work hard."

"But I'm not *smart,*" Haydee said. "I don't just know things, like some of those people do. And I don't just understand. Sometimes, you know, with stuff in Dr. London's class, even, and that's English. Narrative arcs. Mythic archetypes. Getting the stuff in, say, 'The Second Coming.' Do you remember that poem?"

"I remember it," Kenny said. "I thought it was going to kill me."

"Well, it's like that poem," Haydee said. "Some people just get it. They read it and understand it. And I don't. And I talked to Dr. London about it, and she said it was 'cultural context.' Or maybe 'cultural literacy.' Anyway, she said there are all these things out there in the world to know about, and the more of them you do know about the easier it is to read, because writers are always just assuming that readers will know stuff. And if you don't know it, then it won't make any sense when you read it."

"All right," Kenny said.

"But that's the problem," Haydee said. "How do you learn all that stuff? And I think some people have parents who already know it and so they learn it growing up just because they do, you know. Just because it's stuff their parents talk about. But then what happens to the rest of us? Have you ever thought about that? What happens to the rest of us who don't have parents who already know? How do we find out about all that? Shouldn't they be teaching that in school? But they don't teach it in school."

They were pulling into the front entrance of Mattatuck–Harvey Community College. The billboard was still there, the one with

Chester Morton on it. Haydee hadn't realized they'd left the place with the signs.

"It's like that thing you were telling me," Haydee said. "About the tree, the Judas tree —"

"The flowering Judas," Kenny said.

"I didn't even know who Judas was until about three weeks ago. We didn't go to church. My mother didn't care about religion. I wouldn't have known what you were talking about. But that's not stupid. That's just ignorant. And that's the thing, you see. That's the thing."

They were pulling into the Frasier Hall parking lot. Students were not allowed to park in the Frasier Hall lot until after five.

"You'll get a ticket," Haydee said.

"I'll drop you off and then go park in C lot," Kenny said. "This way, you won't have to walk too far. I still don't think you're okay."

"I keep thinking that it might have been different. She might have been different. My mother, I mean. If her parents had known things like that, you know, so that school was easier for her. I don't know. I don't know. You can't just ignore the things she decided to do. I didn't get any of that stuff and I didn't get pregnant in high school. I didn't drop out at sixteen and then just — just. I don't know. You can't ignore the fact that she made choices, it's just that if things had been different she might have made other choices. I'm not making any sense. I'm not making any sense at all."

"You're making perfect sense," Kenny said.

Haydee bent over and put her forehead on the dashboard. The air conditioner was on in the truck. The dashboard felt cold.

"I've got brothers," she said. "Did you know that? I've got three older brothers, at least, and I may have one younger one. I don't know. They all disappeared a long time ago. How am I going to find them? How am I going to find them and tell them? Do they even want to know?"

"Haydee —"

"I have to go to class," she said. "Thank you for the ride. Thank you for the lunch. Thank you for everything, I guess."

Then she opened the truck's door and slipped out.

2

Darvelle Haymes did not go into the office the way most people did. That wasn't the way a real estate office worked, and besides, there was very little to do at a desk if there wasn't a client on the horizon. Darvelle did not have a client today. She did not have paperwork to prepare for other clients. She did not have cold calls to make. She did not have anything to do at all. She went into the office anyway, because it was better than sitting alone in her house waiting for the ax to fall.

Waiting for the ax to fall. That was the way Darvelle's mind put it when she tried to think and even when she did it. The phrase seemed to be swirling around and around inside her skull as if she had a ping-pong ball up there. It bounced and rattled. It made her want to bend over double and cry.

Her desk was the closest one to the big front window that looked out on West Main Street, and she had always liked it like that. In fact, years ago, when she was very new to this firm, she had done a lot of wrangling to get this desk for herself. She'd had to wait until old Miss Fanshaw was out of the way. She'd expected the old biddy to retire, but instead she'd had a heart attack at this very desk, and been carted away in an ambulance to St. Mary's.

There was coffee at the back of the room. It was a big room, long and open, taking up almost the entire first floor of the building. There was a bathroom in the back, and a little place to store records, and a big sink.

Darvelle got herself coffee when she first came in. Then she sat down at her computer and bent over it as if she had a lot to do. Then she played Solitaire, and FreeCell, and Spider Solitaire, and even Hearts, with herself. Then she got on the Internet and went to Pop-Cap Games and played Dynomite and Zuma and Alchemy and Tip-Top and Bejeweled in three different versions. She kept the sound off. She made predictions for herself. If she got to thirty-three thousand points on Dynomite, everything would be all right. If she got thirteen coins in Zuma, everything would be all right. If she won three Solitaire games in a row, everything would be all right.

Nothing was going to be all right. She lost every one of the games, and the more she lost the more tense she got. The muscles in her arms were slammed tight and hard. They ached just hanging by her side. Her head felt like it was going to explode.

Waiting for the ax to fall. That was what she was doing. Waiting for the ax to fall. It didn't matter that they hadn't killed anybody. Kyle was right about that. It didn't matter because everything else they'd done had been so screamingly wrong, both twelve years ago and now. They'd been behaving like children who can't control anything they do, who get themselves into more trouble the more they try to get out of the trouble they had. But what were they supposed to do? What? None of it had been their idea, and none of it had been their fault. All they'd ever wanted was to steer clear of the whole mess and act like they knew nothing about it.

Twelve years ago, Kyle had been in favor of leaving for California. That had been his best idea. They should pack up their things and drive West and settle down somewhere where nobody knew them.

"You know what the Mortons are like," he'd said. "You know what they're like. This is never going to go away. Not ever."

Darvelle changed her standards. She didn't need to win three Solitaire games in a row. She only needed to win one out of three Solitaire games. As long as she won one out of three, everything would be all right.

She lost three in a row. She sat and looked at the computer. She picked up the phone and punched in a number she should not know, but that she knew by heart.

The phone rang and rang. Darvelle told herself she was being an idiot. Nobody would be home in the middle of the day. Charlene wouldn't be home. Charlene would be at the business, because she always was. The woman spent all her time at work.

The phone was picked up. Charlene Morton's voice said, "Yes?"

Darvelle hung up.

Somewhere on the other end of the room, women were gathering around a computer. Darvelle paid no attention to them. They were looking at The Daily Kitten site, probably, or at one of those "lolcats" pictures. The women in this office were always looking at pictures of cats.

Darvelle picked up the phone again. She put it down again. She pushed it away from her. She didn't know what she was doing. She didn't know what she wanted to do. What could she say to Charlene that she hadn't already said?

Margie Cardiff looked up from the computer where all the women were and said, "Darvelle. Have you seen this? Did you know about this?"

Darvelle looked down at her own computer. It was almost two o'clock in the afternoon. She had come in well before noon. She had no idea what she'd been doing all this time.

"Is it a cat?" she asked.

"No, it's not a cat," Margie said. "It's us. Go to Channel 8. Or come over here. We've got it up."

Darvelle did not want to go over there. She wanted to go home — or, maybe, not home, but out to lunch, or shopping, or something. She wanted to find some way to not be anywhere at all. She wiped the Solitaire game off her computer and typed in the URL for Channel 8.

It was up there, right in front of everything, as soon as the page loaded. "Breaking News," it read, in big red letters. Then there was a picture of the dam and next to it a big black pickup truck that she was sure she recognized.

She pushed her chair back. It moved on wheels. She hated chairs that moved on wheels. She pulled the chair closer again and tried to read.

"What is that?" she said after a while.

"Two people shot dead out by the dam," Margie Cardiff said. "It doesn't say who it was, but everybody knows. People have been calling for an hour. It was that terrible Michaelman woman, do you remember her? We had her daughter working here for awhile, and then she came in — the mother, not the daughter; the daughter was a lamb — anyway, the mother came in and she was drunk beyond belief and she chased away two clients, and then we had to let her go.

The daughter, I mean. Oh, for God's sake. You know what I mean. It's those people over at the trailer park. Two of them, this Michaelman woman and somebody else, shot right through the head in a black pickup truck parked out by the dam."

Margie was hanging over the desk now, looking at Darvelle's screen. "There it is," she said. "You can see it."

Darvelle felt as if the skin of her lips had dried out and cracked. It hurt to touch them with her tongue.

"Who was the other person?" she said. "Was it the daughter, the one who used to work here?"

"No, of course not," Margie said. "It was some man. Isn't that something else? A woman like that, and she's always got a man hanging around somewhere. Half the decent women you know can't find a man to go out with, and women like that always have somebody. She's dead now. They're both dead. Isn't that incredible."

"What I want to know about is that truck," Brenda Malloy said, calling out from the other side of the room. "Where did people like that get a truck like that? Do you know what something like that costs? You might as well buy a Mercedes."

"It's probably got orders of repossession

out on it right now," Margie said. "Or maybe it isn't their truck. Maybe it's the murderer's truck. Maybe they were murdered over a drug deal, and the truck belonged to their connection. Drug dealers make enough money to buy a truck."

"Some drug dealers do," Brenda said, "but some drug dealers use up their product, and they're just as broke as everybody else. Besides, who would do that? You don't mess up a vehicle like that? It must have been their truck. You know what people like that are like. They buy everything on credit and then they can't pay for it. The finance company is going to be livid. If the seats had cloth covers they're never going to get the blood out, and if they had leather covers they're going to be shot full of bullet holes. God, can you imagine?"

"Excuse me," Darvelle said.

She got up and walked to the back, past the other women at the other computer, into the little hall. She went into the bathroom and locked the door behind her. She lifted the toilet seat cover and then the toilet seat. She stared down into the water and thought about the truck. Her head was full of helium. Every pore of her body was pumping out sweat.

She leaned over the toilet bowl and threw up.

3

It took her most of the morning to admit it, but Penny London found this whole thing — the motel room of her own; the open account to get anything she wanted from the restaurant — to be really something wonderful. It had been months since she'd been able to settle into an indoor space for more than a single night, and months since she could take as many showers and baths as she wanted just because she wanted to. That was how she spent her time between talking to the boys and noon. She took a shower. She took a bath that lasted an hour and a half. She took another shower. Then she went down to the restaurant and had another of those enormous meals. For some reason, she had to have fried food and butter and a big gooey dessert. Had she been starving herself, all this time living in the car? She didn't think so. She hadn't been absolutely destitute. Money had been automatically deposited to her bank account every other week in term time, and outside of term time there was always at least a little left, and there was tutoring. Still, she was hungry. She couldn't believe how hungry she was. And she wasn't eating like herself. She didn't seem to be able to look a vegetable in the face.

She had told George or Graham or both of them — she couldn't remember — that she had to teach, but she didn't really, not until this evening. After lunch, she went back up to the room and sat on the bed and tried to think. Then she tried to read. Then she tried to watch television. She was too restless. The stories about Althy Michaelman and her man friend — "Slaughter at the Stephenson Dam!" was how Channel 8 put it — came and went. Penny couldn't seem to make them make sense.

She had a book of crossword puzzles. She tried that, but that didn't work, either. That was when it occurred to her that she could get something done. She could do laundry, if nothing else. The laundromat would be open. She could sit there and wait for her clothes to finish going around and around in the dryer.

She got to the laundromat just in time for the noon rush. The washers and dryers all seemed to be in use, except for the two in the back, which were not open to the public. Penny looked around. There was a sign on the wall. The laundromat staff would do your laundry for you, at the price of one dollar a pound, with a minimum of ten pounds. Penny looked at the bag of laundry in her hands. It was really a black plastic garbage bag. That sign had been up there as long as she could remember. She had read it every time she had come into the place. She had read it, but she hadn't taken it in. She complained that her students didn't understand how to read, that they read things and just didn't take them in, and here she was.

She went to the back and looked in at the door where the administrator stayed during the day. Maybe the word shouldn't have been "administrator." Maybe it should have been something like "attendant." There was something she'd never thought of before.

The attendant was a small girl with hair pulled back in a ponytail. She had bright red pimples along the edge of her jaw. She was chewing gum. Penny cleared her throat.

"Could I ask you what the policy is for getting laundry done?" she asked. "I mean, would I have to bring it in in the morning, or —"

The girl looked down at Penny's half-full garbage bag. "Two hours," she said.

"What?" Penny said.

"Two hours," the girl said. "Leave it here and come back in two hours. I can't be any faster than that."

"Oh," Penny said. "Yes." She fingered the plastic of the bag. Could she really do this? It felt extravagant in a bad way, paying somebody else to do your laundry. On the other hand, she hated doing laundry. She hated even more sitting in the laundromat waiting for the laundry to be done. The girl was just standing there, chewing gum. Penny had to do something.

"All right," she said. "I'll be back in two hours."

The girl handed her a plain slip of paper and a ballpoint pen. "Put your name and number on this," she said. "That's just in case I have to call you. I've never had to call anybody all the time I've been here, but that's what I'm supposed to do. Get you to write your name and number."

Penny wrote down her name and number. She passed the little slip of paper back to the girl. Then she just wanted to be out of there. She left the laundromat and went back across the parking lot to her car. She didn't like this parking lot, and she didn't like this shopping center. Too many of the stores were out of business.

Penny turned the car's engine on. She turned the air conditioning on. She turned the radio on. She needed to get up and get out of there, but she had no idea where to go. Usually, when she felt like this, she went in to school. Today, she didn't want to be there.

She had just about decided that she was going crazy in some novel and definitely peculiar way when the radio station she was listening to went to the news, and she was faced with Althy Michaelman yet again.

"Sources that cannot be named inside the Mattatuck Police Department," the announcer said, "tell us that police are proceeding on the assumption that the two deaths discovered this morning are linked to the disappearance and death of Chester Morton, a local man who . . ."

Penny sat up straight in the driver's seat. That didn't make sense, did it? How could those two deaths be related to Chester Morton? How could anything be related to Chester Morton?

Penny looked out the windshield into the parking lot. It was empty. It really was. Two crazed yabbos from the trailer park or the welfare office weren't going to come running in to mug her if she got out of the car.

She got out of the car, went around to the trunk, and opened it. She was still carrying most of her stuff. She hadn't thought to unpack it just because she finally had a room she could count on.

She rummaged through the files of papers she kept in the back of the trunk space — really, all her "stuff" was paperwork from teaching; she owned practically nothing she wouldn't be able to throw out if she ever decided to give it all up to join the roller derby.

She asked herself what had made her think of the roller derby, and then she found it, the file she kept on Haydee Michaelman. Penny kept files on all her students. It was the only way she could keep track of whether or not they were making progress.

She found the first of the papers Haydee had written, the personal narrative, and looked through it. It was all about her mother getting pregnant at sixteen. Penny looked some more and found the copy of the journal entry where Haydee had written about being taken into foster care. She had been six at the time. Penny read through it. Then she took the two papers, closed the trunk, and got back into the driver's seat of the car.

She put the papers out across the dashboard. She leaned forward and read the journal entry.

For me, the really hard thing about the

518

way I grew up isn't the stuff that happened so much. It's that I never seem to feel the way people expect me to feel. When the social workers came and took me away, it was traumatic. I cried for days. But it's not what I really remember. It's not what scared me the most. That was a couple of days earlier, when the social workers took my baby brother away. They took him first, and then they came back for me. And I knew they were going to come back. I knew when they took him that I was going to be next, and for that whole week I hid in my closet at night because I was afraid I was going to wake up and be snatched.

Penny rubbed the side of her nose with her finger. Althy Michaelman was sixteen when she had her first child, but she must have been thirty-four when she had Haydee, and forty or close to it when she had this baby brother. And there was something else, too, in some of the other journal entries, something about older brothers Haydee didn't know because she'd never met them.

And there was the skeleton of a baby that nobody talked about.

And there were two people dead by the dam.

Penny got out her cell phone, found Gregor Demarkian's number in her address book, and dialed.

FIVE

1

Gregor Demarkian took the call from Penny London while he was sitting in Howard Androcoelho's office. After he had heard her out, he asked her to repeat everything so that he could write it down. Then he asked her if she could bring the copies of the essays, or make copies and bring those, or something. He was thinking that it might be possible to send Tony Bolero to wherever she was to get what he needed, but it turned out not to be necessary.

"I'm not far from you at all," she said. "I'm at this awful shopping center with all these empty stores —"

"Out near the trailer park? I know where that is."

"Yes, well, I'm there. And I've got my car. And because of you, I've got my own room at the Howard Johnson and two absolutely furious sons, who are apparently getting on a plane tonight. How did you do that?"

"I waited until you were asleep and then I went in and took your phone. I put it back when I was through with it."

"I know that," Penny London said. "I didn't miss it. How did you know they were my sons?"

"They were California area codes," Gregor said, "and the only ones on the phone. You told me you had grown sons. You told me they lived in California. It wasn't that hard."

"Yes, well. It appears they're coming out here to take charge of my life."

"From what I've seen, somebody has to."

"*Ahem.* I do have a doctorate. I mean, I managed to get through graduate school. I'm not a complete idiot."

"Any sixty-year-old woman who sleeps in her car when she's got family she gets along with who want to take care of her *is* a complete idiot. How long before you get here?"

"Fifteen minutes. You're a very unusual man, Mr. Demarkian."

"My wife says the same thing, but she's usually got a different inflection in her voice."

Penny London hung up.

Gregor put his phone down on Howard Androcoelho's desk. "Who do we talk to to get a rundown of the history of Althy Michaelman with — what's it called here? Child Protective Services?"

Howard Androcoelho was sitting behind his desk, looking deflated and more than a little worried. Now he looked startled. "Here it is. Children and Family Services, OCFS. But they won't talk to us. They can't. Everything they do is supposed to be confidential."

"They'll talk to us if what's involved is the murder of a child," Gregor said. "We've got the skeleton of an infant with its skull cracked. That's the murder of a child."

"But what does that have to do with Althy Michaelman? What does any of this have to do with Chester Morton? I don't understand what's going on in here."

"Well, I'll clear up the Chester Morton thing in about an hour," Gregor said. "I just want to put a few things together first. But as for Althy Michaelman — Chester Morton said he was going to buy a baby. I think we've got everybody agreed on that, right?"

"Yes, right, absolutely."

"Good," Gregor said. "Well, Haydee Michaelman, Althy Michaelman's daughter, takes a composition class from a woman named Penelope London."

"I remember Dr. London," Howard said.

"She taught the class Chester Morton was taking back twelve years ago, too. She was teaching farther back than that —"

"Yes, I know," Gregor said. "And she's the one who witnessed the fight between Kyle Holborn and Chester Morton the last night anybody will admit to seeing Chester Morton alive and around here. I'm going to get back to that in a bit. But as to Althy Michaelman — Haydee wrote a series of essays and journal entries for Penny London's class, and in them she wrote about how her mother had her first child at sixteen. She also wrote about being taken into foster care when she was six. It was a terrifying experience for her because her baby brother had been taken away only a little time before, and she had other brothers who had been taken away and never allowed to come home again."

"Yeah," Howard said. "Okay. That sounds about right. Althy dropped out of high school our junior year because she was pregnant."

"It's all those kids being taken into foster care I'm thinking about," Gregor said.

"With a woman like Althy? Why? She was a raging alcoholic. She couldn't stay in work. She did a fair amount of low-level drugs. She's the kind of person OCFS spends a lot of time involving themselves with."

"I agree. But I don't think that's what happened this time. I think Althy Michaelman sold those babies. Every single one of them."

"She didn't sell Haydee," Howard said. "If Althy was selling babies, why would she keep just that one?"

"My guess is that she was in jail," Gregor said. "That's something else I wanted you to look up. Did Althy Michaelman have a record, did she spend any significant time in jail. By which I mean more than eighteen months."

"Why more than eighteen months?"

"Because," Gregor said, "if you're going to sell babies, you've got to sell *babies.* That's the point. It's difficult to find a white infant to adopt. If the respective adopting parents have anything at all about them that the social service agencies don't like, there's no chance. And that tends to mean that older couples and same-sex couples get the choice of an older child or nothing at all."

"Well," Howard went, "okay. I've heard about that kind of thing. But if she was doing that, shouldn't she have had a lot more money? Didn't I see a *Dateline* report on that where these fancy-ass lawyers were paying hundreds of thousands of dollars to get hold of infants?"

"They wouldn't be interested in getting hold of one from somebody like Althy Michaelman," Gregor said. "People of the kind you're talking about are very careful about this kind of thing. They're not going to want an infant who's been exposed to alcohol and tobacco in the womb, and Althy smoked, drank, and did everything else unhealthy for a developing fetus. Althy would have been dealing with people with far less money. I still think she could probably have charged around, say, ten thousand dollars."

"Ten thousand dollars," Howard said. "You think Chester Morton bought an infant for ten thousand dollars. Where do you think he was going to *get* ten thousand dollars?"

"He got it from the same place he got the rest of his money," Gregor said. "He stole it from his mother. Well, you know, from the family firm. But I've met Charlene Morton. She'd have considered it stealing from her, personally."

"This is nuts."

"I agree. A lot of this is completely nuts," Gregor said. "But let's stick with Althy Michaelman now. I want to know if OCFS ever removed any other children from Althy's home and put them in foster care — any of them. I especially want to know if they removed an infant around the same time they removed Haydee around twelve years ago. You should be able to get them to tell you that. That's not confidential information, and we do have the skeleton to account for."

"All right," Howard said. "I get that. We can probably do that."

"Then I want to find out if Althy Michaelman was in prison for about eighteen months or a little longer around eighteen years ago. I think that's about right. Haydee wrote that she was six when she was taken into foster care and she remembers just when because it was just after the police came and searched the trailer park because Chester Morton was missing. Six then, twelve years later, eighteen now. If she gave birth just before or just after going to prison, the baby would have been put into foster care until she was released — unless there was family? Did she have family to take the child?"

"It's the Michaelmans we're talking about here," Howard Androcoelho said. "They're all like that, except maybe this young one. Althy walked out on her mother when she was pregnant the first time and never looked back. God only knows who her father was. But Mr. Demarkian, I don't get it. If Althy had had all these children taken away by Child Protective Services, why would they have given Haydee back when Althy got out of prison, if she ever was in prison?"

"I don't think Althy did have a lot of business with Children and Family Services," Gregor said. "Remember? I think she just said she did, to cover the fact that she was selling the infants."

"Then why didn't she sell Haydee?"

"Because," Gregor said, "Haydee would have been too old. If Althy went in to prison about the time she gave birth or very soon afterward, and if she stayed there a year and a half or more, she wouldn't have had time to sell the infant before she was incarcerated and the child would have been past the point where people would pay for it when she got out. So there was Haydee. And Althy was stuck with her."

"Honest to God," Howard said.

"Go find out the stuff I want," Gregor said. "I want to commandeer your office for about an hour. I promise to use my own cell phone and not touch any of your papers. Find out if OCFS has any record of removing children other than Haydee from Althy

Michaelman's care. Find out if Althy Michaelman was in prison eighteen years ago. Get the stuff Penny London is bringing in in the next half hour or so and give it to me. Then get Darvelle Haymes and Kyle Holborn into a room for me. I'm going to yell at them."

"Kyle Holborn? Officer Holborn?"

"That's what I said."

"I hope you know what you're doing," Howard said.

Gregor Demarkian knew exactly what he was doing, and he felt good doing it. In fact, he felt good for the first time since he'd arrived in Mattatuck, New York.

2

When Howard Androcoelho was finally out of sight and out of mind, Gregor had the urge to get going and get on with it: call Rhonda Alvarez at the FBI; call Ferris Cole and hear about the bodies. Instead, he reached for his phone and tried first Bennis, then Donna, then Fr. Tibor Kasparian, listening to that strange distant ringing all phones gave you in imitation of what was supposed to be happening on the other end. Of course, it wasn't what was happening on the other end. Bennis and Donna and Tibor all had ring tones they'd bought, little snatches of music, all kinds of things. Tibor's general ring tone was the theme from *Looney Tunes.* Gregor found himself wondering why phones could do all the things they did but not give you the ring tone the person you were calling would be hearing. It was a silly thought, useful for nothing. It was the kind of thing Gregor thought of when he was tired.

When Bennis did not pick up, and Donna after her, Gregor got worried. He had a leaden, sickened feeling that he had failed to check in when he ought to have. He imagined their phones on silent and the ringing going on and on and on, but mute, while old George passed away in a hospital bed while the one person he wanted to hear from was nowhere to be found.

On the other hand, Gregor did not know that he was the one person old George wanted to hear from. In fact, it was unlikely. Old George had family. But still.

Gregor didn't leave voice mail messages for Bennis or Donna. He didn't have to. Their phones would tell them they had missed a call from Gregor Demarkian. He thought he would leave a voice mail for Tibor if Tibor didn't pick up, but then, when the ringing had just begun to feel endless, it cut off, and Tibor said, "Krekor? This is you?"

Gregor took a deep breath and expelled it very slowly. He hadn't been aware that he'd been this tense until this moment.

"Yes," he said. "Yes, Tibor. This is me. I just wanted to check up on, you know, things. I feel like I haven't been checking in anywhere near enough."

"You have been checking in constantly, Krekor. Bennis complains about it. You did not want to call Bennis this time?"

"I did call her," Gregor said. "She didn't pick up. I called Donna, too. She didn't pick up, either."

"They have left the baby with Lida and taken Tommy to the movies," Tibor said. "Then they're going to take him to Chili's to eat. Maybe they're still in the movies."

"Maybe they are," Gregor said, feeling better.

"The movie is called *Cats and Dogs: The Revenge of Kitty Galore,*" Tibor said. "I went with Grace and her friend who plays the violin the other night. It is a really terrible movie, but I liked it. The way I liked Jacqueline Susann. I felt sorry for the friend who plays the violin."

"Why?"

"Because he is in love with Grace," Tibor

said, "and Grace is only pretending she is not in love with the doctor who is an intern at that hospital downtown. You can see the problem there."

"Yes," Gregor said, "I can definitely see the problem there. What about our problem? What about old George?"

"It is the same as the last time you called me," Tibor said. "He drifts in and out, sort of, but he doesn't seem to be getting any worse. He just doesn't seem to be getting any better. He talks to people. He really isn't very confused except when they give him the pain pills —"

"Pain pills? He's in pain? Has he always been in pain?"

"Krekor, please," Tibor said. "They've been giving him pain pills from the first day. You know about this. We have talked about it."

"It's not a good idea, giving a man that age pills that depress his body functions. That's what pain pills do, after all. They —"

"They're not loading him up," Tibor said. "They're giving him the lowest possible dose, in an attempt to keep him comfortable. And it seems to be working. He is comfortable. He is not fading. He is just there. I think maybe he is waiting."

"Waiting for what?"

"For his birthday," Tibor said. "I have seen it in other old people, Krekor, it is not uncommon. They know they are dying and they are ready for it. They are not in that place some people are where they hate the idea and will do anything to fight it. But there is something they are waiting for. Something they want to do first. I think old George wants to wait until his birthday. I think he wants to be officially one hundred years old. And then. Well."

"You think old George is dying," Gregor said. His mouth felt very dry.

"Of course I think old George is dying," Tibor said. "And so do you. And so do Martin and Angela. And so do the doctors. And so does old George, if it comes to that."

"That's horrible."

"No," Tibor said. "What you are dealing with there, *that's* horrible. Murder. Torture. Rape. The things we do to cause each other pain. Those things are horrible. So are the diseases that make people die before they're ready. Cancer. But this is not horrible. This is a natural end of a human life on this earth."

"I'm not convinced that there's any other life but the one on this earth."

"I know, Krekor, but for me it is simpler. I am convinced. But either way, this is not horrible. This is the end of a long good life. You should go now and deal with the things that are horrible. Your murders were breaking news on CNN not twenty minutes ago."

"Right," Gregor said. "Of course they were. How do they do these things so fast?"

"They have local partners," Tibor said promptly. "You hear them talk about it all the time. Go do some work, Gregor. You should come back for the birthday party if you can get here."

"There's going to be a birthday party? For old George?"

"With a cake and those popper things that pop and then throw out streamers," Tibor said. "Angela and Bennis and Donna and Lida and all the rest of them have been planning. And I think that the day after that will be the end."

"Maybe he won't want to go until he sees me," Gregor said. "Maybe that way I could just stay away and he'd live forever."

"Krekor."

Gregor closed the phone and sat back, thinking. *Okay, that last thing had been bad. It had been worse than bad. It had been stupid.*

He picked up the phone again and found Rhonda Alvarez's number in his address book. She picked up on the first ring, sounding a little out of breath.

"I just got the first news in from Atlantic City," she said. "I would have called you, I really would have. I just wanted to go through it."

"Go through it after you give me an overview," Gregor said. "I may have to get some things done here before I get the full report. Did you find the truck?"

"Absolutely. That was easy. Black Ford pickup, approximately twelve years old, registered to a Charles Mason, and an address. Could he really have taken a name so much like his own as Charles Mason?"

"Don't they usually?"

"Not since those true crime shows have been all over TV," Rhonda Alvarez said. "They learn all kinds of things from those shows. Although it's hard to tell. There's that *To Catch a Predator* thing, been on forever, but the guys keep falling for it, over and over again. Maybe it's a good thing so many criminals are stupid."

"I'm sure it is," Gregor said. "Did you run a check on Charles Mason?"

"Absolutely," Rhonda Alvarez said again. "And I got a nice preliminary haul. Worked the casinos for several years and kept getting fired. My guess would be petty theft that they couldn't quite prove, if you know what I mean. Ended up without a job, but I don't see any record that he'd been homeless or anything like that —"

"No," Gregor said, "he wouldn't have been."

"Looks like he had a gambling problem," Rhonda Alvarez said. "A lot of this is squishy. He definitely had a drinking problem, but it never amounted to much. A few arrests for public intoxication, one for possession of an amount of marijuana too small to get a cat high, little things like that, lots and lots of them. Only one serious arrest, for assault. He got into a fight with this guy who does tattoos. The guy called the cops. There was a plea bargain. He got probation. He was still working then, so that was probably why. There really doesn't seem to be much here."

"I didn't expect there to be," Gregor said. "But what I think we do have now is probable cause for a warrant to search his place. It's his truck that was sitting up here with two bodies in it. Do you think that, given that circumstance, you could convince the local cops to get that warrant and search that house?"

"I don't think it would be any problem at all," Rhonda Alvarez said. "Is there something you want them to be looking for?"

Gregor thought about it for a minute. "Try for a bright yellow L.L. Bean backpack. After all these years, it might not be so bright yellow anymore. Look in the basement, in the crawlspace if that's what it is — he has to have kept the body of that infant all this time. Either that or he's been murdering babies systematically for twelve years, and I'm nearly a hundred percent certain that isn't true. He's got to have hidden it somewhere. And he has to have had it with him when he came up here, so it either had to be in the house he was living in at the time or he had to have hidden it somewhere else. I think if it was somewhere else, we're probably screwed."

"But you have the skeleton of the baby," Rhonda said. "You have it with you up there."

"Just the skeleton," Gregor said. "There was no flesh on the bones. It has to have rotted off somewhere, or been removed somewhere."

"Oh, God," Rhonda said.

"Yes," Gregor said. "Well. And he may have lived somewhere else before, and the evidence we're looking for might be there instead."

"I can find out the places he lived."

"I know. I don't know if you could get all

those warrants," Gregor said. "And they might not matter anyway. I don't know how long it takes flesh to rot off a skeleton, and I don't know if the rotting leaves any evidence behind. But at least have the locals get a warrant and search the place he was living in right before he came back here. Maybe they'll find something."

3

It was almost half an hour before Howard Androcoelho came in to say that Kyle Holborn and Darvelle Haymes were sitting downstairs in the "conference room," which was what Howard called any room with a big table and chairs in it. Gregor filed this away on his mental list of grievances over the preciousness of Mattatuck and followed Howard to the meeting place.

"You'd better stay," he said, just as they were going through the door.

"Of course I'll stay," Howard said, looking startled.

Gregor reminded himself that he would be able to get back to Howard later, and went in to find Darvelle and Kyle sitting so close to each other, one of them might as well be in the other's lap. Gregor pulled out a chair directly across from them and leaned over the table.

"We didn't *kill* anybody," Darvelle burst out.

Kyle Holborn grabbed her arm.

Gregor counted to five in his head. Then he counted to ten in his head. Then he reminded himself that there was no way to avoid stupid people in police work.

"I know you didn't kill anyone," he said, "but what you did do is beyond stupidity, and it's caused untold trouble for me and everybody in this police department and it might have been the catalyst that got two people murdered. Now, I'm going to tell you what happened. You're going to tell me if I'm right — and, believe me, I am right — and then you're going to fill in the details. Got it?"

"You can't force us to say anything," Kyle said. "We have the right to have a lawyer present. We have the right to remain silent."

"By all means, let's get a lawyer in here," Gregor said. "Right now, you're just going to be in the ordinary kind of trouble, but I don't see why I couldn't convince Howard here to prosecute you for the stunts you've pulled. At the moment, I think I can promise that that will be off the table. There's just the four of us here. This is the least pressing part of this case and I want it over with. So, take your pick."

"We didn't kill anyone," Darvelle said again, starting to cry.

Kyle Holborn looked away.

Gregor Demarkian waited long enough to make sure Kyle Holborn wasn't going to ask for a lawyer again, and then he started.

"First," he said, "Chester Morton decided to come back home. I don't think the two of you had anything to do with that. And why he decided it doesn't matter for our purposes here, so I'll let that slide. But he decided to come back home, and my guess is that he went straight for Ms. Haymes's house. Am I right so far?"

Darvelle nodded.

"Next question," Gregor said. "Did he ring the doorbell, or did you just come home to find him?"

"I just *found* him," Darvelle said. "And the rest of the stuff. He was — he was hanging, just hanging there, he looked awful. He was just hanging from the lintel, you know, the top of the door to the bathroom, so he was the first thing I saw when I went down the hall. And then there was the other stuff — the stuff."

"The baby's skeleton," Gregor said.

"That and a note," Darvelle said. "The note was about how he couldn't live with himself anymore, and all this total crap. It said that we bought the baby together and that I'd killed it and that that was why he'd run away — but it isn't true. It isn't true. I never saw the baby. Not ever."

"No, I don't think you did," Gregor said. "He was going to get the baby the last night you two ever saw him, the night of the last English class you all had together at Mattatuck–Harvey Community College."

Darvelle nodded.

"And that's what the fight in the parking lot was about," Gregor said. "It wasn't just that Chester was harassing you, it was that he wanted you to come take delivery of this baby, which he'd already bought, and you," Gregor nodded toward Kyle, "didn't want to see Darvelle in that kind of trouble."

Kyle stirred for the first time. "You have no idea," he said. "God, but Chester was an asshole. Really. And I could just see it. Darvelle's life ruined. Everything a mess, and why? Because the guy was a lunatic?"

"Was he a lunatic?" Gregor asked. "Do you think Chester Morton was crazy?"

"I wouldn't know how to tell," Kyle said, "not the way a psychologist would. But he was sure as hell the ordinary kind of crazy, if you know what I mean. He did incredibly risky, dangerous crap all the time, and he sucked people into it."

"All right," Gregor said. "Let's get back to the present. You came home, you found him dead and hanging in a doorway, and then you called Mr. Holborn here. And Mr. Holborn came over."

"Right away," Darvelle said. "He wasn't working, thank God."

"My guess this was about two days before Chester Morton's body was found hanging from the billboard. Which means you must have stashed it somewhere cold."

"We put it in my freezer in the basement," Darvelle said. "I've got one of those big long ones. I buy things in bulk and freeze them. It's cheaper. Except there wasn't much of anything in there, which was good, because after the body was in there I had to — I had to throw everything out. I had to. I couldn't."

"All right," Gregor said. "So you put the body in the freezer, and then you tried to figure out a way to point suspicion of any kind away from yourselves."

"People would have thought she'd killed him," Kyle said. "Or they'd have thought we both had. We weren't being entirely stupid."

"You were, indeed, being entirely stupid," Gregor said. "But let's see how this goes. Chester Morton either didn't have the yellow backpack with him or he had it but it was unusable for some reason —"

"He didn't have it," Darvelle said. "He didn't have anything. We searched the truck later, and there wasn't anything."

"All right," Gregor said. "So one of you went out and bought a bright yellow backpack somewhere."

"Kmart," Kyle said.

"— and put the skeleton of the baby in it. Also the books. Where did you get the books?"

"They were mine," Kyle said, "I still had them from the class. They weren't even out of their shrink-wrap yet. They were brand new."

"Did you two think to wear gloves when you were handling them?" Gregor asked.

"We wore latex gloves the whole time, when we were handling everything," Kyle said. "I don't think you could have found a thing to trace us to the —"

"Oh, for God's sake," Gregor said. "Of course we could have found stuff to trace to you two. You can't pull as much nonsense as you did without leaving something behind. Experts would leave something behind and neither of you are experts. You bought the backpack. You put the skeleton and the books in it. You did what with the note?"

"I flushed it down the toilet," Darvelle said.

"Then you had the truck. Was it parked in your driveway?"

Darvelle shook her head. "If it had been in the driveway, I'd have known he was around before I came into the house. We had to go looking for it. I mean, we knew he had to drive something and we didn't want it near the house. But it was the same truck. At least it looked the same. It was parked around the corner. And the keys were in Chester's pocket, so we —"

"I drove it over to the place, you know, the business," Kyle said. "Morton Rubbish Removal. Whatever it's called. I drove it over there and left it in the employee parking lot way in the back near the brick wall."

"I followed him in my car and after he'd parked he just got in and we left," Darvelle said. "It wasn't hard. There aren't any security cameras or anything."

"And all this time, the body was in Ms. Haymes's freezer," Gregor said.

They both nodded.

"So," Gregor said. "You went back to Ms. Haymes's house, and you tried to figure out a way to dispose of the body, and a way to dispose of the backpack. But first you shaved off a small amount of hair near his nipple and spider-tattooed MOM onto it. Why?"

"That was me," Kyle said. "I thought, all along I thought, we were safest the more bizarre it all was. If it was really strange, people would pay attention to the strange instead of just looking for the obvious, if you see what I mean. And then there was Charlene, you know. I can't stand Charlene. Nobody can. So I thought — well, let's get everybody thinking about Charlene. But it was just a little thing. The whole process took less than fifteen minutes, some ink and a straight pin. It wasn't like he was going to call out in pain."

"All right," Gregor said. "So, first you gave him a tattoo and then — then you must have gotten rid of the backpack. You put the backpack at the construction site, to make sure it would be found. I've got the security tapes from the site. I take it I'm going to find one extra, out-of-schedule police run."

Kyle shook his head. "I just picked up the car and went with it," he said. "Nobody asked any questions. Nobody ever does."

"Did you take Chester Morton's body to the billboard in a police car?"

"Yeah," Kyle said. "Really early in the morning, right after I dropped off the backpack. God, it was surreal. I thought somebody would see the damn thing right away, but it hung up there for hours and hours and hours. I thought I was going to go insane."

"Wait," Howard Androcoelho said. "I thought the medical examiner said it had only been hanging up there for two hours."

"You don't have a medical examiner to speak of," Gregor said, "but the time frame would be off given the coldness of the body —"

"It was frozen *stiff* when I put it up there," Kyle said. "I never realized before that that was meant literally."

"And how could he have done it without anybody seeing?" Howard asked.

"Oh, that's the easy part," Gregor said. "I went over there and looked the other day. The billboard is positioned slantwise to the road. It's very large, and its scaffolding reaches down into a dense clump of trees. You can do anything you want behind that billboard and nobody from the road can see you. The miracle was that nobody driving by saw the body as it came up over the top, because Kyle here had to be literally swinging it."

"Yeah," Kyle said. "All right. That."

"Fine," Gregor said. "But then we've got the disappearing corpse. I take it the two of you see that as my fault, you removed the corpse because —"

"How were we supposed to know what was going to happen?" Kyle said. "I see those television shows. And I know the real thing isn't that good, but you were talking about sending the body to the state medical examiner's and I couldn't figure out, neither of us could, what that would mean. So —"

"So," Gregor said, "you just drove up to Feldman's and took the body out. And it was simple, because you were in uniform and you had a police car. Didn't it occur to either one of you that too much of the stuff you were doing could *only* be successful if somebody was in uniform and had a police car? Dropping off the backpack. Getting the body out of Feldman's. Putting the body in Chester Morton's old trailer. Try any of that in anything *but* a police car and you'd have been nailed midstream. It's something of a miracle you were never nailed anyway. Is that the end of it? Are the two of you sure I'm not going to find something else wandering around that you should have told me about?"

Darvelle shook her head. "We got a little scared. Especially after moving the body. I mean, you know, from Feldman's. It just didn't feel safe anymore. If you see what I mean."

"Right," Gregor said.

"Wait," Howard Androcoelho said. "Just a minute. Are you telling me that Chester Morton committed *suicide?*"

"Exactly," Gregor said.

"But then, I don't get it. I mean, we can't arrest anybody for a suicide, well, unless they live, you know, and —"

"Those two people in that truck didn't commit suicide," Gregor said. "Why don't you try wrapping your mind around that."

Six

1

Shpetim Kika heard the news on the little television set he kept in the construction site. The set was always on, but he didn't watch it much, because it didn't have cable. Once there had been a time when there was no cable. Everybody in this area and everyplace else in the United States had relied on their antennae. How had that worked? The antenna was useless as far as Shpetim could see. The set filled up with snow. It made buzzing noises. Sometimes it just went mute. It was impossible at least half the time.

It was just after lunch, and Shpetim had been watching Nderi and Anya, standing together near the edge of the site, near the new parking lot where cars would be when the building was open. Anya had taken a big box of something out of the trunk of her car. Then Nderi had taken the box from her. Now they were both walking across the site toward him, but they were walking very slowly. It reminded Shpetim of something. He wasn't sure of what.

The television broke through its snow for a moment and someone said, "This just in. Sources inside the Mattatuck Police Department are reporting that an arrest will be made this afternoon for the murders of two local residents near Stephenson Dam just hours ago. Sources also tell us that these murders are connected to the disappearance and death of Chester Morton and that the break in the case was obtained through evidence provided by the infant's skeleton found on a construction site near Mattatuck–Harvey Community College."

Shpetim Kika had lived most of his life in a Communist country. He knew when the news was complete and utter bullshit. He thought what he'd just heard was at least half that. What made him happy was that somebody had mentioned the baby. It was as if he had been trying to push a boulder uphill and it had finally budged.

There was a guy, Shpetim thought. From literature. He pushed the boulder uphill over and over and over again, and as soon as he reached the top, it fell down again. Well, Shpetim decided, he'd beaten the guy from literature. He'd pushed his boulder up to the top of the hill and it had gone straight over.

Nderi and Anya were coming up to him now. Anya was chattering away, and smiling. Nderi was staggering a little under the box.

"Hey," Nderi said, reaching the construction shed. He put the box down on the ground in front of the door. "Anya brought food. She and Mom have been cooking all morning."

"I have the day off from work," Anya said. "There was a funeral. One of our people died. We got off for the funeral and then there was the reception, but I didn't go to any of it. It wasn't somebody I know."

"Heart attack," Nderi said solemnly, looking down at the box of food.

"At forty-six," Anya said. "It was truly awful. You'd think he'd know better, being in the medical profession. But you can't tell with people. And even the ones you think are doing everything right, they die, too. And then there are others who break all the rules, and there they still are at eighty-seven."

"My grandfather lived to ninety-five," Shpetim said. "And he wasn't senile, either. He lived to ninety-five and scared the hell out of all of us to the end of his life."

"I don't remember any of my grand-fathers," Anya said. "They both died in jail."

Nderi picked up the box again and came into the shed with it. He put it on the little desk and looked inside it. "I keep telling her she should think of them as martyrs," he said. "I mean, it's not the same as dying because you're upholding the honor of God, but it is, in a way, because they wouldn't have been arrested if they hadn't been Muslims. I mean —"

"It's all right," Anya said. "I understand what you're getting at."

Shpetim looked into the box and came up with an enormous loaf of bread and then what looked like a vat of lamb and beans. There were utensils at the bottom of the box. That was a good thing.

"Ah," he said. "I forgot. I heard it on the television. Yeah, yeah, I know. But you could hear it a couple of minutes ago. There's going to be an arrest this afternoon, you know, an arrest about all the nonsense, not just Chester Morton but —"

"Oh," Anya said. "Those two people out near the dam. Wasn't that awful?"

"Listen," Shpetim said. "Maybe it was awful and maybe it was not. These people. You

hear things. The people in that trailer park
—"

"You can't look down on people just
because they're poor," Nderi said. "You told
me that yourself. You used to be poor."

"I don't look down on people because
they're poor," Shpetim said. "I have never
done that. It's not the poverty, but the way
they live. Having children where there is no
marriage. Living off the government when
they could be working. And the alcohol.
And the drugs. You know what I'm saying.
You do not know what those people are.
You can't say it was terrible until you know."

"No," Anya said, "I think it was terrible
anyway. I think it's terrible when anybody
dies, and as for the way they lived. Well. You
don't know what happened to make them
like that. And even if nothing did, even if
they decided for themselves to live badly,
isn't that a tragedy, too? God gives us life.
It's terrible when we waste it."

"Yes," Shpetim said, caught again by the
fact that he was being reminded of something. He still couldn't think of what. He
turned to the television set and waved his
hands. "Anyway," he said. "It came on the
television. There is going to be an arrest.
There is a break in the case. The break in
the case came through the skeleton of the

baby. See? I was right all along. The baby was important. And now, since we went and talked to Mr. Demarkian, they will be able to arrest the evil man who did these things, and everybody will be safer. It's America, the way I told you. In America, you go to the police, you state your case, the right thing gets done."

"But we didn't go to the police," Nderi said. "We went to Mr. Demarkian."

"Mr. Demarkian is a consultant hired by the police," Shpetim said. "He is the police here for as long as he is hired. And that's a good thing, too, don't you see? The regular police are not quite up to the job. The patrolmen who came here are clueless. The police commissioner is an idiot with spaghetti for brains. You don't have to worry. They know all that themselves. They bring somebody in with a good mind and the work gets done."

"I wonder what it's all about," Nderi said.

"I can't imagine behaving like that," Anya said. "Not the people at the dam. I can't imagine behaving like that, either, but I was thinking of Chester Morton. Running away from your family like that. Disappearing into thin air and not seeing your own mother for twelve years. Your own mother."

She went to the box and began to set

things up properly. There were paper bowls for the lamb and beans, wider paper plates to put the bowls on and bread and butter. There were smaller paper plates for the pastries at the bottom. Shpetim watched in amazement as *stuff* just kept coming out.

"I brought real forks and knives and spoons," Anya said. "We thought the plastic ones were too — I don't know. Skimpy. The tines of the forks kept bending. I'm supposed to gather these up and bring them back when you're done."

"They wreck their families," Nderi said. Then he blushed. "I shouldn't say 'they' like that. It's not everybody, not all the Americans. But a lot of them do. You can't imagine running away and not seeing your mother for twelve years —"

"Well, you know," Anya said. "Except for a politcal thing. If the authorities were hunting you and you were going to be killed. For politics. Like at home during the war."

"Yeah," Nderi said, "but I've heard all about Chester Morton. I didn't really know him or anything, but I've heard. And the other Morton kid, too, Kenny, I've heard the same thing. And the Mortons aren't the only ones. They hate each other."

"Hate each other," Shpetim said. "The families do?"

"The Mortons all hate their mother," Nderi said. "And they talk about it all the time, even to strangers. And you can see why. I've met Charlene Morton. I've seen how she treats people. How she treats her own children. She hates them as much as they hate her."

"I don't believe it," Anya said, very definitively. "How can a mother hate her own children? Her children are a mother's life."

Shpetim took the bowl of beans and lamb she handed him, and the fork, and then he got it. He knew what he kept being reminded of.

Anya reminded him of Lora, all those years ago, when they first knew each other. And Nderi reminded him of himself.

And, Shpetim thought, it was a good thing he'd listened to reason and decided not to oppose this marriage.

2

When Howard Androcoelho called to say he was bringing over Gregor Demarkian, Charlene listened, and told him she'd be at home, and then hung up. The air in the office felt very still. There was a fan pumping away somewhere, and the air conditioning was on, but the air didn't feel as if it were moving at all. It was odd to think how long it had been since the first day she had sat in this office, knowing that Chester was gone. Charlene remembered that day as if she'd just lived through it. The air had felt very still then, too. Her skull had felt as if it were cracking open.

Charlene waited for what felt like a million years. Then she got up, got her pocketbook off the top of the metal filing cabinet, and headed out to the parking lot to her car. Stew saw her leave. Charlene saw him see her, and stand up as she passed, too. She went by as if he weren't there.

Out in the parking lot, Charlene got into the brand new Focus and turned on the engine. She checked the rearview mirror. She checked the side mirrors. She looked at the nail polish on her fingers. It was an ordinary pink color. It was not like all those new things the girls had on their hands these days. She did her nails herself in her own bathroom once a week. That said something. That was true.

She got the car out onto the road and drove the long back way to Sherwood Forest. Just a couple of hours ago, she had been yelling at Kenny because he would not come home and be part of a united family front. That was how she had imagined this happening. They would all be together. They would be solid against the world. How had it happened that she had failed to instill that sense of family into any of her children? First Chester. Then Kenny. But really, all of them. Mark and Suzanne weren't anywhere around when she needed them, either.

She parked her car in the driveway and went up to the house by the front walk. She liked that approach. The front doors were double doors. They were wide enough so that, if you propped them open, you could drive the Focus itself right into the foyer. Charlene remembered building this house. She remembered sitting at the kitchen table in the old place, the place that was closer to the office, and spreading out the blueprints so that she could go through them with a magnifying glass. The children were all in bed. Stew was in the living room, falling asleep in front of the television. The house, like the business, had been her idea to begin with.

She went into her living room and looked around. There was the big couch, and the love seat, and an overstuffed chair for Stew. There was her own wing chair, with its upright back, that made her feel safe. Charlene didn't like relaxing, the way most people did. Relaxing made her feel like her life was going to hell.

She crossed her legs at the ankles. She folded her hands in her lap. She stared straight ahead. When she heard a car in the driveway, she didn't even flinch. It wasn't their car. It was Stew.

Stew came in through the side door, through the kitchen, the way he always did. He called out "Charlene?" as soon as he was in the house.

Charlene unfolded her hands and looked at the palms of them. "I'm in here," she said.

Stew stumbled through the kitchen and then out into the hall. Stew always stumbled. There was something about his body that did not work right. It never had, even when they had all been in high school.

Charlene looked up when he came through the archway from the dining room. She folded her hands again. She didn't smile.

"You could have told me you were leaving," Stew said. "I'd have come with you. I never said I wouldn't come with you."

"I asked you before," Charlene said. "I asked you and Mark and Suzanne and Kenny. Kenny hung up on me. Did you know that? I think he was with that girl. That girl he met at the college. Another one from the trailer park. What happened to our children, that all they want to know is people from the trailer park?"

"That isn't true," Stew said. "Suzanne is married to a very nice boy. You practically picked him out yourself. And Mark —"

"What about Mark?" Charlene said. "It will probably turn out that I'm responsible for that. Mark without a girlfriend. Mark without a girlfriend for years. Maybe he's gay. Maybe I made him that way. It's what everybody will say, in the long run."

"I don't think Mark is gay," Stew said, "and I'm pretty sure you couldn't make him that way if he wasn't. You're not thinking."

"I'm thinking fine," Charlene said. "They'll be here any minute, and then we'll have to listen to the whole thing, all the bilge, everything. It would have been different if he had died. Then, I mean. It would have been different if they'd have found him dead when he went missing. It wouldn't have been like this, then."

"And that's what you wanted? You wanted him to be dead?"

"He came here, you know, before he went over to that girl's house. He left me a note. Maybe if I'd have been here, it would have been different."

Stew sat down on the love seat. Charlene tried to remember what it had been like sleeping with him, but she couldn't. She could remember a time in her life when sleeping with somebody was the biggest decision any girl could make, and girls talked about it in the bathrooms at school, talked and talked about it, as if talking about it would make it disappear. She hadn't talked about having sex with Stew, because she hadn't had sex with Stew. Not until the night they were married.

"Charlene," Stew said.

"I was thinking about high school," Charlene said. "You and me and Howard and Marianne and Althy Michaelman. Girls getting pregnant. Girls getting kicked out. Boys telling lies. I suppose I thought it was normal. Boys always tell lies."

"What are you talking about?"

"I burned the note," Charlene said. "I did it as soon as I heard he'd been found hanging from that billboard. I knew he'd committed suicide. I knew it as soon as I heard he was dead. She must have strung him up there herself, just to laugh at me."

"Herself?" Stew said. "Do you mean Darvelle? Darvelle couldn't have gotten Chester's body up on that billboard. She's a tiny thing."

Charlene shrugged. "Then she got that boyfriend of hers to do it for her. It doesn't matter. Why would it? I did everything but

561

cut out my own heart to make things right for him, and in the end I might as well not have bothered. He accused me of it. Did you know that? He accused me of it."

"Accused you of what?" Stew said. "Charlene, honest to God, you need to go lie down for awhile. You look white as a sheet."

"I'm not going to lie down. They'll be here any minute."

"They? Do you mean the police?"

"Howard, and that Mr. Demarkian person. I knew that was going to be trouble. I knew it. What could Howard possibly have been thinking? Bringing in somebody like that, somebody who's been on television — maybe Howard thought he'd end up on television, too. God. Does Howard think? Does he?"

"Charlene."

Charlene stretched out her legs. They felt stiff. Her ankles hurt. "Howard Androcoelho, of all people," she said. "He couldn't even get Marianne to marry him, and it's not like she's going to get any other offers. You spend your whole life building up. Building up a family. Building up a business. Building up a life. You work and you work and you work and in a moment it's gone."

"Nothing's gone," Stew said. "Except

Chester. Chester is gone. He was more troubled than we realized. He ran away. He got himself in some kind of trouble. He was depressed. It's a sad thing, but it doesn't mean that everything is gone."

Charlene smiled. Out past the tall, thin windows that flanked the double doors, there was no sound on the street at all.

3

Howard Androcoelho was moving very slowly. He was moving so slowly that it felt as if the air around him had turned into molasses. Nothing made sense, except it might — and if it did, that was worse.

Marianne was still in the building, waiting in his office. He came up to her and closed the door. Of course, the door didn't have a lock. Anybody could walk in at anytime. He still felt better with the door closed.

"Well?" Marianne said.

Howard leaned against the door, as if that could keep somebody out. "He says he knows who killed Althy and Mike," he said.

"Is that all he knows?"

"I don't think so."

"Crap," Marianne said.

Howard didn't usually have trouble being short of breath. He was a fat man, but he thought he was also a fit man. Maybe that was not true. He was having trouble breathing now. "We've got a call in to Charlene," he said. "Well, to all the Mortons, I guess. He wants to go over there."

"And?"

"And I'm going over there," Howard said. "Of course I'm going over there. He wants to bring a patrolman. Or a couple. Or something. I don't know. Do you remember me telling you about that thing, about the ground around the trailer being all dug up about the time we found Chester Morton dead?"

"I think so."

"I included a picture of it, some pictures of it, in the material I sent him when I asked him to come up here," Howard said. "I was just trying to cover all the bases. It was that trailer and it was the timing so I threw the pictures in there. He was just looking at them and that's when he said he'd made a mistake, but we'd better go see Charlene and the Mortons first. I don't like this. I don't like the way this works."

"Nobody likes this," Marianne said. "I kept trying to tell you. Every department that works with him has reason to regret it, even when they get what they want and then have him back again. He sees things. He sees things that nobody else does because he isn't used to them, so they stand out for him where they wouldn't for us. Do you get it?"

"I think we're going to end up having to have a regular medical examiner," Howard said. "And a morgue."

"That was going to come eventually."

"Yeah, I know. But I thought maybe it could come after we'd both retired."

"Where is he and what is he doing?"

"He's upstairs looking through his file," Howard said. "It's incredible how much time he spends doing that. He looks through the file and looks through the file and looks through the file. Then he moves pictures around. It makes me want to scream."

"Get back to him," Marianne said. "I'd better get back to the office. You can't have the mayor away from her desk for half the day, not even in a little town like this. We'll think of something. Don't worry. We'll think of something."

"You don't have to think about it," Howard said. "It was my fault, wasn't it? It was all my fault. If I'd suggested it instead of just losing my mind, you wouldn't have gone along with it. You'd have knocked some sense into me."

"If you'd been able to think ahead to it, you wouldn't have done it," Marianne said, "and I helped you in the end, so I do have to think of something. But for God's sake, Howard, don't do that thing where you just shoot your mouth off and —"

"I won't do that," Howard said.

"Good." Marianne got her purse off the floor and walked across the room to where Howard was still leaning against the door. He moved away to let her pass. "I'll call you tonight," she said.

Howard watched her walk out into the main part of the station. He'd known her all his life. They'd met in kindergarten, when they were both five. Maybe they should have done something about it sometime along the way.

Marianne left and Gregor Demarkian returned, almost simultaneously. He was carrying photographs in one hand and a briefcase in the other. Howard wasn't sure what was going to happen next.

"Mr. Androcoelho," Demarkian said. "Come look at this for a minute."

Howard moved aside so that Gregor Demarkian could go through the office door without interference. "I made the call to the Mortons," he said. "Charlene says she'll meet us at the house. I don't suppose there's anything wrong with that. I don't blame her for not wanting to gum up the business with a murder investigation."

Gregor Demarkian went over to the desk and dumped the photographs on it. They were the same photographs of the ground being dug up around Chester Morton's trailer he had been looking at before.

"Nobody ever mentioned this," he said. "But it's interesting, don't you think?"

"I guess," Howard said.

"I was wrong about New Jersey," Gregor said. "I knew this all had to be about the baby, but I thought Chester must have taken the dead body of the infant when he left here. He took it. He stashed the body somewhere it would not give itself away, in a plastic bag in other plastic bags, in the ground, somewhere so that it wouldn't smell. And then when he wanted to come back here, he dug it up and took it with him. I was so sure of that, I got a Bureau agent to go talk the police in Atlantic City into getting a warrant for Chester Morton's place of residence to check for traces of it."

"Chester Morton was in Atlantic City?" Howard said.

"Yes, he was," Gregor said. "But the body of the baby wasn't. The body of the baby was here. All these years."

"And we never noticed it?" Howard said. "What was it, out in the woods, or what?"

Gregor Demarkian shook his head. "It would have made sense, wouldn't it, to have taken it out into the woods somewhere? But then, maybe not. Kids stumble over stuff in the woods. Hunters do, too. So if you absolutely did not want it found, if you did not want anybody to connect you to the death of an infant, maybe it would make more sense to keep it where you could keep an eye on it. Like in the ground around the trailer."

"So that's where it was? Buried under the trailer? Chester went and buried the body of an infant under his trailer? I think you're crazy."

"I'd think I was crazy, too, if that was the kind of thing I was going with," Gregor said. "In the first place, Chester didn't bury the body. In the second, the body wasn't buried around the trailer. It couldn't have been. People in that trailer park will hide from the police. They'll close their blinds and play dead while Kyle Holborn runs around doing whatever he wants to do with a full-grown adult corpse, because he's got a uniform and a patrol car and they don't want anything to do with the law. But if one of their own was burying something in the middle of the night, or the middle of the day for that matter, they'd have been all over it."

"He wasn't one of their own," Howard said reflexively.

"He lived in the park," Gregor Demarkian said. "That was as close to being one of their own as he needed to get. Let me shove some of this back in my briefcase and then let's go. I need to talk to Charlene Morton."

"But where did he bury the body?" Howard said. "You've still got the corpse of an infant wandering around. Where did he put it?"

"He didn't put it anywhere," Gregor said. "He didn't bury it and he didn't know where it was buried. Although I think he might have thought he did."

"He thought it was in the ground around the trailer."

"That's right."

"But maybe it was," Howard said. "I mean, maybe he found it when he went looking for it. Look at those pictures. The ground is dug up everywhere. Maybe —"

"If he'd known where the body was buried," Gregor said, "if he'd buried it himself, he'd have had a better idea of where to dig. Those are pictures of a blind search. Everything is uprooted everywhere. And not just around his own trailer, but around the one next door. If he'd found the body, he'd have stopped digging. But he never stopped digging. Not until he had the whole area completely unearthed. So he didn't find it there."

"It wasn't a body anyway," Howard said. "It was a skeleton."

"Let's go over and talk to the Mortons," Gregor Demarkian said. "I need to get back to Philadelphia for a birthday party."

SEVEN

1

Gregor Demarkian did not go out to Charlene Morton's house in Howard Androcoelho's car. He'd had enough of Howard Androcoelho on any level. The last thing he wanted was to be stuck in a small space while the man asked him questions while trying not to actually ask him and pumped him for information he didn't actually need.

Instead, Gregor sat next to Tony Bolero and punched numbers into his cell phone one after the other — to Bennis, because he wanted to hear her voice; to Ferris Cole, to find out what could be found if you searched a place where a body had decomposed; to Rhonda Alvarez, to explain why the police probably weren't going to find what he'd hoped they'd find in wherever Chester Morton had been living in New Jersey.

"I really wish the world was like *CSI*," Ferris Cole said, "but it isn't. Of course, it's to our advantage if criminals think it is. The death penalty may not be a deterrent, but fear of exposure through test tubes certainly is. Although I wish it were more of one. I'm so sick of exploding meth labs, I could give up this work to run a Dairy Queen."

"So we wouldn't be able to find anything at all?"

"I wouldn't say that," Ferris Cole said. "I haven't had a look at the skeleton, but you keep telling me it has a crack in the skull. Cracks leave fragments, or they frequently do. Of course, it depends on just how young an infant this was. If it was just a day or two, the skull would have been fairly soft. That wouldn't get you what you wanted. If it was a couple of weeks old, though, you might get fragments. And the fragments would have been left in the soil when the skeleton was taken out. It's a long shot. The police would have to shift through the soil with a flour sifter. But at least it's possible."

"I'm with what you said," Gregor said. "I wish the world were like *CSI*, too."

"You've got to understand, it's not that there would be no evidence at all of a body having decomposed there," Ferris Cole said. "There would always be something left behind. It's just that it would be incredibly hard to detect, and even if you did detect it, it isn't likely that it would tell you anything more than that *something* had been there. Then it would depend first on the judge, to let the prosecution enter evidence that was that vague, and then on the jury. The jury watches *CSI,* too. When you can't nail it the way they do on television, juries are likely to decide that that amounts to reasonable doubt."

"Marvelous," Gregor said. "Half the time they ignore evidence because it's not like the science fiction stuff they see on TV, and half the time they convict without evidence because they're sure that nobody could be arrested if they hadn't done *something* wrong. Tell me again why this is the best possible judicial system."

"It is, though," Ferris Cole said. "Let me get this stuff going and see what I can find. You should try to come up with an alternative approach, that's all. Something that doesn't rely on the skeleton."

"All right," Gregor said. "But it annoys me. The aesthetic is wrong. This whole thing, from the beginning, was about the baby. Well, no, not from the absolute beginning. But — oh, never mind. I'll explain it all later. I'm in a car."

"You're not driving, I hope. Not while you're talking on a cell phone."

Gregor let that go by. He never drove —
or almost never — but everybody wanted to
tell him not to do it on his cell phone.

Rhonda Alvarez was nearly out of breath.
"I'm here," she said, when she picked up. "I
was just thinking of you. I'm here, we're all
here, we've been here for half an hour."

"Where?"

"Chester Morton's house," she said. "It's
a house, too, not an apartment. Out in the
country in this little town. He was renting it
and he still is, technically. He didn't give up
the lease or anything. Anyway, I yelled and
screamed and acted hysterical and insisted
this was priority and rush and all the rest of
it, and the locals got a warrant in no time
flat and we came right out here. We've been
here for half an hour. God, the place is a
mess."

"A mess?"

"Forget vacuuming. The man never picked
up his garbage. You wouldn't believe it. Fast-
food wrappers and boxes everywhere, and
some fast food still in them, going to mold.
Old magazines. Those magazines, if you
know what I mean. He loved beaver shots.
Everything's trashed. The bathroom stinks."

"Could somebody have been trying to
search the place?"

"It doesn't look like that, no," Rhonda

said. "It's not that kind of mess. And anybody who had been trying to search the place would have found what the police found, because it wasn't like it was hidden."

"And what was that?"

"Guns and ammo," Rhoda said. "Two rifles under the bed — just under it. Not in cases or bags or anything, just shoved there. Several, I made at least four, handguns. A double-barrelled shotgun. Three tasers."

"For God's sake," Gregor said. "What was the idiot doing? Had he joined the mob? Did he owe money to the mob?"

"He owed money to everybody, from what we've been able to tell," Rhonda said, "but I don't think that's what this is. There's a lot of ammunition in boxes, but I'm willing to bet, even after just a first look, that most of these things haven't been fired in years. And some of them are brand new. They've never been fired."

"I don't suppose he bought any of them legally and registered them," Gregor said.

"We haven't checked yet, but my guess would be no. He doesn't seem the type, if you know what I mean."

"Yes, I know what you mean."

"I would say, though, that you had a good call that the gun you've got up there would be a gun he brought with him and not anything somebody up there had. My guess is that he was packing most of the time. It probably made him feel important."

"Probably," Gregor said.

"And we also found drugs," Rhonda said. "Not a lot. Not a little, either. It's not impossible that he was dealing a little on the side, some marijuana, maybe some cocaine, but it wouldn't have been anything dramatic. He was definitely using. And his refrigerator was full of beer. And there was an entire bookshelf of the hard stuff, Patrón, Johnnie Walker. Most of those were better than half empty."

"Was there any money?"

"Nope. Were you expecting us to find any?"

"Not really," Gregor said.

"I don't know if any of this helps," Rhonda said, "but this guy was in no way the kind of person who loves the outdoors and wants to go hiking all the time. If he was doing even half the stuff there's evidence of him doing around here, he wouldn't be able to hike for half a mile without falling over dead. And, for what it's worth, I don't think the house being out in the country means he was fond of the wilderness, either. I think it just means —"

"That he wanted to be far away from

people who could pry into what he was doing?"

"Like that," Rhonda said. "You can't think
this guy killed your two, right? Because this
guy was dead first."

"I know who killed my two," Gregor said,
"I'm just trying to find a way for the prosecution to make their case."

"Well, good luck with that. I'm going to
go now. They're going to take out a wall in
the bathroom."

Gregor didn't ask what they wanted to
take out a wall in the bathroom for. He
sympathized with the landlord who was going to have to clean up at least some of it
when all this was over.

Tony Bolero was making his way through
the tree-lined streets of a neighborhood that
practically screamed "best place to live in
town." The houses were all large, if vaguely
old-fashioned: ranches; split-levels; "con-
temporaries" that must have been built in
the Sixties.

Tony pulled into a driveway that already
had too many cars in it, but not enough for
Gregor. There was no patrol car here. There
was no Howard Androcoelho.

Tony pointed ahead to the long, low
ranch. "This is it," he said.

Gregor was looking at something else. The

yard was wide and deep. What he was looking at was almost invisible from the driveway. He got out of the car and went to the side of the garage. Then he just stood there and stared.

"My God," he said.

"What is it?" Tony Bolero materialized at his elbow.

Gregor pointed across the back lawn. "It's a greenhouse," he said.

It wasn't just a greenhouse.

It was a big one.

2

The other cars drove up almost immediately — Howard's, and then the two patrol cars. Nobody's siren was blaring. Nobody's lights were pumping. It was all very quiet, as if what was about to go on here was a pool party or a barbecue, the kind of thing people who lived in the kind of place Sherwood Forest was did on any given weekend.

Except that it wasn't a weekend.

"Did you bring a search warrant?" Gregor asked.

"It's coming. I sent one of the detectives to get it. Did you really get on the phone and call a judge? Did you really do that?"

"Of course I did," Gregor said. "I had to do it, because you won't."

"If I think there's a decent chance that I'm going to find evidence of a murder investigation, I'll get a search warrant," Howard said, "I'll get a search warrant. Are you honestly standing there telling me that one of the Mortons — Charlene, I'd guess, from the way you've been going on — killed Chester Morton and then blew away two completely pathetic people with a gun for — what, exactly?"

"Chester Morton killed Chester Morton," Gregor said. "I already told you that."

"Yes, I know you did," Howard said. "But that doesn't make any sense, either. If Chester Morton committed suicide, then Althy Michaelman and what's his name —"

"Mike Katowski. You ought to read your own reports."

"I don't give a damn what the man's name was," Howard said, "if Chester Morton committed suicide, then what did either of those people have to do with anything? What did they have to do with Charlene Morton? Do you really think somebody like Charlene Morton would have had anything to do with people like that?"

"Sure," Gregor said.

The front door to the Morton house had opened, and Charlene Morton had come out, followed by the stooped tall man

Gregor assumed was her husband. The stooped tall man seemed to be shrinking with every puff of wind. Charlene Morton seemed to be growing taller. She came down the walk to the driveway. She stepped off the driveway onto the grass and walked to where Howard and Gregor were standing.

"Well," Howard said. "Charlene, we're sorry to bother you, but Mr. Demarkian here —"

"Mr. Demarkian here thinks you ought to be arrested for the murders of Althy Michaelman and Mike Katowski," Gregor said.

"You're out of your mind."

"Am I?" Gregor took off across the lawn. The greenhouse was almost all the way at the back. That was why it was hard to see from the road. Once you had seen it, though, you'd never miss it again. It was the size of the greenhouses nurseries used. It was a greenhouse for serious business.

"You can't go in there," Charlene Morton said, catching up to him. Gregor pulled open the greenhouse door and she put her hand on his wrist. "You can't go in there without a search warrant."

"We'll get a warrant," Gregor said. "But thank you for reminding me." He turned back to Howard Androcoelho, who was just

580

puffing up, out of breath and looking angry. "You're going to have to call your detective. You're going to need a warrant specifically for the greenhouse."

"Why?" Howard said. "What are you doing here? What do you think you're going to find in a greenhouse?"

"Evidence of human remains," Gregor said, pointing through the open door to the large, flowering tree that seemed to be growing out of the middle of the floor. "Under that."

"Under that," Howard said. "You think you're going to find a body under that."

"No," Gregor said. "The body is gone. The body is that infant's skeleton we have. It was buried in there for twelve years."

"You really can't be serious," Charlene said.

"I'm very serious," Gregor said. "The first thing you have to know is that Chester Morton was never missing. Mrs. Morton here knew where he was from the beginning, because she sent him there. She gave him the money to leave. She told him where to go. She kept in touch with him all this time. Then she pretended to be looking for him."

"Do you think those billboards are signs of pretense?" Charlene asked.

"Yes," Gregor said, "I do. They were local billboards, which were fine because Chester was no longer in the locality. There are no other billboards anywhere else that I know. And in spite of all the talk you did about calling in the FBI, you didn't actually do it. You made demands. You made a big fuss. You went on local television. You never did the kinds of things people actually do in your situation. You only pretended to."

"It doesn't look like pretending when you see me on television," Charlene said. "It didn't look like pretending to that little whore who turned Chester's head around and made him a traitor to himself and his family."

"The only person who made Chester a traitor to himself and his family was Chester," Gregor said. "Maybe with your help. But Chester was acting out long before Darvelle Haymes came along. You tell everybody Chester wanted to move out of the house and you wanted to stop him, but that's not true, either. Your son Kenny remembers the fights that went on in the weeks before Chester left your house, and I'd be willing to bet I could find other people who remember, too. Lots of fights. Lots of yelling. All about money."

"We never begrudged our children

money," Stew Morton said. Nobody had seen him come up. Gregor was startled. "We gave them all they wanted. We gave them jobs and let them earn even more."

"You couldn't possibly give Chester as much as he wanted, because Chester gambled," Gregor said. "He also took drugs and drank and did a lot of things you didn't want him to do. And when you tried to cut him off, he just stole. So the situation got worse and worse, and you threw him out."

"Charlene would never have thrown him out," Stew said. "She would never throw any of our children out. She's not that kind of mother."

"You did throw him out," Gregor said. "That's what happened. And he rented that trailer, and then the two of you started a fight that lasted for months over the way he was living and the way he was behaving. You weren't going to back down unless he cleaned up his act, and Chester was willing to do anything but clean up his act. That's when Chester started looking for a way to get what he wanted without having to give up the liquor or the gambling. Especially the gambling, I think. That's when he came up with the idea that he should get married and give you grandchildren."

"I didn't want grandchildren from that

little tramp," Charlene said.

"Oh, come on now," Gregor said. "You had nothing against Darvelle Haymes. Under other circumstances, you'd have liked her. She's hard working. She's conscientious. She's frugal. She's all the things you probably would have wanted in a daughter-in-law, if you'd thought she was capable of turning Chester around. But she wasn't capable, because Chester wasn't really in love with her. She was just convenient. Unfortunatly, she wasn't convenient enough. She refused to get pregnant.

"And that's where the real trouble started. Chester was obsessed with his plan to give you a grandchild and get you to come around that way, and when Darvelle wouldn't help he found another way to get a baby. He was living right next door to a woman who had sold every one of her children but one. Sold them as infants. Sold them to get money for liquor and drugs and just fooling around. She was pregnant. She made Chester an offer. Chester took it. He needed some money. My guess is between five and ten thousand dollars. He needed it, and he knew where to get it. He could get it from you."

"If I'd really thrown him out of the house," Charlene said, "do you think I'd have given him even five thousand dollars, never mind ten, to buy a baby to pretend was my grandchild?"

"No," Gregor said. "I think he stole it. He still had access to your house. He still had access to your business. It wouldn't have been all that hard. Of course, doing it right, so that he got away with it, would have been harder, but I doubt if he even tried. He got hold of the money. He got the baby. Then he was going to bring the baby to you and say it was your grandchild, when you figured out he had taken the cash.

"So, instead of going home, here, to talk to you about it all, he suddenly found you on his own doorstep, loaded for bear. You were furious. You weren't going to put up with it. You knew the baby wasn't his and you weren't going to have any part of it. But the baby was there, and it was crying. And you picked it up by the feet and smashed it against the trailer wall, and then it was dead."

"You can't possibly know that," Charlene said, "never mind prove it."

"I don't have to prove everything, Mrs. Morton, I really don't. A lot of these things are details and they're not going to matter in court. But I'd stake my life that you killed that infant, and that you then convinced

Chester that nobody would believe you'd killed it. They'd all think he had. You convinced him that he had to go away and stay away. And he didn't mind that, at first, at any rate. You were going back to supporting him. He could go on living the way he was living. Why not?"

"Why would I bother?" Charlene asked. "Nobody cared about that baby. Nobody even realized it was gone. If we'd really done what you think we'd done, nothing would have happened to us because of it."

"You couldn't be sure of that," Gregor said. "Especially not at the time. You had no reason to think that nobody would miss the baby. And over all these years, that missing baby, the possible pregnancy, the baby-connected-to-Chester hasn't ever completely gone away. It's been here, always, waiting for somebody to pay attention to it. People were wrong about whose baby it was. The general idea was that it was Darvelle Haymes who had had a child — for those people who accepted that she was pregnant at the time Chester disappeared and was lying when she said she wasn't — and you encouraged that, just like you encouraged stories about Chester's love for the outdoors and lifelong ambition to live in Wyoming or Montana or one of those places, safely in the wrong direction from where he really was and safely in the wrong kind of venue. He went to Atlantic City. You enabled the hell out of all of his problems."

"So first I threw him out of the house because of his problems," Charlene said, "and then I enabled him?"

"Enabling was better than going to jail for child murder, or seeing Chester go to jail for child murder, or even just having to weather the scandal. You fed the local media one set of nonsense and you fed Chester another, saying that you were keeping him safe. And, I think, you told him that he had to stay away as long as he did because Darvelle Haymes was going to turn him in as soon as she found out he was alive."

"You think Darvelle Haymes was there when Chester and I murdered an infant," Charlene said.

"No. I think Darvelle Haymes knew all about buying the baby, and that's a crime in itself," Gregor said. "Anyway, eventually things began to come apart. Chester was getting worse and worse and he wanted to come home. The bogus 'search' for him was getting hard to keep bogus. First a television program got interested in the case, a national television program. Then the FBI stepped in and agreed to look things over.

Eventually, somebody was going to recognize him. And you didn't want him to come home. He wasn't better. He might even be worse. As soon as he got back to Mattatuck, you'd have all the same problems with drugs and liquor and hysterical behavior and, yes, stealing from the business. So you were juggling a lot of balls, and you didn't know what you were going to do.

"And in the meantime, Chester just got in his truck and came back. He was strung out. He was depressed. He had money problems from the gambling. And he was convinced that he wasn't going to be able to come home because Darvelle Haymes was a bitch who wanted to destroy him. So he came back. He didn't tell you about it. He just came.

"He wanted to do something dramatic to ruin Darvelle's life, so he went looking for the body of the baby. He started by digging up the ground around his old trailer and in the vicinity. I think you'd told him that that was what you'd done to the body. But it wasn't there, and Haydee Michaelman ended up thinking it was Mike Katowski trying to find the money she'd saved up.

"But Chester started thinking, and when he realized the body wasn't where he thought it was, he started wondering where it could be. And that's when he remembered this. A great big greenhouse, and a tree called a flowering Judas. You're the one who goes around telling everybody that they're traitors to the family. Judases. You buried the baby in the greenhouse and left it there until Chester figured out where it was and dug it up. Then he took it with him, went to Darvelle Haymes's house and hung himself from the bathroom door frame. He left her a note making it seem as if they'd killed the baby together, or as if she'd been responsible for it — she burned the note, so we'll never be sure. But he tried to incriminate her, and because of that she and a friend moved the body to the billboard.

"And from there," Gregor said, "there isn't that much to say, is there? Everything else was just a lot of smoke and mirrors until you killed Althy Michaelman and Mike Katowski."

"And I did that, why?"

"Because Althy Michaelman made the first of what you knew was going to be a series of blackmail demands, threatening to go to the police about the baby, her baby, the one she sold to Chester. That, and the fact that you were at the trailer the night Chester supposedly disappeared, and the fact that Chester was at the trailer the night before he actually died. Althy wasn't good at putting two and two together, but she was good at remembering the things she knew might make her some money. So she did. And first, my guess is that you gave her some cash, but you didn't give her everything she wanted. She had cash, and that had to come from you. But you agreed to meet the two of them to hand over the real payment, and you got them down by the truck, and you shot them. They were drunk as skunks by then. They couldn't have put up much of a fight."

"I've never had a gun in my life," Charlene said. "And you can't say I have."

"No, I can't," Gregor agreed. "But Chester had lots. They found an entire cache of them at his house in New Jersey this morning. The gun was in the glove compartment. You found it when you found the truck, parked where Darvelle and her friend had left it, in your own back lot. It was always that truck that was going to get you in trouble."

"The truck?" Howard said. "What is it about the truck?"

"It was the one thing she couldn't control," Gregor said. "Chester loved that truck. He wouldn't leave without that truck. So she managed to find a way to get it to him. She pretended to be sick of looking at it. She told people she'd sold it to some kid off the street. Nobody challenged her and she got away with it, but if you think about it, you've got to wonder why. This is a woman who rented her son's trailer for twelve solid years, supposedly because she wanted to have it waiting for her son if he was ever found — and she gets rid of his truck in no time flat? Why? Chester Morton didn't give a damn one way or the other about his trailer. He loved his truck."

"You're still not going to be able to prove any of this," Charlene said. "Not in a million years. And nobody would believe it."

Gregor looked back through the greenhouse door at the flowering Judas tree. "Oh, I don't know," he said. "You'd be amazed at what we can do if we know what we're looking for."

■ ■ ■ ■

EPILOGUE

■ ■ ■ ■

Evil is real, like concrete.

— Philip K. Dick

1

On the day of old George Tekemanian's one hundredth birthday party, Gregor Demarkian sat down to write Howard Androcoelho an e-mail.

This was not as easy as it should have been. The promise that if Gregor would only go away for a while Bennis and Donna would deal with the arrangements for renovating the new townhouse had not been fulfilled. The apartment was still full of stacks of carpet samples, stacks of tile samples, dunes of bathroom fixture samples, swaths of curtain materials, stacks of countertop samples. Gregor thought he would never want to hear the word "sample" again, and that it was going to take him years to relax in the new house. He'd never be able to turn on a faucet without remembering all this.

He couldn't use the computer in the

bedroom. That would wake Bennis, and it was only four o'clock in the morning. He couldn't use the computer in the living room. There were samples on it, he wasn't sure of what. He couldn't open his own laptop on the kitchen table, because there was no kitchen table left. It was buried under . . . stuff.

Finally, he went downstairs to what he and Bennis still referred to as "Bennis's old apartment," although the two apartments had been knocked together years ago. He brought his laptop, and told himself that this was a sign he should have caught. They'd knocked the apartments together, but they'd never lived as if they had both spaces to do what they wanted with. They had been destined to buy a house.

Down in Bennis's apartment, the sample situation was a little better, but not by much. He removed a few of the stacks from the coffee table in the living room, but Bennis's taste in coffee tables was too bizarre to make writing e-mails comfortable. The table was in the shape of a gigantic book. It made Gregor feel as if he were Alice in Wonderland, after she'd eaten the whatever it was that made her very small.

He went out into the kitchen and looked at the stacks on the table there, but there

were very few of them. He took these off —
they seemed to be more carpet; he had no
idea why they needed to have so many
samples of so many different kinds of carpet
— and set the laptop up there. He knew
enough about himself to plug the thing in.
He never finished whatever he wanted to do
in half an hour or less. He didn't understand
why the people who made laptops couldn't
find a battery that would go for a day or
more. Then he brought up his e-mail program, clicked on the link for a blank e-mail
form, and typed Howard Androcoelho's
e-mail address into the little box. These
programs had been made to be used by
idiots. Gregor appreciated it.

Dear Howard *(he started),*
    I've spent the last couple of days think-
ing about this. Part of my reason for
writing is to be sure that you understand
what happened in the disappearance of
Chester Morton and the deaths of Althy
Michaelman and Mike Katowski, and
that's easy to do.
    All you have to remember is that Char-
lene Morton is one of those women who
needs to build a fortress around herself,
and one who needs to make sure that
her life and that of her family is seen in

public as being beyond reproach. And to make that happen, she needed her children to be her children forever, or maybe even longer than forever. She needed them to do what they were told. She needed them to be what she wanted them to be.

Chester was not those things — for what it's worth, I don't think Kenny is, either — and he was not those things in the worst possible way. He acted out. He went to hell. He did things that were certainly dangerous and that were sometimes illegal.

The first indication I had that Chester was light years away from being what Charlene Morton wanted to think he was was when I heard the story of buying the baby. Actually, even before buying the baby, the story about getting Darvelle dressed up to look like she was pregnant in order to fool Charlene Morton into thinking she was about to have a grandchild was a clue.

And it was a clue not just to Chester Morton's character and frame of mind, but to the nature of the breach between him and his mother. At one point when we were at the house that last day, Stew Morton said that Charlene Morton would never kick one of her children out of the house, that she wasn't that kind of mother And that was true. She would never do something like that.

That left us with a puzzle. Charlene wouldn't throw a child out of the house. Chester had left and wanted to come back, but she wouldn't let him come back. She wanted us to think that he was still living in that trailer because he refused to come back, but that made no sense. He was working so hard to get home.

That meant that there had to be some reason why Charlene would throw her son out, and the only reason that made any sense was that he was not just out of control on alcohol and drugs and gambling, but that he had started to steal when he couldn't get her to supply him with the money he wanted.

And he had to be stealing from the business, and not just from Charlene personally, because he must have needed large sums of money on a fairly regular basis. That was, in fact, a reason why Charlene might throw him out. The business is the basis for everything in her life. If the business goes bankrupt, if the business is in trouble, then everything Charlene cares about goes completely to hell.

So Charlene threw him out, and Chester got crazier and crazier in his attempts to get back in, and then there was the baby. Chester found a way to steal money from the business even though he was shut out of the house. He bought the baby from Althy Michaelman, and then, just as he was about to produce it as Charlene's new grandchild, Charlene showed up at his door.

I'll be convinced, to the end of my life, that it was Charlene and not Chester who murdered that infant. I think she did it in a blind rage. Buying a baby is a crime. It's a serious crime with a long prison sentence attached. I think she just exploded, picked it up and hit it against the wall. And then the baby was dead, and things went as I outlined them back in Mattatuck.

Charlene and Chester faked the disappearance. Chester got the money he wanted for drugs and gambling, a lot more of it than he could have gotten if he'd stayed here. Charlene was desperate for him to lie low and keep his mouth shut.

I don't think Chester ever realized that

this was, from the beginning, a temporary thing. Eventually, when she felt safe, Charlene was going to want him to come home and get his act together. The interest of the television people just moved the date forward a little.

But Chester couldn't face it. He didn't want to go to rehab. He didn't want to be back home where Charlene would be monitoring his every move and making sure he couldn't play cards or get high. The very thought of it made him desperate. He wanted to come home and be safe and go on living the way he had been living.

Charlene convinced him that he couldn't do that because Darvelle would expose him if he tried, that Darvelle was still furious at him for what he had done to her and frothing at the mouth for revenge.

Charlene thought that would make Chester toe the line. Instead, it made him want to kill himself, and he did.

But he wanted to use his death to get back at Darvelle, so he wanted to leave her with the baby's body. I don't know if he realized that it would only be a skeleton after all these years. He went to the place his mother had told him she had buried it and dug until there was no more room to dig. When he didn't find the body, he probably had a good idea where it was. He went to the greenhouse and dug it up.

Then he went to Darvelle's — everybody was always saying he wouldn't know where that was; she'd bought a house and moved on since he'd been in town; but it wouldn't have been hard for him to find out. His mother was going over there to put up flyers on Darvelle's street every other day or so.

Chester went out there, wrote his note accusing Darvelle and Kyle Holborn of murdering the baby, and then hung himself off Darvelle's bathroom door frame.

And after that, I think you're pretty clear. This would all have been over a lot sooner, and Althy Michaelman and Mike Katowski would still be alive, if Darvelle Haymes and Kyle Holborn hadn't panicked and started acting like idiots.

As for Althy and Mike Katowski — well. You'll never convict Charlene of murdering the baby, but you should be able to get her on those two, if you're careful about the forensic evidence.

That means calling in the state medical examiner. It means no more amateur autopsies. It means no more playing cop with the fibers and the drops of blood.

Mattatuck has gotten too large for you to go on playing the games you do about how you're a small town with no need of a professional law enforcement operation. It is important that Charlene Morton go to jail. I think I've guaranteed that by calling in the state professionals myself while I was there.

But there will be other Charlene Mortons, and you're going to need professional investigations to catch and convict them. It's time for Mattatuck to get its own full-time coroner and forensics department.

I'm sure that if you and Mayor Glew go to the next town council meeting and lay this out, you'll have no problem at all getting a referendum to approve it. I'm expecting to hear all about it in the next few months. Ferris Cole has promised to keep me posted.

And you aren't going to fight it anymore, and neither is Marianne Glew. Because if you do, I'll get in touch with the people I know at *American Justice* and *City Confidential* and a few more of those shows, and I'll point them in the direction of a supposed murder-suicide that occurred in Mattatuck when you and Marianne Glew were partners.

I say "supposed" because you know, as well as I do, that there was no suicide. A man named Dade Warren killed his wife and children, yes, but you two got to him before he had a chance to kill himself. And my guess is that you just lost it. You lost it, you shot the place up, you killed the guy, and then you and Marianne Glew started to worry that this wasn't going to go over well, that it couldn't really be justified by the circumstances. And you both decided to call it suicide and say you'd seen it.

And since Mattatuck didn't have professional forensics, you got away with it. And you've been getting away with it ever since.

Well, it's been a long time. The truth of it probably couldn't be absolutely proved. But I know something about the media. Absolutely proved or not, that truth can ruin your life.

And if you don't do something about the state of law enforcement in Mattatuck in the next six months, I will do it.

Keep it in mind when you think of me.

Gregor Demarkian.

Bennis came down when he was still sitting at her old kitchen table. The e-mail had been sent. He was just feeling tired.

"Are you all right?" she asked him. "Are you coming to the Ararat?"

"Yes, I suppose I am," Gregor said.

He closed the laptop and stared at the black plastic top of it. "I'm a little tired."

"You've been up for forever," Bennis said. "Are you depressed? Is that it?"

"Tibor thinks that we're going to blow the birthday candles out on that cake and old George is going to just keel over dead," Gregor said. "Maybe not that dramatically, you know, but something like that. That he's been holding on just to get to this birthday party, and when he's gotten to it, he'll be gone."

"Is that really such a bad thing?"

"I think so, yes," Gregor said. "I'm from a generation that thinks of death as the enemy. And death is the enemy. I've heard all that stuff about quality of life and all the rest of it, but in the end, death is the enemy. And we should have thought of something to do about it by now."

"I think that old George lived on his own in his own apartment until he was nearly a hundred years old," Bennis said. "I think he went to the Ararat, and had friends and family, and did all the things people do, and he was happy. I think that's a very good life."

"That's what Tibor said."

"Tibor makes a lot of sense most of the time."

"I was thinking, on the day we took George to the hospital, that he'd lived long enough to see almost everybody he'd grown up with die, and almost everybody he'd been close to for most of his life, too. That we were his second set of friends and family, if that makes any sense."

"It does," Bennis said, "but you're not making much. Go put on some serious clothes and come to the Ararat. We're going to set up a big party right after breakfast and go to the hospital. Hannah made a cake. Lida decorated it. It's got the Statue of Liberty on it, and if you light that it throws sparks. The hospital is going to kill us."

"If there's an oxygen tank within a hundred miles, we're going to kill it," Gregor said.

"There's no oxygen tank that I know of. Come on. Get up, get out, get moving. What were you doing down here anyway?"

"Sending an e-mail." Gregor got up. "You can't do anything at all upstairs these days.

Isn't there ever going to be a point where you make decisions about these things and we can have our furniture back?"

"I'm getting there," Bennis said.

She left the kitchen. Gregor heard her moving through the living room, then starting up the stairs to their usual space.

"Come on," she called, as she went up.

Gregor unplugged the laptop, wrapped the cord into a coil and put the computer itself under his arm.

He was tired and he was depressed and he had this irrational need to not let anyone stage this birthday party, as if not having it would keep old George alive forever. But he'd been having that same idea the other day, and he'd told Tibor about it, and Tibor had not been helpful.

Gregor went into Bennis's living room himself and looked out the big plate glass window on Cavanaugh Street.

It would not be the same place without old George Tekemanian in it.

The employees of Thorndike Press hope you have enjoyed this Large Print book. All our Thorndike, Wheeler, and Kennebec Large Print titles are designed for easy reading, and all our books are made to last. Other Thorndike Press Large Print books are available at your library, through selected bookstores, or directly from us.

For information about titles, please call:
  (800) 223-1244

or visit our Web site at:
  http://gale.cengage.com/thorndike

To share your comments, please write:
  Publisher
  Thorndike Press
  10 Water St., Suite 310
  Waterville, ME 04901